BRIGHT 2

A NOVEL

AUTHOR OF DEADLY DECISIONS & DEADLY DECISIONS II

MIMI RENEE

Ink Game Publications

This book is a work of fiction. Names, characters, places and incidents are products of the author's imagination or used fictitiously. Any resemblance to actual events or locales or persons, living or dead is entirely coincidental. Any and all locations existing are mentioned in the book to give it a feeling of reality.

ISBN 10: 0985311037

ISBN 13: 978-0-9853110-3-2

Cover Design/Vonda Howard /vondahoward.com

Author: Mimi Renee/ www.inkgamepub.com

Editor-in-Chief: Jill Alicea/savafiend76@roadrunner.com

Proof reader: LaMia Ashley/mommamia_08232@yahoo.com

Interior Design: Glenda Wallace/ interiorbookdesigns.com

Acknowledgments

First and foremost I'd like to take a moment to thank my Heavenly Father for his continued, love guidance and blessings. I LOVE YOU! Shout-out to all the loyal readers (Gabrielle Dotson & Claudisia Martin), book clubs and the Pretty Bright's book club for your continued love and support! You guys are wonderful, and make my writing journey an incredible one! You're my motivation to come harder and harder with each release, and my inspiration during those long nights of writing. Without your support novels by MiMi Renee would go untold...I am forever humble and grateful to you all!

Special shout-out to the one and only author **T. Styles** A.K.A Reign! A leading woman and BOSS in the literary industry that continues to release one five-star novel after the next! I truly, truly admire and respect you to the fullest, Diva! I hope to someday collaborate on future project (s) with you! *smiles* Thanks for acknowledging me, reading my work, and for also directing traffic to my name and works. YOU ROCK! I hope you enjoy part two just as much, if not more than the first installment. I'm looking forward to seeing you and the Cartel family again SOON!!

Last but not least I'd like to shout out the names of those that put the time and hard work in to make my work both readable and appealing. Editors, Book cover and Interior designers: Jill Alicea (Lead editor), La'Mia Ashley (Proof reader), Vonda Howard (Book cover designer) Tina Sherri (Interior designer) and Glenda A. Wallace (Interior designer). Thanks for your time, hard work and dedication!

Part 1

2006 Birthday Gift

"DIE, BITCH... DIE, BITCH...DIE!!!" Terrence yelled as he tried choking Bright to death in the hospital bed where she had been lying for almost two weeks, fighting for her life. She was in a coma after being nearly beaten to death by her ex-best friend, Treasure, and her two cousins from Compton.

Terrence was enraged after receiving a letter from Treasure. It explained that Bright had been lying to him the entire time about the twins being his, and also explained that the father was an up-and-coming basketball player named Larry Lane. Enraged and heartbroken, Terrence wanted nothing more than to see Bright dead. On Bright's eighteenth birthday, drunk, high off of ecstasy, and bitter as hell, Terrence crept into the hospital room that Bright had been occupying at Long Beach Memorial Hospital in hopes of ending her life.

"How could you lie and portray me like this, bitch? After everything I've done for yo' stank ass!" He demanded to know, looking from her face to the monitors, waiting for it to flatline. "Hurry up and die, bitch!" Terrence gripped tighter and tighter around Bright's neck, noticing that he was grabbing attention from the nearby nurses' station.

"Sir!" A nurse rushed from behind the nurses' station in his direction, alarming other staff en route.

Immediately, other nurses and other staff members hurried toward Bright's hospital room. After his hands were pried from around Bright's neck, Terrence swiftly fled from the room, knocking medical staff down on his way out. Then he disappeared down the staircase of the hospital's emergency exit in an attempt to avoid hospital security or law enforcement. Having safely made it out of the hospital and out to his truck, Terrence pondered the many ways he wanted to end Bright's life.

"Bitch better hope she don't wake up out that coma, and that's on the Eastside!" Terrence fumed, then climbed in his truck and drove out of the lot contemplating.

Once Bright was stabilized, nursing staff reported the incident to the police. The hospital ordered Bright around-the-clock security to secure her protection, and only family members would be permitted in her room until further notice.

One Week and Three Days Later

After three weeks of being in a coma, Bright had finally woken up. As expected, Bright's memory was clouded, but medical staff was happy with her progress and family members were elated to learn the good news. Three days later, Bright had regained her memory and nearly frightened herself back into a coma after she had seen her reflection in the mirror. With a total of seven missing teeth, four at the top and three at the bottom, Bright wailed franticly as she rubbed and observed the permanent gashes about her forehead.

"Where the fuck are my teeth, and what happened to my face?" Bright ran into the hallway, hectically, crying and questioning the nurses, desperate for answers.

"Do you understand that you almost died, Miss?" an Asian nurse said to Bright in the hopes of calming her down. "These things can be fixed and replaced. You can get teeth implants and have surgery to have the scars removed from your face...you understand? But you cannot come back to life once you're dead, so count your blessings, darling, and be grateful to be alive. This stuff can be fixed," she spoke in a strong Asian ascent as she walked Bright back into her room. "Now you calm down, okay? Everything will be all right...you're still very beautiful."

Bright sat on her hospital bed and cried her eyes out. "Just leave me alone! I don't wanna hear none of that fairytale nonsense. My face is ruined and my teeth are gone!" Bright turned away from the nurse, snatched her arm from her, and then continued to fuss and cry.

As Bright had requested, the nurse left out the room.

Hours later after Bright had calmed down, her brother, Cordell, walked into the room to deliver some very disturbing news to his big sister.

"Queen Bee is back!" He hugged Bright tightly, kissed her on the cheek, and then told her he loved her. "You good, Sis?"

Bright covered her mouth with her hand. She didn't want her brother to see her with a mouth full of missing teeth. "Hi, Cordell; I'm good. Where Ma at...did she come with you?" Bright needed her mother desperately.

Cordell shook his head no. "Mom is in the hospital. She had another stroke, Queen Bee," he regretted to inform her.

Bright's eyes widened with sadness as Cordell's eyes began to water up. "That ain't the worst of it either, Bee. Ramon killed himself. My little nigga hung himself from the light fixture in our bedroom. Seeing that shit, Momma lost it. She had a nervous breakdown, and then a few days later, she had another stroke."

"Oh no, don't tell me that, Cordell! My baby brother didn't kill himself!" Her eyes were filled with tears.

"This shit gets even deeper, Queen Bee. When Momma went to the hospital, Child Services came to the hospital and took us all, even the twins. Mrs. Lane came and got them a few days later - but they split us all up and put us in different foster homes and shit. I ain't seen Deja and Rayonna since we buried Ramon at Rose Hills."

The news was so devastating that Bright couldn't even begin to process and comprehend everything her brother had just told her. All she knew was that the only thing that had ever meant anything to her had been destroyed, and her baby brother, Ramon, was gone. Flashbacks of her brother, Ramon, hollering and crying for her help the day she abandoned her babies and walked out on her mother begin to resurface, causing her to fall to her knees and sob uncontrollably. "Don't tell me that, Cordell, pleaseeee, brother, don't tell me that!" Bright covered her ears and shook her head. Crying, she slid off her hospital bed and onto the floor. The guilt of neglecting her family when they needed her the most tore her apart, and she blamed no one but herself. *I would of, I could of, I should of*...continued to pound her brain.

Cordell pulled his sister off the floor and held her tight in his arms. "Sis, we have to be strong right now for Momma and get our family back together. Ramon ain't ever coming back, but right now, Momma, Deja, Ray, and the twins need us. We're all we got, Bee, and we're the two that are going to have to bring our family back together. I ran away from the foster home. I ain't going back either, Sis. I'm staying wit' you," Cordell told her.

Looking at her brother, Bright wiped her tears away. "You're right, brother...we're all we got."

The next afternoon when Bright was discharged from the hospital, Cordell picked her up in a car that he had stolen the night before. He wanted to be able to pick Bright up and drive her to the motel that he'd been occupying. He had been hustling, selling dope day in and day out to maintain it.

During the ride, Bright bitched and fussed at Cordell about stealing cars, and she nearly lost her mind when he grabbed a gun out of the glove compartment.

"Queen Bee, you can't look at me as your baby brother anymore. I'm knee-deep in these streets now. We have to survive," Cordell said to her seriously.

Bright immediately stopped fussing and reminded herself that, like herself, her brother too would have to transition from a fifteen-year-old boy to a man, quickly, in order to survive. From that point forward, Bright vowed to teach her brother everything that she knew about getting money, and what she had learned watching Terrence get his.

"Me and my nigga Lil Jay gon' rob and kill that Eastside nigga, Ice..."

Bright turned the music down and cut Cordell off in mid-sentence. "Pump the brakes on that one, little brother. Y'all can't rob Ice. That's my money man right there," she shot with attitude.

"Oh yeah, that's what I forgot to tell you. That nigga Ice wanna kill you. In fact, he tried to choke you to death while you were in a coma on your birthday. They must have failed to mention that to you at the hospital." Cordell looked at her seriously. "Now you said what again?"

That's why I had 'round- the- clock armed security at the hospital. Bright was in awe, and after a few moments of silence, she sighed, "Not a muthafucking thing, brother." She smacked her lips, folded her arms across her chest, and then a vindictive smirk spread across her face. "That nigga Ice can get it too, but instead of trying to rob and kill him, I know an excellent way you can get to his ass. I'ma tell you when we get in the room."

"I always knew that I'd have to lay old Cuz down someday." Cordell nodded in agreement.

Once they got near the motel, Cordell ditched the stolen car a few blocks from the room and wiped his and his sister's fingerprints out of the car. Then he and Bright walked the rest of the way to the motel. Cordell knew the motel had surveillance cameras in the parking lot, and he didn't want any evidence of him or his sister riding around in a stolen vehicle. Cordell was an eager student of the streets, and he paid close attention to the movement. He took notice of all the mistakes that sent his homies to jail and learned from them. Rule number one was to never leave any evidence behind.

Inside the motel room, Bright shared her idea on getting Terrence with her brother. "If y'all want to get Ice, y'all gon' have to take a different approach to get him. He's on one. He just lost his wife to cancer, I got over on his ass, and he be on them E-pills and be extra paranoid. He won't be easy to touch...trust me."

Cordell blew off hot air. "That nigga ain't superhuman, Bee. His bitch ass can be touched too, trust that."

"Listen to me, Cordell!" Bright began to get frustrated. "I'm telling you how this nigga rolls, and I'm about to tell you the best way to get his ass..."

To Cordell, it seemed like his sister was underestimating him. Unbeknown to her, he and his boy, Lil Jay, had been robbing and getting niggas since he was twelve. *What my sister think she know about robbing and killing a nigga?* Cordell lit a cigarette and cut Bright off again. "How is that, Bee?"

"Get his ass through his enemy. Y'all have to get Capone, frame Ice, and let him take the rap for it. Find a young bitch to give Capone's ass some pussy, and then kill and rob him. But before y'all do that, get one of yo' little homeboys, since Ice knows you're my brother, to get a job at that new detail shop on the Eastside to get close to Ice's ass so he can later plant the murder weapon in his truck. Ice gets his vehicles cleaned at least once or twice a week."

Cordell was amazed at how brilliantly Bright had laid her plan out. It was more clever than his own plan to catch Terrence getting in his car late at night and shooting him. "Damn, Sis; beautiful!" Cordell applauded her. "And that's exactly the way this nigga is about to exit the scene...twenty-five to life! Brilliant, Bee!"

Bright took a bow and then laughed. "I told you, little nigga!"

After making sure their plan was airtight, Bright asked Cordell to call a cab. She desperately needed to see her mother, and she wanted to go to her brother's gravesite.

Cordell turned to Bright. "Look, Bright, I gotta hit the pavement to keep this room paid for and feed us. Can we do it later?"

"Cordell, I have money, and I ain't staying in this dump overnight." Bright looked around the room, displaying dissatisfaction. "It ain't nothing but dope heads and prostitutes running through this rat hole, so if you ain't tryna have the police take you back to the foster home, or end up going to juvenile hall, you better listen to your big sister." Bright reached for the bag that she had tucked her money in, pulled it out, and spread it across one of the full-size beds in the room. It was the money she had gotten from pawning the engagement ring that Terrence had given her. "That's like eight or nine thousand dollars right there."

Cordell walked over to the bed. "Damn, where you get that shit from, Queen Bee?"

"From the nigga you and yo' homeboy gon' set up!" Bright giggled, covering her mouth. "Now take me to Ma and Ramon so we can start working on getting our family back together." Bright began to pack the money back in her bag.

On the ride to the nursing home, Cordell filled Bright in on Treasure's whereabouts. "Treasure and her grimy-ass cousins are in jail fighting attempted murder cases for the shit they did to you. Them bitches better be happy the police got to they asses before I did, 'cause I was gon' bust that bitch in her head with a brick and then let all my homeboys piss on her ass!" Cordell fumed. "I got the detective's number that is handling your case too. He wants you to call him so he can make sure that bitch gets the max - "

Bright cut Cordell off. "They came to the hospital and I told them I didn't remember anything, and I'm gonna continue to not remember anything every time they pop up... you understand?"

Cordell gave Bright a puzzled expression. He knew about the no snitching rule, but that didn't apply to Bright's situation. "What you mean you ain't gon' remember?"

"Because I'm not, Cordell. Treasure's gon' get what's coming to her."

Cordell began to get angry. "Naw, Bee, I think you tripping, Cuz...fuck that! Them bitches could have taken you from us!"

"Cordell, leave it alone. I'm here, and we have more on our plates to worry about than them bitches. They gon' get theirs. Trust that."

"Well I sho' hope so, Cuz, 'cause if they don't, they gon' definitely get it from me, and that's on the north!" Cordell promised.

When the cab driver pulled up in front of the nursing home on Artesia Blvd., Bright paid him, and then she and her brother went inside to see her mother.

"I knew that bitch would be here sooner rather than later!" A wicked smile crept on Terrence's face as he sat watching across the street from the nursing home. Terrence knew he'd get locked up if he stepped foot back in the hospital, so he had his homeboy watching Bright at the hospital and told him to call him the second she was released and stepped foot out of her hospital room. Terrence was in the middle of getting head from two of his favorite Latino bitches, Summer and Maria, when he got the good news. After shooting his milkshake down their throats, he told them to clean his house and cook him some dinner and that he'd be back in a few hours. Then he drove straight to the nursing home. Terrence knew Bright's mother was there and that she'd run straight to mommy the second she was released from the hospital.

"So now that you done pretty much found this bitch, what you gon' do?" Shawn, his childhood friend and crime partner, asked.

"I'ma set her up for failure, and then watch that bitch fall down and crumble. I wanna see her suffer, then I'ma take her out of her misery...but I'ma need your help. You down, Cuz?"

"Bless these hands with some bread, my friend, and you already know!" Shawn nodded in agreement.

"I have a plan," Terrence said, then directed his attention to Shawn the second Bright and her brother disappeared inside the nursing home.

****

Before opening the door to see their mother, Cordell stopped Bright. "Queen Bee, I wanna warn you that Ma doesn't look so good. Like I told you on the way inside, her left side is paralyzed, her words are scrambled, she can barely talk, and she's on a feeding tube. Ma can't walk and needs help doing everything. She couldn't even lift a cup of water to her mouth if she was dying of thirst;" Cordell nodded sympathetically.

"Damn, Ma is that messed up?" Bright covered her mouth and asked.

"Yeah, she is, and I just want you to be prepared before you go in there. I'ma stay out here and wait for you. I don't like seeing Ma like that."

Bright nodded her head in agreement. "All right, I'll be out in a little while," she said, and then she walked inside the room.

Bright was immediately startled by her mother's appearance. She looked like a totally different woman and appeared to have aged ten years, practically overnight. Her eyes were sunken in, and Bright noticed gray hairs in her mother's head that she had never noticed before. On top of that, she had lost a lot of weight. For about ten minutes, Bright stood in silence staring at her mother, hoping she'd make some type of movement or that she would recognize her...but she never did. Bright walked over to her mother and stood looking at her as she called her name a few times.

"Ma, Ma, Ma…it's me, your daughter, Bright. Do you recognize me?"

Rosette moved her fingertips and smiled at her daughter with her eyes. She was relieved that Bright was alive and well. Rosette received a call from her youngest daughter, Rayonna, every night before she went to bed. She'd keep her updated on everything and tell her how everyone was doing. Then Rayonna would recite the nightly prayer that Rosette had taught her before ending their nightly call.

A big smile spread across Bright's face. She kissed her mother on the cheeks a few times then lay her head on her chest so that she could listen to her heartbeat. When Bright was a child, she would sit on her mother's lap and listen to her heartbeat until she'd fall asleep. Listening to her mother's heartbeat provided Bright the comfort and connection that she needed from her mother at that very moment. "Ma, I'm so sorry that I left you.

This is all my fault. I was being so stupid over Larry and let everybody down: you, Ramon, the twins, Cordell, Deja, and Ray. I'm so sorry, Ma," Bright sniffled. "I really am, and I promise that I'll fix everything and we'll all be back together real soon, Ma, just watch," Bright told her, then she stood up to leave. "I have a lot to do, Ma, but I'll be back tomorrow or the next day, okay?"

Rosette mumbled some words that Bright assumed meant "I love you".

"I love you too, Ma." Bright smiled, and then walked out of the room.

Larry Lane

"How are the babies, Mom?" Larry asked his mother through the phone.

Mrs. Lane took a seat in her favorite recliner chair and smiled. "They are fine, son. How are you doing?"

"I'm better, and I wanna apologize for hanging up on you last week and thank you for taking my children in. If they're even mine," he sighed. Larry wasn't very happy when his mother initially told him that she had gotten custody of them.

"Apology accepted. And, son, they are yours. They look just like you when you were a baby, and the blood test is gonna prove that."

After a few moments, Larry broke the silence. "Any word on her?"

"Last I heard, she was still in a coma."

"How about her mother?"

"Last I heard from her mother's friend, Lyn, Rose was admitted into a nursing home. She had another stroke."

Larry sighed. "Man, that woman can't seem to ever get a break, I feel really bad for her. Can you send her some flowers from me when you get time?"

"I will, son. Did you want me to send Bright anything?"

"Nope. The only thing I want you to do is make sure she doesn't get my kids back, if or when she gets back on her feet. She's not fit or ready to be a mother."

"We'll see, Larry. These are her children too, and I'm sure Bright loves them."

"Ma, I can assure you that Bright doesn't give a damn about the twins. If she did, she wouldn't have ever left them in the first place."

"All right, son, I'll do what I have to do to keep your children safe. Now you get back to practicing, and bring your mother a ring home." She smiled proudly. "I love you, Larry."

"You got that, Mom. I love you, too."

Treasure

From inside Century Regional Detention Facility for Women in Lynwood, Treasure cried to her mother on the phone. "Mom, I just finished talking to my public defender about my case, and he's saying they're talking about giving me ten to fifteen years for attempted murder. I don't wanna be in here, Mama! Can you and Grandma please get me out of here?" Treasure cried. "It was only supposed to be a fight...I swear!"

Treasure's mother, Dawn, had just received the same bad news from Treasure's appointed public defender, just minutes before Treasure's call, and she was just as devastated. Dawn had also been crying, but she knew that now wasn't the time to cry, and that crying would only make things worse. Dawn sat up on the edge of the couch and wiped her tears away. "Treasure! I need you to wipe those tears from your eyes right now, and I want you to listen up, and listen up good! You hear me?" Dawn spoke loudly and sternly.

Treasure wiped the tears from her eyes. "Yes, I hear you, Mom." Her voice cracked.

"Good. Now from this point forward, you gon' have to stop crying and be as strong as possible. Your grandmother and I can't come walk you out of there like we'd love to. There's a process in doing so, and it's going to take some time. I need you to be as strong and as patient as possible...we're going to have to fight! But understand that you're going to serve some time for what you did to Bright. She's in a coma, so right now, we have to pray that she lives. You're a good girl, Treasure, and I'm confident that we'll get your sentence reduced...and that you'll be home in no time. But, baby, I can assure you that if you run around the county jail crying like a little lost baby that just got off her momma's titty, those girls are going to give you hell and make your time hard! Do you follow me, Treasure?"

Treasure sniffed, holding her tears back, and then wiped the few tears that had fallen from her eyes away. "Yes, I follow you, Mom." Treasure looked back at the long line of female inmates that were waiting to use the phone, searching for the girl that continued to go out of her way to be rude and make gestures to her. Having spotted the inmate, Treasure dropped the phone without saying goodbye to her mother, and then walked in the girl's direction. Staring the girl dead in the eyes, Treasure stole off on her without saying one word.

"Bitch!" the inmate named Precious yelled, trying to pry Treasure's hand out of her hair.

Not having any mercy on the inmate, Treasure used her as a punching bag to release her stress. She beat Precious in the face until she was completely bloody and unconscious. Moments later, the correctional officers pulled Treasure off of her and threw her into the hole.

****

"Deja!" Rayonna ran to her sister the second she walked in the Children Services office with their caseworker.

"Ray! Are you all right? Has anybody been bothering you?" Deja hugged her little sister tight.

"I'm better now, because we're together now and are going to be placed in the same foster home!" Rayonna smiled. "They had room for Cordell, too, but he ran away. Have you talked to him, huh, Deja?" Rayonna worried.

"No." Deja noticed that the caseworker was waiting for her response. "But I'm sure he's all right, wherever he is," Deja assured her. They had been looking for Cordell for weeks.

After observing the girls, a few moments later the caseworker walked them to the waiting area, so that she could complete her paperwork and drop them off at their new foster home.

Two Weeks Later

After being cooped up in a hotel room for weeks, hiding from the world, embarrassed of her scarred face and missing teeth, Bright had gone to the dentist and gotten a dental bridge that she'd have to wear until her permanent crowns were ready to be implanted. However, the dentures were taking more time than she expected to get used to wearing. They were tight, uncomfortable, and were always slipping out of her mouth. Her daily routine of eating, sleeping, smoking weed, going to see her mother, and then later having dinner with her brother was beginning to bore her terribly.

So come Friday morning, Bright dressed appropriately in a pink trendy oversized couture sweater, threw on a pair of denim jeans and pink boots, and then drove to the mall. It was a breezy spring morning. When she arrived at the mall, Bright headed straight to the cosmetic department to purchase make-up to cover the scars up with. Having gotten a quick session on applying the make-up, Bright smiled, pleased with how fresh and flawless her face looked. Afterwards, she drove to Walgreen's to purchase some PoliGrip. Inside her mother's car, she applied a generous amount to her dentures, and then swiftly put them back on. Bright would have died if someone had spotted her putting them on. Bright was pleased, though, because the dental bridge and make-up offered her just enough confidence to smile again.

On her way to visit her mother, Bright stopped by the liquor store in her neighborhood to grab a bottle of water and breath mints. Having selected her items, Bright stood in line to purchase them when Treasure's mother, Dawn, walked into the store. Immediately, Bright's heart rate increased as she tried her best to avoid direct eye contact with her. Bright knew that Dawn was not only mad, angry and disappointed with her, but that Treasure was her only child. Dawn made it known in the streets and at their old high school that if anybody had problems with Treasure, she didn't mind fighting minors and would worry about jail later, so Bright knew she wouldn't think twice about fighting her.

After staring at Bright for a few seconds in the store entrance, Dawn walked up on the side of Bright and asked, "Why you do my daughter like that, Bright? How could you, after everything my daughter has done for you, and how she always defended you? How could you repay her like this?"

Bright turned to face her. "I didn't do anything to Treasure, Dawn. I was the one she jumped with her cousins, over some lie a guy told her about me. I would never do anything to hurt her. She was my best friend, and we both defended each other."

They had everyone's attention in the store, including the liquor store clerk and the owner. The two families had been the topic of the city, and everybody was interested in who and what was gonna happen next.

"You little lying bitch, you!" Dawn stomped her foot into the ground she was about to go bananas. "Suge told it, and that boy had no reason to lie to her about you. What she gave you, you deserved! But my baby don't deserve to be in no fucking county jail facing a fifteen year sentence!" Dawn had gotten in Bright's face and backed her into the potato chip rack. "You better pray, Bright, that my daughter doesn't have to serve no hard time, because if she does, I'm gonna kill you my gotdamn self...you understand me?!"Dawn pointed in Bright's face.

Angry and tired of her life situations, Bright begin to snap. "Well, kill me then, Dawn, if that's gon' make you feel any better. Your daughter tried to, I gotta nigga that's trying to, and on top of that, I lost my baby brother, my family life is all fucked up, and my mother isn't doing so well. So do what you have to do and hurry up and help me out of this misery called life, 'cause I'm tired of living it anyways!"

Dawn looked at Bright with a mixture of hate and sympathy in her eyes and began to nod her head. "As much as I hate you, I feel sorry for you," Dawn paused. "You're one sick, poisonous, lying, demon, little girl who doesn't know shit! You didn't come from shit, you ain't gon' never amount to shit, and I bet your mother's suffering and brother's suicide was all because of your shit...and - "

Bright cut Dawn off. "It was not my fault that my brother killed himself!" Dawn had hit a bottom that Bright was unaware she had and she was about to explode.

In a yelling match with Bright, Dawn continued to yell, "I'll be damned if my daughter ends up being a victim of your poisonous bullshit!"

"I loved my brother, VERY MUCH," Bright continued to argue. "And if you really knew me, you'd know that!" Bright threw her items to the ground, and then ran out of the store in tears.

It was that or Bright exploding on Dawn...and right now, her family needed her.

On the drive to the hospital, Bright began to curse Treasure in her head. *Bitch, you are in jail because you almost killed me, not because I put you there! And if your mother threatens me again, I'm going to the police, and you and that bitch gon' fuck around and be cellmates!*

When Bright pulled up to the convalescent home, she parked and manually locked all the doors, since the power locks no longer worked. After locking the back passenger side door, Bright swung around and nearly choked on her own spit at the sight of Terrence standing at the driver's side door with a smirk on his face.

He was dressed in a crisp white T-shirt, a pair of gray Levi's, a clean pair of Ken Griffey Nikes on his feet, and he had his hair braided in two neat corn rolls. Terrence flinched at Bright, causing her to quickly climb out of the passenger side of the car for dear life.

"Where's my ring at, you lying, trifling, no-good-ass hoe?" Terrence had spent over ten grand for it, and he wanted it back desperately.

"I ain't got shit! Now leave me alone, Ice, before I scream for help and yo' ass end up in jail. I know you got warrants!" Bright was so frightened that she began trembling.

Glancing at her purse in the passenger seat, Terrence grabbed it and began to look through it. He really didn't want her money; he wanted to hurt Bright and instill fear in her heart. As he looked at Bright, she began to look like a high-yellow demon to him, and he couldn't understand how he had allowed her to use, lie, and get him for thousands of dollars.

"Help, helpppppppppppppp, I'm being robbed!" Bright yelled and screamed for help. She didn't want Terrence to take her money. It was all she had to her name.

Alarmed, Terrence continued to count the money he had grabbed out of her purse. "I'm taking this twenty-two hundred with me." He slid the money in his pocket. "And every time I see you or yo' little bitch-made-ass brother out grinding, I'm taking his shit too. You just started a war, bitch!"

"Miss, are you all right?" A young, black, nurse that Bright had never seen before ran out the convalescent home with a cell phone in her hand.

Bright was relieved that someone had come to her aid. "No, I'm not all right! This nigga just robbed me, and now he's threatening to hurt me. Please, hurry and call 911!" Bright prayed Terrence wouldn't harm her, and would hopefully give her money back.

When the nurse appeared to be dialing 911 on her cell phone, Terrence took off across the street, hopped in his truck, and burned rubber off the street.

Bright leaned on the car crying. "Why me? Why me? Why me? Fuck!"

Once Bright finished crying her eyes out and feeling sorry for herself, she called her brother to tell him what had happened, then before ending the call, she told him to watch his back.

"Don't worry, Queen Bee. That nigga is walking his last days free on the streets, right now. Come to the room when you're finished. I have some money for you," Cordell told her.

Inside the nursing facility, the nurse that had called 911 for Bright pulled her to the side before she went to visit her mother.

"Did you know that guy? Is he some kind of kin to you?"

"No, he's an ex-loser that I used to deal with." Bright sighed in frustration.

"I'm new here, so I'm not sure who you're here to visit, but that guy came in here asking questions about one of our patients and all sorts of crazy questions. When he couldn't give the patient's last name and I saw that he wasn't on the patient's visitors list, he got real irate and left," the nurse explained.

Bright's eyes bucked. "Was he asking about Rosette Clark?"

"Yes, he was. He asked me if he could go see her, and when the last time any of her children had come to visit her," she explained. "I had just told him to leave about five minutes before I heard you yelling for help."

What the fuck is he up to? Bright pondered as she continued to listen to the nurse.

"What's your relationship to Rosette? She's my girl, and since I've been here, I've been assigned to her and have been taking real good care of her."

"She's my mother."

"Okay, well now that you filled me in on ole boy, I told my supervisor about him, wrote an incident report, and wrote down everything that happened today, and if he's seen on the premises again, he'll be arrested," she said seriously.

"Thank you so much! My name is Bright; what's yours?" Bright extended her hand to shake.

"My name is Diamond." She shook Bright's hand.

"That's your real name?" Bright twisted her lips. It was a pet peeve of hers that she didn't like to call people by nicknames unless she made them up herself.

"That's what it says on my nursing and driver's license," Diamond laughed.

Diamond was tall with large breasts and thin enough to be a model. She was brown-complexioned, with high cheekbones and mysterious eyes. Diamond wore a long weave and had a big smile. Her southern accent and demeanor were very warm, and right off the top, Bright took a liking to her.

"I like you," Bright smiled. "And thank you for taking such good care of my mother. It'll definitely allow me to sleep better at night knowing she's in good care." She smiled, walking toward her mother's room.

"Don't mention it, girl, I love what I do." Diamond winked. Then, before Bright made it to her mother's room, Diamond called out to her. "I'll come get you when the police get here."

Bright stopped in her tracks and turned to face Diamond. "Tell them I left or something when they get here. I don't like speaking to cops."

"You sure?" Diamond asked with a concerned expression on her face.

"I'm positive," Bright nodded her head, and then walked into her mother's room.

Good, 'cause I didn't call them in the first place! Interaction with the law was the last thing Diamond wanted or needed either.

****

Cordell sat at the table in his motel room with his right-hand man, Lil Jay, and his new girlfriend, Tanisha, constructing a final meeting before taking Capone out. Cordell trusted both Lil Jay and Tanisha with his life, and he knew that he could trust them even further than his eye could see. After Bright had told Cordell about Capone's fetish for young girls, Cordell hollered at his longtime homegirl, Tanisha. She was sixteen-years-old, and she had the biggest crush on Cordell. She always told him how much he reminded her of a younger version of the old singer Al B. Sure. She loved the fact that Cordell was a biracial bad boy, with curly hair and big, brown eyes. Tanisha was medium height and dark-skinned. She had tight, brown eyes, full, sexy lips, and a smile that could light up a country night. She was average-shaped with medium breasts, and Tanisha had a perfectly round behind and long, sexy legs. When Cordell approached her about needing her help to set-up Capone, Tanisha agreed.

"I'll help you, Cordell, but you know I'm a virgin and that I've been saving it for you. I don't want Capone to be my first...I want you," Tanisha told Cordell shyly.

Later on that night, Cordell told Tanisha to meet him at his motel room and they made sweet, innocent, passionate, love. The next day when Capone approached Tanisha after school, she laughed and smiled in his face, pretending to like him. Days later, Capone called her and told her to meet him at one of his dope spots to kick it, and as promised, she called Cordell and told him which dope spot she would be meeting him at and the time. He constantly stressed to Tanisha the importance of leaving the door unlocked. "I got you, baby; I got you," she'd kept telling him.

Lil Jay, on the other hand, was Cordell's brother in crime, and they had been friends since Cordell was eleven and Lil Jay was thirteen. They were eighteen months apart, and they were more like brothers than anything. The two had got courted on to their 'hood together, vowed to have each other's backs, and ran the streets together doing everything but good. Whenever there was an opportunity to make money, Lil Jay would be involved.

When Cordell gave Lil Jay the change of plans, he went out and got himself employed at the detail shop. Two months shy of seventeen, Lil Jay could have worked every day, but instead only worked every weekend. When Terrence would frequent the shop, Lil Jay made it his business to give Terrence the best service possible, and he spoke to him every chance he got. Lil Jay would always be mistaken for a basketball player because of his height, and a square because of his mannerisms, but he was the total opposite. He was a school boy by day, and an active criminal by night. Tall, dark with dreamy eyes, he was a smooth talker, and he had no problems getting the girls.

"Aight, Tanisha, no matter what you do, don't hop in the bed with Cuz until you make sure the door is unlocked," Cordell instructed her.

"The door will be unlocked, Cordell...don't even trip," Tanisha replied.

"Good." Cordell nodded his approval and then directed his attention to Lil Jay.

"I'ma noodle the nigga, Cuz, so all you gon' have to do is watch my back, take all the dope and money you can find, and then slide the burner under that nigga Ice's seat the next time you wash his truck at the detail shop."

Paying full attention, Lil Jay rubbed the hair on his chin. "Nigga, we been talking about it, let's do it." He stood up and lit a blunt.

Caught Up in the Poonanny

Friday night, 2:45 am

"Oh... oh... ouch... ouch, Capone. I feel like my pussy is about to bust open and bleed. I'm not experienced; slow down, it hurts!" Tanisha whined in pain.

"This nigga really fucking a sixteen-year-old with his old ass," Lil Jay whispered to Cordell as they peered inside of Capone's bedroom, watching him pounding Tanisha aggressively, ignoring her requests to slow down.

"That nigga beating the brakes off that pussy!" Cordell elbowed Lil Jay and continued watching. He couldn't wait to get inside of Tanisha and make her scream and holler for him to stop again.

Breathing heavily, Capone said, "I'm just breaking the pussy in, baby, take that shit. You a woman now." He continued to penetrate her, on the verge of an orgasm.

When she hooked up with Capone, Tanisha had unlocked the door as Cordell had instructed her to do when Capone's head was turned, and then she climbed in his bed and let him have sex with her.

After Capone busted a nut, he told Tanisha how good her pussy was, and then he got up to use the rest room. He was 6′7″, tall, chubby with a beer belly, and all the girls called him Big Daddy. He was thirty-two years old and had more money than he knew what to do with it. He wore a low-cut fade and he had a smooth chocolate complexion. His teeth were so crooked that people always wondered why with all the money he had, he hadn't gotten any dental work done. "I bet that little pussy sore ain't it?" He looked back chuckling at Tanisha as she lay balled up in the bed, regretting she had had sex with him.

Cordell, you owe me big time for this, Tanisha thought as she looked at Capone and forced a smile on her face.

Before Capone made it out the door, he was approached by the barrel of Cordell's .45 caliber. Startled, Capone froze and threw his hands in the air. "Fuck! I knew one of you little bitches was gon' be the death of me one day." Then he looked back at Cordell. "Do what you came here to do, li'l homie." Capone didn't have any fear in his eyes, and he wasn't afraid to die. He had lived a life that most people only dreamed of.

Boom, Boom, Boom! Cordell let off three stray bullets in Capone's chest, causing him to fall on the ground. Then to assure that he was dead, Cordell let one more off in his forehead.

Having snatched up all the dope and money in the apartment, Lil Jay was ready to make tracks. "Let's get the fuck outta here, before somebody calls the police." He spoke in a low, hushed tone.

Tanisha shivered, afraid for dear life. *What have I got myself into?* She thought as she locked eyes with Cordell. "Now what?" she asked Cordell as he looked over her smooth, chocolate, curvaceous body.

Cordell couldn't help but want to put his dick in Tanisha at the very moment, but he knew they had to get out of there. "When we walk out the door, run out of here screaming and hollering for help. Remember, you jumped out of his bedroom window, you only heard gunshots, but you didn't see anyone," he reminded her to tell the police.

Tanisha nodded her head yes and immediately begin to put her clothes back on.

"Naw, don't put yo' clothes back on," Cordell told her. "Jump out the window butt-asshole naked, baby. A scared bitch wouldn't have time to be putting her clothes back on." He smiled at her.

"Nigga, let's go!" Lil Jay began to grow impatient, peeking out the window for activity.

Cordell and Lil Jay flew from the apartment, firing two shots in the air, wearing black hoodies and Jason masks. Nervous,

Tanisha did as she was told. She removed the screen from the window, climbed out, naked, and begin yelling and screaming for help.

Once in the alley, Cordell and Lil Jay hurried to the stolen car that they had parked behind a dumpster, and then they took off to the Northside.

The Set-up

The next day at the detail shop, Lil Jay was antsy, waiting on Terrence to show up to get his car washed. He worked quickly, drying and vacuuming customers' cars so that he'd be ready to assist with Terrence's car the second he pulled up. In the midst of wiping a truck dry, Terrence pulled into the lot bumping Snoop Dog with a female in the car. Lil Jay hurried and wiped the driver's side of the car, threw the towel in the towel bucket, then made his way to Terrence's vehicle.

Happy about the news that his longtime arch enemy had been killed in one of his dope spots, Terrence wore a big grin on his face, knowing that he'd soon take over the Eastside of Long Beach and be the number one kingpin and shot caller. Seeing the young man that normally washed his car approach, Terrence shouted out to him as he and his lady friend stepped out of his new Escalade. "You got ya hands full today, li'l nigga, so hook the boy up and I'll grease those li'l dry-ass palms of yours," he laughed as he patted him on the head.

Lil Jay smiled with excitement. "Fo' sho', big homie, I'ma take real, real good care of you as soon as yo' whip come out the wash." Then he headed to his locker and grabbed his back pack to fulfill his end of the bargain.

After Lil Jay vacuumed Terrence's truck out, he quickly scanned his surroundings and then swiftly slid the gun and drugs under the passenger seat. Lil Jay nodded his head in satisfaction, and then he yelled out to Terrence. "It's all you, big homie!"

After inspecting his truck inside and out, Terrence told his lady friend to get inside. He wanted to speak to the young man that seemed so eager to please him.

"I told you I would grease them palms if you took care of my shit, and since I'm a man of my word, I'ma give you this hundred dollar bill and then offer you a position in my camp that'll keep them palms greased and yo' pockets fat."

Nigga, we about to take the crown, homie! "For real, man, you serious?" Lil Jay pretended to be excited.

"Nigga, I ain't about no games; I'm about making that green. Lock my number in yo' phone and we'll talk more about it later."

Lil Jay licked his lips to relieve the pain. "I don't even own a phone, big Ice, but I'ma buy me a prepaid phone with this bill you blessed me with after I get off the clock."

Terrence laughed as he opened his door. "Yeah, we gon' get you together, young!" He told the young lady to write his cell phone number down for him.

"Good looking, Ice, man, I'm definitely tryna eat out here," Lil Jay continued to play the role.

"Well, you on now." Terrence passed him a piece of paper with his number written on it, and then he got in his truck and smashed off bumping his music.

Smiling, Lil Jay tucked the number in his back pocket, and then waved his towel in the air, indicating that he was ready for the next car.

****

Shortly after pulling out of the detail shop parking lot, Terrence was pulled over by Long Beach police.

"I ain't did a muthafucking thing wrong! These fools just wanna fuck with a nigga because they think I had something to do with that nigga, Capone's, death!" He fumed as he approached the curb.

"Calm down, baby, you were driving kind of fast," his newest girlfriend, Leslie, said to him. "And they can't accuse you of doing shit 'cause you had been with me all night before you got the call about him being killed. I got your back, baby," she smiled, rubbing her finger up and down the side of his face.

"Yeah, that's a good alibi, but I wasn't with nobody when that nigga got killed." He knew lying would only make him look guilty, and since he wasn't guilty he felt he had no reason to lie.

"Me and that nigga had bad blood, and these muthafuckas is about to be all over me like flies on shit." He knew he'd be a person of interest. Terrence rolled his window down as the officers approached both sides of his truck with their guns out.

"Can I have your license, registration, and insurance, sir?" The Mexican officer suspiciously peered inside his vehicle.

"Man, what the fuck y'all pull me over for, man? I ain't did shit." Terrence sighed in frustration as he reached for his glove compartment to retrieve his registration and insurance.

The officer aimed his gun at Terrence and told him to move carefully, and the officer on the passenger side of the truck told Leslie to get out of the truck with her hands up.

Taken aback by the officer's treatment, Terrence got irate. "The fuck is going on? Why y'all aiming the guns at us and pulling my fucking girl out the truck?"

The officer snatched Terrence's door open and spoke in a hostile tone. "Step out of the car with your hands up where I can see them...now, sir!"

Without further words, Terrence climbed out of his truck with his hands up. He knew he was in a no-win situation.

After the officer handcuffed and searched him, he placed him in the back seat of the cruiser. As they searched his truck and put Leslie in the back of the other cruiser, Terrence thought, *Good thing a nigga wasn't riding dirty today! I can't wait to see them muthafuckas' faces after they dumb asses don't find shit!*

When the officer that was searching Terrence's truck stopped and signaled for the other officer to come over, Terrence began to panic. "What the fuck y'all doing?" he said out loud to himself.

Moments later, the officers were headed in his direction with what appeared to be a gun and a package of some sort.

"Hell naw! Whatever the fuck y'all got ain't mine! I didn't have shit in my car; you muthafuckas tryna set me up!" He continued to yell and scream out of the crack of the window.

Before long, a tow truck had pulled up and taken his truck, and both Terrance and Leslie were hauled off to jail for the mysterious gun and the dope that was found under the passenger seat of his truck.

Sitting in the jail, angrier than words could express, Terrence's mind was going a mile a minute. He had been set up, and only two people could be responsible for it: the police, or Leslie. When they finally took Terrence to the interrogation room to question him, the only words that came out of his mouth were, "Call my muthafucking attorney! I ain't got shit to say to you crooked muthafuckas...Y'all niggas tryna set me up!"

Part 2

The day after Terrence was arrested, Bright gathered her belongings from the five-star hotel she was occupying and went back to their apartment. With Terrence out of the picture, Bright knew she'd be safe there, and that it would also give her the opportunity to pack her and her family's belongings up. Everything they owned was there, and she didn't want to leave them behind.

Even without the police looking for Cordell, he told Bright he'd never step foot back into the apartment again. There were too many bad memories there, and he wanted to leave them behind.

The first day back in the apartment, Bright received knock after knock on the door from concerned neighbors sending their condolences for the loss of Ramon, and checking on the progress of her mother. The neighborhood elders sent food over and told Bright that they were there for her and her family if they needed them. Bright was grateful.

The next morning, after getting dressed and making sure her dentures were tightly secured in her mouth, Bright prepared to go visit her mother and see if she could get any information on her sisters, Deja and Rayonna. She missed them both dearly and wanted to see their faces and hug them tight. She had been calling Mrs. Lane to check on her babies, but she had not received a call back. Frustrated, she left several nasty messages for Mrs. Lane to return her calls. When she got on her feet, she planned on going over to pick her babies up so that her fat checks could start rolling in. Bright had no plans of letting Larry get off that easy.

As Bright prepared to leave the apartment, there was a knock on the door. *Who could that be?* Bright thought as she opened the door.

"Brighttttttttttttttttttttttttttt!" Deja yelled her sister's name the second she opened the door.

"Dejaaaa, I was just thinking about you; I miss you so much!" Bright grabbed her sister and held on to her like there would be no tomorrow.

The two hung on to each other, both sobbing and telling each other how much they loved one another.

"I swear I was just about to find out who I could call to get you guys back. I'm so sorry that I let y'all down, and I'm hurting that baby brother killed himself. He's gone and I can't believe it. And it's all my fault, Deja, I'm so sorry, boo boo; I'm so sorry!" Bright continued to cry.

Deja held her sister tightly. She knew that Bright would blame herself. "Stop it, Bright. I know it hurts that Ramon is gone, but it wasn't your fault. It was them kids at the school. They just picked on him until he couldn't take it no more. He didn't understand what was going on with himself. You are not to blame. You loved Ramon!" Deja cried, wiping Bright's eyes.

"You don't understand, Deja, it was my fault. Ramon came home early that day; he was crying his eyes out to me." Revisiting that day nearly made Bright pass out. "He came to me, Deja, hurt, and beat up, crying: 'Bright, Bright, I thought you said I wasn't a faggot anymore, and that nobody would pick on me anymore.'" Looking Deja in her tear-stained eyes, Bright held on to her sister's shoulders to keep her from falling to the floor. "Deja, I was so fucked up in the head, depressed, hurting over Larry, that I ignored him, Deja! Ramon needed me, and I wasn't there for him!" Bright hyperventilated and sobbed uncontrollably. "All he needed was a hug from me!" Bright hit her chest. "Ramon needed a hug from his big sister, and for me to tell him that everything was going to be all right. He would have still been here today, Deja, and Momma wouldn't have had another stroke. It's fucked up, but this entire situation is on me. It's my fault, and I won't feel better until I fix this."

Deja's mouth hung wide open in disbelief. Baffled, she stepped back and pushed Bright off of her. "Oh my God, Bright, how could you leave Ramon hanging like that? I can't believe you! He really needed you, and all you could think of was yourself!"

"I'm so sorry, Deja. Please don't be mad, don't hate me! I already hate myself enough, Sis. I love you." Bright fell to the floor, pleading, desperate for Deja's forgiveness.

"No! It's always been about you, you, you, and you!" Deja kicked her frustrations in the front door. "Your kids and brother needed you, and you weren't there for them, Bright." Deja wiped her eyes. "Do you really think I wanna be living in some fucking foster home? I could have ran away like you did, but instead, I stayed because Rayonna needs me, just like the twins and our brother needed you that day. All you had to do was get over yourself for just a little while. If you would have just hugged your brother and loved your kids, instead of running from them, none of us would be in the situation that we're in today." Deja turned to leave. The love she had once felt for her big sister was slowly turning into extreme animosity, and looking in her face made her gut hurt. Not only had Bright screwed over her best friend, Treasure, and her boyfriend, Larry, she screwed the only thing they ever had...their family. Deja was hurt, and she didn't know if she could ever forgive her sister for what she had done. "Thanks a lot for fucking all of our lives up, Bright...you're the best!" Deja looked at Bright once more before storming off.

Bright knew that she was wrong, but out of all the people in the world, she knew that if she didn't have anyone at all, her mother and siblings had her back and loved her unconditionally...no matter what. However, Deja made it evident that even her siblings would raise up against her.

"Oh, so you didn't know, Deja?" Bright yelled after her sister. "Welcome aboard 'cause everybody hates Bright Sheldon's ass these days, and I don't give a fuck!" Bright slammed the door, steaming, then headed to the bathroom to fix her make-up. *You either fuck with me or not!* Bright thought as she began to fix her make-up.

****

At the convalescent home, Bright was happy that she had made it in just enough time for her mother's therapy sessions. She wanted to learn how she could contribute to her mother's recovery.

"Well look at you, just a-glowing the second your beautiful daughter walks in the room," Diamond said to Rosette.

Bright smiled. "Mommy!" Bright ran over to her mother and planted kisses all over her face. "You look and smell good," she said, and then she introduced herself to the physical and speech therapist.

Though Rosetta's speech was still impaired, she was happy that she was speaking more. She was on an aggressive rehabilitation program to optimize her functional motor performances. Helping her mother do her leg and arm exercises, Bright was confident that her mom would be back to her old self in no time.

"Your mother is a fighter, honey, let me tell you," Diamond said as she changed Rosetta's bedding. "Oh, and your cousin stopped by today too. She brought those flowers." Diamond pointed to the flowers on the side of the bed.

"Who?" Bright raised her eyebrows.

"Shanna," Diamond told her.

"Aw, she's so sweet!" Bright played with her mother's finger, smiling. "Her and my momma used to be real tight back in their days. They used to be getting they one-two step on, huh, Momma?" Bright stood up, swinging her hips.

Rosetta smiled and held onto her daughter's finger. Her children were the key to her recovery.

"Heyyyy, get it!" Diamond giggled, watching Bright dance. "You gon' have to take me out, I'm not from here and I need to get out."

"You got that, after I get situated and back in the swing of things."

"I'ma hold you to that." Diamond headed toward the door. "I have to make my rounds, and then I'm off to lunch."

"Hey, maybe I can go with you. I haven't eaten all day," Bright said. She really needed someone to talk to.

"Cool, I go to lunch in about an hour. I'll come get you before I clock out."

"I'll be right here." Bright needed a friend, and Diamond seemed like the perfect person to build a new friendship with. For the next hour, Bright and her mother bonded, and even though her words slurred, Bright knew exactly what her mother's heart was trying to express.

"I am, Ma, I'm going to pick my babies up, and we're going to all be back together again real soon," Bright said seriously.

In The Game

With Cordell and Lil Jay in the game, money was coming in abundantly, and almost overnight, the two had blossomed into young, rich Northside stars. Cordell and Lil Jay had started a small organization, fronting their peers drugs for extra manpower and revenue, and they were raking in more money than they all could keep count of. Cordell made Bright his bank, and she was responsible for keeping his money safe. When Cordell and Lil Jay purchased vehicles, it seemed like every girl on the Northside started breaking their necks to ride shotgun with the city's newest stars. Loving the pussy that came with the fame, Cordell and Lil Jay took full advantage of it. The girls and women that Cordell slept with on the side knew of his relationship with Tanisha and knew that in order to creep with him, they'd have to keep their mouths shut.

Up bright and early, Bright showered and dressed, and then drove to the motel her brother was staying at to take Tanisha to the clinic. Tanisha had run away from home to be with Cordell, and he wanted her to get on birth control pills before she ended up getting pregnant. On the drive over, Bright called Mrs. Lane for the eighth time to check on her children. She had been calling her almost every day and still had not received a return call, and she was growing frustrated. After the fourth ring, the call was forwarded to voicemail...again.

"It's me again, the twins' mother, calling back to check on MY babies, and to let you know that I'll be over to pick them up once I get back on my feet. Can you please give me a call back, for like the tenth time...THANK YOU!" Bright hung up.

Pulling up in the motel parking lot, Bright parked in front of her brother's motel room, and climbed out of the car. Knocking on the door, Bright could hear the headboard banging up against the wall and the moans of a female yelling and screaming Cordell's name. Afraid that her brother was drawing a lot of attention to his room, Bright banged on the door louder and called out his name.

Moments later, Cordell peeked out the window and then opened the door. "The headboard knocking means do not disturb!" Cordell laughed, feeling good from the cocaine and kinky sex he and Tanisha were having.

"Yeah, I hope you know everybody and they momma can hear you too!" Bright pushed Cordell back inside the room for more privacy.

Tanisha was sitting in the bed wrapped up in a sheet with a white substance on her nose.

Taking notice, Bright threw her hands in the air. "I know the fuck y'all ain't up in here doing no drugs?"

"Queen Bee, calm down. We only trying the shit before we rock it up to get the bread."

"You're supposed to taste it, not sniff it up your nose! You tryna get addicted and be a fucking junkie or something? Remember rule number one, Cordell...never get high on your own supply!"

Tanisha wiped her nose then went to the bathroom with the sheet wrapped around her.

"I just tried a little bit to loosen up and have a little fun. You tripping! Nigga like me need a little something to escape this bullshit-ass life."

Bright looked at Cordell like he had lost his mind. "I know it's already too late for me to be a fucking role model, 'cause I ain't a good bitch, but I'm telling you, Cordell, that shit destroys lives. So it's up to you: you either gon' be a base-head or a boss...but you can't be both." Bright looked her brother seriously and deep in his eyes.

Hearing the shower water run, Cordell looked toward the bathroom and yelled for Tanisha to hurry up and get dressed. "Just throw your clothes on, Tanisha, you can take a shower when you get back!" Then he directed his attention back to Bright. "Look, this isn't the first time we ever tried it, Queen Bee. We aren't addicted now, and we ain't gon' get addicted. We're about our paper, and we was just having a little innocent fun." Having picked up the habit of smoking cigarettes, Cordell reached for his Newports then stepped outside the room to smoke.

"Cordell - "

Knowing his sister was about to bitch and complain, Cordell cut her off. "Queen Bee, I know what I'm doing, so until you see me looking and acting like a base-head, I don't wanna hear it. Yo' boy got money!" Cordell pulled a bank roll out of his pocket. "I know what I'm up against," he told her seriously. Desperate to change the subject, he switched topics. "You hear from Deja and Ray and check on the twins?" He lit his cigarette.

Eyes narrowed in on her brother, Bright folded her arms across her chest and then she started toward him. "I'm picking my babies up once we get our new place," Bright told him, and then she began to explain what had transpired between her and Deja.

Cordell was baffled. "So you seen Ramon before he killed himself?" His entire demeanor had changed.

Bright nodded her head. "So what, you're about to blame me for his suicide too, Cordell?"

"Hell naw, big sis! Deja acting like you knew that shit was gon' happen." Cordell's eyes began to fill with pain. After his brother's death, he wished he had gotten a final opportunity to make things right with him after all of the verbal and physical abuse he had given him. "I actually think it's real unfair of Deja to put that all on you. You were going through yo' own shit. I seen how affected you were after you and Larry broke up, and I also know for sure that you loved Ramon." Cordell nodded. "Man, you used to be on my head about calling my li'l nigga a faggot and shit." Cordell's head fell down in shame. "Man, if anything, Queen Bee, I could have honestly been a better brother to Ramon. I treated him bad because he was different."

Bright lifted her brother's chin and offered him a warm smile "Before everything happened, you were being a great big brother to Ramon. We all noticed the difference."

Interrupting their conversation, Tanisha joined them outside. "I'm sorry, Cordell, but I had to shower." They had been having sex all night and all morning. "I hope I haven't kept you waiting too long, big sis."

"Not at all. Me and my brother were just catching up." Bright told her brother she loved him, and then waited for Tanisha in the car.

Cordell grabbed Tanisha by the small of her back, kissed her, and then whispered in her ear, "Don't tell big sis how often we get high."

"I won't," Tanisha told him before climbing in the car with Bright.

On the ride to the clinic, Bright questioned Tanisha about her and Cordell's drug use, just as Cordell knew she would. "How often do you and my brother be snorting cocaine? And don't lie to me either, li'l girl!" Bright wanted a precise answer.

"We only did it a couple of times." Tanisha's voice trembled. Bright intimidated her.

"Liar, liar, gotdamn pants on fire! You're a horrible liar, Tanisha." It was imperative that Bright gained Tanisha's trust so that she'd willingly confide in her, especially where her brother was concerned.

"I'm not lying," Tanisha giggled. "Seriously."

"You ain't gotta keep it real with me, but I'll tell you what, if you keep snorting cocaine, you gon' end up being like them base-heads you see walking up and down Long Beach Boulevard, and trust me, not even my brother will want you anymore." Bright shook her head disapprovingly. "I'm so glad my brother ain't tryna have no baby right now."

"Did Cordell tell you that he didn't want to have a baby with me?"

"No. I just don't think y'all need no kids right now. I mean, y'all young, he on the run, y'all both runaways, and having a baby would only complicate things more. Why? Do you want to have a baby right now, Tanisha?" Bright asked.

"Kinda." Tanisha shrugged.

"Why now, though, Tanisha?" Bright was curious to know.

"Because we love each other, and I want to have something that's apart of him," Tanisha said truthfully.

Bright rolled her eyes and sucked her teeth. She remembered having similar feelings. Her current reality was the outcome of that, and it made her mad. "Well, don't be thinking that a baby is a guaranteed ticket on keeping a nigga around, 'cause it isn't. I love my brother and everything, but he still a nigga...remember that." Bright maneuvered the car into the clinic's parking lot and then walked Tanisha inside. *My brother don't need no baby or a baby momma that always got her hand out. Fuck that, he's young and tryna come up!* Bright hoped that Tanisha wasn't pregnant, and that she had talked some sense into her head.

****

Terrence was transferred to the Los Angeles Men's Central Jail, better known as The Los Angeles Twin Towers. He was being charged for the murder of Rashon Willis, known on the streets of Long Beach as Capone, and his bail had been denied. Having received a visit from his criminal attorney, Robert W. Snyder, Terrence fumed as he demanded to take a lie detector test to prove his innocence. Terrence hadn't slept in days in the overcrowded pod he was housed in, concerned about his freedom and trying to figure out the person responsible for setting him up.

"I didn't do this shit, man. Do you hear me? I did not murder Rashon Willis!" Terrence slammed the tip of his index finger on the wooden table. "So I'm not about to plead guilty to some shit I honestly didn't do in return for a twenty year sentence!" Terrence banged his fist on the wooden table that his attorney had his court documents scattered on. "Give me a lie detector test, I'm telling you...I'll pass that muthafucka with flying colors!"

Robert Snyder removed his prescription glasses from his thin, pale face and gave Terrence direct eye contact. "Mr. Collins, I keep telling you that a polygraph/lie detector test is inadmissible, and it will not hold up in a court," he reminded Terrence. "But if you decide to take this to trial, you'll be facing sixty years. Not only were the murder weapon and the victim's drugs found in your possession, but you have motive to have wanted Mr. Willis dead. You two were well-known enemies from rival gangs that have been beefing over drugs and territory for over ten years. With that type of evidence and history, the prosecutors won't have to do much to win the jury over." Robert Snyder stressed the severity of the case to Terrence. "None of the evidence is circumstantial, and I don't even have an alibi for where you were at the time the crime was allegedly committed. I have nothing at all," Robert Snyder said in a matter-of-factly tone, and then he put his prescription glasses back on.

"Do you work for me or the prosecutor?" Terrence was steamed, unable to remove his eyes from his attorney.

"I work for you, Mr. Collins, but - "

Terrence cut him off. "Well fucking act like it, and find something, 'cause I didn't do this shit! I'm innocent!" Terrence stood so that the officer could escort him back to the dorm.

****

When Cordell walked in the room, Tanisha was knocked out asleep in the bed with no clothes on. *This girl is a freak!* Cordell reached for his cocaine stash and placed it on the small table. Cordell leaned down on the bed and kissed Tanisha on the earlobes. "Wake up, baby, I'm home." He loved having Tanisha and her soft, sweet voice to come back to the room to every night after hustling.

"Baby." Tanisha rolled over and hugged him; she was happy to see him. "We're having a baby, Cordell."

"You pregnant, baby?" Cordell gently rubbed her stomach.

"Yes. I didn't tell your sister, though." Tanisha sat up in bed. "She doesn't seem to think that we should even be considering having a baby right now."

"Man, Queen Bee better shut up with all that! She was pregnant when she was seventeen, and she just turned eighteen. Don't worry about nothing...we gon' be straight. I don't want you getting high while you're pregnant, a'ight?"

"I had no intention to." Tanisha lay down, smiling and visualizing their life together with a cute little girl or boy.

****

After dropping Tanisha off, Bright grabbed a few rental applications from various houses and apartments that she was interested in before going to visit her mom. All of the vacancies had four bedrooms and two or more bathrooms that would suit her family perfectly. With Cordell's street success, money was no longer an issue to them. The only problem was that Bright had to provide paycheck stubs and employment references before they would perform a credit check. Bright had neither, but she didn't plan on allowing something as small as that to get in her way of finding her family a new home, and she was sure that she'd find a way around it…even if she had to go into seduction mode.

Once Bright parked and got out of the car, she grabbed her new iPhone to call Mrs. Lane. She had still not received a return call, and she wanted to get her babies back so that her fat checks could start rolling in. However, after having a conversation with her new friend, Diamond, the night before about the effectiveness of a positive attitude, Bright decided to drop her attitude and try a new approach. *This shit better work too, Diamond,* Bright thought as she hit Mrs. Lane on speed dial.

"Hello?" Larry's sister Linda answered.

"Hi, Linda, this is Bright. Can I speak to your mother, please?" Bright forced a big smile on her face to make sure her voice would smile through the phone.

"She ain't here!" Linda shot with an attitude.

"Are my kids there?" Bright asked as pleasantly as possible.

"No. My nieces aren't here either, but I do have a number for you to call, though."

This positive shit really works, Bright thought as she hit the contacts on her iPhone to add the number to her contacts list. "Okay, I'm ready," Bright told Linda once her iPhone keypad appeared on the screen.

"555-6285…that's the number to the social worker assigned to my nieces' case. Maybe you should contact them before calling over here again," Linda shot nastily, and then she hung up.

"No she didn't just do that bullshit to me!" Bright yelled out loud, then she hit Mrs. Lane's number on speed dial again. Bright was so upset that she began to breathe heavily as she cussed Linda out in her head. *Ole, young, dumb, stupid-ass bitch!*

"Hello?"

"You, young, dumb, stupid-ass bitch! You better put yo' mama on the gotdamn phone right now, or give me her cell number or something, or I swear I'm coming over there to beat yo' young, dumb, stupid ass!!"

"Bright Sheldon!" Mrs. Lane yelled into the phone, appalled at the language and tone that Bright was using with her. "You watch your mouth when you're speaking to me! It isn't appropriate, and it definitely isn't the way you speak to the woman who has been taking care of your children!"

Bright was embarrassed. "I'm so, so sorry, Mrs. Lane. I wasn't expecting you to answer the phone." Bright tried to control her breathing. "Linda told me that you and my babies weren't home, and she told me that I had to call some social worker or something before I called over there or picked them up." She began to cry. "Why are y'all making it so hard for me?"

"Linda!" Bright heard Mrs. Lane yell out to her daughter.

A few moments later, Linda's voice could be heard in the background.

"What did you tell Bright when she called here a few moments ago, and why did you tell her I wasn't home?" Mrs. Lane demanded to know.

"Oh my goodness, Momma, Bright is lying to you! I told her that you were upstairs changing the twins, and she went off on me and started cussing me out, calling me the b-word and stuff," Linda flat out lied.

Bright's mouth flew wide open. "Liar! She's lying, Mrs. Lane, your daughter is lying to you, 'cause that is not what happened!" Bright yelled through the phone.

Mrs. Lane could hear Bright yelling through the phone, but she couldn't make out what she was saying. She shook her head in disgust as she put the phone back to her ear. She did not appreciate being lied to. "Go back upstairs, Linda, and take Lori with you," Mrs. Lane told her daughter, and then she spoke into the phone. "You played that lying stuff with my son, but I don't tolerate it. You need to hurry up and grow up, Bright Sheldon. You have children to raise, for Christ's sake! Please don't call my house anymore. You don't have any rights to see your children until further notice from Children's Court."

How I don't have the right to see my own kids? Bitch, I'm getting my kids and half of your son's money, and you can bet on that! Them kids are my meal ticket, Bright thought. "What you mean court, and I can't see my kids?"

"Call the caseworker assigned to the children's case. Good-bye, Bright!" Mrs. Lane slammed the phone down.

"Them fucking dumb, stupid-ass bitches!" Bright swung in the air and cried. She was so frustrated that she could explode, and she knew the only one person that would be able to calm her down was her mother. So like a big baby, Bright ran inside the convalescent home, climbed in the bed with her mother, lay on her chest, and listened to her heartbeat until she fell asleep.

Hours later, Bright was awakened by her mother rubbing her fingers through her hair. Diamond was sitting in a chair next to the bed, sipping a soda, watching the evening news with her mother. Bright lifted up, kissed her mother on the lips, and then sat up and stretched. She felt much better than she did before.

"Thanks for trying to get me fired, laid up in the bed with my patient, who was scheduled for a shower like two hours ago!" Diamond fussed in a pretend manner.

Rosette laughed, intertwining her pinky finger with her daughter's.

"Well I'm sorry, honey boom, but I needed my momma!" Bright stuck her tongue out, teasing back.

"All right, momma's girl, I have to give Momma a shower. I get off in an hour and I don't want the night-shift nurse coming in here talking trash." Diamond stood up, putting latex gloves on.

Bright willingly offered her assistance. "I'll help you, plus I need to cut Momma's kitty-cat hair down. She don't believe in shaving, but she hates long pubic hair."

Rosette nodded her head and smiled. "Right...baby...right..." she struggled to say.

Both girls laughed while preparing Rosette for her shower.

The Next Day

Being young and immature to the dope game, Cordell and Lil Jay had the bright idea to spread the wealth throughout their neighborhood by fronting their peers drugs. The task wasn't as easy as they thought it would be, and collecting debts from their peers was proving to be their biggest challenge yet. Cordell and Lil Jay were growing angry.

"Why the fuck I gotta keep calling this nigga for my own gotdamn money?" Cordell pressed the end button on his iPhone, infuriated that he was being dodged and ignored by his so-called homeboys.

Cordell and Lil Jay took turns collecting and ensuring that weekly money owed to them was paid. This particular week was Lil Jay's week. "I told you, nigga. I been calling E-Roc, Baby Kush, and Rod for the last couple days, no answer...or call backs," Lil Jay steamed. "I'm telling you, Cordell, I'ma end up putting one in one of these niggas...on Crip!" The money, and murder of Capone had turned Lil Jay into a monster, and he was ready to take drastic measures.

After thinking about the whole ordeal the previous night, Cordell had come up with a plan, and he was ready to execute it. "We gon' handle this shit, nigga," he told Lil Jay. Needing Bright's participation, Cordell called and told her his dilemma.

Bright was upset with the treatment that her brother and Lil Jay were getting. When Cordell asked her to follow them through Long Beach with his pistol in her console to search for the guys that owed them money, she agreed. Bright knew there was a likelier chance of Cordell and Lil Jay being profiled and pulled over by the police than there was for her, and she didn't want to risk her brother being caught driving with a gun.

"I'm on my way right now." Bright left the apartment and climbed in her mother's car.

Cordell looked at Lil Jay. "We about to let these niggas know what time it is, nigga."

Lil Jay was amped up. "The li'l niggas with the bread ain't having it!" The OG's had the entire hood calling them "the li'l rich niggas".

When Bright pulled up and blew the horn, Tanisha climbed in the car with her, carefully put the gun in the console, and then filled Bright in on their plan.

Lil Jay climbed in Cordell's recent purchase, an older model Nissan Maxima, and then led the way.

"Fuck waiting, nigga!" Cordell and Lil Jay went over their plan thoroughly, preparing to knock out any wrinkles.

Since Cordell had put up the majority of the fronts owed, he wanted to enforce payment. He decided that if he wasn't paid up what he was owed on sight, he'd use the pipe he had in his trunk to beat it out of them. "Niggas need an example, fine, they gon' get one today, and learn that they must pay the piper." It was all about money and respect in the drug business, and Cordell planned on getting both, even if he had to take it.

Lil Jay nodded his head in agreement. "Pay up or get fucked up, have it yo' way." He peered through the streets carefully.

When Cordell pulled up at a known neighborhood hangout, Lil Jay smirked. "Just the niggas we're looking for!" He climbed out of the car...ready.

"I told you it was payday, nigga." Cordell popped his truck for quick access to the pipe, and then they headed through the fenced gate.

Greeting and dapping their peers, they made their way to the garage, where a rowdy dice game was taking place. Cordell and Lil Jay kept their eyes on Baby Kush, who was shooting dice, and E-Roc, who was engrossed in the game, side-betting.

"What's up, locs, Baby Kush and E-Roc?" Cordell announced with extra base in his voice. He wanted it be known that he was there for business. It didn't take long before the scene had gotten loud and began to get out of hand.

Baby Kush noticed Cordell's tone. "The fuck you mean, locs, and Baby Kush and E-Roc? What, you singling niggas out now?" Baby Kush shot sarcastically as he continued to shoot dice.

Aggravated laughter began to echo throughout the garage. Cordell and Lil Jay didn't see anything funny.

E-Roc saw this as the perfect opportunity to add fuel to the fire. "Li'l niggas letting that money get to their heads. Let me remind you niggas of some valuable information," E-Roc looked at them seriously, "Y'all ain't running shit, and ain't gon' get shit 'til I'm good and gotdamn ready to give it to you. Now run tell dat!" E-Roc pulled a large wad of money out of his pocket and turned his attention back to the dice game with a wicked grin on his face.

In between exchanging words, it was obvious that Cordell's age in particular played a big part in why money owed to him hadn't become a priority. Cordell was fifteen, Lil Jay was soon to be seventeen, and their peers used the difference when making their decisions, even when it came to giving them respect.

Without further words, Cordell headed back to his car and came walking back through the gate with a pipe in his hand. Seeing her brother grab the pipe, Bright put the gun in her purse, and then she and Tanisha bristly walked inside the yard. Swiftly, Bright passed Lil Jay the gun without being noticed.

Silence followed as Cordell stood in the yard with a pipe in his hand. Acknowledging Bright and Tanisha's sudden appearance, everybody in the yard knew what was going down except for E-Roc and Baby Kush, who were still engaging in the topic, using their age and rank to intimidate.

Cordell interrupted their conversation, specifically speaking to E-Roc, who had expressed the most disrespect. "I need my money, E-Roc...right now, today, Cuz, and I ain't taking no for an answer," he demanded.

E-Roc continued to ignore Cordell without even looking in his direction.

"The li'l rich nigga ain't playing!" One of the OG's laughed.

Before E-Roc could get out his next word, he experienced a dazing blow to the head from a cold piece of steel.

"I need my muthafucking money TODAY!" Cordell continued to strike E-Roc over the head like a great baseball player to a baseball.

Lil Jay aimed the pistol. "And bet' not, nah, nigga, even think about jumping in or stopping the homie!" he announced, wearing a hardened mug and holding his gun like a seasoned gangsta. He had the biggest crush on Bright, and he went extra hard to impress her. He even stood in front of her to offer her extra protection.

Bright stepped from behind Lil Jay and pulled her switchblade out. She had to stand on the front line when it came to her brother.

"Come on, Cuz, you gon' kill 'im!" one of their peers yelled in.

"I ain't gon' kill the homie, Cuz!" Cordell took a step back from E-Roc's beaten and bloody body. He was satisfied with the example he had made out of E-Roc. "Now, give me my money, Cuz!" Cordell took a second to catch his breath.

Out of it, E-Roc was unable to respond. His words came out muffled.

Cordell spit on the ground and then called out to Tanisha. When she walked over and stood next to him, Cordell said, "Get my money out of Cuz's pocket, baby."

With no hesitation, Tanisha did as she was told. "How much he owe you, boo?"

"Twelve-hundred-and-fifty dollars," Cordell told her.

Tanisha counted the money out in a matter of minutes and then passed it to Cordell.

"Put the rest back in Cuz's pocket and go on over to Baby Kush. He has something to give you too." Cordell shot Baby Kush a look of seriousness.

After Tanisha put the remainder of E-Roc's money inside of his pocket, she then walked over to Baby Kush and stuck her hand out. Hesitantly, Baby Kush passed Tanisha twelve-hundred-and-fifty dollars.

When Tanisha passed Cordell his money, he put it in his pocket and then looked around the yard like a pit bull ready to attack. "Don't let age come in between you niggas paying me my money, 'cause I'm a gangster...I'm coming to get mine. So let this be a lesson my North niggas. If you eat with us, then you must pay the gotdamn piper!" Cordell held the bloody pipe in mid-air like a trophy of victory.

Bright smiled to herself. *Go 'head, brother, straight, natural, born-ass boss!* She was proud of her brother's gangsta.

Lil Jay nodded his head proudly. "Bravo, nigga, bravo! That shit was brilliantly said, Cuz."

Having made their statement loud and clear, they left the yard and headed back to the motel room. Back at the motel, Tanisha ordered pizza, hot wings, and two-liter sodas from Pizza Hut and then kicked back on the bed with Bright as she rolled a blunt.

"You got you a real boss on ya hands, Chocolate Drop," Bright smiled, having given Tanisha a new nickname. "My baby brother was on his shit!" Bright disposed of the contents from the Swisher Sweets cigar in the wastebasket, and then gave her brother a high-five.

"We out there, Queen Bee, we gotta makes these niggas respect us, man." His sister's approval meant a lot to him.

"Damn straight, nigga!" Lil Jay shot Bright a lustful expression.

Bright rolled her eyes. *Li'l nigga, please, you can't afford this!* She hit the blunt.

Part 3

Having gotten nearly stomped to death in the dorm that he had been housed in at the Twin Tower correctional facility, Terrence asked the young, black nurse for her assistance. His injuries consisted of broken ribs, a broken nose, and several stab wounds to his lower abdominal area that almost punctured his kidneys. It all happened after lunch was served when Terrence was approached by a group of Los Angeles gang members inquiring as to where he was from. Proud of his city, Terrence represented the Eastside of Long Beach to the fullest, but before he could stand up to defend himself, he was being dragged, beaten, and stabbed. When he was being stabbed, one of the members yelled out, "This is for my cousin, Capone, Cuz! Tell 'em Baby-Bo sent you, Long bitch-ass nigga!"

Terrence was happy to be alive, and he planned that once his physical health was back up to par, the Crips that sent him to the infirmary would pay an even worse price than he did.

"Yes, again, Mr. Collins?" The nurse shot him a displeased look as she prepared medication for another patient.

Terrence returned the expression. "When is your shift over?" he complained. He was tired of her poor behavior and attitude.

She rolled her eyes and continued doing what she was doing. "Just like I thought, you don't want anything!"

"Look, man, I need some stronger pain medication, 'cause this Motrin ain't doing shit for me! I'm in pain!" He sighed and moaned in frustration.

The nurse walked over to Terrence and whispered in his ear. "Lay here and hurt for a while to feel five percent of the pain that you inflict on others when you decide to take a life." Then she walked away.

"You must be fucking kidding me?" Terrence lifted himself up into a sitting position, only to cause more pain to his back and abdominal area. "AHHHHH!" he roared, and then he pounded his fist into his assigned bed. "Fucking bitch!"

"You haven't seen the half of it!" she shot back, and then she continued on with her duties.

The Next Day

Earlier that morning, Diamond called Bright and asked her if she could pick her up from work because her car had broken down and she had just gotten fired for clocking a late co-worker in. When Bright picked Diamond up, she was devastated. Bright tried to calm her down, but Diamond continued to behave like it was the end of the world. Before going home to finish packing, Bright stopped at the liquor store, grabbed a few Swisher Sweets, and a bottle of sweet, red wine.

Back inside the apartment, Bright took a break from packing the remainder of her and her family's belongings.

"Girl, quit crying! There is too much money out here to be made to be crying over a job."

"It took so long to find that job, gurl, and my man gon' be mad." She wiped her eyes. "I'm not gon' be able to pay the rent, put money on his books, and I'ma end up having to go back to Texas, too. I'm not tryna leave him, either."

Diamond told Bright that her man had gotten caught transporting drugs, that he was fighting a ten year case, and that he was depending on her keeping her job to help him pay for his attorney.

"Bitch, please, you should be more concerned about taking care of you than him. Hell, he gets three hots and a cot." Bright nodded her head. "I'ma have to help you find a nigga to make it rain on you."

Diamond shook her head in disagreement. "Gurl, I cheated on him in Texas and almost lost him for good. Never again! I love my man; we getting married, gurl."

"He's in jail, you don't have a job, and he needs an attorney, quit playing." Bright hit her blunt.

"I just need to find me another job and find a way to save me some money up," Diamond replied.

"Well, honey, I don't know what to tell you. I just lost a boss and my man, bitch, I'm broke down, but I have to move on. There's so much more you can be doing with your time than crying," Bright told her. No one knew the pain she felt inside, and they never would.

A pessimistic expression spread across Diamond's face. "I need to ask you a really big favor, Bright."

"What's that?" Bright shot her a look. *Bitch bet' not ask me for no money either. She has a pussy; she better go use it.*

"I already told you that I don't have anybody here. It's just me and my nigga against the world. I wanted to know if I could stay with you until I find a new job. I'm not going to be able to afford the weekly rent I've been paying at the motel I've been staying at."

Bright sighed a breath of relief. She thought she'd have to hurt Diamond's feelings if she had asked her for money. "Bitch, yes! It would be fun to have a roommate. Matter-of-fact, when you get your job, you can stay a little longer to save up. That is, unless we start bumping heads," Bright said seriously. "I'm looking for a new place now. I just have to figure out how I'm going to come up on some check stubs."

Diamond stood up, excited. "Give me a computer and printer, and I can take care of that for you."

Bright's face lit up. "Bitch, that's what I'm talking about: teamwork!" They gave each other a high-five.

Diamond leapt on the couch and hugged Bright. "I'm not alone in Cali anymore; I have a friend."

"Bitch, you almost knocked my drink over!" Bright laughed and fussed. She was happy to have a friend again, too.

Throughout the night, the two worked together and finished packing everything up. After they smoked a blunt, Bright tossed Diamond a blanket and told her she could sleep on the couch, and then she climbed into the bed in her mother's bedroom, crying her eyes out, missing and wanting Larry back.

The next morning, Bright awakened to good news. The property manager of the house that she was the most interested in called and told her that he would hold the place for her, and that he would be willing to work with her credit check, as long as she didn't have any evictions and was able to provide proof of income. Bright and Diamond showered and dressed, and then after stopping at McDonald's for breakfast, Bright drove them to Kinko's so that Diamond could make her up some check stubs. It didn't take Diamond long to create and print them out, since she had a master file in her email. They were in and out of Kinko's in twenty minutes tops.

"These look good, bitch!" Bright continued to observe the stubs on her way to the property. According to the paystubs, Bright was a high-paid traveling nurse.

When they pulled on the property, Bright told Diamond that she'd be right back, and then made her way to the house to give the owner the rental application and check stubs. After looking her application over and seeing her monthly wages, he told Bright that she had the place. The house was located in Bixby Knolls, an adjoining area to Long Beach, just further north. Though the rent was slightly steep, Bright was completely satisfied with the residence, and she was even happier that it was tucked away from the 'hood. The house had two bedrooms upstairs and two downstairs. Having caught the older white property owner eying her lustfully, Bright told him to call her if he was interested in giving her a monthly rent reduction. *Yeah, nigga, you can get it a couple of times in exchange for that high-ass deposit!* She walked out and winked at him.

As expected, later on that night, the property owner had called Bright and invited her to a hotel room.

"Gurl, you really gon' sleep with that old man?" Diamond asked after she took a quick shower and dressed.

"I mean, why not? That way I can pocket the deposit money my brother is giving me and start putting me some money to the side. It's called work, bitch!" Bright closed her bedroom door so that she could finish dressing. "And I do need the money." Though it hadn't been long and her brother didn't mind, Bright was tired of relying on her brother's handouts to keep money in her pocket.

"You is wild, gurl," Diamond laughed.

"Naw, bitch, I'm getting paid. You broke and yo' nigga need an attorney...jump on board!" Bright shouted out teasingly.

Wrong, bitch, my nigga is straight, but the problems I'm about to give you is what you should be worrying about, whore. You think you know me, but bitch, you have no idea who you really fucking with. A wicked grin appeared across Diamond's face.

****

"Open this muthafucking door right now!" Tanisha's mother, Donna, banged on the door of the motel that she had learned her daughter was occupying.

"Fuck, fuck, fuck!" Tanisha panicked in a loud whisper as she climbed off of Cordell. They were in the middle of having sex before Cordell went out to hustle.

Cordell's eyes bucked. Not sure of his next move, he quickly stood up and put his pants on.

Tanisha threw on the pajama dress that Cordell had just purchased her then peeked out the window, hoping their silence would send her mother away.

"Open the damn door! I know you guys are in there!" Donna kicked at and banged on the door.

She was being so loud that other occupants started coming out of their room.

Noticing all the attention she was causing, she started yelling, "My daughter ran away from home weeks ago, and I just found out from one of her little friends that her and her underage boyfriend have been staying here."

"Who the fuck you tell we was here?" Cordell began to get angry. He had warned Tanisha not to tell any of her friends of their whereabouts, afraid that something like this would happen.

"I only told one of my friends, but she promised she wouldn't tell anybody." Tanisha was almost in tears. She didn't want to leave Cordell; she never wanted to leave his side. "She's not going to leave, so what are we going to do?" She was in a frenzy.

Cordell begin to think fast, he didn't want Tanisha to leave him either. "Go hide inside the closet or something. I'll tell her you're not here."

On her way to the closet Tanisha grabbed all of her things that were in eye's view, then she hid inside the closet.

Cordell kicked her shoes under the bed, and then he answered the door as if he had just woken up. "What's going on, ma'am? Why you banging on my door?" He yawned. He had seen Tanisha's mother before, but had never been formally introduced to her.

Donna pushed past Cordell, then walked inside the motel room, yelling, "Where's Tanisha at?"

Cordell played dumb. "Oh, you are Tanisha's mother, huh? She isn't here, and I haven't seen her in weeks."

"You know gotdamn well who I am, and where my daughter is at!" Donna yelled as she busted inside the bathroom, snatched the shower curtains back, and looked inside.

"Tanisha isn't here." Cordell followed behind her.

"Well, then why are her panties and bra on the bathroom floor?" Donna began to swung and punch on Cordell, imagining what he and her daughter had been doing the entire time after she had run away.

Had it not been Tanisha's mother, Cordell probably would have restrained her aggressively, but instead, he blocked as many of her punches as he could, wiggled out of the corner she had him in, and ran a few feet to safety.

"Look, Tanisha ain't here. She came over here last night for a little while, but she left."

"You gon' tell me where my daughter is right now, or I'm calling the police on you!" Donna picked up a half-filled two liter of soda and threw it at him. "I know you a little drug dealer!"

Cordell ducked to avoid being hit in the head by the soda. *If this bitch call the police, I'm grabbing my money and dope and I'm bouncing,* Cordell thought as he continued to deny knowing Tanisha's whereabouts.

Donna grabbed her cell phone from her pocket. "I gave you a fair chance, and now I'm calling the police. You going to jail today, Mr. Dope Dealer!"

"No!" Tanisha emerged from the closet, charging in her mother's direction. There was way too much dope in the room, and she couldn't allow her mother to send the love of her life and her baby's father to jail.

Meeting eyes with her daughter caused a range of mixed emotions, and Donna began to slap Tanisha all around the motel room. She was disgusted at the sexy silk and lace lingerie that her daughter was wearing. "So you grown now?!"

Cordell didn't know what to do, but he knew that he couldn't allow Donna to continue beating on his pregnant girlfriend.

Tanisha yelled for her mother to stop, but when she pushed Tanisha on the bed and started punching her in her face, stomach, and legs, Tanisha put her legs up to protect her belly and threatened to kick her mother if she hit her in her stomach again.

Bewildered, Donna decided to take her daughter up on her threat and proceeded to knock sense back into her once respectful daughter.

Feeling it was her responsibility to protect her unborn child, Tanisha yelled for her mother not to hit her in a final attempt before she launched off and kicked her mother. "Please, Momma, please, don't hit me in my stomach; I'm pregnant!"

Simultaneously, Cordell jumped in between Tanisha and her mother in hopes of breaking things up. He got punched in the mouth from Donna and kicked in the back by Tanisha.

"All right, all right, that's enough, y'all!" Cordell knelt down from back pain and wiped the blood from his lip.

Tanisha instantly wished she could take her kick back. It wasn't her intention to hurt Cordell, but she was happy that she wasn't forced to kick her mother.

"You're what?" Donna stepped back and covered her mouth in shock.

Tanisha sat up on the bed and stood up. "I'm pregnant, Momma!" she cried.

Cordell stood by Tanisha's side and held her hand. He knew it was hard for her to tell her mother, and he wanted to support her.

Bewildered, Donna sat at the edge of bed and began to cry silently. Minutes later she stood up, looked at her daughter, and then broke the tense silence in the room. "Get your shit now, and let's go, Tanisha. We're gonna be sitting at the abortion clinic the first thing tomorrow morning. I'm not going to sit by and watch you ruin your life and have a baby with this nothing-ass drug dealer!" Then Donna exited the room.

After Tanisha left with her mother, Cordell called Bright and asked her to go with him to visit their mother. It was a time that he needed to be near her.

****

It had been two weeks since they had moved into their new house and since Cordell had last seen Tanisha. During that time, Bright had also gotten her teeth implants, and they looked great. Cordell had given Bright the deposit to move into the house, and he had agreed to pay half of the monthly rent. But with all the head Bright had given the owner of the house, she was able to pocket the deposit money, had gotten the first two months' of rent knocked off, and he had even given her a few thousand to put in her pocket. Bright didn't feel the need to mention her involvement with the owner to her brother, he was balling and she felt she earned the money rightfully. Bright had let the gray-haired owner eat her out in the middle of her treating herself for a yeast infection. While doing it, she told him to bite her tingling lips and suck her itchy pearl tongue hard for relief. She didn't care about the outcome of it, since she had no further intentions of dealing with him. When she left him that last night, she told him that if he called her again, she was going to his wife about everything. She had completely cornered him. She had gotten what she wanted from him, and it made her sick performing oral sex on him.

Having gotten a little time on her hands, Bright went out and paid for a house full of costly, elegant furniture that she couldn't wait to have delivered. She postponed her search for a new car and went to visit her mother. Until her mother and sisters moved into the house, Bright allowed Diamond to occupy Deja and Rayonna's bedroom downstairs. Bright and Cordell both choose the upstairs bedrooms and left their mother the master bedroom downstairs.

Besides Diamond being a good friend to Bright, she was also a great assistant. When Diamond was around, Bright hardly ever had to do much of anything. She ran all of Bright's errands, cleaned the house, and did most of the cooking. Cordell, on the other hand, didn't care too much for Diamond. He told Bright that besides all the make-up that she wore, and her big feet, that something was very suspicious about her, and that he just didn't like her. Bright told Cordell that Diamond didn't have anybody in California and for him to give her a chance. She hadn't done anything to him besides go out of her way to gain his acceptance.

When Bright pulled up to the convalescent home, she grabbed the teddy bear that she had purchased for her mother and headed inside. She couldn't wait to tell her mother the good news about the house and all the elegant beige, black, and brown furniture she had just purchased.

When Bright got inside the room, she was happy to see her sisters, Deja and Rayonna. Deja was braiding their mother's hair while Rayonna painted her nails and toes. Having caught direct eye contact with Deja upon her entrance, Bright offered her a warm smile.

Deja returned the smile, happy to see Bright. She had been feeling so awful about their last reunion that she had caught the bus over the previous week to make amends with her sister, only to find an empty apartment and a mailbox stuffed with bad news.

Before long, the sisters began engaging in conversation that had gotten loud and chatty. Deja and Rayonna were catching Bright up on their current living arrangements at the foster home and telling her about school. Bright told them the good news about the house, new furniture, and how she had passed her driver's test days earlier and gotten her license.

"I got L's, baby," Bright bragged.

When Deja finished braiding her mother's hair, she told Bright that she needed to talk to her in private. Curious, Bright led her sister out into the hallway. After Deja apologized to Bright, the two hugged.

"I was wrong to blame you. I just really miss Ramon." Deja's voice begin to crack.

Bright held her sister tight. There wasn't a day that she didn't think of Ramon or blame herself for not listening to him. "Baby brother is with the angels now, Deja. We'll see him again."

After the sisters' emotional moment, Deja passed Bright an opened letter from Children's Court. "Larry and his mother have full custody of the twins, Bright. The letter states that you missed two court dates and have not complied with DCF's orders," Deja regretted to inform her.

Bright read the letter three times to confirm that she was properly comprehending the document. "Okay, I see this shit just got real. Mrs. Lane gave me a number to call a social worker a couple weeks ago, but I didn't think that it was this serious. I knew the babies were in the system, but not really in the system like you guys are." Bright paused. She hoped she didn't sound too insensitive. "Not like that, Deja, but you know what I'm trying to say, right?"

"Yeah, you thought Larry was just stepping up." Deja understood her sister fully.

"Exactly! I actually thought Larry and his sorry-ass mother were doing the right thing by the babies because our family was going through a crisis. Fuck that! I'm going to Mrs. Lane's house right now, and I'm about to beat somebody's ass!" Bright steamed. "Larry ass just tryna get out of paying me child support with his dumb, stupid ass!"

Deja grabbed Bright's arm. "We're in the system now, Bright, this stuff is serious! If you want the twins back, you can't be missing court."

"I know that, Deja! Why you think I been busting my butt with the house and everything? I ain't just doing this shit for me." Bright snatched her arm from her sister, "This is on Larry and his mother, 'cause his stupid ass, or his dumb-ass mother, didn't call and tell me anything about court. Matter-of-fact, his bitch-ass mother hasn't even been returning my calls."

Deja shot Bright a crazy expression. "Of course Larry and his mother aren't going to call you, Bright. They're claiming that you're an unfit mother that abandoned your kids. You have to comply with Children's Court and the Department of Children and Family Services. They've been sending you a gang of mail, too. I have a bag full of it in my backpack for you," Deja explained.

Bright had forgotten to have the mail forwarded to their new address. "Abandoned? I didn't abandon my babies!" Bright snapped. "I left them with MY mother so that I could clear my head. I was coming back," Bright lied. Had it not been for the beating that Treasure and her cousins had given her, Bright would have been long gone by now.

"Bright, when you left, Lyn and Gale took turns helping Momma with the twins while we were at school. Momma confided in them about everything that happened the day you left, and later Lyn told DCFS everything. Gale and Lyn aren't even on speaking terms anymore because of that," Deja sadly informed her. She wanted Bright to know exactly what she was going to be faced with.

"Ole stupid, dumb-ass bitch," Bright frowned. "Wait till I see Lyn's old, trifling ass. I'm beating her ass too!" she steamed.

"No, Bright. I know you're upset, but you can't go around cussing and beating everybody up. It will only make you look worse in court. Just call your caseworker today and find out what you need to do to get the twins back."

I ain't have them kids for nothing! Larry, yo' ass is about to pay me! Bright looked at Deja, pretending to have calmed down. "All right, Deja, I said I was calm!" Bright walked back inside her mother's room.

It always amazed Deja how Bright could go from being the strong, motherly, nourishing type to an all-out mean, ignorant, bitch. Bright was stubborn, and when she was mad, she could get evil. Deja nodded her head and followed Bright inside.

Having promised to pick Deja and Rayonna up after school the next day so that they could see the house and spend time with Cordell, Bright walked her sisters out to their ride, and then headed home.

Back at home, Bright bragged to Diamond about how she had gotten two numbers in less than five minutes at a gas station. Then she asked Diamond to make her a sandwich and if she could please run her some bath water. "Bitch, I'm tired, I been ripping and running all day," she told Diamond.

"You want Miracle Whip or mayo?" Diamond asked.

"Surprise me," Bright told her as she stretched across her new couches, smoking a cigarette.

Bitch, maybe I'll surprise you and blow my nose with your bread, you lazy, trifling bitch, Diamond grinned.

When Diamond walked over to Bright and passed her the sandwich, Bright looked at her like she was crazy. "That's okay, you can eat that yourself, bitch; you know I hate the butt of the bread. You wanna go to Jack in the Box and get me a Sourdough Jack combo and curly fries?" Bright passed Diamond the money. "Oh, and stop at the store, get me a pack of cigarettes and get two blunts and a bottle. Oh, and get you something too if you want, Diamond."

"I'm good, I already ate," Diamond told her.

"Ok, but pleaseeee run my bathwater before you leave, Diamond. I love you!" Bright lay back down on the couch, smoking her cigarette, watching the news, wiggling her toes.

Bitchhhhhhhhhh! I'ma find some shit to make your skin peel off your body, bitch, keep thinking I'm your fucking maid! Diamond went upstairs and ran Bright's bath water.

When Diamond walked out of the house she slammed the door. Bright lifted up, looking in her direction. *I wonder if I'm asking her to do too much? Naw, Diamond doesn't mind; she likes to help me out. Maybe I should have asked her to stay until my bath water filled up? Aghhhh... let me get my ass up and turn the water off and hop in the tub.*

****

After picking her sisters up from school, Bright stopped at KFC so that they could all sit down and eat together after they got their tour of the house and saw Cordell. When Bright pulled in front of the house, she was happy to see Cordell's and Lil Jay's cars pulled in the driveway. Excited, they all climbed out of the car and followed Bright into the yard. The girls loved how big the house was, and that it had a big front and back yard. Bright told them that she was going to have a pool put in the backyard. Rayonna jumped in joy; she loved swimming. Once Bright unlocked the front door, they were hit with a thick cloud of weed smoke. Cordell and Lil Jay had the house swarming with females, each smoking their own blunt. Loud music was being played, and lines of cocaine and expensive bottles of liquor were situated on the new cocktail table Bright had just purchased. To say the very least, Bright was pissed.

"Take Ray outside for a second, Deja, and let me clean this mess up." Bright walked inside the house, slammed the door, headed straight to the stereo system, and turned the music off.

"Hey, what happened to the music?" Diamond walked out the kitchen with a tray of snacks in hand.

Bright snapped, "You do realize that you're sitting in here getting high with a bunch of damn kids, and if the police comes, yo' ass is going straight to jail, right?" Bright slapped her hand on her hip, waiting for a response.

Diamond was at a loss for words.

"I ain't hardly no kid," the girl sitting on Lil Jay's lap said.

"I can see. What, you about twenty-five?" Bright shot her a nasty look.

"Man, get out the way with all the dramatics, Queen Bee. You be smoking with a nigga and the homie, Lil Jay, all the time. It's my nigga, Lil Jay's birthday, and us li'l rich niggas is celebrating boss style. Now grab a blunt and some drank and get faded with us." Cordell turned the music back up, and then lit a Newport.

Tingling with frustrations, Bright turned the music back down.

Having grabbed a caramel beauty by the waist to dance, Cordell shot Bright a look of anger that she had never seen before.

"Bee!" he shot.

"Cordell!" Bright shouted back, just as loud. "Your sisters are outside and would like to come in and see you!"

His mean mug quickly turned into a big smile. "Deja and Ray outside?" He dumped his Newport in an ashtray, and then told everybody to straighten up. "Take my personal tray and bottle in my room, sexy girl, I'll be in there in a few." Cordell passed the tray of cocaine and Belvedere to her.

Bright stood there angry, watching Cordell and his conquest move about the house in silence. *Cordell high off cocaine, and he got these grown, stupid, dumb-ass bitches up in here drinking and smoking on my new furniture like this the Crip spot or something! And Diamond, bitch, I'm cussing yo' ass out! I don't play this shit!* Bright fumed inside.

After Cordell sprayed the house with Glade air freshener, he opened the front door and called out to his sisters. "Where big head-ass Deja and innocent, angel Ray at?" He walked off the porch.

Rayonna came running from the backyard to hug him. "Brother, brother, I missed you! I like our new house and can't wait to come back home!" She jumped into his arms. After kissing him, she laughed. "Why your eyes red?"

"'Cause he a bad ass, Ray." Deja playfully hit Cordell in the head and then hugged her brother tight. She missed being with her family tremendously.

"Yeah, your brother is a bad boy, Ray." He pulled a few hundred dollars out of his pocket and passed it to Deja. "Make sure Deja peanut head-ass buy you something with your money too, Ray," Cordell teased, and then told his sister to come inside.

By the time Cordell had come back inside, Bright had made all of his company go into his room. Bright was sitting on the sofa alone, trying to smoke her frustrations away...she was on cigarette number two.

By the time Cordell had given Deja and Ray a tour of the house, Bright had somewhat calmed down. After eating, Deja told Bright that they had to get back to the foster home before curfew. Bright grabbed her keys and asked Diamond to ride with her to drop them off. Before they could get in the car, Cordell and his guest piled back into the living room, turned the music back up, and got back to their wild party. "Cordell's ass is out of order, and I'm all on his ass when I get back home. I don't know what's on his mind, but our home is not his clubhouse!" Bright started her mother's car up, and then took off down the street.

Seven Days Later

For the past seven days, Bright and Cordell had been arguing about the guests he continued to bring into their house. Having not smoked any Kush for five of those days made Bright even more agitated and cranky about everything. Bright had called her children's caseworker, and when she was told to come for a meeting, Bright was handed a stack of referrals to programs that she was mandated by the state to enroll in before she'd be granted supervised visitation. Bright had to submit to random drug testing and take three classes five days a week that varied from drug, parenting, and anger management classes. Then, after a psychiatric evaluation was performed, the psychiatrist referred Bright to seek therapy, because he believed that she suffered from a range of emotional disorders. Bright told the psychiatrist that the only emotional issue she was distraught about was having to go through so much to get her babies back.

Days later, Bright had enrolled and began taking classes, but she felt it would be impossible to live her life and at the same time meet the Department Of Children and Family Services requirements. Bright knew she should have been willing to do anything it took to get her children back, but she was tired of walking around pretending to want her children when she really didn't. It wasn't that Bright didn't love her children, because she did, but she knew they were in better hands than her own with Mrs. Lane.

It was the physical characteristics of motherhood that Bright dreaded. She didn't want the long nights, up feeding them, changing diapers, or having to clothe them every day and drag them around with her everywhere she had to go. Her plate was already filled with her mother and siblings, and until they were all in a better place, Bright just didn't see how her children would fit in her life.

But the big monthly payout she'd receive from Larry each month was her motivation to continue taking classes and stay off of the marijuana. However, Bright would never admit that to anyone...ever.

"Cordell, can I pleaseeeee talk to you?" Bright asked the moment she walked in the house after a long day of parenting, drug, and anger management classes. Again, he had a house full of company smoking weed and hanging all over their new furniture, and she could no longer tolerate it.

Dressed in a fall Banana Republic sweater, dark jeans, and Stacy Adam shoes, Cordell followed Bright to her bedroom, pissed. He was tired of her trying to control him and the house that he paid her the deposit and half the rent to live in.

Bright sat on the side of her bed, pulled her hair out of the ponytail it was in, and then began to massage her scalp with her fingertips as she waited for Cordell. *I can't do this with his ass no more,* she thought.

"What you ready to bitch and complain about now, Queen Bee?" Cordell said upon entering his sister's room. He was just as tired of the situation as she was. *I pay the rent around here too; fuck that,* he thought, staring at his sister as she walked over and pulled an envelope out of her closet.

Bright sat back on her bed and counted out $4,000. Here is your deposit that you paid on the house back. I ain't evicting you, but I'm paying you back for the control in the house, 'cause obviously you can't respect the rules of it, and I can't take it no more. This is our house. Our mother and sisters will be here soon... it's not your Crip clubhouse and hangout."

"How you gon' pay me my own money back?" Cordell laughed. He knew Bright had exhausted the money she had.

"You know how much money I'm holding for you! You wanna count it?" she offered with attitude.

Cordell knew Bright was serious. "You damn right! I know what you holding for me, and I told you that you were welcome to any of it whenever you need it as long as you let me know."

"Well, I ain't used none of it other than a couple grand on the furniture. You want that back too?" Bright begin to count out some more money.

"What's yo' problem, man? I never asked you for this money back!" Cordell threw the money back on her bed. Bright was messing up his high.

Bright stood up, put her hand on her hip, then started rolling her eyes and snapping her neck. "Well, if that's what I have to do in order to come home to a fucking quiet house sometimes, without all them niggas and bitches you be bringing over here, than take it!"

The argument the two were having could be heard in the living room. Lil Jay turned the music off and told everybody to go to the backyard. "We in the backyard, C-Loc!" He called Cordell by his 'hood name.

"Nigga, don't you hear I'm in the middle of something right now?" Cordell shot back.

"Nigga, hell yeah, me and everybody else in the living room, little nigga!" Lil Jay replied, reminding Cordell that he was the older of the two.

Frustrated, Bright grew tired of talking. "Look, I'm on my period, I'm cramping, I ain't had no weed, I'm cranky and I'm tired. I'm about to go to bed!" She walked Cordell to her bedroom door.

"You need me to get you anything before I step out the house, big sis?" Lil Jay asked. He respected and understood her point of view.

"You can get yo' nigga and y'all bitches and bounce! A bitch is tired," Bright told him.

Walking back to his sister's bed to grab the money she had offered to give him back, Cordell shook his head. "Nigga, get off my sister's nuts and stop kissing her ass. You sound like some type of simp-ass nigga." Then he looked at Bright on his way out of her room. "Well, if you put it that way, then I need that." He walked down the hall to leave, fussing with Lil Jay.

Bright sucked her teeth. *Niggas ain't shit!* She thought as she walked behind her brother to lock the front door.

After a couple hours of sleep, Bright was awakened by a disturbing call from Tanisha. "Bright, can you come pick me up, please? My momma is trying to beat this baby out of me because I won't get an abortion. I just left the room, but Cordell isn't there anymore."

"Have you called him, Tanisha?" Bright had enough drama of her own and was tired of dealing with other people's problems.

"My mother took my cell phone, and Cordell doesn't take unidentified calls. I called him four times already."

"I was sleeping, Tanisha." Bright rolled over in bed and laid her head back down. "Catch a cab over here, I'll pay," Bright told her, and then she gave her the directions.

Afterwards, Bright called Diamond into her room and gave her the money to pay the cab when it got there. She asked her if she could keep Tanisha company. She had a headache and didn't feel like being bothered.

"I got you, gurl," Diamond assured Bright. After pouring Bright a glass of water, Diamond got two Tylenol, put them on her nightstand, and then left Bright to rest. Diamond laughed inside. *I didn't even spit inside your water today!* Then Diamond went to the kitchen, grabbed a snack, and waited for Tanisha to arrive.

Diamond sat on the sofa, watched the evening news, and snacked on watermelon and Tajin (a Mexican fruit and snack seasoning). Diamond got up to pay the cab when she heard the driver honk the horn.

After paying the cab driver, Diamond smiled and waved at Tanisha. *Yeah, bitch, talk to Diamond, I'm a bitch's best friend.*

Though the two had never been formally introduced, Bright had told Diamond enough about Tanisha to pinpoint her weakness...and destroy.

"Thank you so much!" Tanisha forced a half-smile as she grabbed her backpack and purse off the back seat of the cab. "You must be Diamond?"

"Yup, that's me." Diamond extended a hand to help.

"Oh, thanks." Tanisha passed Diamond her backpack since her purse was heavy. Tanisha's first impression of Diamond was that she was kind and warm. But she had to agree with Cordell when he told her that Diamond wore way too much make-up. Other than that, Tanisha thought Diamond was pretty and that she had a nice body.

When they walked inside, Diamond turned each room light on as she gave Tanisha a tour of the downstairs portion of the house. Afterwards, Diamond led Tanisha upstairs to Cordell's bedroom so she could put her things away.

Inside Cordell's bedroom, Tanisha flipped out after seeing another female's G-string lying at the foot of his bed. "These are not mine!" she cried. Then she noticed three condom wrappers lying on the floor next to his bed. Tanisha picked them up. "For real, Cordell, you cheating on me?" she sobbed. Tanisha never thought in her wildest dreams that Cordell would ever cheat on her; they were so in love. He called her his wife, and she called him her husband, and he promised that he would never cheat on her. "He's probably out with whoever this female is, right now!" Her heart ached and caused her pains she had never felt before.

When Diamond walked over and hugged Tanisha, she melted in Diamond's arms like butter. *Yeah, nigga, that's for always giving me such a hard time,* Diamond thought while consoling Tanisha.

"How could he do this to me, Diamond, huh? He told me he loved me and, I'm carrying his baby."

"I know the feeling." Diamond rubbed Tanisha's hair from her face.

After a few more moments of crying, Tanisha began to lose her mind. She started walking through the house yelling Bright's name. "What room my sister in?" she asked Diamond.

Diamond led her in the direction of Bright's bedroom.

Pulled from her sweet dreams by Tanisha's loud screams, Bright rolled over in her bed to make sure she wasn't hearing things.

"Bright, Brighttttt!" Tanisha's sobs grew louder and louder as she approached Bright's bedroom.

"What the hell is going on?" Bright finished off the glass of water that Diamond had given her before she closed her eyes again.

Tanisha opened the door crying, fumbling for the light switch, and then she turned it on. "Your brother is cheating on me! He has some bitch's G-strings on the foot of his bed and condom wrappers on his floor. Who is she, where she live at, is Cordell with her right now?" Tanisha's cries were desperate.

Lips twisted, Bright shook her head in disbelief. "Tanisha, calm yo' ass down! Is you really in my room, waking my ass up, crying like a muthafucka got murdered, over Cordell and some bitch's G-strings? Are you serious right now?"

Tanisha cried so hard that she was unable to talk.

"Girl, turn my light back off. I'm going back to bed." Bright lay her head back down on her pillow.

"Bright, he broke my heart. How could he look me in the eyes and say he loves me and even make love to me and do me this way? I love your brother." Tanisha sat on the edge of Bright's bed and cried her heart out. "I wanna know."

Diamond stood in the hallway laughing inside. *Poor girl.*

Oh my God! Bright yelled inside as she rolled back over to look at Tanisha. "Tanisha, I keep telling you that niggas ain't shit, so quit crying like that before you end up having a nervous breakdown or something." Bright sat up, scratching her head with her nose twisted up in the air.

"I thought he loved me! He told me he would never cheat on me, and I'm carrying his baby." Tanisha wiped her eyes and nose with the sleeve of her sweater. "I don't understand, what did I do wrong?"

Bright grabbed a cigarette and lit it. "As long as he's lying and hiding to keep shit away from you, then that means you the bitch he love and wanna be with. Niggas gon' cheat, Tanisha, and the bitches they cheat with don't mean shit to them. He just fucking them bitches, but he making love to you! He gives you whatever you want and ask for, and only gives them bitches what he wants to. So stop all that crying, girl, Cordell is too young to be committed to one girl."

"No, Bright, me and Cordell have more than that. We're best friends; we both know everything about each other. When he's hurt, I'm hurt, and when he's happy, I'm happy. When he's lost, I help him find the way. I was the one that wiped his tears away when he couldn't hold them in anymore. It was me, Bright, me!" Tears continued to flow down her face. "We have something different than that."

"What's different?" Bright sighed. "Aren't you the one sitting here looking like you're about to jump off a damn bridge or something? Girl, pleaseeee!" Bright shook her head. "Niggas gon' lie and cheat, even my brother...I keep telling you that. I know he loves you, but you have to understand, Cordell is young, handsome, and he's coming up in the game. He gon' fuck other bitches...simple as that!" Bright scooted next to Tanisha and put her arm around her. She knew the pains of a broken heart all too well, and regardless of the fact that Cordell was her brother, she wanted Tanisha to know the truth…even if it hurt. "You my little bitch, so I'm gon' keep it real with you." Bright wiped her tears away. "My brother is gon' cheat. So either you leave, find another nigga that's gon' end up doing the same shit, maybe even worse, that might not even give a fuck about you, or you ride it out with a nigga that loves and cares for you. It's your choice, Chocolate Drop."

Looking through tear-drenched eyes, Tanisha fell silent, lost in thought. Love was nothing like she believed it to be.

After Bright put her cigarette out, she put her hand on Tanisha's thigh to comfort her. "You feel better now?"

Tanisha shook her head no. "Can I use your phone to call Cordell?" She desperately wanted to hear his voice.

Bright passed Tanisha her iPhone and told her to call Cordell in his room, because she still had a headache that wouldn't go away. Tanisha thanked Bright, then went to Cordell's room and called him.

Wrong, Bright! It's bitches like you that niggas don't give a fuck about, you gold-digging, lying-ass hoe! Why you think I'm here in the first place, you dumb-ass bitch! I'm about to fuck up your entire world. You ain't gon' even see it coming, Diamond tiptoed down the stairs thinking.

Part 4

Plan for Destruction

Tanisha had been at the house for two days, and Cordell had yet to show his face. He hadn't returned any of her calls, and Tanisha was completely messed up in the head about it. When Bright could not be there for Tanisha and had to go to one of her classes, she asked Diamond to stay close to her.

Outside, it looked like Tanisha had been speaking to Mother Nature, because the supposed-to-be warm, spring, sunny day was as gloomy as Tanisha's mood.

In the car on her way to parenting class, Bright called Cordell and left him a voice message. "Cordell, you better fucking call me back TODAY. Tanisha is at the fucking house, stressed out, pregnant, driving me crazy, and I have my own fucking problems! Please get home to handle yo' shit, and remember, this bitch got yo' dick in her hand and could take us all down!" Bright pressed the pound key on her iPhone to end the call then drove off.

The second Bright drove off the street, Diamond moved from the window and called Tanisha downstairs. *Time to work on this dumb bitch.* Diamond sat on the couch, smiling mischievously.

Tanisha dragged down the stairs, depressed. She hadn't showered, washed her face, brushed her teeth, combed her hair, or even eaten in two days. She felt like her entire world was over. When Tanisha got downstairs, Diamond convinced Tanisha to eat and then offered to brush her hair into a neat ponytail. Later, Diamond convinced her to shower and change clothes. After showering and dressing, Tanisha walked down the stairs and told Diamond that she felt one hundred times better.

"I told you," Diamond smiled, pretending to be snorting cocaine through a rolled-up piece of paper on the cocktail table.

"You snorting?" Tanisha asked, quickening her paced down the stairs. She had been desiring the temporary relief that cocaine would offer her and had been tempted to do so within the past couple of days.

"Girl, shut up!" Diamond laughed, then slid the tray of cocaine under the couch. "You don't know nothing about that!" Diamond stood up to go to the kitchen. "Now I need me a few shots and I'm good."

"Can I have some?" Tanisha stood next to the sofa and asked. Seeing Diamond snorting/using made her decision to indulge a lot easier.

Diamond turned and looked at Tanisha. "Girl, no, Cordell and Bright ain't about to kill me for you getting high."

"I do it with Cordell all the time. Just not since I been pregnant." Tanisha looked down and rubbed her small, growing belly.

"Oh, well if that's the case, then I'm going to leave that up to you, boo boo. I like getting high, so how can I tell you?"

Tanisha slid the cocaine tray from underneath the sofa and eagerly took a seat.

Diamond walked over and grabbed the tray from Tanisha's hand, then stared her in the eyes. "Under one condition, though, Tanisha boo boo."

Tanisha was desperate to snort her misery away. "What, Diamond, what?"

"That you keep this between me and you. You can't tell Cordell or Bright anything about this. I keep my shit on the low."

Tanisha took the tray from Diamond's hand. "I promise I won't say anything." Then Tanisha tore a piece of paper from the message pad sitting next to the phone, rolled it up, and snorted an entire line.

Project teen junkie in the works. Now I have to figure out how the hell I am going to get Cordell to transition from cocaine to crack? Diamond pondered, watching Tanisha snort like there would be no tomorrow. "Take your time, Tanisha, boo boo, there is a lot more where that came from," Diamond said, then walked in the kitchen for a few shots of Patron.

****

Frustrated that her mother's car had broken down while trying to make a left hand turn onto the highway, Bright got out of the car and kicked it.

"Fucking, dumb-ass car!"

"Damn, baby, kicking it ain't gon' do shit but fuck up them pretty-ass feet of yours," a guy in an old Cutlass Supreme pulled on the side of her and said before parking and getting out to offer his help.

"Beautiful lady, beautiful day, and a bad car day...not a good combination," he said as he walked over.

Bright looked at the light-complexioned, medium-height, bald-headed guy approaching her in a dirty work jumpsuit and turned up her nose. *The broke-ass niggas always got something to say.*

"Damn, I know it isn't my best day, but from the looks of it, you could use my help, am I right?" He stopped in his tracks before going any further. He did stop initially because she was fine, but he wasn't in the business of helping those that didn't want to be helped.

"If you can…but it looks like you're only a few miles from a major car crisis yourself." She threw her hand on her hip, directing her attention to his old smoking Cutlass.

"I see Boughetto got jokes, and you're right. I just copped this a few minutes ago, and if I don't hurry and get it to my mechanic's shop, then the engine gonna give. So do you need my help or not?"

"Boughetto," Bright rolled her eyes.

Seeing the expression on her face, he took it that his help was unwanted. "I guess you don't, so you be careful out here, beautiful." He climbed in his car and pulled off. *Ole bougie-ass bitch!* He laughed, watching her in his rearview mirror yelling and signaling for him to help.

"Muthafucking, dumb, stupid-ass nigga!" Bright cursed the guy as he drove away.

Moments later, another man pulled over and tried to give Bright a jump. After three attempts, he recommended that Bright have the car towed to a mechanic's shop then he left, claiming that he was already late for work.

Bright didn't have enough money on her to pay for a tow truck, so she called her brother, praying he'd answer her call. No luck - Cordell didn't answer, and her call was forwarded to voicemail.

"You need help?" a voice alarmed Bright in the middle of leaving Cordell an unpleasant voice message.

"Yes, yes I do," Bright quickly turned and responded. She was tired of sitting on the side of the freeway entrance, looking stupid.

Having attempted to give Bright another jump, the gentlemen offered to call AAA to have her car towed to a local mechanic shop. While waiting on the tow truck to arrive, Bright sat in the car pretending to be asleep to avoid further conversation with the older flirtatious man. He was disgusting. Twenty minutes later when the tow truck pulled up, Bright climbed out of her mother's car and into the passenger seat of the tow truck. Before Bright could get good and comfortable in her seat, the tow truck driver pulled into a mechanic's shop off the next exit in the Eastside of Long Beach. *I hate the damn Eastside, they bitches and niggas! He could have taken me to the Northside,* Bright thought, climbing out of the tow truck with her nose in the air.

A burst of loud laughter grabbed Bright's attention. "Boughetto, is that you?" the guy who had earlier tried to help her with the Cutlass Supreme laughed. "I guess you needed my help after all." He began to walk toward her.

"No, I don't need your help. Where's your boss at, nigga?"

"I'm that nigga." He patted his chest then gave Bright a serious look.

Bright rolled her eyes; she wasn't impressed at all.

"It's obvious that my presence is sinister to you, so let's see what's wrong with your vehicle so we can getcha up outta here," he said in a professional manner.

"Umm hmm...thank you," Bright puffed.

After he directed her to the waiting area, Bright grabbed a cup of water and tried calling Cordell again. No answer. *Damn, I hope everything is all right!* Bright's anger began to turn into worry. Realizing that Deja was at school, she texted and told her to call her when she got out of school, then she called her house to see if Cordell had come home. After the third ring, Diamond answered.

"Hel-lo."

Bright could tell Diamond was buzzing. "What's up, bitch? My brother make it home yet?"

"Gurl, no, and boo boo is about to go crazy!"

Bright rolled her eyes. "That bitch starting to get on my nerves! Shit, for all we know, my brother could be laid up dead or in fucking jail somewhere. So I ain't worried about her right now."

"You so mean, gurl." Diamond chuckled.

"No, I'm just real. This ain't like my brother, and I'm really beginning to worry now."

"Well, don't worry, 'cause, boo boo has called every jail and hospital in the area. Cordell is just out being a nigga, that's all," Diamond assured her.

Hearing the news offered Bright solace. She held her hand over her heart and breathed a sigh of relief. "Well in that case, he better hurry up and get his ass home, before he loses a good bitch."

"I agree. You on your way home?" Diamond asked, observing Tanisha indulge in line after line of coke like a maniac.

"Not yet. Mommy's car done broke down on me. I'm sitting at some mechanic's shop on the dirty-ass Eastside right now, and I know I'm gon' need me a muthafucking drink when I get home...period." Seeing the mechanic approaching her, Bright told Diamond that she'd call her back.

"I didn't catch your name," the mechanic announced once he was in the designated waiting area.

"I never tossed it to you, that's why," Bright teased, followed with a smile. "My name is Karen," she stood up and lied. Ice being an Eastside legend, Bright didn't want the mention of her name to cause any further hardship between the two. She just wanted her car to get fixed so that she could go about her business.

"My name is Tobe, but everyone calls me, T-Roc. Nice to meet you, Karen." Tobe stuck his hand out to formally introduce himself.

"I don't do nicknames," Bright shook his hand, "so Tobe will do."

Tobe began to blush. *This chick is a handful.* Lost in her pretty green eyes, Tobe had lost his train of thought.

"What's wrong with my car, and how much is it gon' cost to fix it?" Bright waved, snapping him out of the trance he was in.

"Oh yeah, nine hundred for the parts and labor. I'm sorry, but you have some very mesmerizing eyes." He was embarrassed.

"Nine hundred!" Bright's eyebrows shot straight up. "What's wrong with it?" She called her brother again, hoping he'd answer so he could bring her the money she needed to have the car serviced.

"The fuel injection system went out," Tobe explained.

"Fuck! His ass still ain't answering," Bright sighed in frustration. "Look, my brother isn't answering the phone. Is there a way you can temporarily fix the car so I can go home and get the money?"

"Unfortunately not; the entire system went out," he regretted to inform her.

Fuck, fuck, fuck! Time to go work and make it happen. Bright bit down seductively on her bottom lip. "T-Roc," she softened her voice. "Is there any way we can cut the cost down? I don't have that kind of cash on me right now." She pressed her body up against his as she whispered in his ear.

"Damn, girl, you gon' get me in trouble!" Tobe pushed Bright to the side so that his brother-in law and other employee wouldn't see their interaction. "I'm a very married man." He struggled terribly to hold his composure

Looking deep in his eyes, Bright exposed her right breast, then grabbed his hand and gently rubbed it all over her breast until her nipple got hard. "Shhh...I won't tell." She licked her lips and winked her eye at him.

"Look, I have something you can do." Tobe led Bright to the tire section of his shop, then told Bright that she could get rid of all the bad tires and stock the good ones.

Bright looked at him like he had lost his mind. "You playing, right?"

Ten minutes later inside of his office, Tobe had Bright bent over on his desk. He was plunging in and out of her wet vagina, slapping her ass until each cheek turned red, and filling his hands up with her full, firm breasts. Tobe had fallen weak to her sweet temptations. "You suck dick good, and got good-ass pussy, too! Ohhh, I'ma make you my side bitch," he moaned.

"Ohhh, yes, baby, yesss, I wanna be your side bitch, you have enough dick for me and your wife to share. I love sucking and fucking that big, ole, giant dick," Bright moaned, giving Tobe her classic performance. "It's soooo big, ohhh, it feels so good inside of me. Ohhh, aww, fuck me, fuck me, fuck me harder, baby, that big dick feel so good to me!" She looked back at him and exchanged fuck faces.

"Ahhhh, you so fucking beautiful, girl!" Tobe bit his bottom lip and took two deep thrusts inside of Bright, nearly taking her breath away. "You gon' bring me this pussy every day, huh?" He slapped her ass then squeezed it, on the verge of cumming.

"Every day, baby, every day!" Bright continued to look back at him, slamming her ass up against him. She contracted her vaginal muscles on his penis until she had him locked inside of her, then squeezed the cum out of him.

"Ahhhh," Bright joined him in unison.

"Karen, that pussy ain't no joke!" Tobe helped Bright off the desk after he pulled the condom off and threw it in the wastebasket. "My wife ain't sexed me in weeks!" He was relieved.

Bright grabbed her purse, retrieved a few packs of feminine wipes, and then began to freshen up. After she was done, she looked at Tobe and nonchalantly said, "My job here is finished. Now how long is it going to take you to do yours? I have a lot to do today." Bright spoke as if she hadn't just experienced some of the best sex she had ever had. If she wasn't mistaken, he had even made her climax.

Tobe gave Bright a look of disbelief. "Damn, like that?" He had never felt so used and insulted by a woman his entire life.

Bright put her hand on her hip, then looked him over with a smirk on her face. "Yup. Now what time will you be finished?"

"After you give me half of the damn money, I'll be finished in less than a few hours. Trust me, I'ma hurry up and get yo' ass up outta here!" Tobe snapped. He was completely turned off by her attitude and deeply regretted accepting her proposition.

Bright's eyebrow shot straight up. "I ain't paying you a dime! We made a deal." She rolled her eyes.

Tobe began nodding his head, "Yeah, to cut the cost. We didn't agree on anything being free, Karen."

"Umm, I was talking about cutting the cost money-wise before you put ya dick in my mouth and pussy." Bright folded her arms across her chest.

"Hoe, you must be out yo' gotdamn mind!" Tobe's bruised ego begin to replenish, seeing the crushed expression on her face. "So it's up to you: you either pay me half, or that piece of shit will sit out there until I decide to junk it." He opened his office door, finalizing the conversation, and then looked at her.

Gazing at the picture of him and his wife, Bright began to think wickedly. *Nigga ain't about to get over on me; head and pussy cost. It's time to play scandalous.* She smirked. "If you don't fix my shit, nigga, I swear I'll start crying and screaming rape...right now." She stood from his desk and slowly started toward him. "I'm sure your brother-in-law would love to tell his sister about it too!" Bright switched past him, batting her eyes.

Nostrils flaring, Tobe aggressively grabbed Bright by the arm and then pulled her close to him. Angry, he knew he was in a no-win situation, and he wanted her to know just how much he despised her. "You one evil, sick, twisted-ass, bitch...you know that? Just trash."

"Trash I'm not, but the last nigga called me 'pretty poison'." Bright yanked her arm from his hold, and then went to sit in the waiting area for her car to be serviced. *These niggas got me fucked up!*

Early the Next Day

"Just drive me to my house, E!" Cordell exclaimed, climbing in the passenger side of his new Beamer, furious. After stopping at Lil Jay's trap spot, the two had encountered their first quarrel, which led to a fist fight.

Lil Jay was infuriated with Cordell's absence on the streets and expressed his dismay privately the moment Cordell approached him for cocaine. "Nigga, you out here moving like a smoker, snorting up all yo' money and tricking on these low-grade-ass bitches, Cuz. You tripping, on the North!" Lil Jay tried to dismiss him.

"Cuz, fuck that!" Lil Jay's statement was one that Cordell's ego couldn't stomach, so he punched Lil Jay in the eye, which lead to a drag-out fight.

Fighting, neither of the two fought at their maximum potential. They fought like brothers that needed to release their frustrations in a slap-box-like manner that later turned into a wrestling match. Worn out from days of little sleep, Cordell was relieved when their peers separated them. Lil Jay had him pinned to the ground, and he didn't have enough energy to break loose from his hold.

"You still my nigga, C-Loc, but you fucking up, my nigga, on Crip, and I ain't about to accept or watch that shit go down, homie!" Lil Jay yelled as Cordell climbed in the car and instructed Erica to drive off.

Inside the car, Cordell steamed, inspecting his face in the visor mirror. His bottom lip was busted and he had a small knot over his right eye. The one day he planned to spend out with Erica turned into a three-day binge on drugs, alcohol, partying, and plenty of hardcore sex. In that time alone, Cordell put $6,000 down on a Beamer that Erica had talked him into getting, spent $1,500 at a high-end hotel that she had begged him to take her to, had lost his iPhone, and together they made close to an ounce of coke disappear, snorting and lacing it in their joints.

Angry, Cordell ranted on and on as Erica drove him home. "Cuz's bitch-ass betta be glad he my nigga, cause I would of popped a cap in his ass, on Crip!"

"I'll make you feel better, baby! We can get some ecstasy and go to my place. You know I know how to make you feel better." She rubbed his thigh, making her way to his penis. Erica was one of his old junior high school homegirl's big sister who had practically snatched him up and seduced him in the backseat of her 2003 Volkswagen Bug. Erica was tall, thick and light-skinned. She had tight gray eyes, and she wore a short haircut. When Erica had spotted Cordell on the block selling drugs, she took an immediate interest in him. She told Cordell that his age didn't matter to her because he was mature for his age, and she was both physically and sexually attracted to him. Cordell enjoyed being with Erica for the most part because she sexed him good, made him feel good, and treated him like a grown man, but at the moment, she was getting on his nerves.

"Mannnn, take me to my house so I can get my money and get back on my grind. Fucking with you, I'm gon' end up broke!" He removed her arm from his leg.

"Damn, baby, don't be like that! I'm yo' boo and remember...we a team now." Erica was infatuated with his money and loved how he'd spend it on whatever she wanted.

Like a ticking time bomb, Cordell snapped on Erica, claiming that they were a couple. He liked her a lot, but had explained to her when they first started messing around that he had a girl. At the time, Erica didn't seem to mind, but after the three days they spent together and him getting the Beamer, she started pressing the idea of them being together. Though it was true that Cordell misled Erica to believe that they were more when they had sex and got high, He had only said those things in the heat of the moment. Tanisha was the only girl that had his heart; any other female that he dealt with on the side was just that.

When they pulled up in front of his house, Erica threatened to take his car and leave, so Cordell took the key out of the ignition and told her to shut the fuck up and come inside while he freshened up, or to sit in the car by herself. But what happened next came totally as a surprise.

****

Having seen Cordell and a girl in a Beamer pull up in front of the house, Diamond hopped up from the chair she was sitting in and ran to the stairs. "Tanisha, boo boo, gurllllll...Cordell just pulled up in a BMW with some yellow bitch!" She entered the bedroom without knocking.

Within a hot New York second, Tanisha was down the stairs and out the door, taking turns swinging on Cordell and the female in the driver's seat. Cordell tried to contain Tanisha, but she was so amped up and full of energy that she was running a marathon on him. Erica got out of the car and the two began to fight in the middle of the street. Cordell grabbed Tanisha from behind, begging her to stop, and started carrying her back into the house.

Erica called both Cordell and Tanisha every bitch in the book, angry that Cordell was giving more attention to Tanisha than her. "Take me the fuck home now, Cordell, or I'm fucking this car up!" She threatened as she began to kick the driver's door with her bare feet.

"Fuck my shit up and I'ma have my sister beat yo' ass!" He replied, practically dragging Tanisha into the yard.

Spit flying from Tanisha's mouth, she desperately tried to break loose from Cordell. "No, let me go, Cordell! On everything I love, on my unborn child, I'ma beat that bitch's ass, and then I'm fucking yo' ass up, too!" Tanisha hauled back and slapped Cordell in the head.

Diamond watched from the window, laughing the entire time, plotting. *Ohhh... I should call the police! Cordell has a warrant, and Bright gon' be pissed when she get home and her brother's ass is in jail, and if she ends up getting evicted behind this...* Diamond stopped in her tracks. *Oh hell no, I'm tripping! I can't afford for them pigs to be in my face either. Hmm... I'll just slip out the back door and disappear when they get here.* Diamond grabbed the phone to dial 911.

Sweating and out of breath, Cordell finally managed to pull Tanisha into the house. When he saw Diamond on the cordless phone, he went ballistic. "Diamond, what the fuck you in here doing hopping on the phone fo', like you don't see what the fuck is going on outside?" Cordell took the keys out of his pocket and tossed them to Diamond. "Drop that crazy bitch outside home, NOW, before somebody calls the fucking police, Cuz! I have a warrant; I ain't tryna see the police right now!"

Diamond grabbed the key, fussing as she headed out the door. *If she didn't hate 'em already, it wouldn't be hard to. Muthafuckas, I see why they Momma ended up having two strokes!*

Crying and punching Cordell every opportunity she had; Tanisha cried, "Is that the bitch you was fucking that left her G-strings in your bedroom?"

Cordell tried desperately to calm Tanisha down without getting his eyeballs ripped out.

Minutes later, Tanisha stopped fighting Cordell and began to sob, asking him why he was cheating on her.

"Baby, she don't mean nothing to me. I was only fucking with her because she gave me the pussy and I didn't have you."

Tanisha's eyes widened. "You was doing powder with that girl, wasn't you?" She began to attack him again. She knew how wild and passionate Cordell could be when he was on cocaine, and it made her ass hurt. "You was having sex with her like you be making love to me all them days, wasn't you?" Tanisha ripped his shirt off of him.

"Naw, man, I ain't make love to that bitch! I don't never make love to other bitches like I do to you, baby, and, if I would have known you were home, I would have been back home," Cordell replied, making distance in between the two of them. He had no energy and he was worn out.

"Oh, so there's more girls than that bitch? Bright was right; even you. You ain't shit, Cordell! And quit acting like I didn't call you like a hundred times!" Hurt, Tanisha walked up the stairs, crying, hurting, and just wanting to be alone. "I should have stayed home!" she cried.

Cordell wanted to beat his own ass. *I did not mean to say that shit, Cuz, fuck!* "I lost my phone and had to get a new one." Cordell followed behind Tanisha, trying to show her his new phone. "I'm home now, baby; I'm home, with you, where I wanna be, and you're right where you belong, right here with me, baby. Everything ends today; no more cheating. We're about to have a baby. I love you." He caught her midways up the stairs and hugged her tight. Tanisha sobbed in his arms.

Diamond stepped in the doorway ready to cuss Cordell out. *I ain't going on no more missions for his little, dumb ass no more!*

Looking at Diamond, Cordell felt the need to apologize for the way he had treated her. She wasn't half-bad and always went out of her way to be kind to him. *Maybe Queen Bee's right; the bitch ain't bad.*

"Aye, my bad for the way I came at you earlier, Diamond. Nigga just needed help. It wasn't your fault. Thanks for your help," he said sincerely. Then he told her to toss his car keys on the table.

"Your keys? I thought that was Erica's car?" Diamond was confused.

Cordell quickly climbed down the stairs. "You gave that bitch my car?" Cordell headed to the window to look outside. He hoped Diamond was either playing with him or that they were having a terrible misunderstanding.

"Hold up, Erica told me that was her car. She showed me the paperwork with her name on it, and told me that she just needed directions to the highway, and then dropped me off on the corner," Diamond explained. "Now what did I do wrong?"

Since Cordell was too young and didn't have a driver's license, after Erica persuaded him to get the BMW, she volunteered to get the car in her name because she was old enough, had good credit, and a driver's license. Having paid a large sum of money on the vehicle, Cordell planned to pay the remaining balance within the next few days after he got his hands on his money, and Erica agreed that she'd go to the DMV with him shortly thereafter to put the car in whomever's name he desired. "I just believe that a boss should ride like a boss," she told him.

This bitch just got me! Cordell hit the wall in anger, causing an expensive portrait to fall to the floor, shattering glass. He nodded his dismay, directing his attention to Diamond with a mean mug on his face. "Cuz, didn't I ask yo' ole funny-looking ass to drop her off? If it was her car, don't you think I would have just asked you to pass that bitch the keys?" Looking at Diamond made Cordell angrier and angrier, and in order to avoid taking his frustrations out on her, he stomped up the stairs, cursing Diamond loudly. "Stupid-ass bitch! Man!"

Tanisha ran behind Cordell in hopes of calming him down. She felt sorry for the way Cordell was speaking to Diamond.

Having made an honest mistake, Diamond pleaded after him, "Cordell, I'm sorry, but I swear, I didn't know that was your car!"

"Sorry ain't gone cut it, bitch, and don't say another muthafucking word to me! It's already taking everything in me not to slap the shit out of you!" Cordell yelled back down then slammed his bedroom door.

Diamond cringed in anger at Cordell's blatant disrespect. *I didn't know that was your car, nigga! The muthafucka wasn't going to be yours for long anyways, since YO' STUPID ASS put the car in her name in the first place. She was already gon' take that shit! But you calling me dumb…negative muthafucka!* Diamond set the broken portrait up against the wall at an angle to ensure that Bright would notice it the second she walked through the door, then she grabbed the broom from the kitchen to clean-up Cordell's mess before Bright returned home.

After a long day out taking parenting, anger management, and drug classes, Bright dragged herself into the house, beat. All she wanted to do was take a couple shots of tequila and go to bed. However, when she walked inside her house, she felt like she had stepped into a war zone.

"Bitch, you were doing cocaine with my girl, bitch, and you see clear as day that she pregnant!" Cordell was close enough to kiss Diamond, and her eyes were as big as quarters.

Bright was tired of having to tolerate unwanted drama every time Cordell was in the house. "What the fuck is going on now? Damn!" Bright snapped. Cordell was in Diamond's face calling her stupid bitches.

Tanisha slid in between the two, trying to break it up. "Cordell, I only said I got high with Diamond all day so that we could do a few lines together. Or at least do a few every once in a while until I have the baby!" She explained. In the middle of pillow-talking, the truth that Tanisha swore she'd keep between her and Diamond slipped out in the hopes that Cordell would get high with her. Instead, her plan backfired terribly. Cordell wasn't having it...and he was heated.

You little bitch! You went there...I got yo' powder-head ass! Diamond looked from Cordell to Tanisha, and then began to play the victim. "Oh my God, no! I would never give a pregnant girl drugs! Mind you, I don't even do coke myself; I only blow weed."

Nodding her head, Bright pointed at Tanisha and yelled, "Why you tryna keep shit up, Tanisha? Didn't I tell you if you wanted to stay here that I didn't want any drama? Didn't I?" She reminded her.

"Tanisha nodded her head yes. "I'm sorry, Bright. I told Cordell I was just playing."

Hearing the tone Bright was using with his girl, Cordell felt the need to defend her. He had already caused her to have a trying day. Cordell immediately stopped arguing with Diamond and looked at his sister. "What you mean IF she wanted to stay here? We fifty-fifty up in here, Queen Bee, and there isn't an 'if' where Tanisha's name is concerned. This is her home too, but this bitch right here..." he pointed at Diamond. "Now this is the bitch's ass you should be getting in. She ain't to be trusted, and I want her ass outta here TONIGHT!" He flexed his power.

"Excuse me!" Bright shot her brother a disbelieving facial expression at his approach to her. "Nigga, you must be out of your mind talking to me like you don't have no sense! You need to check yo' self, like right now!" Bright was furious and was tired of Cordell playing the boss card around the house. Bright had sucked the wrinkles out of an old dick for the deposit, first couple months' rent, and then some, and though she had never disclosed that information to Cordell, she had already given him back half of his money.

"I'm just making it be known that when it comes to Tanisha, my house is her house!"

"And that's fine, but let's get one thing straight, brother. You pay to stay, but I run this muthafucka, and that's why I gave you half of your money back...remember that!" Bright snapped her neck. "Other than part of the rent, I pay everything else, so my word goes around here! And yo' bitch lying 'cause she wanna get fucking high is not my problem, or Diamond's... and I think you owe her an apology!"

Cordell took two steps back and shot his sister a nasty look. "Apology, my ass! Cuz, fuck that bitch, and this house! Matter-of-fact, give me my money, and we'll leave this muthafucka, cuz I ain't gotta be here."

Bright threw her hand on her hip and sucked her teeth. "Cordell, y'all ain't gotta go nowhere! We're family; we roll together! I'm just saying you need to check yo' self, 'cause you going ham on the wrong people, including me, and I'm not having it! Our momma and siblings will be home soon, and we don't need all the drama." Bright didn't want to fight with her brother. They were on the same team, and she just wanted them to be on the same page.

"Naw, you going in on us, yo' family, over this ole straggler-ass bitch, when WE the reason you living in this house, got bread, and is living a carefree life with no worries!" Cordell spat back. "Me and my girl is responsible for that, so don't come at me like I'm some, stupid-ass little boy! I ain't a kid no more. I'm in these streets making shit happen...every day! Now you remember that!" Cordell stared at his sister long and hard.

"Are you really coming at me like this, Cordell?" Bright's eyes began to fill with tears as she and her brother stared in each other's eyes. "Nigga, as far as I'm concerned, Diamond was already outta here after this, 'cause you know what I'm about; family is first. But you..." Bright pointed in her brother's face. "You on some big macho, ego bullshit and you can let the door hit yo' ass on the way out too. I'm the big sister here, and nigga, I'll always be able to hold myself down!" Tears fell from her eyes. With everything that had been going on, Bright relied on a peaceful home and her family to get through the turmoil. But lately, Cordell had only been adding to it.

"Yeah, give me mine!" he yelled after Bright. Then he looked at Tanisha. "Go pack our shit, baby, we outta here." Cordell called his homeboy that he let use his Nissan Maxima and told him to pick them up. *Where I pay, my girl can lay, all day, fuck that!*

Bright passed Cordell his envelope full of money. "It's all there," she told him and then slammed her door. *If he wanna leave, he can go! I can take care of my damn self.*

Hours later, the house was in complete silence. Cordell and Tanisha left and Diamond stayed inside the bedroom. Bright laid in bed, allowing her problems and pain to release from her eyes. She just wanted to be happy, but happiness seemed so far away. Drifting into misery lane, Bright received a text from her sister Deja. It was a picture of her and Rayonna, and the caption read: *WE LOVE YOU, BRIGHT!* Smiling, Bright replied: *I love y'all more and can't wait to be together again!*

Deja texted back: ***Cordell loves you too.***

Bright replied: ***Yeah right!***

Deja texted back: ***Yes he does, we just had a long talk. He's just upset. Ray and I are gonna stop by after school tomorrow okay? I love you, sister, stay strong...we're all we got!***

Smiling, Bright replied: ***Can't wait to see you guys, let's do lunch! And that's right, Deja! We're all we got...and you guys mean everything to me! Sweet dreams, hug yourself and kiss Ray baby for me...Goodnight!***

****

Lying in the bedroom, Diamond located Tanisha's mother's number. Diamond had convinced Tanisha to call her mother earlier that day to let her know she was all right. When Tanisha called her, she told Diamond it went to voicemail. Having found the number, Diamond locked it in and decided to give her a call the next day. *Damn, damn, damn! Her fucking brother left and she still didn't tell me to stay! Okay, I see I gotta make this nigga and his little bitch disappear for a while so Bright can realize that she needs me. Time to let momma know what type of dope her daughter's doing and where the fuck her baby girl is at, fucking big mouth, black bitch! And Cordell, don't worry, you'll be in jail soon!* They were messing up the plan, and now Diamond had to put it back in the right direction.

****

In the middle of the night the doorbell rang, immediately waking Bright up. She was hoping it was Cordell and that he was ready to come back home. *I knew yo' ass would get ya mind right sooner or later.* Bright hurried down the stairs.

Hearing Bright climb down the stairs, Diamond stood in the hallway listening. *I hope that ain't the little boss and his powder-head bitch!*

"Who is it?" Bright said before opening the door.

"It's me, Bright, Lil Jay."

Bright swung the door open, hoping he wasn't coming to be a bearer of bad news. "What's going on, Lil Jay?" she asked with a look of curiosity on her face.

"'Sup, Bright. Cordell here?"

"No, he isn't, why; is everything all right?" Bright told him to come in. He looked like he had a lot on his mind. "Have a seat," Bright told him once they got in the living room.

Lil Jay sat down. "Me and that nigga got in a little tussle today. I been tryna holla at him, but he been ignoring my calls."

Recalling the knot over his eye that she assumed Tanisha had given him made Bright's temperature instantly rise. "For what?" She stood up, demanding to know.

"Naw, not like that; me and that nigga still good, that's why I wanted to holla at him."

"Don't tell me y'all niggas getting into it over no bitches?" Bright sucked her teeth.

"Hell naw! That's my nigga; we like brothers, never no shit like that!" Lil Jay nodded his head.

"It's over money, ain't it? I thought y'all vowed to never allow money to come in between y'all." Bright shook her head in disgust.

"Naw, it ain't over no hoes or money, Bright. That's little shit to niggas like us." Lil Jay stood up and grabbed both of her hands. After a moment of getting lost in her beautiful, green eyes, Lil Jay said, "You know you one of the bombest females I've ever seen in my life? Every time I see you, my dick gets real hard. You gone be mine one day." He grabbed her by the waist.

"Lil boy, pleaseee!" Bright pushed him off of her. "You ain't got enough money to fuck with a bitch like me, and besides that, you my little brother's homeboy. Now sit yo' ass down and tell me what's going on with you and my brother." Bright pushed him down on to the sofa.

Lil Jay laughed ignoring her question. "Damn, like that? Well how much money I have to have to fuck with a dime like you?" He pulled her on top of him.

"Lil Jay, you gon' make me slap yo' ass! Touch me one more time!"

He kissed her on the lips. "Slap me now; that was worth it."

SMACK!!! Bright slapped him so hard that his dark brown skin turned hot red. "Now get outta here! Yo' ass went too far tonight!" Bright pointed to the door.

Lil Jay stood up and emptied his pockets on the table. "Let me kiss them lips one more time, and it's all yours," he said seriously.

Bright looked at the money, eyeballing it to be a couple grand, and then looked at Lil Jay. "Come get it."

Lil Jay turned his fitted cap to the back, walked up, grabbed Bright by the waist, and kissed her lips. Though he knew he wasn't supposed to, he slid his tongue inside her mouth to steal a tongue kiss from her. To his surprise, Bright indulged in it passionately. Lil Jay squeezed her ass, pressing her up against his hardened penis. He wanted her badly. "I wanna fuck you so bad," he said in between breaths.

Bright slid her tongue out of his mouth then bent down to retrieve her money. She was low on funds and she needed it. "There's the door...now use it."

"Bye, girlfriend, I'll be back for the pussy next time." He smirked, visualizing his dick in Bright's mouth.

"Goodnight," Bright waved at him nonchalantly. Once he walked out the door, Bright locked it then went upstairs to count her money before she went to bed.

Diamond stepped out of the hallway to grab a glass of water, thinking, *Damn, Bright is a monster about her money! I wonder how much money I'd have to drop on her to get in between them thighs. I got something for her ass to suck on, all right!* Diamond giggled and then tiptoed back inside the room.

Happy Birthday, Rayonna

"Happy birthday to you, happy birthday to you, happy birthday dear Rayonna, happy birthday to you!"

The siblings clapped, having lunch at the Olive Garden to celebrate Rayonna's birthday. This had been the first time in almost two weeks that Bright and Cordell had seen each other since their falling out. During that time, Tanisha kept in touch with Bright to let her know that they were all right, and that was the only reason she hadn't gone out to search for them herself.

"I love yo' mean ass, Queen Bee," Cordell told Bright when he arrived at the restaurant with Tanisha.

Happy, Bright stood up and hugged Cordell tight. "I love you too, young boss, and remember, you'll always be little brother to me," Bright told him after kissing him on the cheek.

In the midst of all the joy, seeing her family sitting together at the table, Rayonna's smile began to tremble, and then cracked. "I miss Ramon! He's supposed to be here too!" She cried.

Deja hugged Rayonna and told her everything was going to be all right.

"I wish someone had been there for him! Maybe he'd still be alive!" Rayonna cried. "I miss him so much!"

Hugging Rayonna, Deja instantly looked at Bright. She had never mentioned Bright being inside the apartment the day Ramon killed himself, and she didn't want Bright to begin to feel bad. But it was too late; Bright's eyes were full of tears. She stood from the table, excused herself, and then walked to the restroom.

Cordell stood up. "Come outside and let me talk to you, Rayonna." Cordell pulled her seat out as he watched Bright make her way to the restroom.

Rayonna stood up, wiping her eyes. Cordell held her hand and led her out the door.

Deja wanted to be there for Bright, but she couldn't. She had forgiven Bright and she loved her, but deep down inside, she still blamed and resented Bright for Ramon's loss, no matter how much she tried to reason with herself otherwise.

"I'll be back." Tanisha stood up. Bright looked disturbed, and Tanisha wanted to comfort her. Bright was always calling to check on them, and for once, she wanted to be there to check on her.

Inside the restroom, having stopped herself from shedding tears, Bright leaned over the sink, trying to pull herself together. *It wasn't your fault, Bright. How could you know Ramon would kill himself?* she continued to tell herself.

"You all right, Bright?" Tanisha said once she entered the restroom.

In need of a hug, Bright quickly faced Tanisha and hugged her tight. "Yes, I'm better now; thanks, Choc. I love you."

Bright had never told Tanisha she loved her, and whether she knew it or not, Tanisha looked up to her as a big sister and cared for her a lot. "I love you too, Sis."

When Bright and Tanisha got back to the table, Cordell and Rayonna had already come back inside and he had Rayonna and Deja cracking up, laughing. Bright hugged Rayonna from behind and kissed her all over her cheeks. Joining in on the laughter, Tanisha took her seat.

Later, Cordell blessed everybody at the table with money, and then they all headed to the mall. He told Rayonna she could get whatever she wanted. While shopping, Bright told Cordell to come back home.

"Diamond has been gone since you left. There is no use in you wasting money at a hotel when you and Choc have a home to come to."

Cordell nodded in agreement. "Our room is paid up for the month already, but I'll be back next month, fo' sho', Queen Bee."

Part 5

Back on the Prowl

"Queen Bee, I'm in jail," Cordell said to her through the phone while she was driving to parenting class.

Bright had a court date coming up and she was desperate to get her kids back so she could get paid. Her money was low because she was unable to get high, and she grew tired at the thought of working niggas for money without her Kush in her life. But she had bills that needed to be paid, her mother's old car was beginning to give her problems, and since she had her license and desperately wanted a brand new car, she pushed forward in her search for elite men that could swell her purse and pockets back up. Other than her new boss, Marion, that drove a Mercedes, whom she had met at the mall, her brother had been her only other outlet for money. She even tried to reel her white-haired property owner back in, but he told her that after the number she did on his lips, all he wanted from her was his first-of-the-month rent.

"Oh my God; in jail for what?" Bright asked nervously.

"Man, I got caught with an ounce of dope on me! I'm straight though. I need you to pick up Tanisha from the room, Sis. Look out for my girl, Queen Bee," he stressed. "She got that bread I was saving up and I added some more money to it too. It should be about twenty-five grand. Use half of the money to pay an attorney for me and the other half for rent, bills, and you and my girl. Make sure you give her something to put in her pocket, Sis, and keep her away from yo' homegirl. Pleaseeee, Queen Bee, my baby is depending on you, all right, Sis?"

"I got you, brother. We'll be up there to see you too, all right? I love you." Bright's eyes watered and she sniffled.

They had just made up at Rayonna's birthday lunch and were supposed to move back into the house the following week.

Bright shed tears. She was heartbroken that her brother was in jail.

"Quit crying, Queen Bee! I'm a monster, so don't cry or worry about me. Lil Jay has my work and gon' hold me down. Tell that nigga to keep money on my books while I'm in here, and if y'all need anything while I'm gone, hit him up, all right?"

Bright wiped her eyes. "You know ya sister got this; I stay keeping the niggas paying. I'll relay the message to Lil Jay, and whatever money he gives me, I'll put up for you until you get home. I'll get at the attorney right after I pick up Tanisha from the hotel. I'ma take care of her ass like she's one of my own little sisters; that's my bitch, so don't worry about her. Call us all day and night too."

"Thank you, Sis. I'll just have Cuz drop all my bread off to you, and don't hesitate to use whatever you need to keep shit going. You ain't gotta be out there like that. I love you. Kiss Ma for me," Cordell said before hanging up.

After the phone call with her brother, Bright called her parenting instructor to let her know that she wouldn't be making it to class due to a family emergency. Since Bright called out over six times and never made any of her classes up, the instructor advised her that if she missed class again, she'd be dropped from the class and would have to re-do the entire class over.

I'm sure the judge will understand. Shit, I ain't smoked no weed and been going to all my other classes, so fuck it! Bright thought, heading to the motel to pick up Tanisha.

****

"One down, two to go!" Diamond laughed, having just gotten off of the phone with a distraught Bright, who was crying her eyes out because her brother had gotten charged for distributing drugs and had been taken to jail. Diamond played the good friend role, listening to and consoling Bright like any good girlfriend would, but inside, Diamond was as happy as could be. Having gained valuable information from Bright and Tanisha on Cordell's whereabouts and knowing his hustle, Diamond made an anonymous call to the Long Beach police and tipped them off on Cordell's illegal activity and drug use, and she even mentioned that he was a foster kid and runaway from placement. Now it was time to get rid of Tanisha so that Diamond could get back into the house.

Bright told Diamond, "I wished you still lived here with me, bitch. I miss you and hate being alone over here, but if Cordell and Tanisha ain't here, it just don't seem right to have you here, especially since he left because of you."

Diamond smiled. Don't worry, you'll realize just how much you need your help back in a minute, baby. I'll be back soon to continue fucking your world up and smiling in your face...I promise you that. I just have to make a call to Tanisha's mother. I'm sure she'd love to know where her pregnant runaway daughter is at and how much powder boo boo can snort up one nostril at a time. Diamond laughed. "This is beginning to be too easy. Sorry, Bright Sheldon, but you fucked with the right one this time, and I'm going to see to it that your life is truly a living hell!"

****

After paying the criminal attorney a retainer to take Cordell's case, Bright took Tanisha to the house and then prepared for her date with Marion. He had fat pockets and loved to spend on Bright, doing whatever made her happy. Bright's new game plan was that she was a traveling nurse, so whenever Marion wanted to play, he'd always offer to pay her wages for her time. So instead of telling him that she was out of state like she did the last two times, she told him that he was right on time.

Bright admired herself in her bedroom mirror. Marion was much older than Bright, and outside of the usual hustlers she normally attracted, Marion was a married orthodontist, and he had come from a long line of highly educated and top-paid professionals. Bright was intrigued with the idea of having a professional man on her team. Now she just needed a few more bosses so she could add two more bosses to her roster, then she'd be set. *Time to work, bitch!*

Having allowed her hair to hang to its natural curl, Bright dressed provocatively in an all-white, mini cocktail, designer dress and matching white heels. Her accessories consisted of her all-white jewelry and a pair of one-carat, white-gold diamond earrings that Marion had gifted her on their second date. Her smoky eye effect made her eyes pop and sparkle even more than the diamond earrings in her ears, and her shimmering lips gloss made her full lips look wet and ready. Bright was dressed to kill and get paid. She hadn't had sex with Marion yet, but she planned to break him and put on a performance of a life time. When Marion texted her to tell her that he was outside, Bright made her way downstairs.

"You look pretty, Bright...oohwee!" Tanisha said once Bright walked into the living room.

"Thank you, Chocolate Drop. I'ma hook you up too so when my brother get out, he gon' be screaming, oohwee too!" Bright giggled. "I may be out for the entire night, so don't wait up for me and be good."

"I will." Tanisha smiled, admiring Bright.

Outside, Bright sashayed seductively to Marion's smoke-gray Mercedes S-Class, allowing him to get an eyeful of her sexy legs.

"Damn, you make me feel under dressed." Marion stepped out of the car to open the door for Bright.

Bright gave him a hug and smiled. "I think you're right. Should I go back inside and change clothes or something?" She winked

"Hell naw, you look good enough for the both of us," he teased, dressed nicely in Kenneth Cole from head to toe. He was wearing a black blazer, white T-shirt, a pair of washed denim jeans, and black dress shoes.

Later, after hanging out with the rest of Marion's married professional friends and their mistresses at the hotel bar, Marion took Bright to the thirty-fifth floor of the hotel and went to work. Inside the luxury hotel suite, Bright was butt naked in between Marion's thighs, sucking the skin off of his penis while she allowed her breasts to massage his balls. His dick was nice and thick, and Bright enjoyed making him moan, squirm, and curl his toes. She hoped her second round of head would spare her from having to spread her legs to him. She was in no mood to be fucked. But after he climaxed all over her breasts, he told her to lie down and nipped all over her body. He told her he wanted to please her too.

The second he began to nip on her pearl tongue, Bright pretended to be on the verge of an orgasm. She wanted to get it over with, quick. "Ohhh, right there, yes, yes, suck it, suck it, lick it, suck it! I'm about to cum!" Bright made her legs tremble and told him how good he had made her feel.

Marion wiped his mouth. "I would have loved to make love to you, but you sucked all the life out of my dude," he teased, revealing his limp penis.

Smiling, Bright pretended to catch her breath. "No worries, baby. I came sucking your dick and while you feasted on my treats. I feel good." She told him to lie down, and then she laid in his arms. It was time for part two of the game. "I really like you, Marion, seriously. I like you so much that I dumped my boyfriend tonight."

"You did what? Why did you do that?" Marion stuttered.

"We've been going out regularly, we talk on the phone every day, you've been spoiling me and treating me like a princess, and I really enjoy being with you. I'm ready to take it to the next level." Bright smiled, feeling his heart rate increase. "I may even be able to be wifey one day." She rubbed her finger down his chest.

"Wait, hold on, Bright, I think there is something I should have told you from the start. Marion sat up and then turned the lamp on.

Hurry up and tell me that you're married so I can bust out crying and yo' ass can write me a fat check and take me the fuck home. Bright sat up with a confused expression on her face. "Tell me... what, baby?" She held her hand over her chest.

"Bright, I like you a lot, but - "

Bright cut him off. "Don't tell me that you're breaking up with me, Marion!" Bright pretended that she was about to cry.

"No, baby, you're special to me, I'd never break things off with you. Matter-of-fact, I plan on spending a lot of time with you, spoiling you, taking you around the world, loving you and treating you well, but I have to tell you that...I'm married." He grabbed her hand.

Time to work, bitch. "Married? Are you serious, Marion?" Bright hit him with her pillow and then climbed out of bed. "I left my man of five years for you, 'cause I wanted to be with you. How could you go all the way with me, knowing this? Even after I expressed how special the bond of sex was to me? I would have never…" she sniffled. "I would have never went this far with you, or left my man, if I knew you were married, Marion!" Bright sat at the end of the bed and begin to bawl and sob.

Marion felt horrible. He climbed out the bed and fell to his knees in front of Bright. "That's why I'm telling you now. I'm sorry, baby, but I was afraid if I told you I was married from the start, you wouldn't have ever given me a fair chance. When I saw you at the mall, I just couldn't resist."

"You didn't give me a fair chance, Marion...you lied to me. And I better not have lost my job either, because I called off three times since I've been dating you...just to be with you. And remember, I don't have a man to rely on anymore." Bright stood up and put her clothes back on, fussing and crying. "To think I spent all this money on this dress and these damn seven-hundred dollar shoes just to go out and look nice for you."

Marion didn't want their night to end this way. "I'll re-pay you for all of those expenses, baby. I'll take care of you too; just don't leave me. You make me feel young and happy again," he said as he grabbed her.

Bright shook her head no. "You can't buy me, Marion!"

"I'm not trying to. I just wanna spoil you and make you happy. Don't leave me."

After Bright allowed him to hug her, Marion wiped her tears away. Later he wrote Bright a generous check and then dropped her off at home. When he walked her to the door, he kissed her lips. "Whatever you want or need, I'll do for you. You're now a priority in my life too. I'm here to make you happy, and baby, I promise I'll make this worth the ride."

Bright had him right where she wanted him. The four-figure check he had given her and the talk of the new luxury car he had planned on buying her proved it.

"Just don't break my heart, baby. I just wanna be loved," Bright told him. Then she went inside the house, took a bath, and went to sleep.

Treasure

Having run into a familiar face in the county jail, Treasure was relieved to have gained a friend to help her cope and pass time. Treasure and Tabitha used to go to Hamilton Middle School together, and were both fighting long-term sentences. Though they weren't the best of friends in middle school because they had stolen each other's boyfriends, they were each other's backbones in the county jail. Treasure was fighting a fifteen-year attempted murder case, and Tabitha was fighting a ten-year drug trafficking case. She had gotten caught up transporting drugs for her boyfriend. They would be together from sun up to sun down, picking one another up when they needed a lift and continuously giving each other words of encouragement. Today, Treasure needed that lift.

"Come on, Tres, don't lay here and do this to yourself again. We may be in here, but we could be in much worser places. There is still hope for us." Tabitha kissed Treasure on the cheek, making sucky noises on it.

"I'd rather be fighting in Iraq than to be lying here on this uncomfortable-ass bed in this overcrowded-ass dorm. I just wanna go home," Treasure sniffed.

"I know you do. I do too, baby." Tabitha looked away to keep from crying, then turned to Treasure and said, "Yo', there go the hoe, Bright!"

Treasure immediately sat up in bed. "Where?" Killing Bright would make her time worth it. But being locked up while Bright was on the streets potentially living a good life was killing her softly.

Once Treasure sat up, Tabitha started busting up laughing. "I knew that would get you up!"

"You bitch!" Treasure playfully hit Tabitha in the head.

"Don't hit me! Shit, what would you do if that bitch came through these cell doors?" Tabitha wanted to know. Talking about Bright always gave Treasure that extra will she needed to go on.

"I'd bash her head in the ground until her head busted wide open and started bleeding. Then I'd look her in the eyes and say, 'was it worth it?'" Having had this dream many times before, Treasure knew exactly what she wanted to do to Bright. "They could even add another ten on my sentence for that, and I'd do the time with honors." Treasure laughed.

"And I'll pull my pants down and piss on that bitch for you," Tabitha added.

Later they played spades and speed and then wrote letters to their loved ones. Life behind the wall was hard.

Locked Up

The next morning while making herself a bowl of cereal, Tanisha was alarmed by a loud knock on the door. "Who is it?" she asked as she opened the door. But when she saw her mother, two of her brothers, and the police, she knew she was in big trouble.

"Who is it?" Bright asked on her way down the stairs, talking on the phone with Diamond. She was on her way out to get drug tested and go to her first therapy session. When Bright saw the look on Tanisha's face, she swung the door open wider to see what was going on. Seeing the woman and the two boys at the door that resembled Tanisha accompanied by two police officers, Bright knew she was in trouble, and she immediately begin to stutter. After telling Diamond she'd call her back, Bright asked what was going on.

"Are you the lady of the house?" the police officer asked Bright, reaching for his handcuffs.

"Yes, I am. Now can someone explain to me what the hell is going on? I have places to be this morning."

Tanisha's mother begin to yell and point in Bright's face. "Yo' ass is going to jail for harboring a runaway is what's going on right now!" Then she looked at her daughter. "And your fast-tail-ass is going to juvenile, since you like running away from home and doing dope. Where is that little dope-pushing boyfriend of yours?" She poked her head inside and yelled for him to come out.

Eyebrows flared, and with hands on her hip, Bright replied. "I ain't harboring nobody, and I ain't going to nobody's jail! Tanisha just came over here this morning, and I ain't know shit about her running away. Did I, Tanisha?" Bright tapped her on the shoulder to get her full attention.

"Yeah, I just got here this morning," Tanisha stated. "I been staying somewhere else."

Donna butted in. "Officer, she's lying! This is her boyfriend's sister's house, and they all live here. Arrest both of them!" she demanded.

"Ma'am, if we don't have anything inside the house that proves that Tanisha hasn't been residing here, I can let you go about your day. Otherwise we'll have to take you in for contributing to the delinquency of a minor," the officer said as he began to walk inside.

"You won't be stepping foot inside my house without serving me a warrant first!" Bright blocked the officer's path.

"Miss Sheldon, you have a runaway in your home. I have probable cause to search the premises." The officer brushed past her with Tanisha's mother on his trail, and they began to search each room for Tanisha's belongings.

Bright begin to yell for them to get out of her house. "I know my rights! This is illegal, and I'm suing!" Bright threatened.

Moments later, Donna yelled from upstairs in Cordell's room. "Arrest her ass, 'cause that's all my baby's stuff right there!"

Bright leaned on the couch and dropped her face in her hands. *How the fuck am I gonna get out of this mess?* Her eyes watered up.

Once he came back downstairs, the officer read Bright her Miranda rights, handcuffed her, and put her in the backseat of his cruiser. Next, Tanisha was handcuffed and was being placed in a separate police cruiser. Her mother yelled, "Let's see if you can run away from juvenile hall! I'ma see to it that you have that baby in there, too!"

After the police officer calmed Tanisha's mother, Donna, down, both girls were hauled off to jail.

****

After spending two days in the jail, Bright had been transferred to Century Regional Detention facility for women in Lynwood until her court date. After being housed in the holding tank known as the horseshoe for forty-eight hours, the inmates were sent to shower, given prison uniforms, and then they were housed in different pods and dorms throughout the facility. Thrown into a dorm with close to two hundred other inmates, Bright found her less-than-comfortable bed and sat on it. Observing the women in her surrounding area from various walks of life, Bright decided to make friends with the toughest bunch in the dorm.

"Wrong bed, White Girl, that's mine," a middle-aged, heavy-set black, woman said to her. "Hit the top bunk." She pointed to the bed above hers.

"Sorry about that, I thought this was the bed I was assigned to." Bright stood from the bed. "My name ain't White Girl, it's Bright; what's yours?" She offered a warm smile.

"Well, it's White Girl to me, and my name ain't none of your damn business!" the lady spat, giving Bright a nasty look. "Now get the fuck out of my way; I'm tired!" She pushed past Bright.

Noticing they were beginning to grab attention from other inmates, Bright thought, *fuck, it's either check this bitch now or get fucked with by the rest of these bitches until I get out of here.* Bright pushed the woman back, "Let's behave like ladies and watch our fucking manners! Now I think the proper words you were looking for were 'excuse me'!" Bright stepped in her face.

Immediately the lady began to laugh in Bright's face. "Is that right?"

"Yeah, that's right!" Bright stood her ground. She didn't see a thing funny.

The lady continued to find amusement in Bright's remarks and continued to laugh in Bright's face.

Bright sucked her teeth and rolled her eyes. "Fucking weirdo!" She spat as she proceeded to climb on the top bunk. But before she could take her next step, a force had slammed her head into the bunk.

"Bitch, you better fix yo' lips before you step in here speaking to me like you don't have no gotdamn sense!" The lady continued to bang Bright's head into the bunk.

The crowd began gathering around, rooting the fight on, and Bright had to find some way to get herself out of the situation she was in before she got lightheaded and passed out. Bright was always taught that fighting wasn't fair, and she fought dirty. After catching a visual of the woman in front of her, Bright reached up and dug her nails into the woman eyes. She tried to pull her eyeball out, and then started kicking her in between her legs as hard as she could. The woman grabbed Bright by the hair and tried to pin her in between her legs, but Bright rammed her like a bull in the gut, dropping her to the ground. Then, before she could climb on top of the woman and commence to making her face turn purple and blue, armed correctional officers appeared through the crowd and separated the ladies.

"That bitch did her ass in!" Bright heard a girl say as she was being carried out of the dorm.

"Let's see what's gon' happen after they get out the hole," Bright heard another inmate say. Then she heard another yell, "There go that bitch, Bright!"

Before being dragged completely out of the dormitory, Bright looked around to see who had said her name. She was met with a face from her past, her old best friend, Treasure. *My bitch!* The two locked eyes and stared at one another until Bright was out of eyesight. Treasure was the last person that Bright wanted to face, and she hated wasting energy to hate, because deep inside, Treasure was still a part of her.

Being thrown into a small room known as the hole, Bright tried to mentally prepare herself for war. It was either that or she wasn't going to make it out of there alive. *Fuck, I need to get out of here!*

****

"That really was that trifling-ass bitch!" Treasure steamed with excitement. Hair freshly braided in corn rows, Treasure was ready for war. "She in here with me now, and I can't wait to see her face again!"

Tabitha began to worry that Treasure would make good on the many ways she wanted to kill Bright. "Look, I know you want her head, but Treasure, that bitch ain't worth your life. Your attorney already said you have a good chance to do as little as five years. You don't want to ruin that now, do you?"

Treasure looked at Tabitha seriously. "How far would I really be able to advance in life with a manslaughter felony on my record, huh, Tab?"

"You can get that shit expunged." Tabitha stood in front of Treasure and looked her seriously in the eyes.

"NO! That bitch ruined my fucking life!" Treasure gritted her teeth, "And girl, all I wanna do is fuck hers up too." Then Treasure walked off to inquire about Bright. She had been dreaming about this moment for months, and she wasn't going to allow the opportunity to slip through her fingers. *Your next stop is the morgue, Bright. I'ma kill yo' ass, and that's on my momma!* Treasure thought, searching the overcrowded dormitory cell for a correctional officer.

Cordell

"My sister and my girl are in jail?" Cordell punched the concrete wall in the phone area. "Cuz, on Crip, I'm about to fire on any nigga that look at me the wrong way today. I'm heated!" Cordell had been taking his attorney's advice to stay out of trouble in juvenile while he worked his case for the minimal sentence, but that would all change today.

"Nigga, I got bread to get your sister out. I just have to find somebody to post her bond. Ain't nothing I can do about Tanisha, though. Her momma put her in jail." Lil Jay told Cordell over the phone. He had a jail prepaid account set up on his cell phone to keep in contact with Cordell. Though he hated that his boy was locked up, Lil Jay hoped his time spent in juvenile would help him kick his cocaine habit.

"A'ight, cool, my nigga, cool. Look, hit my momma's homegirl, Gale, up to get my sister out." Cordell read the number out to Lil Jay. He kept in touch with Gale because she kept his mother and family's best interests at heart. She had been trying to get temporary custody of them since they had been in the system, but her record was making it difficult. "When Queen Bee steps out, tell her to check on my girl and put some bread on her books, man. Aye!" Cordell burst out and said, remembering what he wanted to ask Lil Jay, "You seen that bitch Erica?"

Lil Jay nodded his head. "Yeah, that gold-diggin'-ass trick still riding around in yo' shit, and now she's claiming she's pregnant by you."

"What?" The absence of cocaine made Cordell easily aggravated. "How that bitch pregnant by me?" He blew off hot air. "Nigga only fucked her a few weeks ago. Man, fuck her ass, Cuz, and aye! Tell Queen Bee to get my shit from that bitch too, Cuz. If she can't get it, torch that muthafucka, on the Norf." Cordell nodded his head.

Lil Jay laughed. "Nigga, you a fool! I got you, though, real business. Hit ya boy later on, I should have some good news for you by then."

"I'ma holla." Cordell ended the call.

Bright

Bright had been in the hole for eight days, and it was driving her insane. "Why am I still here?" She yelled out loud. She had done everything she possibly could to remain calm, cool, and collected, but none of it worked. She did push-ups and jumping jacks, braided her hair in tiny plaits and then took them all out one by one...she had even started counting sheep. She knew it was time to get out of there when she started talking to herself and found herself answering back. The food they served was horrible and made her sick, and the sandwiches had moldy bologna on them. Bright had gone days without a shower and she desperately wanted to soak in a hot bubble bath. She had been unable to use the phone since the one call she had made to Diamond when she was first arrested.

Diamond's ass can't do a damn thing for me! Why didn't I call Gale? She could have borrowed the money from someone to get me out of here until I got home! Bright regretted that, and then began to cry. "I can't take this shit anymore."

In the middle of feeling sorry for herself, the slit in the metal door opened up and a correctional officer told her to stand up and put her hands through them. She was about to be transported back to the dorm. Bright stood up and wiped her eyes. *Anything is better than this,* she thought as she did what she was told.

Having been thrown back into the same dormitory, Bright asked if she could be placed in a different dormitory. She didn't want to be placed with the woman she had fought days earlier, and she definitely didn't want to face Treasure. Bright knew Treasure like the back of her own hand, and knowing her, she had something malicious up her sleeve. "Can I please be placed somewhere else?" Bright made a final attempt before she was forced inside.

"Look who's back," a girl with a familiar face smirked upon Bright's entrance.

Trying to figure out where she knew the girl from, Bright gazed at her. "We know each other from…?"

"Hamilton Middle School. I'm Tabitha. Now weren't you best friends with Treasure?" She raised her brow and twisted her lips.

Bright's blooming smile had suddenly turned into an expression of one who had the sun beating down on their face with nothing to block it. "Did you come over here to say hello, or to start messing with me?" Bright cut straight through the small talk.

Tabitha gave Bright a puppy-dog expression and then smiled at her. "Naw, I'm sure Treasure can handle her own. I just wanted to stop by and say hello." Tabitha walked away, seeing that she had gained the attention of the correctional officers. "Take care." She winked at Bright.

"Ole fucking, stupid, dumb-ass bitch!" Bright said under her breath, then she went to search for her bed. She planned on keeping to herself and sleeping with one eye open.

After the beat down Bright had given the woman - whose name, she learned, was Judy - and was in on her third DUI. Bright had become quite popular amongst the inmates and had been invited over to join the ongoing spade game that took place in the dormitory the vast majority of the day. Needing something to help her pass time, Bright accepted the offer and she was engrossed in the game, having been set twice. She used to play with her mother and friends and considered herself something of a Spadeologist. She was so caught up in the game that she didn't notice Treasure creeping up on the side of her with an inmate-made shank, ready to stab her in the neck. Everybody in the dormitory knew what was going on and had no plans of standing in Treasure's way. In fact, the girls that invited Bright over to play spades were merely setting her up to get comfortable so that Treasure could get a quick and clean shot at attacking her.

Something seemed very odd to Bright. She saw the peculiar facial expressions of the inmates that were moments earlier rooting her on. They narrowed their eyes and focused their attention on her in an intimidating manner. It startled her, causing her to drop her cards. *Fuck that, I'm done playing cards, these bitches is up to something,* Bright thought, leaning down from the chair, quickly picking her cards up from the ground.

"Get that bitch!" Bright heard a girl yell seconds before a body flew over her head and hit the ground.

"What the fuck?" Bright hopped up in full defense mode, seeing Treasure emerge from the ground with a sharp object in her hand.

Bright tried to wiggle out of the crowd, but the inmates stood around her like a brick wall. Bright yelled and screamed for help while Treasure attempted to penetrate her with the object.

"I fucking hate yo' ass, Bright; I hate you! Hurry up and die, bitch!" Treasure had gotten her on the ground and was on top of her, jabbing Bright in the side of the head.

Dazed from the hit her head took from hitting the ground, her weak punches to Treasure's face didn't faze her one bit.

"You ruined my life you nasty, trifling bitch!" Treasure tossed the contraband, mad that it wasn't as effective as she thought it would be, and proceeded to bang Bright's head into the ground.

Bright's eyes widened with fear. "Somebody help me!" She yelled, and the correctional officers once again forced their way through the crowd and separated her from another fight.

Once pulled up off the ground, the correctional officer that had previously thrown Bright back inside the dormitory said, "Let's go, Sheldon. You don't seem to be to a very popular person in here!" She hauled her out.

"It wasn't my fault! Please get me out of here; they gon' kill me!" Bright said incoherently as blood dripped down her ear.

Treasure had to be pepper-sprayed for resistance. "Let me have that bitch! Bring her back to me! I swear to God, I'ma kill that bitch...I'ma kill her!" Treasure kicked and screamed.

Inside the infirmary, Bright was glad to learn that her wounds were minor and she didn't have any internal bleeding, missing teeth, black eyes, bumps, or bruises. She came out of the fight clean and had no plan to complain when they took her back to the hole. She actually preferred to do her time alone. When Bright was finished being patched up, she was walked down to the release area and was given her clothes. She was being released on bail. Excited, Bright screamed, “Thank you! I ain't never coming back here...ever again!” After going through the release process, Bright was sent to retrieve her personal items and then she was set free. The nightmare was finally over...at least, that’s what she thought.

Ice

"Damn, baby, you got tight-ass pussy," Terrence told the nurse that once hated his guts as he slid his finger up her skirt and inside her tight opening.

"Quit being bad," she giggled, showing off her dimples while taking his vitals. After being around him for a few days, she had no other choice but to grow fond of him. She did everything in her power to keep him in the infirmary so that they could spend time together. Jackie had been sneaking him in outside food and weed, and she had even gotten him a cell phone so that they could keep in contact when the doctor finally released him back to regular population.

"When you gon' let me hit that?" Terrence fondled Jackie's pearl tongue as he looked her lustfully in her dark brown eyes. Jackie had jacked him off a few times, but he wanted the real thing.

"Iceee..." Jackie smiled, allowing his name to roll slowly off of her tongue. "You know I want it more than you do." She bent down to sneak a kiss in.

"Make away, baby. I'm serious," Terrence said when Jackie gave him an impossible look.

"I'm going to try." She removed his hand from underneath her nursing uniform, and then started to walk away.

Terrence grabbed her arm. "Don't try, make it happen," he said, then he let her arm go. He needed to start dicking her down and getting in her head so that he could add another valuable player to his team before he was transferred to prison. He figured if he married her, she'd eventually be willing to kill for him, and he needed as many killers on his team as possible...especially women. They always proved to be the loyal and most trustworthy.

Within the last few days, Terrence had his people wire money into Jackie's bank account and sent flowers to her at work. On top of that, he had long, intimate conversations all about her and her wants and needs. Terrence spent a lot of time complimenting her and making her blush. He was willing to do whatever it took to get Jackie on his team and make her happy.

"I'm going to make it happen," Jackie assured Terrence, removing the silly schoolgirl grin she had on her face.

"Good. Now that's what I like to hear!" He winked at her. "Now get back to work before you get us caught up," he teased.

****

Diamond packed while waiting for Bright to call. Bright had already called her and told her that she was being released on bond, and Diamond knew that she'd be calling back when she got in her big empty house, begging Diamond to come back. *No Cordell or his little bitch in the way to interfere... just me and you bitch.* Diamond smiled.

****

After talking to Gale in the Century Jail parking lot for twenty minutes, Bright hugged her and thanked her for coming down to get her out, before climbing in the car with Lil Jay. Gale had to go back to work.

"I guess they didn't allow you to take a shower in jail, huh?" Lil Jay rolled his window down to allow the breeze to sweep Bright's strong, musty body odor out.

"Fuck you too, Lil Jay!" Bright sucked her teeth and rolled her eyes at him, and then subconsciously closed her legs and folded her arms tight. She knew she smelled, but it wasn't on her own accord. She hadn't been allowed a shower the entire time she was in the hole.

Lil Jay laughed. "Naw, not like that, I'm just saying. My girlfriend is always on point, smelling and looking good ...you know what I'm saying?" He offered her a half-smile.

Bright sucked her teeth and blew out hot air. "Boy, take me home please. I got the money you used to bail me out at home," she told him, and then she looked out the window the rest of the ride to her house.

Lil Jay looked at Bright. *My little mean, ungrateful bitch!* Then he turned his music back up.

When Bright got home, she paid Lil Jay his money back, locked the door, and then soaked in a long, hot, bubble bath while she talked to Diamond on the phone.

"Bitch! It was going down in the County. I had two fights. I had one the second my fine ass got thrown in that stanking-ass dormitory with some older bitch, and, bitchhh, I whooped her ass!" Bright yelled, slapping water all over the place. "Then, after being confined in this tiny-ass space they call the fucking hole, bitchhh I ran into that dumb, stupid-ass bitch, Treasure - the ex-bestie that I told you about that crossed my ass. Well yeah, bitch, that hoe seriously tried to kill my ass. Bitch tried to fuck my nigga, but she mad," Bright lied, sucking her teeth. "I was crying and screaming for help, like hurry up and get a bitch up outta here! I ain't made for this jail shit...at all!" After Bright told Diamond about her full jail experience, she begged Diamond to pack her things and to come back to her house. She didn't like being alone and she loved Diamond's company. She was a best friend, therapist, assistant, and maid all in one, and Bright loved it.

Diamond smiled. *Just as I expected, bitch.* "You sure, gurl? I don't want no problems with baby boy and his little lying-ass girlfriend," Diamond said.

"Bitch, I didn't tell you, huh?" Bright sat up in the tub and grabbed a cigarette. "Tanisha is in jail too. Her momma put her in juvenile and told her she was gon' have the baby in jail." Bright sucked her teeth then lit her cigarette. "So bitch, it's just me and you. Now hurry and get ya ass over here!" Bright said playfully.

"Okay, if you insist, gurl. I just don't want no problems." Diamond laughed inside. "I hate that you been going through so damn much. I'ma start fucking up anybody that messes with you in the future. I'm so serious; you don't deserve all this crap.

You're going through enough already," Diamond said sympathetically.

"See you in a minute, bestie, and we can beat that bitch Erica's ass, 'cause bitch, I need my brother's Beamer like ASAP," Bright said before ending the call.

In the middle of towel drying her hair, she heard a knock on the door. In a pair of booty shorts and tank top, Bright slid her slippers on her feet and then ran down the stairs to open the door.

"My Diamond's back!" Bright opened the door, but she was wrong; it was Lil Jay.

"Naw, it's me, girlfriend." Lil Jay cracked a smile.

Bright told him to come inside. *Nigga, you ain't about to hit, so what the fuck you want?* she thought, standing in the foyer with him.

Lil Jay pulled a cuddly stuffed bear cub from behind his back and passed it to her. "Just wanted you to have something to hold on and cuddle with at night when you're alone. I know you been going through a lot."

Bright thought that was one of the sweetest things a guy had ever done for her. "Aw, thanks Lil Jay, you are so sweet!" She grabbed the bear and hugged it tight. "Soft and cuddly, I love it!" She smiled happily.

Lil Jay was happy to put a smile on Bright's face. Reaching for his pocket, Bright stopped him.

"I'm not in the mood to make any money tonight, Lil Jay." The last time he paid her to kiss him, he told her he'd be back for her pussy, but she didn't want to sleep with him. He was her brother's best friend.

Lil Jay gave Bright an odd look, and then he passed her the money she had given him back, chuckling. "I just wanted to give you your money back. A nigga should never take money from his girlfriend," he said playfully yet seriously.

Bright stared at Lil Jay for a few moments before taking the money back. "Thanks, Lil Jay, I appreciate that." She kissed him on the cheek then walked him to the door.

Halfway down the walkway, Bright called out to him. Lil Jay stopped in his tracks and asked her what was up. Hand on her hip with her stuffed bear cub in the other hand, Bright said, "Don't be catching no feelings for me. It's always business with me, never personal." She felt the need to warn him. Love had beaten Bright down so much that she didn't believe in it anymore. She was all about getting paid.

Lil Jay gave Bright an intense look. "Well, it's already too late. I'm head over heels over you," he told her, then he climbed in his car and left.

Bright shrugged her shoulders and raised her brow. *Don't say I didn't warn yo' ass, nigga,* she thought as she closed the door.

Later when Diamond got there, they went out for dinner and drinks, and they were attracting men left and right. When they got back in the car, Bright said, "Follow my lead, bitch, 'cause we about to be some rich-ass bitches! Welcome to Bright's acting class 101…cha-ching!" Bright burst out laughing.

Diamond laughed too. "Let's see what Bright's acting class can do for me, 'cause I'm one horrible actress."

Part 6

Children's Court

Early the next morning, dressed in an all-black Anne Klein suit, Bright walked with Diamond through the security check at Children's Court and they went to the designated floor. They waited for Bright's court-appointed attorney to call her to discuss the case. She had verification that she had enrolled in the classes that the Department of Children and Family Services had recommended.

"Don't be nervous. You gon' get your kids back, girl, I'm sure of it," Diamond told Bright seeing her bite down on the tip of her acrylic nails.

"Hopefully all his money, too, the ole stupid, dumb-ass nigga!" Having been told at the last minute that Larry would be at the custody hearing gave Bright butterflies in her stomach. She hadn't seen him since she had the babies, and she didn't know how she would feel seeing him after he had left her hanging on a limb.

Lost in thought, Diamond had to tap Bright on the shoulder to get her attention and tell her that her attorney had called her name.

"I knew I needed you here, Diamond! I'm all disoriented this morning." Bright stood up and walked over to her attorney.

Standing at the side of the packed hall, the attorney found an area for the two of them to speak briefly. Looking over paperwork that she had gotten from a file, she shook her head in a displeased manner, and then looked at Bright. "This doesn't look good."

Throat dry, Bright gave her a look of confusion. "What doesn't look good? I've been drug-free and have been doing everything the department has been telling me to do."

"You've been kicked out of parenting class, haven't gone to therapy, and have only gone to a few anger management and drug classes. You were doing well with your drug testing, but then you missed two tests." The attorney threw the paperwork back inside the file. "I can tell you now that the judge isn't going to allow you to have your kids back. I'll see if he'll grant you visitation. I'm sure it'll be supervised," she warned Bright.

Bright stuck her nose in the air. "Wait, I've been doing all of this just to possibly get supervised visitation?" She was appalled. "I want my kids and my child support checks, immediately."

"I'm afraid that won't happen just yet. The department hasn't recommended you get your kids back. You haven't finished any of your classes, and being kicked out of parenting class and having missed two drug tests doesn't make this case any better, Miss Sheldon."

"Doesn't seem like you're trying to help me at all. I probably should have hired my own damn attorney!" Bright rolled her eyes. She didn't realize it would be so difficult to get her kids back.

"I'm sorry you feel that way, Miss Sheldon, but I'm really the wrong person to be fighting with. I'm here to help you, but I can't help you get your kids back until you've completed everything the department has recommended you do. This is your progress report," she held the file in mid-air, "and I'm just letting you know that it doesn't look good. So what I'm going to do is ask that the judge give you more time to finish your classes and grant you supervision to see your kids."

Before Bright could speak, Mrs. Lane, Larry, and a high-powered-looking attorney walked past discussing the case. Seeing Larry made Bright's knees buckle and her heart beat increase. "We were supposed to be together," Bright said to her attorney while gazing at Larry as they passed by. He was dressed in a smoke-gray designer suit and he wore a black pair of dress shoes. His goatee beard gave him added sex appeal and masculinity, and his smile was one of a classic Kodak moment. A true star in his own right, he was the man of Bright's dreams that had left her, never to return.

"Miss Sheldon, over here!" Her attorney whistled while forcing a smile on her face. "That's all I'll be able to do today. I'll see you inside." She walked away.

Bright walked past and stared at Larry, pulling his attention from his attorney to her. She looked amazingly beautiful, but when they locked eyes, he realized just how much he hated her. She was a liar and cheater, and everything that he ever felt for her was piled under enmity. Before joining back in the conversation with his attorney, Larry gave Bright a look full of hatred, causing Bright to pick up her pace. When she made it back to Diamond, she sat in silence.

"You all right?" Diamond kneeled down in front of Bright.

Allowing a stream of tears to fall from her eyes, Bright wiped them away and sniffed. "He never loved me in the first place; fuck him!" She sat back in her seat and waited for her case to be called in court.

Inside the courtroom, Bright felt it was her against the world. She was called every kind of negligent parent in the book, and no one was on her side. Her attorney just sat there and listened. She didn't try to fight, and Bright refused to continue to just sit there and listen anymore.

"Excuse me, Your Honor!" Bright stood from the hard wooden chair, cutting Larry's attorney off. He had just brought it to the court's attention that Bright had just been released from the county jail for contributing to the delinquency of a minor. "The only reason this man, with his dumb, stupid-ass is even in here saying all of these things about me," Bright rolled her eyes then looked directly at Larry, "is because I cheated on him with a guy for his money so that his ass wouldn't have to work a simple nine-to-five job. If I'm a bad parent for leaving my kids with my mother until I cleared my head, then what does that make him? He's the one that left me and his kids at the hospital and never came back! He neglected us. So why is everybody in this room glorifying Larry? Because he's a famous NBA player? Like he's such a great father raising his kids, when in fact, his mother is doing his job?!"

"Order in this court!" The judge continued to hit his gavel against the block, but Bright continued to speak.

"Miss Sheldon, you are going to be thrown out of this courtroom! Please conduct yourself in a proper manner and take a seat," her attorney warned her.

"No!" Bright yanked her arm from her attorney. "The only reason I'm being prosecuted today is because I lied to you, but I loved you, Larry! And everything I did was for us, so that you could be successful!" A tear rolled from her eyes. "I never loved Terrence. I used him, but I loved you, and even though you would probably never believe me or understand it...it's true! You wanna take everything from me to hurt me, but I rightfully deserve the lavish lifestyle that your ass is living too, because I helped you get to where you had to go to get what you have today!"

"I worked!" Larry looked at Bright, angry, forcing the rest of his words back through clenched teeth. His mother patted his back and told him to calm down. Larry knew this was neither the time nor the place to discuss their past and differences. He would walk out of the courtroom with class and respect.

"Remove Miss Sheldon from this courtroom for contempt...NOW!" The judge ordered. "The children are to remain in the custody of the father and grandmother until further notice. Visitation for the mother has been denied! Miss Sheldon is to have a psychiatric evaluation performed immediately! It's my belief that Miss Sheldon is in no position to be around or to properly raise her children until her mental issues have been addressed and resolved. Court is adjourned!" The judge hit his gavel one last time before going into his chambers.

"Does it make you feel good to hurt me, Larry? To take my life and my kids from me? Huh?" Bright yelled as the bailiff dragged her out the courtroom. "Fuck you, fuck you, you can have them kids! I'm not gon' fight you anymore; you won, they're yours!" Bright yelled and cried before she was thrown out of the courtroom.

Pulling herself together, Bright wiped her eyes and tried to calm herself down. She was so upset that she was trembling and hyperventilating.

Spotting her, Diamond ran over to her and helped her to a nearby seat. "Oh my God, are you all right?" Diamond asked in a concerned manner.

"No!" Bright sniffled, trying to control her breathing. *You can have them, Larry; I don't have no kids anymore.* "I need some weed. Let's get out of here." Bright stood up and headed to the elevator. She never wanted to see Larry's face again.

Diamond grabbed Bright's things and then followed behind her.

'07... One Year Later

It had been a year since Bright had last seen Larry in Children's Court and the last time she attempted to get her babies or his money. For those that knew of Bright's previous life, she made it a rule to never mention Larry or her children to anyone, not even in conversation with her. She left them in her past and had blocked them from her mind. She told people she didn't have any children and thanks to her grandparents, she was able to erase and block them from her memory and mind, as if they never existed.

Bright was working on her own luxury life, and so far, she was doing quite well for herself. Bright had three major bosses that she called her top three, and they contributed to her lavish lifestyle abundantly: Marion, her married orthodontist; Big Poppa, her married business owner/ loan shark; and her gangsta, drug kingpin from Compton, Dime, who was crazy in love with her. But because they all believed that Bright was a traveling nurse, they were all understanding when it came to her time. At nineteen-years-old, Bright had a house, a newly-developed condominium in Brentwood that Marion put her in to be closer to him. She also had two cars, plenty of money to spend, and a savings account with over $ 60,000 in it. Life was good.

After a long battle, cooperating and living up to Child Protective Services and Children's Court standards, Gale had finally been granted custody of Deja and Rayonna. They had been residing with her and her family for the past eight months in her Long Beach home, and they spent every weekend at Bright's house doing sisterly things. When they came over, they'd all sleep in the bed together. Having had an attorney on his case, Cordell's sentence had gotten reduced from three years to sixteen months. Currently in juvenile hall finishing out the last few weeks of his sentence, Cordell was scheduled to be released into

Gale's custody when he got out, and his sisters couldn't wait to reunite with him.

At seventeen, Deja had graduated from Long Beach's Jordan High School at the top of her class, and she had been accepted to various universities. She had decided to go to Santa Barbara University the following semester, and Bright had purchased her sister a brand new car and spoiled her with whatever she wanted. She was very proud of Deja. Rayonna was her normal, happy self, and like Deja, she excelled in school. A sixth grade student at Hamilton Middle School, Rayonna continued to stay focused through all of their family's triumphs and transitions. She continued to sing in the church choir, and she went to a prestigious ballet school in Los Angeles. She told Bright she wanted to be a ballerina, and Bright paid her costly tuition monthly, seeing to it that she made it to practice three times a week...faithfully.

When the sisters, family, and friends begin to notice how slowly Rosette was recovering in the convalescent home, Bright took matters into her own hands and had her mother transferred to a respected stroke recovery center two hours away, in Palm Springs. They had one of the top recovery teams in the county. Bright paid the balance that her mother's insurance would not, and since being there, Bright had noticed the difference. Every other weekend the girls, Gale, and sometimes Cousin Shanna would drive out to Palm Springs to go visit her. For once, life was looking up.

In New York, in a presidential suite with one of her tops, Big Poppa, Bright stepped into the room from the bathroom smiling shyly, plotting and up to her old tricks. "Big Poppa, I don't understand how this happened, but we're pregnant." Bright had met Big Poppa months earlier, when she and Diamond drove out to Las Vegas for all-star weekend. After spotting them, Big Poppa and his boy had shown them a good time, and then later the two hooked up. Since then, he had been flying Bright all over the country to wine, dine, and fuck her.

"How did that happen? You're still on the pill aren't you?"

Those are for show...but don't worry. I don't trust yo' dirty-dick ass. I use a female condom every time we fuck, you fat bastard! Bright smiled. "I do, but when we were in the Bahamas for New Year's, I accidentally missed two days." she hunched her shoulders. "See what happens when we're having a great time?" Bright sat next to him on the bed and then showed him the pregnancy test. She had decided to reap all she could from her bosses before she got an abortion the following week. Marion cut her a fat check and then gifted her with a four-carat "promise to love you forever" diamond ring. Dime surprised her with a Lexus after she lied and told him that she had a miscarriage. He wanted nothing more than to have a baby with her. Bright was working on her ultimate boss, Big Poppa. Six foot and four inches tall, Big Poppa was three hundred pounds of pure muscle. He was light brown, bald-headed, arrogant as hell, and had money growing out of his ass. On top of being a wealthy loan shark, he also had lucrative businesses from New York to California, and he was Bright's hardest challenge.

"You already know the deal, baby. We're just having fun. We can't have any kids. I'm a married man," he reminded her, and then after a few moments of silence he patted his bedside and told her to get in bed. "You know what you have to do," he said, referring to an abortion.

Time to work, bitch. Bright stood from the bed and begin to pack up her belongings, slamming, closets, drawers, and doors. Big Poppa rolled over to see what was going on.

"What the fuck is wrong with you?" He gave her an agitated look.

"I'm leaving, Poppa! I'm tired of being your fucking bed whore! You don't give two shits about me!" She threw her things inside of her designer luggage.

"You knew that from the gate! I'm a fucking married man. You're my entertainment. I pay you to accompany me, so quit acting like you don't know what time it is!" He stared at her long and hard. "Now cut the crap, and get yo' ass in bed and take care of me. I have a long day ahead of me tomorrow." He rolled back over and lay down.

Bright's eyes begin to water. Big Poppa had angered her and hurt her feelings deeply. She wasn't used to such treatment, and though she was only in it for the money, she didn't like how low he had made her feel when he looked and spoke to her.

"I ain't getting in shit!" Bright swung her luggage shut in a fit of rage. "I'm going home! Call yo' wife, you short-dick, muthafucka, and let that bitch suck yo' little-ass dick!" She took off the sexy night gown that she had purchased hours before he had arrived and begin to put her traveling clothes back on. Cussing loudly, telling him how much she hated sucking his little dick and pretending to enjoy having sex with him, she pulled her pants up. Not having seen Big Poppa roll out of the bed and creep up behind her, Bright suddenly found herself gasping for her next breath.

Big Poppa had her gripped by the neck and he had her held up against the wall. "Let's get one thing straight…bitch!" When in my presence, you are to do what I tell you and pay you to do. Nothing more, nothing less. Do we have an understanding?"

Tears coming from her eyes, desperately needing air, Bright mustered up all of the energy that she possibly could and slapped Poppa in the face… SMACK!!! Bright slapped him so hard that she knew he'd strangle her to death, but instead, he released her neck, watched her slide down the wall, allowed her to stand up, and then slapped her back down to the ground.

"You must not know what kinda nigga you fucking with, bitch! I'll kick the pregnancy out of you!" Big Poppa stopped himself from kicking her in the stomach. He didn't get off on beating women, but he would if they got out of line with him, especially one he was paying for services.

Bright folded up in a fetal position and begged him not to hurt her. Her lip was bleeding and she was trembling for dear life. "I'm sorry, Big Poppa!" she cried.

Seeing that Bright was visibly shaken, Big Poppa was confident that Bright had learned her lesson and would never pull such a stunt again. "I know you are. Now put your nightgown back on and come get in bed," he ordered.

The next morning, Bright lay in the hotel room, restless. She hadn't gotten a wink of sleep the previous night, and she had lock jaw from giving Big Poppa head all night. Before he had left that morning, he told Bright to get on all fours and then he ejaculated inside of her. "Since you're already pregnant, I guess there's no need to fret." Then he tossed a credit card on the nightstand and told her to go on a New York shopping spree. "Have fun, but be back in the hotel by seven and ready by nine. I'm taking you out to dinner tonight," he told her before leaving the hotel room.

When he left, Bright pulled out the condom that she had secretly inserted inside of herself moments before Big Poppa had awakened that morning. She flushed it down the toilet. *I don't want your baby or diseases...you fucking pig!*

After spending the afternoon racking up thousands of dollars' worth of charges on Big Poppa's credit card in Manhattan at the high-end clothing stores, Bright caught a taxi back to the hotel to rest. Afterwards, she smoked a blunt and prepared to get dressed. She knew Big Poppa's patience was wearing short and she wanted to make up for the night before. Bright couldn't afford to be replaced; she had too much on her plate. At the hotel, Bright dressed sharply in a pink, designer, short, flirty, lace dress and pink and gold heels, Bright selected minimal pieces from her gold jewelry collection. Her hair was flat-ironed and swept over her right shoulder. Bright's make-up was flawless, lips shimmering. She was ready to command Big Poppa's eyes and mind. She looked like exquisite eye candy.

Having received a call from Big Poppa, Bright reached for her iPhone, answered, and spoke in a soft and sweet manner. "Dressed and ready, baby where you at?"

"You sound ready, too. Aye, check this out, I'm tied up over here in Brooklyn. I'm not gonna make it for dinner on time, but I made reservations. I still want you to go."

Bright rolled her eyes. "Wow, daddy, I know you don't think I'm that hard up to go out and have dinner alone." She sat on the bed and prepared to kick her heels off. "Before I do that, I'll hop in the bed butt naked, order take-out, and just wait for you."

"My business partner from Japan is meeting me there, so you won't be alone. Go hang out with him and keep him company."

"Keep your partner company?" Bright sucked her teeth. She didn't like the direction the conversation was headed.

"Yeah, keep him company. You know, show him a good time, let him take you around for the evening. Help me keep my business deal in place, baby. If I could be there right now, I would, but what I can't do is lose this deal."

No this nigga ain't tryna fucking pimp my ass! "Big Poppa, you better be playing with me, baby."

"Bright, you like money; you know what time it is. Don't let me down. Big Poppa gon' take care of you," he cut to the chase.

Before Bright could get another word in, the doorbell begin to buzz. She looked at the door and then said, "Hold on, someone's at the door."

"Bright, I sent a car over to pick you up. Let's make this money, baby. You're the star, and I'm depending on you."

This nigga is really serious. Bright gritted her teeth, looking at the buzzing hotel door. "Big Poppa!" Bright yelled into the phone. She could not believe what he was asking her to do.

"I have to go, baby, don't let me down!" Then he hung up the phone.

"Hold on!" Bright yelled toward the door as she stood in place, weighing her options. *Fuck it; if I don't go, Big Poppa gone cut me off, or even possibly have me killed. I need him more than he needs me, and it ain't like I'm new to this. This is how I eat.* Bright sucked her teeth. Go to work, bitch! Then she texted Big Poppa: ***I'm going, but bet' not shit happen to me, and since you pimping, I need my money when I get back to the room!***

Big Poppa texted back: ***Ride for your boss, baby; I got you when I get back to the room. Wear a condom, too. I don't need that sushi eating muthafucka nutting all in my pussy.***

Bright tossed her phone in her handbag and headed to the door. *Nigga, unbeknownst to you, I wear protection every time I fuck yo' ass. What makes you think this nigga ain't about to strap it up?* Bright headed out the door and into a private car. Inside, she took three shots of Patron and smoked a cigarette, thinking, *A Japanese dick...now how about that!*

****

At the Long Beach Airport, Bright was happy to be back home. Pulling her iPhone out of her Versace purse, she powered it on and called for a ride. "Deja, tell Diamond to come pick me up. I'm at Long Beach Airport!" She yelled happily through the phone once Deja answered.

"She ain't here. When me and Ray got here yesterday, she was on the phone crying and arguing with her jailbird boyfriend, and she hasn't been back since then."

"I keep telling her that niggas ain't shit!" Bright sucked her teeth. "I'll check on her when I get home. Come pick me up, Deja. I got you some nice-ass shit from NY too." She loved spoiling her siblings.

"I like your kind of nice," Deja smiled through the phone. "I'll come pick you up. Where are your cars at? Mine has no gas."

Bright shook her head. "You should tell your boyfriend to keep gas in your car, Deja, since he's always riding around with you when I fill it up." Bright sighed before telling her sister where her car keys were at.

"I broke up with him. You're right, he's a bum. See you in a bit; we're on our way." Deja hung up.

She finally listened to me, Bright smiled. Deja had been dealing with him for the past six months, and he was always leeching off of Deja. Though Deja made it clear that she wasn't interested in dating guys for their money, Bright told her that she should at least get one that could afford to take her out sometimes. Bright couldn't understand to save her own life how someone as beautiful as Deja continued to stumble upon one loser after the next.

When Deja pulled up in her Lexus with Rayonna in the front seat, Bright's happiness reflected on her face. After hugging her sisters, Bright put her belongings in the trunk of her car and Deja drove them home.

At the house, Bright stretched across her bed. She was tired, and within minutes, she had fallen asleep. Hours later, awakened by a knock on her door, Bright rolled over in bed and yelled, "Come in!" Lil Jay walked in her room, looking like he was slightly under the weather.

Bright sat up in bed and lit a cigarette. "What's up, Lil Jay?"

"You pregnant, aren't you?" Lil Jay sat on her heart-shaped vanity chair, wanting to know.

"Is that any of your business?" She shot, unbuttoning her pants. She yelled for someone to bring her a bottle of water.

"Because it's mine, and I been having your fucking pregnancy symptoms again, that's why!" He shot back. "Were you even going to tell me this time?"

"Well, maybe it's some other bitch you fucking with this time, because it ain't me."

It all started one night six months earlier when Lil Jay stopped by the house to give Bright some money to put on Cordell's and Tanisha's books. When he came inside, Bright hugged him and remembered thinking, *Damn, this nigga getting finer and finer every time I see his ass, damn! I might have to add him to my client list.* He had status around the city, money, he had moved out of his father's house and into his own spot, had two cars and a truck, and he was much more mature then his seventeen years. Lil Jay had stopped coming around as often after Bright continued to reject him time and time again. After Lil Jay passed Bright a stack of money, he headed toward the door, telling Bright that he had his girl waiting in the car.

Immediately, Bright began to get jealous. He hadn't paid her much attention and he didn't even try to hit on her, and she missed it. Bright sucked her teeth and then grabbed Lil Jay by the arm. "Have fun with yo' girlfriend, and when you get yo' money up, come fuck with a real bitch." She opened her door for him to leave. "That is, if you're ready."

Lil Jay thought he'd never hear those words come out of Bright's mouth after she had continued to reject him. He told her he'd be back in twenty minutes.

Since Bright was home alone, she thought, *Why not?* After looking at the time on her iPhone, she told him to be back in fifteen minutes or she'd be gone. Seventeen minutes later, Bright climbed in her car and left. *Nigga, I said fifteen minutes!* Now you gon' have to chase a bitch, she thought as she saw Lil Jay flying back up her street.

Later on that night after Lil Jay blew her up half the night, Bright texted him. ***Take a shower and have my money ready, baby. I'm on my way to you. I hope you're not busy with one of your bitches.***

Lil Jay texted back: ***I'm about to drop her off at home, have that ass over here when I get back, or you gon' miss out. I'ma pay you well and fuck you better. Been waiting on it.***

Bright texted: ***Pay me better, and fuck me well. Here I come.***

From then on, the two would be all over each other like wild animals. Lil Jay would suck her nipples until she came all over herself. He would pay her knots of money to come to his apartment and cook him breakfast butt naked while he played his Play Station 2 and smoked a blunt. One weekend when Bright had thrown a barbecue at her house, she and Lil Jay crept off to her room for a quickie while his girlfriend was in the backyard with her sisters and the rest of her guests. It was that type of thing that made sex with Lil Jay that much more pleasing. Bright liked what she couldn't have. It was always intense, and Lil Jay was hooked. He was the only guy that Bright would slip up with and have sex without protection because it was always in the heat of the moment.

Months later, their relationship began to blossom into more than fun, wild sex and stacks of money. Bright enjoyed sleeping with him, cuddling in his arms, and she loved waking up to see him in bed with her. When it was time to part ways, Bright would experience the traits of separation anxiety, and he'd constantly be on her mind. She was falling in love with Lil Jay, but no matter how much Bright felt for him inside, she made it a priority not to let him in. It was supposed to be business and nothing personal. Besides that, he was her brother's best friend, and she knew he'd never approve of them.

Lil Jay shook his head no. "Naw, I stay strapped with everybody else. You know we've talked about that already. I keep this dick clean for you."

Bright dumped her cigarette in the ashtray and avoided eye contact. When Lil Jay said things like that to her, it made her long to be in his arms.

After Rayonna brought Bright a bottle of water, Lil Jay told her that he was about to leave.

"Come take care of me later, baby. Let me suck them nipples 'til I go to sleep. I'm sick. I'll make it worth your time," Lil Jay told her.

Bright smiled. "I'll be over after my sisters go to sleep."

"I love you," Lil Jay said as he headed out her door.

"Boy, get outta here!" Bright rolled her eyes, laughing at him, but it was really her way of telling him she loved him too.

****

The next morning while preparing to take Rayonna and her friend to Knott's Berry Farm, Diamond told Bright that Tanisha was calling her. "Hey, gurl, looks like your sister-in-law is calling." Diamond tossed Bright her iPhone, and then went back to folding Bright's laundry.

Deja walked in the room and immediately started helping Diamond fold her sister's laundry. *Bright is such a diva, I don't know how Diamond tolerates her half the time.* If Diamond wasn't ripping and running errands for Bright all around the city, she'd be in house, acting like her live-in maid.

Bright nodded her head at Diamond. "Be nice, bitch, that was so long ago. She admitted she was wrong and apologized to you, dang!" Bright shot as she grabbed her phone.

"Why are we folding the Queen's clothes anyways?" Deja teased, swinging a pair of Bright's thongs in the air.

"Shut up, hater, and get to folding. I take care of you bitches!" Bright stuck her tongue out at Deja as she answered. "Hey, Chocolate Drop!" Bright smiled through the phone. She hadn't seen Tanisha since she had gotten out of juvenile hall or had the baby, and Bright missed having her around.

"Bright, I need to talk to you, it's important. Do you have time?" Tanisha cried.

"I have time. What up, Choc? I'm just getting ready to take Ray and her friend to the Knott's Berry Farm today. You are still coming over later on so I can finally see the baby, aren't you?" Bright walked back into the bathroom to put her make-up on.

Tanisha cried hard into the phone. "Bright, this baby isn't Cordell's."

Bright stopped what she was doing and froze, staring at herself in the mirror. "Of course he is, silly, what are you talking about?"

"He's not, Bright. He don't look anything like Cordell. He doesn't have his good hair, his complexion, nothing!" She sobbed hard. "He's even darker than me, Bright, and is starting to look just like Capone," Tanisha sniffled into the phone. "That's why I haven't taken him to see Cordell or brought him over there yet."

Bright's mouth flew wide opened. "Bitch, y'all didn't use a condom?"

"Nooooooo!" Tanisha cried. "I told Cordell we did, but we didn't. Capone wouldn't put one on, and I knew Cordell and Lil Jay were on their way. I just wanted everything to go as planned, so I let him!" she cried. "What am I gonna do? I love my baby, but when I look at him, it reminds me of what I did to his father, Bright, and it's gonna kill Cordell"

"Oh my God, I can't believe this! Look, I know your mother doesn't want us in her house, but we have to talk in private. Is there any way you can get out the house?"

"Yeah, I can, I'll come over later. I have to get myself together." Tanisha sniffled. "I'm not bringing the baby, though. I don't want your sisters or Diamond to see him."

"I understand, Tanisha," Bright nodded her head in agreement and then whispered into the phone. "Don't mention this to anybody, all right, Tanisha? Or we'll all end up doing big time."

"I haven't, and I won't. I would never do anything to harm you and Cordell. I love y'all."

Bright smiled and sighed a breath of relief. "Good. I love you too, baby. Now stop crying your beautiful eyes out. It isn't the end of the world, and we gon' get through this."

Tanisha stopped crying, "Thank you, Sis, I'll see you in a little bit," Tanisha said before hanging up.

When Rayonna's friend got dropped off, they all piled up in Bright's Infiniti truck for a day out at the amusement park.

At the amusement park, they rode just about every roller coaster imaginable. After taking a break, they stopped and had lunch at Johnny Rocket's for hamburgers and fries. Diamond was acting like a sourpuss because her wig had fallen off her head while on one of the rides. She wanted Bright to drive her home, but instead Bright took her sequined fedora hat off and passed it to her. "I keep telling you, if you can't grow it, then sew it, but just don't throw it on." Everybody at the table laughed. Diamond picked up the plastic squeeze ketchup bottle and squirted it in Bright's face. "Laugh at that!"

Shocked that Diamond had squirted her in the face, Bright froze. "You bitch!" She picked up the mustard bottle and squirted it in Diamond's face.

"Food fight!" Rayonna yelled, and then joined in throwing pickles and lettuce off of her hamburger at her friend Kimberly.

Everybody at the table indulged in a messy food fight, and before long, they were all asked to leave the restaurant. Walking out of the restaurant, laughing in food-stained clothes, they all made their way to the car and headed home. They had had a blast!

Later That Night

Bright was sitting at the park with Tanisha and Lil Jay. The duo sat in silence, all trying to come up with a sound solution.

Breaking the silence, Lil Jay spoke. He knew his homeboy was going to go ballistic once he found out that the baby he had been waiting and bragging about for nine months wasn't even his. "Damn, Tanisha, Cuz. Why you just didn't let that nigga know that y'all didn't use any protection in the first place?" He shook his head.

"Because I thought if I told him, he wouldn't pursue me anymore." Tanisha began to cry. "You think he's gonna break up with me, Lil Jay?"

This nigga ain't no kind of help! Bright shot Lil Jay a nasty look, stopping him from saying his next words. "I know my brother is hot-headed, but you've had his back since day one, and you wouldn't even be in this situation if it wasn't for him putting you in it. I'm confident that even though shit may seem extra complicated right now, that it will work out." Bright hunched her shoulders. "I mean, it wasn't like you cheated on him or anything."

"Yea, Bee is right, Tanisha. You didn't ask for any of this, and was just being down for yo' nigga. You that nigga's Bonnie and he's your Clyde. You guys will make it through this." Lil Jay nodded his head. Lil Jay knew that Cordell wasn't innocent in his relationship and withheld secrets from Tanisha too, so this should make them even. Or at least, he hoped it would. He just didn't want Cordell to end up making a decision that could possibly send them all to prison...for a very long time.

After deciding to be Tanisha's moral support when she broke the news to Cordell, Bright rode with Lil Jay to drop Tanisha off at home. When they pulled up in front of her house, Bright got out of the car and hugged her tight. "Don't stress; everything will be all right."

"Thanks for having my back. I love you." She looked at Bright. After thanking Lil Jay for his support and the ride home, Tanisha went inside her house. Her mind was heavy.

On the ride back home, Lil Jay looked at Bright and asked, "You sure you're not pregnant?"

Even though Bright wasn't keeping the baby, she didn't want to keep lying to Lil Jay and felt she owed him the truth. Bright took a deep breath, "Fuck it, I ain't gon' even lie about it anymore. Yes, I'm pregnant, Lil Jay, but I'm not keeping it."

Lil Jay stopped immediately and pulled over on the side of the street. "So the abortion clinic is your second home now?" He was in love with Bright and wanted nothing more than to be with her and start a family. Without her telling him, Lil Jay knew that she held deep feelings for him too. She hardly ever put her hand out for money before or after they made love, and she'd lay in his arms for hours talking about everything under the sun. Many times she'd call him crying for a hug, and though she'd never mention it to him, he knew she'd be shedding tears for her children. Then, whenever she cooked, she'd call or text him to tell him that she saved him a plate. Their relationship was very much so different from the beginning to now, and without saying it, their status changed from business to personal.

"You already know how I feel about kids. I don't want any, and it's why we should start using protection." She avoided eye contact with him.

"What in the world would be so wrong with you being with me and having my baby, huh, Bright? Look at me!" he demanded.

"My brother for one, and for two, I don't even take care of the - " She stopped herself in mid-sentence. "Not tonight, Lil Jay. Please respect my wishes and understand that I don't want any babies."

"Cordell…and what else is stopping us from being together and having a family?" Lil Jay wanted to hear her mention her kids. "Because my nigga knows how strongly I feel for you, and always has! So trust me when I say that he'd be the first one offering us his blessings."

"Lil Jay, do you understand what I do to make money? I fuck niggas to get paid! Why would you wanna be with a bitch that does that?" Her eyes watered. It hurt her to look him in his eyes and say those words. "That's why I told you from the start not to get your feelings all tied up in me! I don't work well with feelings. I'm about my business...it's never personal with me," she tried to remind him.

"You could have fooled me, 'cause I ain't paid for the pussy in a long time."

"That's because I fuck you for leisure," Bright spat, not having anything else to say in her defense.

"Oh, is that right?" Lil Jay started his truck up and looked at her. "Well, you can show me better than you can tell me, because if you get rid of my baby, I ain't fucking with you no more, and that's on everything I love." He blasted his music and then drove her home.

__*Weeks Later*__

With Diamond out of town staying closer to the prison so that she could visit her boyfriend more often, Bright found herself spending more time at her condominium, fixing the place up. It gave her something to do, since she was hardly ever there, and felt it was time to furnish the place. So while waiting on her new furniture to arrive, Bright decided to call Lil Jay. She missed him tremendously, and after ignoring a few of his calls and text messages, Bright was sure that by now he was missing her too and was fully aware that she called the shots in their relationship. *I run this, little boy, not you!*

"Lil Jay, meet me at my condominium later on. I'm waiting for my new furniture to arrive. My brother gets out in a week, I'm getting fat and I'm still pregnant, and we have yet to speak since our last little altercation or whatever," Bright spoke in a slightly nonchalant manner.

Occupied, Lil Jay replied, "I'm out with my girl right now, Sis. If I'm not too busy, later on, I'll stop through."

Bright laughed to keep from crying. "Nigga, what the fuck ever! Stay out with yo' bitch! I'm about to call my nigga. I'm gone." She hung up before her voice began to crack. It didn't take much to hurt Bright's feelings or make her cry these days, and it was another reason why she hated being pregnant.

Later when her furniture arrived, Bright poured herself a glass of punch and admired the place. She had gotten a modern black leather sectional, two glass end tables both with built in lights, and a large black-and-white-striped rug. Now all she needed was a flat screen TV for the living room. Both bedrooms were furnished, and inside of the master bedroom was a queen-sized heart-shaped bed that Marion had delivered to her for Valentine's Day. The second bedroom was furnished with a basic full-sized bed, and nightstands. Bright's iPhone ringing grabbed her attention, and without looking at the caller ID, she answered, chewing ice.

"You back in town yet, baby?"

It was her Compton boss, Dime. *Time to go to work.* Bright forced a smile on her face. "Hey, baby, I was just on my way to Maryland. I have a two week case. I was going to call you when I got back in town. I miss you so much, and I'm so glad you called me."

"Two weeks? Hell naw, I haven't seen you in weeks. How much the sick fucks paying you to work? I'll double they pay."

"Baby, you know it's not about the money to me. I love my job and what I do. I've already committed to the case, and as much as I'd like to spend time with you, I don't have coverage. And if I call off..."

Dime cut her off. He had heard that same old song over and over again. "If you call off, you'll lose your job," he said agitatedly. "I'm getting tired of your fucking job, you know that? In fact, I blame that muthafucka for the reason you lost my baby."

Bright rolled her eyes in the back of her head. "I know, baby, but you know I have to work. I have bills," she said sweetly.

"Fuck that job, find coverage! Tell them bitches that I'll make it worth their time to go. I need to see you," he told her.

Bright smiled. *Coverage is on the way, nigga.* "Well, let me call the office and see who I can find to work for me. I'll call you in a half hour."

"You do that," Dime said before ending the call.

Dime would put one in mind of the rapper The Game, from the tattoos all over his body on down to his hard core, sexy, thug exterior. Bright had been kicking it with Dime for about seven months, and she would have actually spent more time with him, getting his money, if his attitude was tamer. Dime walked with his chest out, had a constant chip on his shoulder, and held a lot of animosity toward others. His macho persona made Bright sick. He loved being in his city, riding around, making money, clowning, showing Bright off, and while she'd been with him, she never knew if she'd be laughing and smiling, fucking and faking, or hiding and dodging bullets. So she milked him for as much money as she could while she could and she was never ecstatic about going back. Unless she needed money, Bright would always use her nurse card on him.

Forty-five minutes later, Bright called Dime back. "Baby, you're the best boyfriend in the world! I found coverage, and when I told the nurse that you'd pay her two thousand dollars to cover for me, boy, was she dripping with envy! I have to be one of the luckiest girls in the world." Bright laughed and smiled through the phone. When she was with Dime, she acted like she didn't have or know anything. She even pretended not to know how to straddle a dick, and instead would just lay there and stroke his ego.

"You gotdamn right, baby! Now where you at? I'm about to drop this qwap off to you so you can pay the bitch and we can go about our day."

"I'm at my uncle's house. Hurry up and drop the money off and I'll meet back up with you later. But you have to be quick; my uncle is a pastor," she lied.

Thirty minutes later, Bright received a knock on the door. When she opened it, she was surprised to see both Lil Jay and Dime standing at the door exchanging mean mugs.

"Oh hey," Bright forced an awkward smile on her face. She wasn't expecting Lil Jay to show up.

"Baby, who dis nigga?" Dime mean-mugged Lil Jay, sizing him up.

"Nigga, who is you?" Lil Jay sized Dime back up.

Bright stood in between the two. "Lil Jay, this is Dime. Dime, this is Lil Jay. He's like a brother to me." She smiled and then looked at Lil Jay. "Go on inside. I'll be in in a second."

"Like a brother, huh?" Dime stood in a gangsta stance, trying to peek Lil Jay's lingo.

Lil Jay walked in the house, intentionally left the front door wide open, took a seat on the couch, and then folded his arms across his chest as he continued to exchange mean mugs with Dime.

Dime wasn't feeling Lil Jay, and he felt there was more going on than Bright was willing to tell him. "Give a nigga a kiss, girl. I been missing yo' fine ass," Dime said as he guided Bright by the back of her head to his lips. Roughly and passionately, Dime guided his tongue into Bright's mouth for a tongue kiss. When she was fully participating, he removed his hand from the back of her head, put his hands on her ass, and squeezed it.

Bright slowly backed out of the kiss. "Baby, we can't be behaving like this in public, let alone in front of my uncle's house. I told you, he's a pastor." She spoke in a low and shy manner.

"Yeah, you right, baby. I guess we can pick back up where we left off later on tonight." He kissed her lips one last time and then slapped her hard on her ass.

Blushing, Bright smiled. "I can't wait."

Yeah, this nigga knows whose bitch this is! Satisfied, Dime passed Bright two grand and then told her that he'd take care of her later. "Go pay that bitch, baby, so we can play catch-up. Don't keep a nigga waiting too long, a'ight?"

"I promise I won't." Bright blushed, waving Dime out of the gate. *Fuck, that was awkward as fuck!* She took a deep breath and then turned to walk into the condominium. *It's business, bitch, nothing personal,* she continued to remind herself. Casually walking inside, Bright avoided direct eye contact with Lil Jay. She could feel his eyes burning a hole through her. She walked straight into the kitchen, and then after refilling her glass with punch, she spoke. "Why you didn't call and tell me you were coming over?"

"Umm, because you called and asked me to come over!" Lil Jay shot, walking up behind her. "Is that yo' nigga or something?" It killed him inside to see another man's hands and lips on Bright, and he never wanted to see it again. He was tired of playing games; he wanted Bright all to himself.

"Lil Jay," Bright turned to face him. "First off all, I didn't think you were coming, and secondly, don't you have a bitch?" She shot him a nasty look and then pushed past him. "I keep telling you about working with them feelings." She crunched on a piece of ice.

Maintaining his composure, Lil Jay agreed. He would play Bright at her own game. "You right, and I was wrong. It's all business...nothing personal. Let me quit playing and get what I came here for." Lil Jay pulled a bundle of money out of his pocket. "Get butt naked, and then get on them knees and give a nigga some head." He was going to treat her how she required to be treated.

Bright looked at Lil Jay like he had shit on his face. "Say what?"

"Get on them knees and give a nigga some head so I can go on about my day." He threw a few hundred on the end table and pulled his dick out.

Bright's heart sank in her belly at the way Lil Jay had addressed her, but she wasn't going to allow him to break her. Instead, she was going to play his game and give him what he wanted. Standing in front of him, Bright took her clothes off, grabbed his hardened penis, and then got on her knees. Looking up into his eyes, Bright placed his penis in her mouth. Sucking on his penis alternately fast and slow, Bright slobbed on his knob until she devoured him. When finished, she stood up, grabbed her money and told him to have a good day.

Disappointed that Bright chose money over love, dignity, and respect, Lil Jay nodded his head while he put his dick back in his pants. *I'm done with this bitch.* He looked at her. "Aye, and about the baby, you right. Hurry up and get rid of it. You ain't mommy material, and I'm cool on having one with you," he told her before walking out of the condominium.

The degradation of showing yet another man that she was in love with that she was nothing than a heartless, high-priced whore came with a price that she wasn't willing to face or deal with at the moment. She didn't know or understand why she did the things that she did when it came to love, but the painful reality of her actions was beginning to hurt her deeply. *This baby is outta here next week!* Bright prepared to get dressed. There was money to be made...

Dime's Time

Dressed like a schoolgirl, all smart and savvy, Bright climbed in the Lexus that Dime brought her and then headed to Compton. Dime was proud of Bright's so-called nursing profession and with the fact that she was a so-called nerd, and he would be all over town bragging about her to his friends. "My bitch has brains and beauty," Dime would always say. So Bright continued to dress and play the role. After putting her hair in a neat, tight, bun and putting on a simple pair of pearl stud earrings, Bright put on a pair of jeans, a wife beater, a blazer, wore a pair of her loafers, and then threw on a pair of her reading glasses to complete her look.

Later on that night, Dime had gotten Bright a pair of designer heels delivered to his house for her from a guy named Eric. "This nigga only dresses the city's elite. I'ma get him to start styling you," he told Bright before he instructed her to put the high heels on and to get butt naked. "I'm about to put you on some doggy-style tonight."

Butt naked with the red high heels on, Bright stood in front of Dime. "Now what do I do?" She grabbed his blunt from in-between his lips and asked him if she could hit it.

Dime took his blunt back from her. "I don't want you smoking no weed; you a nurse. You don't need this herb in yo' life, girl. I already can't stand that you smoke them stanky-ass cigarettes." Then he stood up and blew the weed in her face. "I'll let you get a contact." He grabbed her by the waist and kissed her gently on the lips.

Bright laughed inside. *Nigga please I could smoke ten of them and you'd never know it,* she smiled. "You protect me and make me feel so good and special," she said honestly. If there was one thing about Dime that she did love, it was his over protectiveness of her and how good he always tried to make her feel about herself. If she was into tough gangsters, Dime would be her number one pick, but since she wasn't, she was going to assure that he got his money's worth.

"Oh my goodness, babe, does that mean you're going to have sex with me from the back?"

"Yeah, baby, now stand up and bend over on the bed."

Bright looked at him. "Is it gonna hurt? The nurses at work say that it does." She pouted.

"They probably getting hit in the booty, baby. I'm just about to poke it from the back. I'll be gentle." He gently pushed her back down, and then he slapped her hard on the ass. "Spread them legs."

****

The next evening, after lunch with Dime's homeboy, Scrap, and his girl, Monique, they all went back to Scrap's house for cocktails. Monique was tall, dark, classy, trendy and very beautiful. Her man took care of her, and she was able to stay home and shop all weekend. Something about Scrap - Bright later learned his name was Cameron - turned her on. He wasn't rude and impolite like Dime. Instead, he was a smooth, laid-back, classy gangster that enjoyed a good cigar, cognac, old school funk, and smooth music. On top of being dark and fine, Scrap had businesses, nice cars, owned his newly built home, and his mannerisms made Bright's pussy wet. Whenever she got a chance, she locked eyes with him and hoped he'd get lost inside of them, but he never did.

After a few cocktails, Dime told them that they were about to leave. He had a 5 p.m. fitting set up at his house with his stylist, Eric. Bright was always excited about getting new clothes, so when it was time to go, she held on to Dime like a woman in love, and they walked out the door.

Back at Dime's house, the gay stylist, Eric, and Bright hit it off well. He styled her in top designer dresses and suits that were all to Dime's liking. Happy with her new items, Dime paid Eric and he left.

"Thanks for all of my new things, baby. I don't know when the last time I was able to go shopping was."

"As long as we're together, you're gonna always be taken care of and look good." He kissed her on the lips. "Now let me take you on a ride in my Six-Four. It's time for you to learn how to give yo' man head on the highway. We gon' be taking plenty of Las Vegas road trips."

Boy, please! I've sucked more dick in Ice's Six-Four low-rider than I have on my knees and in bed combined... quit playing! Bright looked at Dime and smiled. "Interesting, baby, I've never done anything like that before."

Part 7

Welcome Home, Cordell

Tanisha was so nervous about seeing Cordell that she felt like her stomach was tying in knots. She hadn't eaten in days and she rode in silence the entire ride to Juvenile Hall. Here it was supposed to be one of the happiest days of her life, being reunited with her man after sixteen long months. Yet she felt as if she was being escorted to the electric chair. The fear of what Cordell would do, feel, and say once she revealed to him that their baby was not his was driving her insane.

"Damn, Tanisha I can hear your heart beating way up here." Bright turned and looked at Tanisha from the passenger seat of Lil Jay's truck. "Calm down; everything is gon' be all right."

Turning into the facility's parking lot where he was instructed to pick Cordell up from, Lil Jay looked at Tanisha through his rearview mirror and offered her a comforting smile. She looked a nervous wreck.

"There go my brother!" Bright yelled out the window, looking back at Tanisha excitedly.

Having been released into Gale's custody, Cordell and Gale stood in the front of the detention center, laughing and talking, waiting for them to pull up.

"Nigga all yoked up and shit!" Lil Jay grinned as he parked and then climbed out of his truck.

Tanisha took a deep breath and got out of the car. Looking at Bright jumping all over Cordell hugging and kissing him all over his face made her smile. He had gotten buff and let his hair grow out.

Spotting Tanisha standing near Lil Jay's truck and smiling at him, Cordell yelled out to her, "Why my baby ain't over here giving her nigga no love, though? You don't miss yo' man or something, girl?"

"More than you'll ever know." Tanisha ran into his arms. She was an emotional wreck. The two hugged and then allowed their lips to reunite them. Happy to be in his arms again, Tanisha hung onto him as they made their way to Lil Jay's truck. "Baby, you got buff," Tanisha smiled, rubbing his chest. "You gon' keep your hair?"

"If you gon' keep it braided up. Otherwise, I'm chopping this shit off." He playfully pulled Bright's ponytail. "I'm almost catching up to you, Queen Bee."

"Yeah, right, that Mexican hair don't grow as quick as mine," she teased.

Once they got in the car, Tanisha laid her head on Cordell's chest. "You get that place set up for me and Tanisha, Queen Bee? Nigga ain't really about to be at Gale's spot like that. I'm tryna be with my girl and baby." He kissed Tanisha on her forehead.

Tanisha looked up at Cordell and stared into his eyes. Cordell sensed something was wrong.

"I keep telling you to save your money. Since you don't want to be at the house, y'all can stay in my condominium, Cordell. I hardly ever go over there. I was going to let Diamond stay there since you're back home, but it's up to you. I just don't want you going back to Juvenile until you're eighteen." Bright explained.

"You know I'd love to be at the house, but Tanisha's moms already know where the house at, so that's a no go too. She'll be at the house every day giving a nigga hell," Cordell explained. "I ain't tripping off Diamond no more. That's yo' homegirl, fuck that bitch, I ain't gotta say shit to her."

Lil Jay laughed. "Diamond cool."

"That's what I keep tryna tell him, Lil Jay," Bright nodded her head. "That's my bitch."

"Fuck that bitch, Cuz, I just don't like her ass," Cordell looked at Tanisha lying on his chest. "Why you looking all sad and shit, baby? You ain't happy that I'm home?" He lifted her face and then kissed her lips again.

Everybody in the car got silent, and tears began to fall from Tanisha's eyes as she looked Cordell in his. Bright looked back at

Tanisha in the passenger seat, grabbed her hand, and told her everything was going to be all right.

Cordell looked from Bright to Tanisha. "What happened...what's wrong?" he was curious to know. "Is it my son?"

Tanisha began to sob. "I don't want to lose you, Cordell. I love you, baby," she continued to say.

"I love you too, baby, now tell me what's wrong?" Cordell wiped her eyes. "Is my son all right?"

When Cordell couldn't stop Tanisha from crying, he began to panic and asked Bright what was wrong.

"Wait until we get inside, Cordell." Bright told him.

When they pulled up to the house, they all walked inside. The aroma of Cordell's favorite home-cooked meal lingered throughout. One by one, they all sat on the couch. Lil Jay hurried and lit the blunt he had rolled for Cordell and then passed it to him. He knew he'd need it.

Cordell hit the blunt and held the smoke in his lungs. "I'm listening." He had a feeling something was terribly wrong with his son since the mention of his name made Tanisha bawl uncontrollably.

"We're here for you, Tanisha; tell him." Bright got up and sat next to her on the couch. She wanted to give Tanisha her full support.

Tanisha wiped her eyes and then looked in Cordell's. "The, the, the," she stuttered. "I mean the baby, the baby isn't yours, Cordell. He's Capone's son, but I swear I didn't know it until after he was born." she tried to stop herself from crying.

"What??" Cordell removed her hands off of him and stood up. "What the fuck you mean my son is Capone's baby and you didn't know?" His nose began to flare and his face was turning red. He was very confused.

"I didn't know he wasn't your son until he was born and started looking like Capone. I didn't know, I thought he was our baby," Tanisha stood up and explained.

Cordell shot Tanisha an evil eye. "You fucked that nigga without a rubber, Cuz?" He was boiling inside.

Even though Bright told Tanisha to lie and tell Cordell that the condom came off, she just couldn't bear to lie to him. It was killing her inside, and she couldn't bear to look him in the eyes and lie to him. "No, Cordell, no," Tanisha snuffled wiping her eyes. "I told him to put a condom on, but he wouldn't."

Bright eyes widened. *Stupid, dumb-ass bitch! I told yo' ass to say it came off! This nigga is about to go ham!* She rested her head in the palm of her hands. *Stupid bitch!*

"The fuck off of me, bitch!" Cordell pushed Tanisha off of him. "I asked yo' dumb ass back then if Cuz hit without a condom, and you told me no!" The sight of Tanisha began to disgust him. "I thought you was better than that, but I see you just another lying, trifling-ass bitch!"

Dazed from Cordell's words, Tanisha broke down hysterically and cried, "How can you talk to me and treat me this way? Cordell, I love you," she sobbed.

"Come on, loc, Tanisha did it for the team." Lil Jay stood, hoping to bring solace to the room.

Nerves bad, Bright lit a cigarette. "I feel you, Cordell, and you have a right to be upset. Now I don't know why Tanisha didn't tell you the truth in the beginning, but I do know she loves you very much, and that y'all need to sit down and try to work this out."

How the fuck would you know anything about love? Lil Jay shot Bright a sour face expression, and then directed his attention back to Cordell and Tanisha. "I gotta agree with big sis, loc. If it's love, than it's worth riding fo'."

"Man, fuck that and this bitch, man! This bitch straight out lied to me! She could have told me that Cuz hit without a rubber back then when I asked her ass instead of lying to me! At least I would have known what I was up against, and we could have sat down and figured that shit out then! But it's too late right now and I ain't tryna hear none of this shit, man!"

"On God, Cordell, I didn't know, he pulled out and everything." Tanisha continued to sob and plead her case.

"You knew Cuz didn't wear a rubber, though, didn't you?" Cordell stared Tanisha in her crying face.

"Yes, but-but-but," Tanisha cried so hard she was unable to make her words out.

Cordell nodded his head at her pitiful face. "We may not have a son together, bitch, but I'll tell you what I do have." he pulled a picture of his and Erica's daughter out of his back pocket and threw it in Tanisha's face. "You ain't the only one that had a baby outside of the relationship. A nigga has a beautiful daughter by Erica, and she look just like her daddy."

"Come on, nigga, let's take a walk." Lil Jay wanted to prevent the scene from getting volatile. He was fully aware of Cordell's daughter with Erica, which was, in fact, the only reason Cordell had told Lil Jay not to follow through with his plan of torching the BMW that Erica had previously taken from him.

Seeing that he had crushed Tanisha with his words, he stormed out of the room. He was hurt. "Yeah, get me the fuck up outta here, Cuz. Take me to see my daughter!"

Mouth wide open, Bright was speechless. She didn't have any knowledge of Cordell having a daughter. *That's why Cordell's ass told me not to fuck that bitch Erica up or trip off the car when he was in jail. I bet Lil Jay's ass knew about it all along and didn't even tell me.* "That's fucked up, Cordell!" Bright helped Tanisha to a seat on the couch, and began to rub her back. He had broken her down completely. "You wrong for that, Cordell, brother or not, I don't give a fuck, you wrong!"

"Naw, this bitch wrong for lying to me! I know whores that know who they baby daddies are," Cordell said before walking out of the house.

I know a whore that keep track of her baby daddies too. Lil Jay looked at Bright on his way out the door.

"Y'all both lied, Cordell!" Bright yelled after him.

Frozen in shock, Tanisha stared at the picture of the little girl that she had just learned was Cordell's daughter. She looked just like him. She had his complexion, his eyes, and hair. Their baby was supposed to look just like her, but instead Tanisha had a child by a man she helped set up to be killed. *I did this for Cordell's love, and now I'm losing him over it. How could this be happening to me?* "Our baby was supposed to look like that baby, Bright," Tanisha began to cry on Bright's shoulder.

****

On the highway, headed to the Northside of Long Beach, Lil Jay and Cordell indulged in a serious conversation.

"Man, just take me to the 'hood! I ain't tryna see that bitch Erica's ass either. I don't need to be around Tanisha right now, though. I can almost imagine myself slapping the dog shit out of her ass for lying to me, man. Bitch tell me everything else, but she couldn't tell me this shit! If she would have told me this shit in the beginning, instead of fucking lying to me, man, I would have told her to terminate the pregnancy. I ain't tryna be with her ass and raise that nigga Capone's kid. I murked that nigga. What the fuck I look like? I'm done with her ass!"

"Nigga, I know you're upset, but think of it like this," Lil Jay paused. "If Tanisha wouldn't have pulled this off, that nigga Capone would still be alive, Ice would still be running the streets, Bee could have possibly been killed, and nigga, we wouldn't be rolling like we are now. Niggas is straight balling, gotdamn me!" Lil Jay hit his console. "So let's just be real about it, nigga."

Cordell nodded his head in agreement. "You right, nigga, and right now my only regret is that I wifed Tanisha's lying ass up instead of pimping her ass out... on Crip!"

Lil Jay couldn't help but laugh. "Nigga, you a fool."

Cordell continued, "I ain't gon' never walk around my hood or family with the female whose virginity I took, the girl I loved and spoke highly of, pretending that another nigga's baby is mine. And the only way I would consider being with Tanisha is if the baby disappears from the picture. It's either me or the baby, but one of us definitely has to go," he said seriously.

"Nigga, you raw!" Lil Jay nodded.

"Nigga, I'm real. If Tanisha gets rid of that baby, I'll fuck with her again, and I bet after that, that bitch won't ever lie to me again." Cordell didn't see any other way around it.

"That's a bit extreme, nigga, but let me leave this on your mind. Tanisha has our freedom in her hands, and all of our asses can be serving some serious-ass time if she decides to talk," Lil Jay warned Cordell as he pulled up in the hood.

One Week Later

Lil Jay's eighteenth birthday celebration had been the big buzz on the streets for the past several days. Having rented out the Grand Ballroom at the Marriott Hotel in Long Beach, Lil Jay's auntie came in town to assure that her nephew's celebration was a lavish one. It was an all-white party, and since Bright had plenty of brand new white dresses to wear, she woke up bright and early to pick up Lil Jay's spectacular, heart-filled birthday gift from the mall. The two had not spoken or kicked it since their last encounter at her condominium, and besides the few times he had stopped by the house with Cordell, the two had not had any contact. It took everything in Bright not to call or text Lil Jay. She missed him terribly and couldn't wait to knock his socks off with her appearance at his party that evening. She was even going to let him know how serious she was about him.

After watching Diamond walk up the walkway and start knocking on the door, Cordell finished the orange juice he was drinking, headed back upstairs to his bedroom, and knocked on Bright's bedroom door. "Your homegirl at the door."

Bright swung her bedroom door open with a cigarette hanging in between her lips, nodding her head. "Let me guess: your hands were too damn full to open the door for her, right?"

"Hell naw, they weren't! You know I ain't fucking with that bitch."

"I asked you to behave nicely, Cordell. That is my friend." Bright started down the stairs to let Diamond in.

"Shit, I am behaving. Why you think I don't look or speak to the bitch, Queen Bee?" Cordell replied before closing his bedroom. Since Tanisha and Cordell were no longer together, he no longer felt the need to move into his own place. He was only getting it in the first place so that he and Tanisha would have a home to go to that the police or her mother knew nothing of. So instead, he moved back in with his sister. He'd only go to Gale's house when the caseworker was scheduled for house visits, and when he wasn't in the streets, Cordell would be at home resting...which that wasn't very often.

"Bitch you look good! I missed you so much. Don't you leave me that long again." The two hugged.

"Look who missed me!" Diamond giggled. "I missed you too, boo boo, I really did, but I had to see my man. He convinced me to stay in Cali, but bitch, I have to hurry up and find me a job or else I'm going back to Texas. I can't get by living off of you and him having his people wire me money."

They walked into the living room and sat on the sofa.

"Why you can't?" Bright sucked her teeth and asked. "That's yo' man; he's supposed to look out for you by any means necessary, and bitch, what, you don't like being my maid no more?" Bright asked teasingly, but she was serious as a heart attack. Diamond cooked, cleaned, washed her laundry, ran all of her errands, ran her bath water, was one hell of an advice giver and friend, and Bright didn't mind taking care of her at all. "Bitch, I look out for you because you stay looking out for me, so don't even trip, and you bet' not go back to Texas. I keep telling you that I can hook you up with a few bosses that would love to make it rain on you until yo' nigga get out. But no, yo' scary ass rather be broke and lonely."

Bitch, I clean up and keep shit tight so that yo' dumb ass don't notice how much I really be rearranging yo' life, you dumb-ass bitch! Keep thinking I work for yo' nasty, trifling ass. I been slacking, but bitch, I'm back in full force! Diamond began to laugh. "That's just that nurturer in me. If I had a job and paid rent to live with you, I'd still do those things. That's just me, but gurl, you already know I ain't about to cheat on my man. They find out shit quicker in there than out here, and I ain't tryna risk that."

"Yeah, I see why yo nigga ain't tryna lose you. You a good ole faithful house bitch," Bright teased. After sending Diamond to get her designer bag off of her bed, they left and went out to Bright's Infiniti truck.

During the ride, after begging Diamond to stay in Cali, they smoked a blunt, and then Bright broke down and told Diamond about her and Lil Jay's secret relations. She planned on making it public, so she figured why not start with Diamond? Tanisha and Cordell's break-up was Bright's wake-up call, and it reminded her to never take true love for granted. Diamond was completely surprised. Walking inside the mall, Bright wrapped her arm around Diamond's, laid her head on her shoulder, and began to pout. "Now who the hell am I gonna have to dish all my dirt out to if you leave me?"

"I keep telling you that I'm going to stay." Diamond giggled. "I swear, you working with my dude to keep me here. You're my girl, Bright, and I'll always be here for you."

"My bitch!" Bright jumped up and down like a little kid, and then dragged Diamond to the jewelry store to pick up Lil Jay's birthday gift. After purchasing her merchandise, Bright found a bench in the mall for the two of them to sit, and then showed it to Diamond.

"This is so nice!" Diamond approved of the birthday gift that Bright had purchased for Lil Jay. It was a four carat, white, yellow, and gold diamond ring with an engraving inside that read: *If it's love then it's worth riding for.* They were the very words that came out of Lil Jay's mouth when trying to help Cordell reconcile with Tanisha, and Bright cherished them. She was in love with Lil Jay and she was tired of trying to hide and fight it. Lil Jay loved Bright for who she was and accepted her for what she was, and since she had pushed him away, she was going to do her best to reel him back into her life.

Diamond was in awe. "Are you going to propose to him, gurl? Is this an engagement ring?"

Teary-eyed, Bright nodded her head yes. "If he'll take me, I will. I fucked love up once, and I'm not gonna let it slip away a second time. I really love him, Diamond."

"What about your tops?" Diamond asked, astounded.

"I've saved up enough money from all of they asses to quit them now. I love Lil Jay, and in case you didn't know, his ass has cake!" Bright boasted.

"So you love him so much that you're willing to give it all up?"

"All of it!" Bright teared up. "Every last bit of it. Bitch, I got my whole 'fit laid out. I'm about to be on some Cinderella type shit. I got my glass slippers and everything. I'm just gon' be the one to pop the question to my Prince."

"Oh shit, my gurl is really in love!" Diamond hugged Bright. "I'm so proud of you, gurl, and I am really happy for you...I really, really, really, am."

Bright hugged Diamond back tightly and began to tear up. "Thank you, girl. I love him so much. I'm even having his baby!" She cried, full of emotions.

"Oh my God!" Diamond's eyes widened in disbelief. "You pregnant, too? I knew yo' ass was getting a little thick about the waist, but I know how sensitive us girls can be about our weight at times, so I wasn't going to mention it."

"Yeah, bitch, thirteen weeks today." Though her pregnancy wasn't noticeable, her hips were beginning to spread. "This is going to be his best birthday ever."

****

Tanisha drove her mother's car to see Cordell after telling her that she was only going to the store to get the baby some milk. When she pulled up and parked, she immediately begin to steam when she saw the BMW that Cordell claimed he bought for her parked in front of the house. Bright's Infiniti truck wasn't parked in the driveway, so Tanisha knew that she wasn't home. *I hope Bright and Erica aren't new best friends now, but if Erica's butt is in that house, I'm beating the brakes off of her ass on sight. I won't be eighteen for another few weeks, so after I beat her ass, I'm putting her old ass in jail!*

Tanisha climbed out of the car steaming hot. After she banged on the door, Cordell opened it wearing a pair of basketball shorts with no shirt on. Looking as handsome as ever, his hair was braided in corn rolls and his neatly trimmed sideburns gave him an extra grown man sex appeal.

Dressed in a trendy, short, purple romper and a fresh pair of Vans, Tanisha's hair was neatly hanging in an eighteen-inch weave ponytail that hung down her back. Her eyelashes and nails were freshly done how Cordell liked it, and the MAC lip gloss that Bright purchased her adorned her full lips. After making sure that Cordell got a good look at her, Tanisha looked at Cordell. "I know that bitch, Erica ain't up in here?" She snapped with lots of attitude.

"If she was, then what? We ain't together no more," Cordell replied. After seeing his daughter, Cordell paid Erica the money she used to pay the car off and she gave him his car back as she told him she would when she would bring his daughter to visit him in Juvenile Hall.

"I don't care if we aren't together. If I see you with that girl, Cordell, I promise you I'ma beat her ass, every time I see her." Anxious to get inside to see Erica for herself, Tanisha brushed past Cordell in search of her. When she didn't see her in the living room, kitchen, or in the downstairs bathroom, Tanisha made her way upstairs to check Cordell's bedroom.

Cordell slammed the door. "Aye, ain't nobody in here but me, and if my baby moms was over here with my daughter, you ain't doing shit to her. Now what you want, and who told you to come over here?"

Tanisha ran down the stairs, irate. "Yo' baby moms?" She spat. Cordell had never put another girl before her, and it hurt her deeply to hear him protect Erica. "Fuck her, fuck that, bitch, I'ma whoop her ass!"

"If she whoops yo' ass, then that's gon' be on you, but if you touch her while she has my daughter, then I'ma fuck you up myself, Tanisha." He stared her in her eyes full of pain. "Now go home and take care of your son." He walked to the door and opened it for her.

"So you really don't love or wanna be with me anymore, Cordell...we're really over?" Tanisha held her tears back.

"Yeah. I love you, Tanisha, I can't lie. But the only way we'll ever be together is if you get rid of the baby," he said to her seriously.

"Get rid of my baby? What are you talking about?" Tanisha looked at Cordell like he was insane.

"Put him up for adoption, is what I'm talking about. It's either me or him?"

"That's not fair, Cordell. I'm not asking you to choose that baby you have with Erica over me. Am I? So why are you trying to make me choose between you and my son?" Tanisha couldn't help the river of tears that streamed from her eyes.

"Because you can't. You already knew that I fucked Erica?"

"Yeah, I did, but you never told me that you guys didn't use protection, either!"

"You never asked if we used protection...I did!" Cordell yelled back. "So like I said, it's either me or your son, and if you ain't willing to give him up, then you need to leave, because you've lost me." Cordell opened the door for Tanisha to leave. "I ain't never about to raise another nigga's baby or be with a bitch that has a baby by another nigga...on Crip."

Tanisha was speechless. "How could you be so heartless and cruel to me after everything I did for you, Cordell?" She managed to say. "I got in a bed and fucked a man I didn't even know so that you could rob and kill him...and this is how you treat me?!" Her voice cracked.

Cordell hit his chest. No matter what he said or how tough he acted, it hurt him just as much to be without Tanisha, and even more so that she had Capone's son and not his. "What I'm tryna understand is why would you want to raise this nigga's kid, Tanisha? Didn't you tell my sister you could barely even look at the baby because of this shit, man?"

Tanisha nodded her head yes. When she looked at her son, she saw Capone, which in most cases made it very hard for her to sleep at night. The thought of adoption came to mind a few times, but fear of what others would think or feel about her came into play. She didn't want to be looked upon as a bad person, and even though raising her son was the hardest obstacle she had yet to encounter, Tanisha would always hope and pray that the next day would be better than the day before. "It's very hard, Cordell." She sniffed and wiped her eyes. "I didn't want this!" She put her head down and cried.

"So why you think I wanna see or raise this nigga's kid, then...huh? Look at me." Cordell lifted her chin so that they could look each other in the eyes. "He don't deserve us and we don't deserve him. Let's leave our past in our past and move on, baby."

Cordell's words made more sense than anything in Tanisha's life at the moment. Her son didn't deserve to be raised by his father's killer, and she didn't deserve to raise him. Tanisha wanted to be free of the guilt she experienced raising him every day, and she wanted to be happy again. Her mind was made up; she was going to give her son up for adoption. In her heart, she knew that she'd never be good enough for him. Tanisha fell into Cordell's arms, sobbing uncontrollably. "I'm ready to leave the past in the past and move on with you, baby."

Cordell hugged her tight. "I missed the fuck outta you, Tanisha." His eyes watered up.

The Birthday Bash

Dressed to impress, Bright looked around the living room feeling like she was surrounded by angels. They were all dressed in white from head to toe in designer dresses. Having met up with her stylist Eric, whom she met through Dime earlier that day, Bright treated both Deja and Diamond to new dresses, and they looked fabulous. Bright wore a sexy, white, strapless, evening mini dress, and she wore a pair of heels that looked like glass slippers. Deja wore a sleeveless, short, white mini dress, and Diamond wore an all-white pants suit. Bright had treated them all to the salon and had gotten their hair done. Bright had a head of loose curls and side bangs. Deja had gotten her hair flat-ironed and layered, and Diamond had her hair pulled up into an elegant up-do. They were all stunning and took lots of pictures while waiting on Cordell and Tanisha to arrive.

"I hope the limo doesn't leave us, 'cause Cordell and Tanisha are way behind schedule," Deja said after Diamond took a picture of her Bright.

"I know, but who's really tryna be on time? I know I'm not." Bright sipped from the champagne glass full of Vintage Barefoot bubbly. She promised that after tonight she was quitting cigarettes, weed, and alcohol all together. "Roll up a blunt for the ride, Diamond, a bitch need to be high."

Diamond grabbed the weed from Bright's antique silver tray and began to roll them a joint.

"Finally!" Deja stood up from the couch and said. "Here come the lovebirds! And why haven't I seen the baby yet?" Deja went to open the door.

Bright stopped Deja in her tracks. "Deja, please don't mention anything about the baby tonight. It's been a lot going on. I'll tell you about it later. Let's just enjoy ourselves tonight."

A curious expression spread across Deja's face. "All right," she agreed, and then opened the door for them.

Hyped up, Cordell entered the house. "Damn, everybody looking good tonight, we on!" He boasted. "Check out Diamond!" Cordell smiled at her. "You even looking good tonight, girl!" He twirled Tanisha around. "Look at my baby, though...stuntin'!" Having his girl back in his life made him his happiest.

Bright and Diamond's mouths flew wide open. Cordell had never said anything nice about Diamond, let alone smiled at her.

Bright stood up. "My baby brother is feeling good, looking good as a mutha, and his bitch is styling and muthafucking profiling too! What is that, Prada or something?" Bright walked up to hug the two, examining Tanisha's silk, white, one-shoulder mini cocktail dress.

"Naw, my baby got me Gucci!" Tanisha smiled and planted another kiss on Cordell's lips.

"You banging, Tanisha, and my little brother is killing the game in that all-white Gucci suit with the satin lining."

Blushing, Cordell said, "You know I gotta keep it Northside clean. Nigga stay fitted."

After taking a picture with Cordell and Tanisha, Diamond snapped a picture of them all together and then they grabbed their birthday gifts, made their way out of the house, and entered the white stretched limo that Cordell had ordered for them.

The ride was nice and smooth and everybody kept their glasses filled with champagne.

When they pulled up to the hotel, the driver let them out and they all made their way to the Grand Ballroom. Since Lil Jay's cousin worked security at the hotel and was assigned to his party, he allowed Lil Jay and his requested underage guests inside. He told them to bring ID's and that he'd ignore their ages. Having just turned eighteen, Lil Jay was ready to celebrate and get faded and he wanted his homies to be able celebrate with him too.

In line, they all showed their ID cards to the bouncer as instructed, and they were all allowed inside. Though they were all under twenty-one, they didn't dress like it and had all possessed enough grown-up swag that no one would have ever thought they were a day under twenty-one.

"This shit is nice," Deja grabbed Bright's hand and headed to the bar. Everything was all white inside the elegantly dressed Grand Ballroom. The tables, the chairs and even the balloons that flowed evenly throughout were white. The room looked like heaven.

After placing their gifts on the fancy gift table, Lil Jay's auntie wrote their names down on small cue cards, placed them next to each of their gifts, and explained. "You'll all be a part of the five hundred dollar best gift contest," she told them. She passed them each a raffle ticket. "Write your names on the back of your ticket, and then drop them inside the silver drawing bowl at the end of the table for a chance to win eighteen-hundred dollars," she smiled excitedly. Lil Jay was giving away one-hundred dollars for each of his eighteen years. Bright returned the pleasant smile at Lil Jay's aunt.

"Thanks. I love money, too... I sure hope I win."

"Good luck, honey, and by the way, you ladies look amazing!" She gave them a thumbs up before directing them to the drawing bowl.

"Thanks," they all said, smiling in unison, and then they dropped their tickets inside the drawing bowl.

Having spotted Lil Jay out near the DJ booth talking to her brother and Tanisha, Deja shouted out, "What's up, birthday boy!?" They made their way over to them.

"'Sup, Deja," Lil Jay smiled, checking her out with a big smile spread across his face. "From the looks of it, I might have to be your private bodyguard tonight, 'cause these goons up in here may try to eat you up alive," he teased, hugging her.

Cordell joined in. "All right, nigga, get up off my sister before you taint her with your bad ways. That's college girl right there!" Cordell bragged. He was proud to have a future college student in the family.

Lil Jay draped his arms around Deja's shoulder. "It's too late, nigga, we're already in love and planning to get married, ain't that right, Deja, baby?" Lil Jay playfully kissed her on the cheek and laughed.

"That's right, little brother, Lil Jay is really in the family now," Deja teased.

The play between the two made Bright uncomfortable and Diamond noticed it right away. *Look at this jealous bitch!* Diamond laughed inside.

"Yeah right, nigga!" Cordell chuckled. "But I have to admit that y'all niggas do look cute together, and if my sister chooses to go with a street nigga over a college-educated brother, then you'd be the only nigga that I'd trust with her," Cordell said seriously. "You a good nigga, man."

Trust, that shit won't be happening! Bright steamed inside. "Happy birthday, Lil Jay." She split the two up, and then hugged him tight.

"You look amazing tonight, Big Sis," Lil Jay told her.

"Don't I always?" Bright teased, observing him from head to toe. "You clean as a whistle tonight. I'm very impressed, boss." She hugged him again. He was dressed in an all-white Dior suit and matching dress shoes. He had a freshly lined-up fade and side burns and an exquisite pair of two-carat, invisible-diamond earrings adorning his ears. Lil Jay looked like a true boss.

"Damn, nigga, not both of my sisters!" Cordell teased. "It's either one or the other."

Lil Jay looked in between the two sisters. "That's a hard choice, nigga. You know you have two of the finest sisters in Long Beach," he laughed.

Bright sucked her teeth. "Try Los Angeles County!" She rolled her eyes, full of confidence. Bright wasn't happy with the attention that Lil Jay was giving her, or with the amount of attention he was giving her sister.

"Damn, Big Sis said in L.A. County, that's right, y'all hot!" Lil Jay nodded his head. He could tell that Bright was getting extremely jealous, and he was enjoying it. *I wonder how the fuck she thought I felt when she was all down that nigga's throat at her condominium that time? Yeah, two can play this game, baby!* He smiled devilishly.

Cordell popped his collar. "I got the city's best kept secret." He grabbed Tanisha by the waist and looked her deep in the eyes. He was very much in love with her.

Lil Jay smiled happily at the two. "Nigga, I'm glad y'all back together. I kept telling you that Tanisha was the one, Cuz. She keeps you happy, and now you won't be running around the 'hood like you on your rag no mo' either, nigga," Lil Jay teased.

After complimenting Diamond and telling her how nice she looked, Lil Jay told them all to enjoy themselves and that he was going to mingle with the rest of his guests.

"A'ight, nigga!" Cordell yelled after him. Then he and Tanisha took seats at their reserved table filled with tasty appetizers.

"I'll be back." Bright walked off to the restroom to get herself together. Her feelings were truly hurt.

Deja and Diamond headed back over to the bar to grab another drink.

"Gurl, I didn't realize how fine Lil Jay's ass was, but I can sure tell he has his eyes on you."

"Gurl, I didn't realize how hot his ass was until now either. Hmm, I might have to make him my boo," Deja replied, searching for him through the crowd.

"Don't mention that to my sister, though. She only wants me to interact with and date college guys. She swears street niggas ain't no good and that my picks are the bottom of the barrel type niggas." Deja nodded.

"I already know how she feels. I won't mention a thing. Now why don't you go over there and dance with Lil Jay and those girls? I bet he'll kick them all to the curb to dance with you, Snow White."

"I should, huh?" Deja drank the rest of her drink and then headed over.

Project fuck up a bitch's night is in full effect! Diamond took back a shot of Patron and giggled.

When Bright came to the bar, she got pissed when she spotted Lil Jay and Deja dancing. "Okay, nigga wanna play, let me find the finest nigga up in here so I can smile all up in his face." Bright looked around the Grand Ballroom.

"Don't do that, Bright you love him, gurl. But it does seem like Deja is kinda throwing herself all over him, though."

"Fuck that, he knows not to fuck with me! Keep an eye on them two, I'll be back." Bright sashayed around the room and accidentally bumped into one of the sexiest men she had ever laid her eyes on. *Damn, this nigga is fine as fuck! Tall, dark, and beautiful with light brown eyes...Lord have mercy!* "Excuse me," Bright smiled.

"No need to apologize. I've kinda been hoping you'd bump into me since you walked through the door." He extended his hand.

"My name is Shawn, but everybody calls me S-Man."

Flattered, Bright blushed. "I'm Bright. Pleased to meet you, Shawn,"

"Are you here with someone? I don't have my fighting clothes on," he teased.

"I'm here with my siblings and best friend to celebrate Lil Jay's birthday."

Shawn nodded his head. "I don't personally know the man of the hour, but my partner does. I'm glad I came with him now. Let's have a drink and pick each other's brains. I'd love to get to know more about you."

Bright forced a smile. "I'd like that." *Too bad my heart has been caught, and that I'll only be using you for the night, with ya fine ass!*

After he pulled a chair for Bright to sit in, they emptied an entire bottle of Dom and talked flirtatiously for over an hour. During the time they spoke, Bright learned that Shawn was a very wealthy man.

"It was good familiarizing ourselves with each other, but I have to go. My phone has been vibrating non-stop, and I'm sure it's my siblings or best friend looking for me." Bright stood up, feeling tipsy. She knew Lil Jay was blowing her up, and she was ready to pounce all over Lil Jay. "Care to walk me to the main bar, new friend?" Bright asked Shawn.

"It would be my pleasure."

Once he stood up, Bright wrapped her arm in his and sashayed back to the bar area. Sure that Lil Jay had caught a glimpse of her openly flirting with Shawn, Bright waved good-bye and then went to find Diamond at the bar. *Yeah, nigga, now how you like that!?* Bright smirked. She didn't bother to look on the dance floor or around the ballroom in search of Lil Jay. She didn't want to give him any indication that she was searching or thinking of him. She knew by now his eyes were glued to her.

Where the fuck is Diamond? I told her to keep her fucking eyes on Lil Jay and Deja, and her ass isn't even here. I'm cussing that bitch out! Bright steamed and begin to look about the Grand Ballroom.

"Bright, gurl, I was calling you 'cause I lost they asses." Diamond approached her from behind.

"What you mean you lost them?"

"First they were dancing, and then Deja walked off the dance floor and headed toward the ladies room. A few seconds later, Lil Jay headed in the same direction with some light-skinned chick with long hair. I seen Deja, she's around here somewhere, but Lil Jay and that other chick been missing in action for about twenty minutes now," Diamond explained.

Bright tried to calm herself down. *This nigga bet' not make me look stupid and be booed up with some other bitch while I'm about to propose to his dumb, stupid ass!* Both of her brows were flared. "That was probably one of Lil Jay's homegirls you seen him with, but just in case, come with. I'ma pretend to be looking for Deja so I can nose around for his ass. Nigga ain't about to make me look stupid. If that's the case, I'll get my ring and go." They walked off.

"Yeah, you're right, Bright. Lil Jay loves you, gurl. I even seen that little twinkle in his eyes when he looked at you tonight," Diamond smiled. "He ain't tryna lose you, 'cause like he said: if it's love, than it's worth riding for. He's riding for you, Bright."

Having checked both the ladies' and men's restrooms, Bright's mind began to wander. Lil Jay wasn't on the dance floor, at either of the bars, or the restrooms. They searched all over the entire Grand Ballroom. *That nigga wit' some bitch!* Bright boiled.

"What's back there, Bright? I hear some noise coming from behind there." Diamond pointed toward a dark area where the utility room was.

Bright followed Diamond toward the utility room, and the closer they got, the louder the sounds became. Bright looked at Diamond in horror when the sounds turned into moans. Seconds away from the door, Bright took a deep breath as she reached her hand out to open the door. *Please don't let this be Lil Jay with no other bitch!* She thought and then opened the door up.

The sight before her made her scream. "Oh my God!" Bright covered her mouth. Lil Jay's pants were down, his shirt was unbuttoned, and he had Deja up against the wall with her dress halfway up, fucking her like their lives depended on it.

Unaware of her sister and Lil Jay's relationship, Deja caught her breath and spoke, "Close the door, Bright, we're almost finished."

Lil Jay looked like he had just seen a ghost.

Standing there, Bright didn't know what to do or say. *Should I confront Lil Jay? Should I tell my sister about us? Or should I just walk away?* These were the questions that pounded Bright's mind. Holding her stomach, Bright felt the need to throw up. She instantly felt sick as a dog. "I was just looking for you to tell you that I was about to leave. I'll see you back at…at...at home." Bright closed the utility door, grabbed Diamond by the hand, and then ran out of the Grand Ballroom crying, leaving a glass slipper behind.

Standing in front of the hotel, holding Bright as she cried her eyes out, Diamond laughed inside. *Yeah, bitch, I knew Lil Jay fucking your baby sister would blow your mind...bitch!* Diamond had seen the two walk off within minutes of each other in the same direction after dancing provocatively on the dance floor together. Diamond just didn't mention it to Bright because she wanted what Bright had coming to her to come as a total surprise.

"How could he do this to me, Diamond? How could he do this?" Bright continued to cry. It was a true Cinderella moment, but instead of losing just one of her glass slippers, Bright had in fact lost her Prince Charming too.

****

After fixing their clothes, Lil Jay and Deja came out of the utility closet and then separated to go to the restroom to freshen up. After washing his hands, Lil Jay leaned over the sink and threw water on his face. *How the fuck did I let that shit happen?* He dried his face with a paper towel. He was only dancing and flirting with Deja to make Bright jealous. Then, while dancing, Deja whispered in his ear, to meet her by the restroom in five minutes. Though he was faded at the time, he didn't think anything of it, but when he met her there, Deja walked him to the utility room, grabbed him by his tie, and said, "I want you to fuck me, Lil Jay." The next thing he knew, they were in the utility closet going at it like two wild animals and Bright had caught them.

Cordell, Baby Kush, Blu, and E-Roc all mobbed in the restroom looking for Lil Jay. Though they had not all gotten along in the past, they had made amends for the sake of the 'hood and continued to make money together. They respected the little rich niggas, and always paid the piper on time.

"'Sup, man? Niggas been looking all over for you. I thought you dipped out to get some pussy or something, nigga." Cordell stood in front the urinal and took a piss.

Lil Jay forced a laughed. "I was mingling with the guests," he lied.

"Baby Kush joined in. "Yo' aunt told us to come find you so that you can crack open them gifts and do the raffle."

"And a nigga like me ready for some of that cake, Cuz, so hurry yo' slow ass up!" E-Roc teased as he headed out of the restroom with Baby Kush, E-Roc, and Blu.

"Tell my aunt I'm on my way out!" Lil Jay yelled after them.

Cordell washed his hands. "You the man, nigga! You got bitches lined up and ready to give you that birthday sex...all night!" He chuckled as they walked out the restroom.

Back in the Grand Ballroom, the party was still going strong and Deja was sticking to Lil Jay like flies on shit. She continued to flirt with him relentlessly. At the moment, he wished Deja were a fly so that he could swat her away. *Fuck, why did I do this to myself?* Lil Jay looked at her and thought. He didn't like clingy girls that didn't give him space and overwhelmed him. Deja was nothing like Bright. Before starting the raffle, Lil Jay pulled Deja to the side and asked her to get ahold of herself. He didn't want to give anybody the impression that they were together, especially not Cordell.

"What are you saying, Lil Jay?" Deja grabbed his hands. She thought they were at the start of a new beginning.

Lil Jay took his hand from her. "Look, we fucked, but that was it. You're the homie's sister, and I don't even know why I allowed myself to take it there with you. You know I have nothing but love for you, Deja. You're a beautiful, smart girl with a bright future ahead of yourself. I'm sure the right guy is out there for you, I'm just not him." He paused. "So let's just leave what happened between us tonight in the utility room, a'ight?" Lil Jay offered her a warm smile. He didn't want to hurt her feelings, but he knew he had to keep it real with her, and the only way to do that was to give it to her straight with no chaser.

"Really, Lil Jay?" Deja looked at him through cold, hurt eyes. "Fuck you! I thought you were different." She threw the half-filled glass of champagne that she was sipping from in his face, and then walked off, leaving the party.

"Bitch," he said through gritted teeth, and then he grabbed a napkin from a nearby table and began to blot his suit jacket dry. *Good thing her champagne was light,* Lil Jay thought, heading back over to the raffle table.

After selecting a raffle ticket from the drawing bowl, Lil Jay's auntie read the name out over the microphone. "The winner of the eighteen-hundred dollar cash prize giveaway is...Bright!"

Everybody in the room begin to clap and wait and look around the room for the winner.

"Come and get your money, baby!" Lil Jay's aunt repeated.

"Where my sister at?" Cordell said out loud while browsing the ballroom with his eyes. Having been unsuccessful in his attempts to locate Bright, Cordell stepped up to receive his sister's winnings. "I'll see to it that the Queen gets her green," he teased, and then he passed the envelope to Tanisha and told her to put it in her purse.

"Time to open gifts!" Lil Jay's auntie announced over the loudspeaker, preparing to pass Lil Jay his gifts. Lil Jay was giving away five hundred dollars to the person that the selected four judges decided brought him the best gift. Taking pictures, all of the guests began to gather around the table, hopeful to have won the contest.

"This gift is from Bright Sheldon," Lil Jay's aunt passed him an extra light, large, perfectly wrapped silver-and-white gift box. Lil Jay opened it. Inside was a small jewelry box that had a white, gold, and yellow man's diamond ring inside that almost blinded him. *Hell naw, this isn't what I think it is? Lil Jay said to himself as he read the small note attached to the box: Your words have captivated me for days and have inspired me to hold tight to true love and to do the right thing by it. Read the engraving inside the ring, and oh, will you marry me and allow me to have your baby? He or she is still within me, and for you, I'm ready to start a family. Happy birthday, baby...I love you very much!* Lil Jay was so touched that his eyes almost began to water. He read the engraving inside the ring. *If it's love then it's worth riding for.* Lil Jay could not believe how the best day of his life ended up turning into his worst. Sitting there staring at the ring, Lil Jay begin to get lost in deep thought. Bright had consumed his mind heavily.

Startling Lil Jay, his aunt broke his train of thought. "Hello, nephew, can you share the gift with us and tell us what you got? Judging from your reaction, it must be one hell of a gift," she laughed.

Patiently, his guests stood, silently, waiting for Lil Jay's response. Lil Jay forced a smile on his face. "My bad, everybody, Bright got me a nice pair of gold cuff links with ya boy's initials engraved on 'em," he lied. He wanted nothing more than to leave and find Bright.

"Niceeee," his auntie sang. "Well, hold 'em up and show everybody," she told him.

Pretending to have dropped them, Lil Jay slid the ring in his pocket and began to search the floor. After what had just happened, he knew it wouldn't be appropriate to share. *The bitch of my dreams just proposed to me...on my birthday…and I just fucked that all up,* Lil Jay kneeled on the carpeted floor, mentally beating himself up. *On Crip, I need to get the fuck outta here!*

Seeing that Lil Jay was having a hard time locating the cufflinks, his aunt told him that it was time to move on. "I'll help you look for the cufflinks after we get the remainder of these gifts open. You got plenty of them to open," she told him.

E-Roc yelled out, "Yeah, and I'm still waiting on that cake, Cuz,"

After quickly opening up the remainder of the gifts and seeing Cordell on his iPhone, the four selected judges decided that Cordell's gift won the best gift contest. He had purchased Lil Jay a brand new set of Asanti, multi-piece, twenty-six inch chrome rims for his new '08 Suburban truck, and he had his Mexican homeboy put them on while they attended the party. When he was finished doing the job, he texted Cordell a picture of Lil Jay's truck with his new chrome on them.

Everybody in the room loved them.

Pleased, Cordell nodded his head, and then held his glass up to propose a birthday toast to his boy. Everybody held their glasses high. "You're more than my nigga; you're my brother. Toast to the good life...happy birthday, nigga!"

After everyone toasted him with their glasses, they all gathered around Lil Jay's cake to sing happy birthday to him. Once he blew out the candles, he crept out of the Grand Ballroom unnoticed to find Bright, hoping that she'd still be his wife.

Part 8

The Pain

"Gurl, Lil Jay been coming to the house acting like he's been looking for Cordell, morning, noon and night, and he has been calling the house every hour on the hour. The poor boy has been running around, looking like a sad-ass puppy dog, gurl. He's hurt, Bright, and I really think you should give him a chance to explain, or just at least hear him out." Diamond sat on the sofa next to Bright in her Brentwood condominium.

Sitting in her satin pajamas with her hair all over her head, Bright wiped her eyes and replied, "His ass been even coming over here, too, knocking on the door, screaming my name. But I been acting like I ain't even in here. I ain't turned on no lights, or TV. Bitch, it's just been me, Newport's, my Kush, and a bottle of tequila." Bright's eyes were puffy and red; she had been wallowing in her condominium for three days, sobbing in misery, hurting. No one knew where she was other than Diamond. Her family thought she was out of town with one of her bosses. The visual of Deja up against the wall with her dress halfway up and Lil Jay's pants down to the floor, shirt unbuttoned, fucking her sister in the utility room, continued to replay in her head, each time hurting and causing more pain than before. Bright wanted to tell her sister what had been going on between her and Lil Jay, but with each attempt to call or text her, Bright would back out. She didn't want to hurt Deja, or chance having her brother involved in a potential homicide. Deja was still recouping from her last break-up, and Cordell was an automatic live-wire who valued his family and did things without thinking when it came to them.

"Poor baby." Diamond nodded, giving Bright a sympathetic expression. "Are you gonna try to talk to him, or at least get your engagement ring back from him? That ring was expensive."

On the edge of tears, Bright lit a cigarette and wiped her eyes. "Lil Jay's bitch ass can keep that shit as a token of what he fucked up and lost. Matter-of-fact, all the pussy he paid me for, he bought it."

Diamond's cellphone begin to vibrate. "Hold on, gurl, Deja's calling me. She's probably worried sick about you." Diamond answered, putting the phone on speaker. "Hey, Lil Sis?"

"Hi, Diamond, where you at? I'm at the house. Are you with my sister?"

Bright tapped Diamond on the arm and rapidly shook her head no.

Diamond told Deja no. "I told you, she's with one of her tops. She'll be back in town in the next day or so. She did tell me that she had bad service where she was at though. Is everything all right?"

"Yeah, I just wanted to tell y'all about Lil Jay's sprung ass." Deja laughed.

With the raise of the eyebrow, Diamond looked at Bright suspiciously.

Having quickly grabbed a piece of paper and pen, Bright jotted down a few questions she wanted Diamond to ask her sister, questions she was dying to know.

Reading the questions on the paper that Bright wrote down, Diamond nodded her head and began to ask Deja the questions. "Have you and Lil Jay kicked it since the night of his birthday, and have y'all been seeing each other and talking on the phone?"

"Gurl, yes! He picks me up from Gale's house and we be in his truck tonguing it up for hours! And he calls me every day, at least three or four times a day. I'm not even going to mention all the texting we do. SPRUNG!" Deja laughed into the phone.

Diamond looked at Bright sadly and then asked her next question. "Whattt? Have y'all slept together since his birthday?"

"Yup, twice, and he's picking me up later on tonight so we can do it again," Deja spoke through the phone, full of energy.

"Damn! Y'all must be getting serious." Diamond read Bright's last question and asked Deja, "So you must like him a lot then, huh?"

"I can't lie, I really do. He's so cute, sexy, and baby got pipe for days," Deja tried mimicking Bright.

Hearing Deja's words crushed Bright to the lowest degree she had been to in days, causing tears to rapidly pour down her face. *I let Lil Jay's young ass stick his dick up in me...for free! I listened to all his bullshit lies and believed everything he told me, and all along, all that nigga was doing was running muthafucking game on me, telling me how much he loved and wanted to be with me and how he wanted me to have his baby! Now this lying, dumb, stupid-ass nigga is fucking my little sister and running the same game on her too? I ain't gon' let him hurt us both; I'll kill his ass first.* Bright was beyond devastation.

"I'ma call you back." Diamond quickly got off the phone, seeing Bright going into convulsions. *Don't die on me yet, bitch, the worst of it has yet to come!* Diamond grabbed Bright and hugged her tight. "Everything gon' be all right." Diamond rocked her.

"This nigga is gon' get hurt, I swear to God!" Bright stood up sniffling. "How this nigga still blowing me up, leaving me sympathetic, I love you, I'm sorry, Deja-was-a-mistake type of voicemails and text messages, but yet he's still fucking and trying to pursue my sister?" Bright shook her head angrily. "I don't play that shit; fuck him! Lil Jay ain't worth another one of my gotdamn tears." Bright wiped all her tears away. "I'm not gon' never stand by and allow anybody, especially a nigga, to come in between me and my siblings, 'cause at the end of the day, we're all we got!" Bright's pain began to brew into extreme aversion and hostility. "I gotta go see this dumb, stupid-ass nigga, Diamond. He fucked me over, but I won't allow him to do the same to my sister." Bright went to take a shower and get dressed.

This Is Good-Bye

Tanisha had been speaking to an adoption specialist that she found in the newspaper, and after meeting her at the adoption agency a couple of times, asking questions and getting familiar with the entire adoption process, Tanisha had finally gotten comfortable enough to give her son up. She was able to tailor out an adoption plan that she felt would best suit her and the well-being of her son. She wanted him raised out of state, but not out of the country, to a middle-aged, married, black couple that couldn't have children of their own. And though she didn't want to be in contact with her son or the family after the adoption was final, she did have one request: she wanted to receive pictures and letters every five years.

Preferring to leave her child in the custody of the adoption agency, Tanisha held him in her arms and kissed his chocolate face for the last time. "You'll never understand how complicated this is for me to give you up, but I promise you, it's for the better. Your new family will look like you and will take very good care of you. I will always love you, Cordell." Tanisha kissed his lips and said a silent prayer, holding him tight in her arms. Taking her final look at him, she had tears in her eyes, unsure if she was doing the right thing. *You're doing the right thing, Tanisha,* she told herself, and then she passed her son to the adoption specialist and left the room, crying.

****

Banging on Lil Jay's apartment door, Bright waited for him to open the door. "I know yo' sneaking, lying ass is in there! Open this muthafucka!" She kicked his apartment door.

Once Lil Jay had seen that it was Bright at his door, he quickly climbed out of the shower, threw on a pair of basketball shorts, and then opened the door. Mad or happy, Lil Jay was just glad to see her face.

"Bright, come in, we need to talk," Lil Jay said in a serious and respectful manner.

SMACK, SMACK, SMACK! That was Bright's response to his words. "Muthafucka, you ain't shit! You called yourself playing me, but you're playing the game with the wrong muthafucking bitch, and nigga, I ain't going for it! SMACK, SMACK! Bright slapped him again, hoping to slap the taste out of his mouth. Having had her switchblade in the other hand, she wished like hell that he would put his hands on her.

"Bright! All right now, Cuz, that's enough!" Lil Jay rubbed his stringing face and backed up a safe distance from Bright. She had actually made him see stars. "I'm sorry, all right, that shit just happened, but it meant nothing to me!"

Eyes wide, Bright went into a frenzy. "You fuck my sister and then have the nerves to sit in my fucking face and tell me that it meant nothing to you? Nigga, what type of bitch you think you dealing with?" Bright charged at him with her switchblade, ready to attack.

Lil Jay dipped and dodged Bright as she wildly swung her blade at him. "Bright, put that shit down, Cuz, before you ending up hurting a nigga!"

"That's the whole idea, you stupid, dumb-ass nigga!" In trying to cut Lil Jay, Bright slashed his leather sofa, missing him by inches. "If you think I'm gon' allow you to play my sister, then nigga, you got life fucked up!"

Lil Jay wrestled Bright down to the couch, pinning her hands above her head on the arm of the couch, in order to prevent her from stabbing him. "Look, I ain't tryna play your sister, a'ight, and to be honest, I ain't been worried about her either. I been worried about you and my baby!" He looked directly in Bright's eyes. "Now stop all this bullshit and talk to me." He lowered his voice, having gotten her attention.

"Get off of me, lying-ass nigga!" Bright attempted to wiggle from underneath him.

"What am I lying to you about, Bright? Let a nigga know...Talk to me!"

Out of breath, Bright avoided eye contact with Lil Jay as she yelled and screamed for him to get off of her. His eyes mesmerized her and she was in no mood to be mesmerized.

"I ain't letting you up until you tell me what I lied about first, Bright! I don't want Deja; I love and want you," Lil Jay said, full of passion.

"You tryna be with my sister, fucking her and seeing her, but yet you calling and texting me all muthafucking day and night talking about how much you love me and wanna be with me! Nigga, get the fuck outta here!" Bright tried getting from underneath him. "I ain't crazy, and I ain't gon' let you hurt my sister!"

Lil Jay's face immediately screwed up with confusion. "Hell naw! I ain't tryna be with Deja! I ain't fucking her, and we aren't seeing each other, either, Bright. I don't even have Deja's number in my phone, and that's on my mother, rest in peace!" Lil Jay never put things on his mother, but he felt the need to do so at the very moment so that Bright would believe him and hear him out. "Now if you wanna get mad and slap a nigga for that shit that popped off on my birthday, then do that, because that's all that happened and all it was. Me and Deja don't have shit going on!" Lil Jay stood up and let Bright up.

Bright sat up, fixed her clothes, and then set her switchblade on the table. "Well, why would my sister lie about that, Lil Jay? You must have did or said something to make her feel this way."

"Why would I lie? On my mother, Bright, when you know how much I love her, and how much she means to me?"

"'Cause niggas lie, that's why!" Bright knew how much his mother meant to him and how much he loved and missed her. On her death anniversary last year, he called her on the phone and said, "Come through, I want to introduce you to my mother." When Bright got there, Lil Jay had countless photo albums spread across his cocktail table, and then, when she sat down with him, he showed her numerous pictures of his mother and told her many wonderful things about her. When his eyes started to water up, Bright hugged him and they silently released tears of hurt and pain. It made Bright think about her little brother, Ramon, and how much she missed him and regretted not being there for him the day he took his life.

Lil Jay took his phone and tossed it to Bright. "I would never mix my mother's name with lies. I thought you knew me better than that," he said, then walked inside his room.

Nigga, I thought I could trust you enough not to fuck my sister too, but you did, Bright looked at Lil Jay wanting to say, but she allowed him his moment. He looked genuinely hurt from her last comment. She was dying to get her hand on his phone the second Lil Jay disappeared from her vision. Bright picked up his phone and begun strolling through his contacts. When she didn't see Deja's name in his contacts, she went to his text messages and practically read every text that he had sent and received that month, and not one of them were to or from Deja. However, Bright got extremely jealous of the sex-texting and provocative pictures from girls named Crystal and Layla. *Bitch!* Bright sat at the edge of the couch and put Lil Jay's phone back where she got it from. *Why would Deja just lie about something like that?* Bright thought. *But even if so, Deja likes him now. His dumb, stupid-ass fucked her, knowing what we had going on. I'm cool on this nigga...fuck him!* Bright stood, preparing to leave. He wasn't going to hurt her sister, and though she did feel better knowing that nothing was going on between them, Lil Jay had still hurt her by having sex with her sister in the first place.

Seeing Bright standing at his apartment door to leave, Lil Jay stepped into the living room. "So you just gon' come over here, slap a nigga around like some sort of bitch, cut my couch up, accuse me of some untrue shit, go through my phone, and then leave without saying good-bye or giving me a chance to change this entire situation and make it right?"

"It can't be made right. You fucked my sister, Lil Jay," The images of them in the utility closet began to run through her head again and make her heart ache.

"Bright, yeah, I was wrong for fucking your sister because me and you do business together," he reminded her of her very own words. "But it would have never happened if our relationship was more personal, and you were always pushing a nigga away, feeding that bullshit in my head."

"So do you think that made it right?" Bright turned to face him with tears in her eyes. "I don't give a fuck if we were business, personal, or whether you were fucking or making love to me, Lil Jay! You should have NEVER crossed that line and had sex with my sister!"

"Well, why you kept feeding that shit in my head like you didn't give a fuck about me, huh?"

"Without words or confirmation, nigga, you knew what we had!" Bright tried hard to keep from crying.

"Well, I'm a nigga, a young wild one at that. I don't work off all them sensitive, fucking female emotions. I needed confirmation. I needed you to tell me that you loved me, or that you wanted to be with me. Hell, as crazy in love as I am with you, you could have even given a nigga a rain-check. Let me know something!" Lil Jay hit his chest and explained.

"Well, I was wrong, because I thought what we had was magical. I thought you were one of the only niggas in this world that really knew and loved me, truly and wholeheartedly for me!" she cried. "And whether or not you apologize or admit that, yo' ass was dead wrong for fucking my sister." Bright's voice cracked. "You hurt me, Lil Jay; you hurt me bad, and I didn't expect you to ever hurt me. I trusted you!" She cried.

Caught up in emotions, Lil Jay's eyes began to water up. He hated that he hurt Bright when all he ever wanted was her. "Can I hold you?" Lil Jay asked before taking Bright in his arms. "I'm sorry, Bright, it meant nothing to me, I swear it didn't. Deja offered it up, I was faded, she was ready, and I was wit' it. I'm not gon' lie to you. When you caught us and I seen the pain in your eyes, that shit fucked me up inside. But what killed me was when I opened your gift." The hurt could be seen in his eyes. "And when I seen the ring, and then read the note you attached to it, mannnnnn, I felt like I had just won a billion bucks and then lost my mother all over again." He held Bright tighter. "That's how happy I was just to know that you loved a nigga, how hurt I felt for the pain I had caused you." Lil Jay looked in her face, wanting nothing more than to see her smile. "We all make mistakes, baby. Let's ride for our love?" He kissed her softly on her forehead.

Those words practically made Bright melt. "I want to, Lil Jay, bad, but it was my sister. If it was anybody else, I wouldn't give a fuck, but it was my baby sister. She looks up to me..."

Lil Jay interrupted Bright's words, kissing her on the lips, "Shhh. Shhh". Gently, he slid his tongue in her mouth and allowed their tongues to fight their battles. "I can't lose you, Bright. I been wanting you and waiting on you for too long to just let you go," he said in between breaths.

Bright held on to Lil Jay, knowing it would be their last time together. She knew after this encounter, she'd never be able to do or see him anymore. Her family was everything to her, and no matter how scandalous or conniving she could be, she would never allow anything or anyone to stand in between her and her family. They had been through too much, lost more than they should have, and were at a very vulnerable place. Bright refused to be the cause of any further breakage. However, she would make love to Lil Jay. She wanted to feel him inside of her one last time.

"Let's make love to each other, Bright. I wanna make you feel good." Lil Jay began slowly massaging her breasts as he kissed and sucked on her neck.

Fully indulged, Bright was lost in his kiss, rubbing the side of his face and all over his chest. "Take the cookies, Lil Jay, take 'em," she said seductively.

Lil Jay picked Bright up and took her inside of his room. Using one arm, he swept his clothes from the bed onto the floor and then carefully laid Bright down on it. Butt naked, he enjoyed the view. Removing his basketball shorts, Lil Jay joined her in bed. Spreading her legs, he rubbed in between them as he looked deep in her beautiful eyes, kissed her soft lips, and then sucked on the spot on the right side of her neck that made her climb the walls. "Get on top, wifey. You know how much I love watching you perform with my dick inside of you."

Instead, Bright placed her pussy on his face and then leaned forward to kiss his fat, long dick. *I'm gonna miss sucking on you.* She sucked and slurped all over it. Sucking her way up each side of his dick, she then long-stroked it in her mouth, allowing it to reach her tonsils. Then she grabbed it with both of her hands, slobbed all over it, and sucked it fast, softly biting the head of it on her way back down. "I love the way yo' dick taste and feels inside of my mouth, Lil Jay." Bright licked and smacked on it while Lil Jay ate her until she was nearing an orgasm. Unlike most women, nothing was as satisfying to Bright as sucking on a big, fat, juicy dick, and she sucked it with deep passion.

"Suck on yo' thang, baby, but don't make it cum," Lil Jay said, out of breath. Holding on to each of her booty cheeks, he spread them open and started licking her from her asshole back down to her juicy pussy.

"Ohhh, yes, Lil Jay I'm about to cum!" Bright held his dick in her jaw and moaned.

"I love this pussy! I don't never wanna share it with another nigga again." He sucked on her pulsating clitoris while he messaged her ass, making her cum all over his face.

"Ahhhh!" Bright's body went into small convulsions as she rolled off of him, holding his dick in her mouth like a woman in need of nourishment.

"Don't let this little nigga wear you out!" Lil Jay slapped her on the ass as he guided her back on top of him.

Bright popped his dick out of her mouth. "Never that! You know how much I like playing with it in my mouth." Bright sat on his long, hard dick and they got lost in each other's eyes. Slowly moving her hips, she wanted the moment to last forever.

Lil Jay let his hands wander all over her body, cupping her breasts with his palms and then fondling her nipples. "Yeah, baby, make love to it, do it soft and slow." Then he told her to take her ponytail out of her hair. She was his true sex goddess, amazingly beautiful, and he could never get enough of her. He had never enjoyed having sex or being with another woman as much as he did with Bright, and he was in love with everything about her.

Doing as she was told, Bright bit on her bottom lip, sure to keep his member nice and stiff. Picking up the pace, Bright's moans grew louder and louder, "Ohhh, ahhhh, yes, I love it!" Riding at her maximum speed, she just couldn't get enough.

Feeling himself about to cum, Lil Jay told Bright to slow down. "I ain't ready to cum yet."

Ignoring him, Bright leaned forward, resting her hands on his chest, "I'ma miss fucking you, Lil Jay."

Lil Jay didn't like what he was hearing and instantly rolled over on top of Bright. Lying on top of her, he allowed the head of his penis to rest in her opening. Looking her dead in the eyes, Lil Jay held her face in his hands. "What you talking about, Bright? This ain't the end; this is the beginning for us. I hope you don't think I'm about to let you go. We going public," he said, full of emotion.

Knowing that their legacy would never happen, tears begin to pour down Bright's face. "Make me remember this dick, Lil Jay." Bright turned her face from his.

Lil Jay penetrated her harder and harder, taking long, hard, deep thrusts inside her, and then he started biting and sucking on her neck and ears and tenderly kissing her lips. He held her tight, telling her how much he loved her and planned to take care of her. "I ain't going nowhere; we personal now," he whispered in her ear.

"Harder, harder, hit the back of this pussy," Bright begged him." She no longer wanted Lil Jay to make love to her; it was making her too emotional. She wanted him to hurry up and bust his nut so she could leave and be done with it. The enjoyment of making love, being in love, and the deep feelings that she had for Lil Jay continued to shift back into hurt, pain, hate, and visions of him with her sister. It made it all that more difficult. Tuning out, Bright lay there in silence while Lil Jay stroked and kissed her. Tears streaming from her eyes, she began to think that she had done too much to actually gain true happiness and love. Larry, Treasure, Terrence, Chrome, and Capone all began to trouble her mind.

"Lil Jay, you in here, nigga?" Cordell pushed his bedroom door open with a burner in his hand. He hadn't heard from him in two days, and he had begun to worry about his friend's well-being. Since he had a set of keys to his place, Cordell decided to stop by and check on him.

Totally taken aback by her brother's sudden presence, Bright reached for the sheet and hurriedly covered herself up. Speechless, she didn't know what to say.

"What the fuck! Bright?" Cordell had a look of confusion on his face.

Lil Jay reached for his basketball shorts. "Hold up, nigga, I'm about to come out."

Tanisha and Deja quickly ran into Cordell's direction. "What's wrong?" Deja asked.

Eyes wide, Bright's heart skipped a beat, *Oh shit, not Deja!* She reached for her clothes. "Close the door, Cordell." Bright managed to say. She didn't want Deja to see her naked.

"Bright in there?" Deja peered inside the bedroom, immediately locking eyes with her sister. Seeing her sister in Lil Jay's bed, naked and covering herself up with a sheet made Deja's jaw drop. Her world stopped for a second; she couldn't believe what she was seeing. Hurt, Deja thought, *how could she do this to me?* Then, without further words, she stormed in Bright's direction and slapped her. *SMACK...* "I see you just had to get your turn too, huh, Big Sis?!" Deja said sarcastically, looking at her sister with disgust.

Bright held her face, "All right, Deja, I'ma take that one. Now let me explain!" She wrapped the sheet around herself and then stood up.

"Explain what? How you fucking a nigga after me!" *SMACK!* Deja slapped Bright again.

"Put ya hands on me again, all right!" Bright pushed Deja, causing her to trip and fall on the bedroom floor. Immediately feeling bad for her actions, Bright offered her hand to help her sister off the floor.

"Don't fucking touch me!" Deja swatted Bright's hand away from her as she scrambled up off the floor. "I knew you fucked all of Treasure's boyfriends, but now you hopping in bed with niggas after me too...your own sister?" Deja stared her sister in the eyes. "But I see now that I am no different in your book than the friends that you stabbed in the back! You ain't shit, Bright."

"Treasure? Are you fucking serious, Deja? After that bitch tried to kill me...not once, but twice? Fuck that dumb, stupid-ass bitch!"

"Wasn't like you didn't push her to it," Deja rolled her eyes.

"You little bitch!" Bright delivered the first strike, igniting a fight. She was angered by Deja's words and disrespect to her, after everything she had done and was about to give up for her. "You don't even know what the fuck is really going on, and you gon' come at me like this after everything I've done for you? Bitch, I'm your sister!" Bright barked, fighting her sister in the nude.

"Fuck you!" Deja yelled as she and Bright continued to punch, scratch, and pull each other's hair. "Fuck you, slut!"

"Help me break them up!" Tanisha yelled to Cordell and Lil Jay, who were in the midst of their own argument, near blows. Having gotten their attention, Cordell and Lil Jay continued their argument as they split the fight up. Lil Jay grabbed Bright and Cordell grabbed Deja.

"You a'ight, baby?" Lil Jay asked Bright in between arguing with Cordell.

"Fuck that, Cuz! Give my sister some muthafucking clothes to put on, nigga!" Cordell didn't want to see his sister naked, and he didn't appreciate seeing Lil Jay's hands all over her nude body either.

Lil Jay passed Bright her clothes. She briskly put them on.

The affection that Lil Jay displayed to Bright made Deja drip jealousy. "Let me go, Cordell! I'm getting the fuck up outta here," she said, and then looked at Bright. "Don't call or come around me anymore. I don't want to have nothing to do with you, ever again, you, worthless, back stabbing, whore!"

"I may be a lot of things, but worthless is what I'm not. Go check my bank account with yo' little young, stupid ass!" Bright was tired of turning the other cheek to Deja's verbal beatings, and figured that since she was bold enough to dish them out, then Bright would no longer bite her tongue.

"I know yo' ass is a sorry-ass mother, bitch! Go get your kids and raise them. Better yet, why don't you call them and check on them from time to time." Deja smirked, seeing the sadness that spread across Bright's face. "So go ahead and brag about your fat-ass bank account that your loose-ass pussy made for you. But you'll never be able to brag about the shit that counts, like being a good mother, person, friend, or girlfriend. Hell, you aren't even a good sister. You let Ramon down, and he ended up killing himself. But you can think of me as dead too, 'cause I'm outta ya life for good!" Deja exited the room in tears.

"I can be all that, but bitch, I ain't never done shit wrong to you! Leave without knowing the truth!" Bright yelled after Deja.

Not knowing what to do or say, Tanisha passed Bright a cigarette in hopes of calming her down. She had never seen her so upset before. "Y'all just need time, everything will be all right," Tanisha laid her head on Bright's shoulder. She had just given up her son and she was in a lot of pain too.

Cordell didn't know what messed him up the most: the dishonor from his friend that he called his brother, the fact that his sisters had both fucked his homeboy, or the fact that his sisters had just fought. Full of animosity, Cordell grabbed Lil Jay's attention, aiming his gun at his head. His mind was going a mile a minute. "Nigga, both of my sisters, Cuz?"

"You know what they say, loc. If you gon' point it you better be willing to use that muthafucka."

Making the sound effect of a shooting gun, Cordell shot Lil Jay a look of war. "Bop, bop, bop. "Yea, nigga, we gon' handle this shit on the streets," he assured him before going after Deja.

"I love you, Bright." Tanisha kissed her on the cheek and then followed after Cordell.

****

Back at the house, Diamond was in the kitchen moonwalking, taking back shots of Patron, celebrating. *Yeah, buddy, my timing is right!* Diamond smiled and then poured herself another shot, laughing uncontrollably. Deja had just called Diamond crying about how when they went to check on Lil Jay, he was in the house fucking Bright. She said they had gotten into a physical altercation and that she was never going to talk to her again. *Yeah, Lil Sis, that's why I suggested y'all go check on the nigga when yo' bitch-ass brother was walking around worried about Lil Jay. I knew Bright would be over there giving up the pussy!* Diamond thought as Deja cried her heart out.

Shortly after Cordell and Tanisha had come home, they went straight upstairs and started packing all of their belongings. Diamond didn't have to ask why, but when Tanisha came downstairs, Diamond sat a twenty piece of dope on the kitchen counter and pretended to be smoking dope out of a glass pipe. Tanisha begged her for a hit. "I can't fuck with you. Loose lips sink ships. I almost lost my best friend sharing with you last time, gurl, and yo' man just started speaking to me. Can't do it."

"I promise I won't say anything this time. Let me try it before Cordell comes down here tripping."

"Nope, I can't trust you anymore." Diamond walked out the back door and waved good-bye to Tanisha. An hour later, when Cordell and Tanisha left the house, Diamond walked back in the kitchen, and as expected, the dope was gone. Diamond knew Tanisha would eventually turn Cordell out. *Now I need to work on that little ballerina, and if Bright doesn't kill herself after that... then I will!*

Downward Spiraling

The next few weeks had been hectic ones. Tanisha had fallen into a complete depression. She had full support from Cordell's siblings, who didn't know the full depth and reason for her giving her son up for adoption (other than Bright). Tanisha had been disowned by her mother after breaking the news to her, and every time she heard Cordell speak to his daughter on the phone or brought her around, it messed her up mentally. Dope was her only refuge. The addiction to dope had completely empowered her. Whenever Cordell was out in the streets hustling, she'd hopped in the new car he had just purchased her for her eighteenth birthday and head to the other part of town in her hunt for drugs. Tanisha would smoke an eight ball of crack a day and could hardly wait to get her hands on her next eight the following day.

Having gotten herself an eight-ball for the day, Tanisha hurriedly drove home to hers and Cordell's new two-bedroom town house in Long Beach. After the revelation that both sisters had slept with his ex-best friend (now enemy) Lil Jay, Cordell felt it was in their best interest to move out of the house with his sister, Bright, and into their own place. He was disappointed in both of his sisters for their ratchet behaviors, especially Bright's, and he felt that his homeboy had crossed ignoble lines, having slept with not one but both of his sisters. It was a very damaging blow to their friendship, and the two had fought more than four times since the startling revelation. They were at the point of gun play.

When Tanisha got out of the car, she ran inside their townhouse, sat at the kitchen table, and put the flames to the pipe and inhaled.

Walking out of the bedroom and into the kitchen, Cordell's eyes widened with bewilderment, seeing Tanisha sucking on the tip of a crack pipe, he went completely berserk. He had been noticing Tanisha's strange behavior over the last couple of weeks and had actually thought she was cheating on him or was still mad because he didn't want to celebrate his birthday. So after leaving earlier that morning, Cordell decided to go back home and see what Tanisha did with her time while he was out. When he got back home and she wasn't there, he went to lie down until she came back home.

"Oh shit!" Tanisha dropped the pipe on the kitchen floor and watched the scene that seemed to play out in slow motion right before her.

Cordell ran across the kitchen floor and slapped Tanisha so hard that she fell out of the chair and onto the floor. "You smoking dope now?" Cordell roared in a fit of rage. He knew that in the past, he had gotten her to use cocaine with him, but after doing his time in juvenile, Cordell decided that cocaine would eventually lead them to the path of dope, and he no longer wanted to indulge. Tanisha asked him on many occasions to do a few lines here and there and he always told her no, and that he didn't want her using either.

"The fuck you doing, man?" He stood over her.

"Nothing." Tanisha shivered on the floor, blocking her face, afraid of what Cordell might do to her.

Cordell picked up the pipe and busted it on the kitchen floor. "Nothing my ass, bitch, 'cause to me it looks like you in here smoking dope! Get yo' ass up!" He demanded.

Tanisha got up from the floor and looked at him with shame. "I'm sorry, Cordell. I just been needing something to help me ease all this pain!" She cried.

"Bitch, if I catch you sucking on a muthafucking pipe again, I'ma beat yo' ass!" Cordell reared his hand back to slap her again.

Tanisha ran to the side of the refrigerator and yelled and screamed for him not to hit her again. He had never hit her before, and from the look in his eyes, he was about to hurt her bad.

"So that's what you been doing with my muthafucking money, huh...smoking the pain away? Cuz, fuck that!" He knocked the glass to the kitchen floor, heated. He felt like everything was going wrong in his life, and it angered him deeply.

"Yes, Cordell, I'm hurting!" Tanisha stood firm and cried. "I gave my son up and now my mother and my entire family has disowned me!"

"Well, why you didn't keep yo' baby then?"

"Because he wasn't your son, and I didn't want to lose you! He was Capone's son, a baby of deceit. How could I raise him? Now my mother hates me and she doesn't even know why I gave him up." Tanisha sat down at the table and slipped a piece of dope in her pocket without Cordell noticing it. She relied on the drugs to make her feel numb to the pain she experienced every day.

"Well, maybe you need to go talk to a muthafucking shrink or something, but smoking dope ain't gon' change shit but make you lose a whole lot more." Cordell stared in her eyes. He couldn't help the feelings of guilt that he was feeling at that very moment for not only Tanisha's drug use, but for the entire situation she was in. He was so upset that he was unable to comfort her the way he wanted to, and after grabbing her keys to make sure she wouldn't leave, he stormed out of the house. "I bet' not catch you smoking that shit no more either!" He slammed the door shut, and then headed to his truck. His mind was on overload and he needed the one person that he knew he could always count on, no matter what...his sister Bright.

****

"I'm all right, bestie, don't worry about me. How is your family?" Bright asked Diamond as she stretched across Dime's bed, sucking on a fat blunt. He still didn't know that she smoked weed, but since he was scheduled to be out for hours, she figured she had enough time to get high. Bright had been spending much of her time with Dime, needing comfort. She had Deja and Cordell pointing the finger at her, and since Diamond was in Texas for her grandmother's funeral, Bright ran to the next best person that always showed her lots of love and protected her: Dime.

"Everybody is coping, but you know, I had to check on you. My momma is tryna make me stay, and I keep telling that I can't leave you hanging. You're going through too much for me to leave now, and I'm still sad you aborted my god-baby last week."

"Bitch, that baby had to go, right along with Lil Jay's ass!" Bright sucked her teeth. Having had the abortion performed last week, Bright had no regrets about it. "I love you, though, Diamond. You've been the only person to help me make sense out of all the bullshit I been going through. Thank you so much, and when you get back I have a surprise for you." Bright smiled. Bright valued Diamond's friendship now more than ever, and she had bought her many things to show her appreciation.

"No more gifts, Bright. I'm serious, it makes me feel like you tryna buy me." Diamond laughed.

"Is it working?" Bright teased. In the middle of their conversation, Bright received a call on the other line from her brother, and she told Diamond that she'd call her back.

"Okay, Missy, be nice and call me whenever; I'm here for you." Diamond said.

"Thank you, friend. I'll call you later on tonight. Kiss your mother for me too," Bright said then answered her brother. They had spoken a few times since the incident at Lil Jay's house, and each time it turned into a shouting match.

"Yes, Cordell?" Bright answered sarcastically, preparing herself for battle.

"Queen Bee, where you at? I need to holler at you - serious business, too," he said in a somber tone.

Bright sat up in bed. "Are you all right?" she asked, full of concern.

Cordell sighed. "I'd rather talk to you in person. Where you at?"

"I'm at Dime's house, in Compton. I can be at the house in like fifteen minutes, though." Bright began to put her shoes on her feet. Cordell knew of all her tops, and she made sure he had their phone numbers, cell numbers, and home addresses.

"A'ight, I'll be inside waiting on you."

As Bright prepared to walk out of Dime's four-bedroom, newly-renovated house, she was met by a very familiar face. *The muthafucking mechanic from Long Beach that I fucked and then blackmailed to fix my mother's car last year? What the fuck is he doing here?* Bright thought, completely taken aback by his presence.

"Can I help you?" Bright asked pleasantly. She put her game face on. She had immediately decided to play the dumb role and act as if she had a twin sister if necessary.

"Don't I know you?" He looked at her suspiciously.

Bright looked him over, shaking her head no. "No, I don't think so."

"Aren't you Karen? You have a Honda and had it worked on at my mechanic shop last year?" His face began to slowly grow into a mean mug.

Bright begin to laugh. "Oh goodness! If you know my twin sister Karen, then it must not be good." Bright extended her hand to shake. "I'm Bright. Are you friends with Karen?"

"Hell no!" He retorted, and then immediately calmed himself down. "I mean, not at all. Being her twin sister can't be a good thing at all. She's bad news."

Bright laughed. "Your name?"

"I'm Tobe." He continued to observe her.

I know who your stupid, dumb ass is, nigga! Bright smiled. "I'm always being mistaken for Karen. I just recently took her to court for using my identity." She shook her head in disgust. "Are you a friend of hers? And how much money does she owe you?"

"She owes me six hundred dollars for fixing her car. You sure you're not Karen?" He asked suspiciously.

Bright pulled her driver's license out of her purse and showed it to him, and then he returned it back to her. She told him that Dime was out, and that she'd tell him that he stopped by.

"Yeah, you do that." Tobe looked at Bright as she walked away. He wasn't completely convinced.

That was close as fuck! Bright thought as she climbed in her car and drove off. Feeling the need to be cared for, protected, and showered with love, Bright told Dime that she had a week's vacation from work and wanted to spend it with him after Diamond had gone back to Texas. Her siblings were both at her throat, and Lil Jay would not leave her alone. He called her day and night and would pop up at her house at all hours of the night after Diamond made the mistake of telling him that Cordell had moved out of the house. When Bright told him that they could no longer see each other after everything that had gone on, Lil Jay flew into a fit of rage and told her that he'd kill any nigga he saw her with. When Bright pulled onto her street and parked, Lil Jay pulled up on the side of her, bumping her old-time favorite songs by Keith Sweat. After he turned the music down, he rolled his passenger-side window down and told Bright he loved her.

Seeing him for the first time in weeks, Bright's heart melted and a slow smile begin to peek from her lips.

"You don't have to tell me that you love me back, baby. I know you do." Lil Jay winked at Bright revealing the ring she had bought for him on his ring finger. "I do..." He looked her deep in the eyes. "I can't wait to marry you. I'm working on a few million for us right now."

POW! POW! POW! Three loud gunshots broke the intense gaze that the two were sharing, causing them both to duck for cover. Lil Jay yelled out and asked Bright if she was okay. Bright yelled that she was fine.

With his gun aimed, Cordell emerged from the porch. "Muthafucka, don't be riding up showing your face at my muthafucking house like we partners or something, nigga!" He fumed. He told Bright to go inside the house.

Lil Jay smashed off the street, tires screeching. Bright stood apprehensively, preparing to walk inside the house.

Cordell aimed his gun at the back of Lil Jay's truck and let two bullets rip through the back of it. "Muthafucka!"

"Cordell, you gon' get me put out of here doing crazy shit like that! Lil Jay and I aren't fucking anymore."

"I bet his bitch ass won't be bringing his ass around here anymore!" Cordell pulled his gun to his side and then followed Bright inside while she fussed at him.

Inside the house, Bright took a shot of tequila and chased it with a glass of water. Having just had a quick argument about her and Lil Jay again, Bright asked Cordell if he was hungry. She knew Tanisha wasn't much of a cook, and that they ate out most of the time.

"Naw, man I'm cool." Cordell tried to calm himself down before going at it with Bright again. He had a bigger problem at hand.

"So what's up, Cordell? Did you come over here to fight with me again or what?" Bright stood in the living room entrance with her hand on her hip.

"Naw, I actually came over here to call a truce, Queen Bee. I'm still heated about everything, but you still my sister and I love you." He stood up to give her a hug.

"Aw, shit, what's going on, Cordell? I know you didn't just come over here to tell me how much you love me." Bright could see the pain in his eyes.

Cordell sat on the couch, shaking his head as a single tear jerked from his eyes. "Tanisha is smoking dope, man. I caught her hitting the pipe earlier today." He put his head down. He was hurt and didn't know what to do.

"Oh my Godddddd, are you serious, Cordell?" Bright sat next to her brother with her mouth wide open, her heart slowly sinking into her gut. Over time, Bright had really developed strong, genuine feelings for Tanisha. When everybody was upset with Bright, Tanisha still made it her business to display nothing but love and support to her.

Cordell told Bright how he loved Tanisha more than himself, that he felt responsible for her entire situation, and that he needed her help to help Tanisha. He had even shed a few tears when he explained to Bright how devastating it was for him to see her lips on the pipe, that he went ballistic and slapped her out of the chair she was sitting in. Bright had never seen her brother so disturbed in her life, and she wanted nothing more than to help him make things better.

"Let's go to your house and let me have some time alone with Tanisha, Cordell," Bright said to him as she stood up from the couch.

After Cordell grabbed his keys from the table, they headed out of the house, climbed in his truck, and drove to his house. When they got there, Tanisha was nowhere to be found.

"I took her keys; where the fuck she go on foot?" Cordell fretted, looking around the apartment.

Bright shook her head. *Damn, bitch, what the fuck, why dope?* Were Bright's current thoughts. "So if she's on foot, Cordell, let's get in the car and find her," Bright told him in a comforting tone in the hopes of calming Cordell down. He was beginning to lose it.

"I bet' not see her out there on a dope mission, Bright, I'm telling you, 'cause I swear to God, I'ma beat her ass!" He locked his house up and they walked back out to his truck. Cordell's eyes were watery and full of pain.

Inside his truck, Cordell drove like a maniac, peering at all of the high-traffic dope spots in North Long Beach. Bright had to tell him to slow down before he attracted attention from the police and ended up getting his truck impounded for driving with no license. He had already lost one of his cars for driving with no license, and he was told the next time he would be locked up.

"Queen Bee, quit bitching please. You know my head is already fucked up, and I got a million things running through my mind at once."

"That's why you need to calm down. Pull over and let me drive so you can vent, cuss, fuss, and clear your head," Bright said in a compromising tone.

"There her ass go right there! Is she buying dope from that nigga?" Cordell spotted Tanisha on the opposite side of the street stopping in the middle of the street, holding up traffic. Cordell climbed out of his truck, dodging oncoming traffic, and ran across the street.

"This crazy-ass nigga!" Bright yelled, having climbed over into the driver's seat to move her brother's truck out of the middle of the street to park it.

"The fuck you doing, Cuz?" Cordell fumed, seeing Tanisha exchanging money for dope. He knocked the dope out of her hand and slapped her silly. "The fuck I tell yo' ass about fucking with this shit, Cuz?" Cordell flexed, ready to punch her, but the dope dealer intercepted.

"Aye, homie, you gotta take this shit somewhere else...you making my spot hot." He picked up the two pieces of dope off the ground that were knocked out of Tanisha's hand and put them back into his dope pack.

Frustrated and in a desperate need to release some of his pent-up stress, Cordell took his fist into the guy's jaw, landing him on the ground, and then immediately started stomping him.

Unable to find her dope on the ground, Tanisha got up and tried to escape from the scene.

Having just pulled up and parked on the street, Bright grabbed Tanisha by the arm. "No you don't!" Then she opened the passenger side door for Tanisha to get inside. "You can't be doing this shit to yourself, Tanisha, and be having my brother out here fucking up every dealer that supplies you." Bright got nervous when she saw a mob of niggas running out of an apartment building, headed toward the fight Cordell was having.

"Where does Cordell keep his gun at, Tanisha?" Bright begin to fumble through his console and glove compartment. She remembered him mentioning he kept one inside.

Tanisha hurriedly pulled a book from under the passenger seat, opened it, and revealed a black .38 nestled comfortably in the book where the pages had been carefully carved out around the gun for its perfect fit.

Not knowing what to do with the gun, Bright put her game face on and ran toward the approaching crowd, aiming the gun. "Won't be no jumping my brother today! Now back y'all little dusty asses up!" She demanded.

"Cuz, I knew I should have brought the burner down," one of the rowdy gang bangers deeply regretted, shaking his head.

"Let's go, brother, your wife is safe in the truck." *Nigga got me out here like this while he acting a damn fool! I'm cussing his stupid, dumb ass the fuck out when we get in the truck!*

A loud sound of screeching tires and the sound of a honking horn grabbed everyone's attention at once. "What the fuck?" One of the gangbangers said, looking in that direction.

"Oh no! Tanisha just got hit by a car! Come on, Cordell!" Bright ran over to the scene.

Heart racing, Cordell beat Bright to the scene and almost lost it when he saw Tanisha lying out in the street in a puddle of blood, unconscious. He knelt down by her side, cursing the driver out, and he tried to move her. He wanted to put her in his truck.

"No, Cordell!" Bright yelled to him while she was on the phone with an emergency dispatcher. "Don't move her; just talk to her." Bright had learned that in junior high school.

Cordell carefully removed his hands from under Tanisha's body and began to talk to her. "Tanisha, baby, open your eyes, talk to me baby, let me know that you're all right." Cordell massaged and held her fingertips.

Eyes fluttering, Tanisha wiggled the finger that Cordell was holding on to, letting him know that she was all right. He bent down to kiss her forehead, "I'ma take care of you, baby. I won't ever leave you; you gon' be all right," he told her, full of passion and love.

Having lost the battle to her demons while sitting in the truck, Tanisha had swiftly climbed over to the driver's side and tried to creep out of it unnoticed. When she climbed out of the truck, instead of watching for oncoming traffic, Tanisha kept her eyes glued on Cordell and Bright, praying that neither of them would see her. She had proceeded to run across the street when she was hit by a car traveling at forty-five miles per hour.

When the paramedic showed up on the scene, Bright was relieved. The gangbangers continued to peer at her evilly. One of them pulled his T-shirt up and revealed a gun to her. She kept her game face on, but feared that at any moment he would pull his gun out and use it. Once the EMT's strapped Tanisha to the gurney and put her in the back of the ambulance, Bright took the wheel of the truck as Cordell climbed in the passenger seat.

Passing the gangbangers, Cordell threw his hood up and yelled, "Northside Crips, bitch!"

Part 9

Boss Behind the Walls

Having been transferred to Kern Valley State Prison, Terrence sat in the visiting area in the midst of having a low, heated discussion with his partner Shawn. After months of requesting that Shawn come to visit him, it took a threat that Terrence put out on one of his most cherished family member's lives in order to get him there.

Wearing a grim expression on his face, Terrence spoke in a low and stern voice. "I see I have to threaten you bitch niggas to get shit done these days." Terrence shook his head in disgust. He had just had one of his suppliers robbed for over two millions dollars in dope and money for not delivering his paid load off to a designated spot for one of his partners to distribute. He was even in the process of having a couple of longtime business partners killed that owed him thousands of dollars' worth of money from fronts and interest rates. "Y'all niggas think out of sight, out of mind, but what you dumb muthafuckas forget is that bosses still shot-call from behind the wall, nigga." He pounded his index finger on the table and spoke through gritted teeth. "But I want you to grab a newspaper and keep ya eyes on the obituary section, 'cause some familiar muthafuckas is about to start disappearing off the face of the earth one by one."

Shawn began to get flustered. "Ice, but my baby momma and daughter, what they got to do with this? Homie, you know I'm good, I just been tryna get my family back..."

"Nigga, I'm in this bitch fighting a life muthafucking sentence. Now do I look like a nigga that really give a fuck about you tryna to get yo' little fucked-up-ass family back? I want that bitch's life destroyed! I want her mother, her little Northside-ass brother or somebody in that family to come up missing, do you understand me? And I'm giving you - "

Shawn cut Terrence off. "Please, man, I'ma handle this, but you know that it's going to take time. Let me build the bitch up and then break her down like you initially told me to," he pleaded. He didn't want a ridiculous time frame on a job that would later only send him behind prison walls.

"I'm tired of hearing how this bitch, Bright, is living a carefree life. She got money, houses, and cars, and her little bitch-ass brother, Cordell, is on the Northside balling. I gave you a year and haven't been satisfied yet, so we gon' do this shit my way now. I'ma be generous and give you eight months to fuck that bitch's world up and start making her family disappear. Eight months," Terrence repeated firmly. "And I'm being that nice because I like to be entertained and I wanna see that bitch suffer, but not a day over." Terrence slid a picture of Shawn's daughter to him. "Or you'll be going to her funeral first." Terrence stood from the table. He had said all he needed and wanted to say.

How the fuck this nigga get a picture of my daughter? I just moved them in a new house three weeks ago. Shawn was confused.

Terrence laughed, nodding his head. "Yeah nigga, just 'cause I'm in here don't mean I don't have eyes and ears out there," he pointed toward the window and began to walk off. "Time for me to go back to my cave." He stopped in his tracks and looked back at Shawn, who had fear written all over his face. "By the way, nice-ass house, homie. Four-bedrooms with a pool in the back-yard...real nice!" He winked at him before being escorted back inside the prison.

The Next Day

"Dime, I've never mentioned my twin sister, Karen, to you before, because she and I don't get along, let alone speak to each other." Bright had stayed at the hospital all night with Cordell and left the following afternoon when Tanisha was stabilized. She wanted to go home, shower, and roll up and smoke a blunt before picking her sister up from ballet class and heading back over to Dime's house.

"Well next time, baby, keep me in the know of things like this, all right? I don't need another guy telling me shit about the bitch I call my lady, all right?"

"I promise, baby, but geez, I don't know why it makes me hot and horny when you call me the b-word!" Bright giggled through the phone, going into her Valley girl, nerd mode.

"That's 'cause I'm bringing the freak out of you, baby. I hear your sister has no problem in that department, though, with her ole freaky ass." Dime laughed.

"So I assume your friend Tobe told you more about Karen than her owing him money to fix her car yesterday?" Bright laughed to herself.

"Girl, your sister is a hardcore freak! I heard she can suck the skin off a dick and fuck a nigga to an orgasm in less than five minutes. She bad!" He continued to laugh.

"If you had met her and me at the same time, would you have preferred her over me?" Bright pretended to sound sad. "The guys have always picked her over me."

"Hell naw, baby, I only fuck bitches like your sister! I wife 'em up when they're like you though."

After playing the insecurity role, Bright then told Dime that she'd be back at his house within two hours. She had to pick Rayonna up from ballet class.

When Bright got off the phone, she smoked her blunt and then called to check on her mother. Tears came to her eyes listening to her mother pronounce her words like a small child learning how to pronounce her words. "Some days are better than others, but your mother is working very hard toward her recovery, so be patient," the therapist would tell Bright when she questioned about her mother's up and downhill progression.

Since the siblings had not been getting along, Bright had only driven up to visit her mother once with her little sister, Rayonna, and missed her terribly. When the therapist got back on the phone, Bright began to vent. "It's been over a year since my mother's stroke. When is she going to fully recover? It didn't take this long for her to recover the last time! What am I paying you guys for?" Bright yelled, crying over the phone.

"I understand your frustrations, Miss Sheldon, but please be patient and understand that each stroke patient and stroke is different..."

"I'm tired of hearing that same old story," Bright interrupted. "I'm coming to get my mother. She'll probably rehabilitate quicker at home, with her family!" Bright slammed her house phone down on its cradle and walked out of the house to pick up Rayonna. *Diamond was right; they just taking my money, and she would recover a lot faster at home seeing the faces of the people she loved,* Bright thought, climbing inside of her Infiniti truck.

Inside the car, after calling Diamond and telling her that she was going to take her advice and bring her mother home, Bright asked her if she would still be willing to help her care for her mother when she was out. Diamond was enthused.

"Gurl, I been telling yo' ass that she needed to come home, and you already know I got yo' back with this. I love your mother, and in my opinion, when she was under my care, she sounded a whole lot better."

"She seen me more often, too," Bright agreed.

"Exactly! Hurry up and get Momma Rose home. I'll be back in Cali in a week," Diamond told Bright before hanging up.

The second Bright got off the phone with Diamond, she received a disturbing text from Lil Jay: ***I need to see you before I end up killing your brother. Get at me ASAP!***

"Nigga, what?!" Bright immediately hit Lil Jay on her speed dial as she drove on the highway.

"Nigga, I know you ain't threatening my brother, Lil Jay!" Bright yelled at him the second he answered his phone.

"The shit that nigga pulled yesterday was uncalled for, Bright! I gave him two passes pulling a burner out on me; I won't allow him to do it a third time." Lil Jay spoke in a stern tone.

"You know my brother would never hurt you, Lil Jay. You're like a brother to him, and you know good and damn well that he's only acting out of anger, 'cause if he really wanted to kill you, I'm sure he would have used his gun on you by now!" Bright snapped through the phone.

"Well, take this as a warning and talk to his stubborn ass, 'cause I just got tired of accepting his shit."

"Lil Jay!" Bright yelled through the phone. "You better watch what you say about my brother to me!"

"Fuck that shit! Cordell ain't the only nigga angry 'bout this shit. I just lost the girl of my dreams, so you tell that nigga we both mad now," Lil Jay said before ending the call.

<u>Days Later</u>

Having spent the remainder of the week with Dime, Bright left him to supposedly go back to work when Cordell told her that Tanisha was at home and had been released from the hospital. Bright was happy that other than her broken arm, leg, and sprung neck that she hadn't incurred any major medical problems. Cordell hadn't left Tanisha's side the entire time she was hospitalized, and because of it, Bright had not mentioned the last conversation she and Lil Jay had. She felt today would be the best time to do so. Anxious to see Tanisha, hug her, and curse her out for using drugs, Bright knocked on their door, calling out their names. "Hurry up and open up the door."

Cordell came to the door moments later, happy that Bright had come right over. He needed his sister's support and wanted to thank her for always having his back, even when it seemed that he didn't always have hers.

"Where my bitch at?" Bright walked in the house.

Cordell grabbed Bright by the arm and hugged her real tight. "I love you, Queen Bee."

Bright smiled with her eyes. She knew her brother was having an emotional moment with her. "I love you too, brother," Bright kissed him all over his face and then ran inside the bedroom to see Tanisha.

"I know you mad at me." Tanisha pouted the second Bright walked in the bedroom. Cordell had her propped up in bed comfortably with a cold drink and remote on a TV tray within her reach.

Bright held and kissed her face and then pretended to slap her up. “Hell yeah, I'm mad at you Choc!” Bright took a seat on the other side of the bed. “Now talk to me, Sis, tell me what's going on with you, and why dope?”

“I don't know, Bright. I just been going through so much lately, and when I use, it takes all the pain away and makes me numb to everything,” she said honestly.

“What kind of pain are you feeling, Choc?” Bright asked, full of concern.

“Really just everything: me giving my son away, my mother and family disowning me, Cordell and his daughter, just a lot,” she sighed.

“Bitch, you have no idea of all the bullshit I have been through in my life! I've been through more than you could imagine, but you don't see me relying on a crack pipe.”

“I'm not as strong as you, though, Bright.”

“Who said I'm strong? I just know how to keep it moving. I have a family that relies on me.”

“How do you cope with not being able to see your kids?” Tanisha asked.

Moments of silence filled the room before Bright spoke. Tanisha's question had caught her off- guard. She had made it a rule to never ever bring her children or Larry up. They were her past, and it was her way of leaving them in it. “It never bothered me to let them go, because somewhere deep inside, I never wanted them to begin with,” Bright gazed off and said in a hypnotized manner.

Though it appeared that Bright was looking and listening to Tanisha thereafter, her mind had actually drawn a blank. Tanisha looked like a blur, and her words seemed muted.

Tanisha continued to talk on and on. “I wish I would have never stolen that piece of dope from Diamond that day, otherwise I wouldn't even be in this situation.” Tanisha covered her mouth. She didn't mean for that slip out. “Please don't tell her I told you she uses, Bright.”

Snapping out of the daze, Bright tuned into what Tanisha was saying to her. It was one of the strangest things she had ever experienced before. Her mind had gone to a whole other dimension.

Tanisha grabbed Bright's hand. "Promise me that what I told you today will stay between me and you, Bright?"

Bright nodded her head. "I promise I won't say anything; it's between us. So are you finished with drugs?"

"I'm sure going to try to. I just have to stay away from you-know-who, and learn how to fight harder than my temptations. It's hard."

"You can do it, Chocolate Drop, just keep fighting." Bright stood up from the bed. "I have to speak to Cordell about something. I'll be back before I leave to pick up Rayonna from ballet lessons." Bright walked out of the room.

Having found Cordell on the couch engrossed in a game on his PlayStation 3, Bright sat next to him and repeated Lil Jay's words to him word for word. Cordell tossed his controller on the couch and told Bright that Lil Jay could kiss his ass.

"Fuck that nigga, Cuz! He running around the 'hood talking about how I'm butt hurt 'cause he fucked both of my sister's days apart from each other, but he acting like what he had for you was real?" Cordell shot Bright a disbelieving facial expression. "Fuck, Cuz's bitch-made disloyal ass, on Crip! He telling niggas in the 'hood that you broke the bank and copped him an expensive-ass engagement ring for 'im and that you begged him to marry you. Niggas already know about how you get down, so they wasn't even believing that shit, but now some sex tape is supposed to be surfing around the 'hood that he showed a few of the homies of you and him. So yeah, nigga, I'm heated, and every time I see Lil Jay's ass, I'm serving him. And if I feel like shooting him or his muthafucking truck up...I will! Cuz already know what time it is with me. Fuck him!" Cordell stood from the couch, heated. "I see I'ma have to put this nigga in a hole a lot sooner."

Bright could not believe what Cordell was saying to her. She just looked at him through bucked eyes, wanting to cry her eyes out. *For real, Lil Jay? You ole dumb, stupid-ass nigga! You played me once by fucking my sister, but now this, a sex tape? And you clowning me all through your 'hood, for real? Nigga, they don't call me Pretty*

Poison for nothing, but now I guess it's time I introduce you to her! "I can't believe him, with his young, dumb, stupid, lying ass!" Bright spat. "Yeah, I was wrong for messing with your boy in the first place, but it's always business with me, never personal, and his ass was breaking off loot, every time. I can't even believe he said I bought him a ring, and that I asked him to marry me. Nigga, pleaseeee!" Bright lied to keep what little dignity Lil Jay had left her. "But a sex tape, though? Really? Now I just got mad too!" Bright stood, forcing herself to laugh before she broke down and cried. Her feelings were extremely hurt. Mind working overtime, Bright knew it was time for her to go. She was in desperate need to release the pain she was feeling inside. Afterwards, she'd start plotting her next move. *Lil Jay, baby, yo' ass is...through.* Bright told her brother good-bye and that she'd call him later, and then left his townhouse.

Two Days and a Plan Later

Bright called Cordell. "Brother, where you at?"

"At the house with the homies, playing the game. Why, what's up? You still gon' come over here later and keep Tanisha company while I get out in the streets?"

Good, his friends are there, he'll have an airtight alibi. Bright smiled. "Yeah, I am, but in a minute, I'ma start charging you. I know the only reason you want me around the house while you're out is to make sure Tanisha don't hit them streets," Bright teased.

Cordell laughed. "You got me, that's real, but you know I'll take care of you, Paper Queen," he teased back.

"Okay. I need to talk to you before you leave, too," Bright told him before hanging up.

Bright had been plotting for days, and now it was time to put her plan in action. Getting out of her car, Bright called Lil Jay from a corner pay phone. When he answered, she smiled through the phone.

"Hey, you, I guess somebody doesn't love me anymore, huh?"

"I'll always love you," Lil Jay said.

"Well, why you ain't riding fo' it, then?" Bright laughed seductively.

"I am, but I can't keep riding for it alone. I miss, you girl."

"I miss you, too, baby, a lot. I been keeping my distance to keep everything between you and my brother down, but my heart aches without you. Let's go to Vegas and get married and get away for a while."

"Hell yeah, baby, I'd love to, let's do it!" Lil Jay said excitedly.

"You sure you ready to marry me, Lil Jay? I mean, we won't be able to tell anyone, at least not right away anyways."

"What I look like, some type of bitch, baby? I ain't saying shit to nobody. Let's go get married!"

"I'm so happy...woooooo!" Bright yelled.

Lil Jay smiled.

"Lil Jay, I don't want my brother to find out that we're about to get married unless he hears it from me first. I'd like to have that moment. Can you promise me that you won't tell none of y'all little homeboys? Because you do know that niggas talk like bitches. All I want to do is be happy with you and not have my siblings down my throat in the process," Bright said convincingly. So I need your word on this one."

"On my momma, rest in peace, I won't mention it to a soul until after you tell your brother first."

Just what I wanted to hear, you ole dumb, stupid-ass nigga! An evil grin appeared across Bright's face. "I love you so much! I'm so happy! I love you, Lil Jay, I love you!" Bright told him, and then she told him where to meet her at. *You fucking with Pretty Poison now, baby.* She walked to her car.

Lil Jay

Having just gotten to his apartment from the block, Lil Jay ran inside to pack a couple weeks' worth of clothes. "Yeah! I told y'all niggas Bright was loving a nigga like that!" Lil Jay said out loud to no one in particular. He couldn't wait to get back from Las Vegas to show his niggas proof of his and Bright's marriage, and he could imagine the expression Cordell would wear on his face after he found out they were married. It was true that Lil Jay loved Bright and genuinely wanted nothing more than to be with her, but after he found out that Cordell had slept with one of his main girls, Lil Jay decided to belittle and tarnish his and his sister's names in the 'hood. Besides demeaning his and Bright's relationship, Lil Jay revealed a sex tape that he had secretly recorded of them without Bright's consent to a few of his homies and then bragged about how he had Deja in the utility closet on his birthday, yelling and screaming his name. "Cuz, I didn't even have enough time to wipe Bright's pussy juice off my dick before Deja jumped all on it. Did I mention that the big sister gives much better head than the little one does?" Lil Jay remembered telling his homies.

However, after he and Bright got married, Lil Jay planned on cleaning up everything that he said about the sisters. *I'ma confess that I spoke on the situation out of spite and anger and reveal my true feelings for Bright. Hopefully after that, the nigga Cordell and I will be able to make amends and let bygones be bygones. It ain't like niggas aren't about to be brother-in-laws.* Lil Jay grabbed his luggage and headed out of his house.

On the ride, Lil Jay began to experience a strange gut feeling. Something was telling him to go back home, but instead, he turned his music up and kept it moving.

****

An hour earlier, Dime had received a disturbing call from his girlfriend, Bright, crying about how she had just been raped the day she left his house by a close friend of the family. She was so devastated when they talked that he could barely understand her. When Bright told him that she was going to call the police, he begged her to let him handle it.

"I knew that nigga wanted my bitch when I seen his ass at her uncle's house months back, Cuz!" Dime told his homeboy as he rode to the park that Bright told him Lil Jay normally hung out at during that time of the day.

His homeboy nodded his head. "This nigga is wicked, raping bitches, and then got the balls to be posting up at parks and shit."

"Nigga probably looking for his next victim. I see he gets off raping innocent, nerdy type of bitches too, 'cause my girl don't do shit but go to work. She don't even have no female friends." Dime pulled into the park location in North Long Beach.

"Well, I guess the state of California can thank us for getting rid of this sick son of a bitch," Dime's homeboy said.

"Hell yeah, nigga! Now go put in that work, homie. Quick and easy...close range," Dime instructed his homeboy, who was dressed like a bum before pointing him in Lil Jay's direction. He was sitting on a park bench smoking a blunt.

****

Choking on the top-notch Kush that he was smoking while waiting on Bright to arrive, Lil Jay picked up his cell phone. He wanted to call and find out what was taking Bright so long to get there. While looking through his recent calls, he found himself confused, noticing the number she had called him from. *What the fuck?* He thought as he watched a bum near him go fumbling through the garbage. *Maybe she changed her number,* Lil Jay thought, calling the number. But when he got an answer, he was told that he had called a phone booth. *Why the fuck would Bright be calling me from a muthafucking pay phone? Something ain't right.*

"You got some change, homie? I'm tryna get something to eat," the bum that was in the garbage approached and asked, disturbing Lil Jay's thoughts.

"Naw, I ain't got shit for you." Lil Jay waved him off. He was trying to figure out what was going on.

"What can you give me for this?" The bum pulled a large object from inside of his heavy coat.

"Nigga, get yo' ass the fuck away from me! I told you I ain't got shit for you!" Lil Jay looked in the bum's direction. When he saw what appeared before him, it immediately confirmed the gut feeling and doubt that Lil Jay had ignored the entire ride and time he had been sitting at the park waiting on Bright to arrive. *That bitch done set me up,* he thought, unable to make the words come out of his mouth. Lil Jay tried to get up and run, but the disguised gunman had let off two hollow tips that knocked him back on his butt and made his chest explode wide open.

"You'll never rape another bitch again!" The gunman said and then briskly fled the scene.

"I didn't rape nobody...help!" Were Lil Jay's last words before he took his last breath and his heart stopped beating. He was only eighteen.

****

When Bright walked in her brother's house, he and his homeboys were too engrossed in the game to acknowledge her. So she grabbed herself a bottle of water and headed to the room with Tanisha. Tanisha was so antsy for dope that she was popping attitude all over the room. Ignoring her, Bright stared at the happy face that Dime had texted her minutes earlier, indicating that Lil Jay was dead, and it made her numb. *What the fuck have I done?* Bright continued to say to herself. *You played me, Lil Jay, and that shit hurt, but regardless of that, my brother was going to kill you anyways. He took a life for me, and I for him. I'm sorry that it had to end this way.* Bright cried inside.

"Cordell ain't gon' keep me locked up in this house like this," Tanisha fussed, hopping around the room on her crutches.

"Bright, take me to the store. I need a drink or something." Tanisha continued to pat Bright on the shoulder. "Bright, gotdammit can you hear me?" Tanisha opened the bedroom door, walked in the living room and started fussing with Cordell.

"That nigga Lil Jay just got murked, Cuz!" One of Cordell's homeboys said after reading a text message.

"What?" Cordell immediately turned his attention to his homeboy and asked.

"They said he got dumped on at the park, they don't know by who yet though, Cuz," His homeboy continued to explain. "I bet it was one of them Eastside niggas, Cuz, 'cause they lieutenants been dropping like flies lately, homie."

"Hell naw, Cuz, the homie dead?" Another homeboy stood up and paced the floor.

Using the opportunity to get out and get her hands on some dope, Tanisha quickly made her way out of the living room and swiftly out of the front door.

Cordell was in a deep state of shock, eyes watering. Though the two were at war that would eventually lead to gunplay, Cordell couldn't help feeling that he had just lost another brother. They would never see each other again or be able to make amends.

Part 10

Momma's Home

Weeks after Lil Jay's murder, Bright had just come out of the pharmacy in Walgreen's from getting her mother's prescription drugs and a prescription of Xanax for herself. As a result of setting Lil Jay up to be murdered, Bright relied on a daily dose of Xanax to keep her stabilized. Otherwise, her brother's words would repeatedly rewind themselves in her head night in and day out, causing her to experience sudden anxiety attacks that would often leave her full of sorrow and pain.

"Mannn, I was so hot and felt disrespected after I found out that Lil Jay had hit both of my sisters that I went out and fucked his main girl. I put that bitch on a few lines of that shit, recorded me fucking her in the ass with my .45, got her butt naked in the truck, and then dumped her ass off to Lil Jay at his trap spot late one night," Bright remembered Cordell telling her a day after Lil Jay's murder while they were smoking a blunt.

That nigga loved me before he was killed, were Bright's immediate thoughts, realizing that Lil Jay had only begun to tarnish her and her sister's names in the hood after Cordell's ignominious act. "Would you have killed Lil Jay if he were still alive, Cordell?" Bright looked her brother in his eyes and asked him seriously. For some reason, she could never bring herself to tell him that she had set his murder up.

Cordell nodded his head yes. "The city was getting too small for me and that nigga's ego, so eventually, one of us would have ended up dead. Better that nigga than me," Cordell told her honestly.

To ease herself and the pain, Bright would always say to herself, *Our love was doomed anyway, Lil Jay.*

"Excuse me, Cinderella, is that you?" A man yelled out after Bright as she proceeded to get in her Infiniti truck.

When Bright turned to face the man, she immediately remembered him. He was a guy named Shawn that she had meet at Lil Jay's eighteenth birthday bash: tall, dark, fine, and rich.

Not really in the mood to be flirted with or bothered, Bright told him that it was good seeing him again and proceeded to get in her truck.

"I've been looking for you, literally, for months. What a coincidence running into you at a Walgreen's, of all places." Shawn offered her his million-dollar smile. He had one very similar to Larry's.

Tired-ass game! Bright shot him a sarcastic look. "We only met once." She put her things inside her truck.

"Yeah, and you gave me a wrong number, and I've been literally looking for you since then."

Corny-ass nigga! "Well, it was nice seeing you again, but I have to go." Bright climbed into her Infiniti and proceeded to back out.

Standing behind her truck so that Bright couldn't back out, Shawn asked. "Wait, can I take you out on a date?" He waved his hands to grab her attention.

"This is not funny! Now move yo' ass from behind my car!" Bright yelled out of her window and demanded.

Shawn put his hand to his ear. "You said you wanna give me your number? Okay." Shawn pulled his cell phone out of his pocket, pretending he didn't hear what Bright had asked of him. "I'm waiting; what's the number?"

Frustrated, Bright continued to honk her horn. "Keep playing with me, you stalker-ass nigga! I'ma run yo' ass over in a minute!"

After putting up a fight, Bright was literally forced to give him her true number. She had attempted to give him another fictitious number, but he wouldn't get out of her way until he heard her voice on the other end of his cell phone.

Two months later, after dodging Shawn's calls and him popping up everywhere she would be, Bright decided to go out on one date with him after much of Diamond's convincing.

"Girl, go out and have fun! You've ignored your tops' money and the world long enough. Lil Jay is gone boo boo; he isn't coming back. Now get pretty and go out and enjoy yourself. You know me and Rayonna will take care of Momma Rose," Diamond said to her. Since their mother was in the home, DCFS and the courts allowed Rayonna to move into the house, and though she had her own room, she slept with her mother almost every night.

Later on that evening, Bright dressed in a tight, black pencil skirt that she had gotten from her stylist, Eric, on her last visit; she wore a white tank top that she tucked in, rocked a pair of red designer heels, and wore accessories and red lipstick. "Okay, I'm feeling a date right about now. I have been cooped up in the house long enough," Bright announced, walking down the stairs.

"Go out and enjoy yourself," her mother agreed, smiling at how beautiful her daughter looked.

Since Rosette had been back home, she had been progressing well. Though her speech was still impaired and choppy, she could be understood in conversations, both in person and on the phone. She relied on her electric wheelchair to get around, and rarely ever used her walker. She liked the independence of getting around quickly. Rosette helped out as much as she could in the kitchen. She loved baking, she dusted a few times a week, she enjoyed going to the mall with her cousin, Shanna, and she went to church on Sunday. With the help of her family, she was able to live as normally and independently as possible. Seeing her children's faces every day was her strength to continue to fight and her will to live. She was glad to be back home.

Bright kissed her mother on the cheek and forehead and then sat next to her on the couch while waiting for Shawn to arrive. *I don't know why I'm letting this nigga pick me up from my house. He's already a fucking stalker. I guess I'll lie and tell him that this is a family member's house and for him to never come here again.*

"What's going on outside?" Cordell and Tanisha walked inside.

Rayonna ran to the window and her eyes lit up with amazement. "Beautiful!" Then she told her mother to come look out the window.

"What gon' on?" Rosette maneuvered her electric wheelchair to the window.

"Is this super extra-out-ass nigga here for you, Queen Bee?" Cordell said with a hint of jealousy, seeing how fascinated Tanisha was at the entire scene.

"Boy! You better watch yo' mouth; cussing like Mama ain't sitting right here!" Bright stood to see what all the commotion was about. When she made her way to the window, she froze in great surprise at the unexpected sight. Shawn had come to pick her up in an all-white chariot that had a full canopy, drawn by two white horses, and a coachman dressed in a black and white tuxedo.

Emerging from the carriage dressed in black slacks, an all-white, designer, button-up shirt, and a pair of white penny loafers, Shawn walked up the walkway with a glittery object in his hand. Standing at the door speechless, Shawn stepped on the porch and passed Bright a pair of glass slippers.

"Oh my God! I've been looking for my shoe for so long." She reached for the pair.

Shawn smiled. "You left the right shoe behind the night of the bash, in the Grand Ballroom. It took me months to find the matching shoe, but now that I've found you, it was worth all the hassle."

Bright jumped in Shawn's arms and hugged him, her eyes watering up. No one had ever gone to such extreme measures to impress her on a first date before, and for once in her life, Bright felt like she was a true princess. "You are just full of surprises! It's so beautiful! Oh my God, thank you Shawn!" She said to him.

"Now you understand why it was so important that I found you?" Shawn looked her in her beautiful eyes.

Bright nodded her head yes, gazing intensely at him.

"The chariot awaits." Shawn put his arm out for Bright. He was a true, hopeless romantic.

Bright wrapped her arm in his and then told her family good-bye. Shawn stopped in mid-step and told Bright that she had forgotten something.

"What's that?" Bright wondered.

"Your glass slippers. You forgot to put them on, Cinderella."

Bright went to grab her shoes and then quickly slid them on her feet.

Cordell busted out laughing. "Niggas don't do this in the 'hood, man!" He stepped on the porch and yelled after them. "You overworking yourself. All you had to do was pull up in a Bentley and smash off, bumping with some of that stanky," he teased. "'Cause all this Cinderella and Prince Charming shit is corny as hell, man!" Cordell continued to laugh.

"Shut up, Cordell! I think what he's doing is extremely romantic." Tanisha came out of the house and stood next to him.

"See, nigga, now you gon' have my girl thinking I'm about to roll up on her in a chariot, man." Cordell grabbed Tanisha by the waist and kissed her. "Naw, for real though, y'all have fun, be safe, and oh, be back by twelve before ya carriage turn into a pumpkin and you lose all that Prince Charming swag, nigga!"

Inside the carriage, Cordell had Bright and Shawn laughing to tears.

"A'ight, black man, we gon' do that!" Shawn yelled out to Cordell as the carriage made its way down the street.

This is it; Shawn's my prince. He found my glass slipper. Bright looked into the sky, and having seen a shooting star, she made a wish for happiness.

Months Later

Though Deja was still not speaking to Bright, she felt complete, having her entire family back under the same roof again. Cordell had moved back into the house since Tanisha struggled to maintain her sobriety and was constantly in and out of the drug rehab. Deja had eventually transferred to Cal State Dominguez in Carson. Not only did she want to be closer to her mother and family, but she also moved into the house so that she could assist her siblings in their mother's full recovery. Deja shared a room with Rayonna in the downstairs bedroom next to their mother's room. Bright occupied the same room in the house that she always had when she spent time there, and still had her Brentwood condominium. Diamond, on the other hand, had moved into the condominium with Bright. However, since Diamond was always in and out of town, visiting her man in jail or her family in Texas, she was rarely there.

If Shawn wasn't at Bright's house, she would be with him at his penthouse having romantic breakfast and dinners on the terrace overlooking the entire city of Los Angeles. She assumed that Shawn was a drug dealer. He told Bright that he was a part of his family's legacy in the diamond business; he was very wealthy. He treated her well, loved her, gave her whatever she wanted or asked for, and was slowly but surely making her believe in love again. She told him that her previous relationships made her distrust love. He promised Bright that he would show her better than he could tell her. Because Bright cared for Shawn, she didn't make it her business to drain his bank account. What they had was more than money, and her mind was made up that the second he proposed marriage to her, she'd retire the lifestyle altogether.

While at her condominium one night, cooking dinner while Shawn was in the shower, Marion popped up without calling her. Bright told him to leave because she had company. The sad part was that Marion actually believed that even though he was married, Bright was supposed to be faithful to him because he gave her money and paid the lease on the condominium. Upset, Marion stormed out the door. When he got in his car, he texted Bright, told her that they were over, and that he would no longer pay the lease on the condominium. The next morning after Shawn left, Bright returned Marion's call. She told him that he could be done with her all he wanted, but if he stopped paying the lease on the condominium he would lose a lot more. Then she hung up on him and sent him various pictures of her performing oral sex on him and a snippet recording of them having sex, and she told him that she wouldn't mind forwarding the pictures to his wife. Bright knew sooner or later that Marion would pull a stunt like that, since he was always demanding her time. That was why she took the flicks and recorded them in the first place.

Big Poppa started paying Bright to spend more time with his business associates than he actually spent with her, so she'd let most of his calls go to voicemail. She exclusively dated bosses and ballers who kept her bank account fat, and she didn't like the feeling of being looked upon or treated like a prostitute. Dime, on the other hand, had just gotten released from prison on drug charges, and until he got his money up, Bright would continue with her traveling nurse role until he could afford to pay for her time.

After helping her mother shower and dress, Bright helped her in her electric wheelchair so that her mother could go about her day. "Ma, are your besties coming over today?" Bright said, referring to her mother's cousin, Shanna, and best friend Gale.

Rosette laughed. "Shan-na coming by to-day, Gale tired, she's been work-ing a lot."

"Well, don't forget Shawn wants to take us to dinner after you get back from church on Sunday."

"I like Shawn. You talk to Lar-ry? I wan' see the twins, Queen Bee. I haven't seen them?"

"Ma, I keep telling you Larry took them from me and that I can't see them. Please, please, please stop asking about them all the time, dang!" Bright vented, and then walked out of the bedroom.

"Quit yelling at her!" Deja walked into her mother's bedroom from the living room. "Just because you never mention or think about your own kids...don't mean we don't!" Deja yelled after Bright as she stomped up the stairs.

"Keep talking to me, Deja, and watch what I do to you!" Bright yelled down to Deja, and then she slammed her bedroom door. Her mother had been home for almost three months and had asked her that question at least twice a month. It was the reason why Bright kept pushing their dinner date with Shawn back and stayed at her condominium most of the time. Shawn didn't know Bright had kids, and she planned to keep it that way. Bright put her shoes on, grabbed her designer bag, and decided to go to her condominium. She didn't want to upset her mother any further or end up slapping Deja into next week.

Once downstairs, Bright brushed pass Deja and kissed her mother on the forehead. "I'm sorry for yelling at you, Ma. It wasn't my intention to get you upset." Bright offered her mother a smile. "I'm going to go to my condominium for a couple days. I'll call you, but call me if you need me. I love you."

"I love you too, Queen Bee. Just try to see when we can see, Lari and Lori, all right?"

Bright bit her tongue and walked out the room. "All right, Ma."

Deja laughed. She knew how mad Bright got when anyone brought the twins up.

"Stupid bitch!" Bright said under her breath as she walked out the door.

"Bright!" Tanisha yelled running up the street. "Please take me with you, wherever you're going! I just jumped out of the truck with Cordell. He about to beat my ass! Please?" She had tears in her eyes.

Observing Tanisha, Bright nodded her head. She was slowly turning into a full-blown crackhead. "You just ain't gon' learn, are you?"

"Bright, please!" Tanisha begged. "I've been in the streets for two days, I'm hungry, I'm tired, and you know I don't have anywhere or anybody else to go too. Please?"

"Come on, Tanisha, but if Cordell comes to my house looking for you, you gon' have to leave with him. He ain't about to kick yo' ass in my house or get me put out." Bright rolled her eyes, and then got in her Infiniti.

When Bright got home, she made Tanisha some food to eat and then gave her some clothes to put on after she bathed.

"You can lie in my bed, Tanisha, but throw a sheet over my comforter. You be sweating and shit after them little missions, and I don't want it all over my bed."

"Thanks, Sis. I appreciate you so much!" Tanisha hugged her and then spread a sheet over her bed.

"Yeah, I love you too." Bright flared her eyebrows. "But bitch, I sure hope I ain't getting you rested up for your next mission."

"I'm done after this. Matter-of-fact, after I get some rest you can call Cordell so he can beat my ass and take me back to the rehab. I really want help this time," she said sincerely.

"Get some rest, Choc. I'ma about to call my man." When Bright sat on the couch and observed how out of place the condominium was, she lit her cigarette and yelled to Tanisha, "When you wake up, you can thank me by cleaning this dirty-ass house up!" *I sure hope Diamond hurry up and get back home. This place ain't never like this when she's here.* Bright dialed Shawn.

After getting off the phone with Shawn, Bright decided to run to the store to get her some cigarettes, a blunt, and a new bottle; hers were low. Shawn wasn't due back in town for two days, and she knew she'd have to keep a good eye on Tanisha so that when she returned her to her brother she'd be in good condition.

Before Bright walked out the door, she stopped in her tracks. *Bitch ain't about to steal shit from my house to get high with, fuck that!* After a few moments of thinking, Bright decided to handcuff Tanisha to her bed. Tanisha was so knocked out that she didn't even realize that she had been handcuffed.

After seeing Bright's truck parked in her assigned stall, a masked intruder made his way to her apartment, missing Bright exiting the opposite side of the building by seconds. Having walked to her door, the masked intruder carefully let himself inside her condo using a key. *Ice said set up a rape, but bitch, it's gonna be an honor to violate and take that pussy from yo' slutty ass!* He crept through the condo, light on his feet. Peeking inside of her room and seeing a pair of feet hanging off her bed, the intruder laughed. *This is gonna be easy; this bitch is knocked out asleep.*

Tiptoeing inside the room, the masked intruder was suddenly disappointed upon seeing Tanisha lying on the bed. *Fuck! I guess this crackhead pussy gon' have to do today, 'cause I need to get this one off. I hope you like 'em long, hard, and skinny.* The masked intruder released his pants to his feet and began to message his limp penis, thinking about Bright. Immediately, it got nice and hard.

Carefully lifting Tanisha's pajama T-shirt up, the masked intruder noticed that one of Tanisha's hands was handcuffed to the brass headboard. *Damn, Bright, if I knew you were into women, we could have made that happen a long time ago!* Trying to build up the courage, the masked intruder decided to ram his dick straight up her rectum. *No, that might wake the bitch up screaming. I'm just gon' put it in her pussy, and when she moves and start screaming, I'll just knock her out. Hopefully I'll be finished getting my nut off by then.* So he decided to ram it inside of her vagina instead.

Positioning himself over Tanisha, the masked intruder easily spread her legs apart and swiftly slid his penis inside of her opening. *Ohhh, this feels good!* He began to penetrate her nice and slow. *Oh, it feels good!* Loving the way it felt inside, he took a quick deep thrust, causing the bed to shift. *Fuck it, it feels so good!* The masked intruder had to take control of himself; Tanisha's pussy was making him go crazy. *Maybe this bitch won't even wake up,* the masked intruder thought, and he began to quicken his rhythm. It felt so good that he wanted to scream, but instead, he allowed soft moans to escape from his mouth. Waking up out of her sleep, Tanisha began to thrust him back. Excited, the intruder began to go faster and faster.

"Oh, Cordell, baby, you not mad at me no more? Baby, I'm sorry! Oh, it feel so good!" She started squeezing and tightening her vaginal muscles.

"Ahhhhhh!" the masked intruder accidentally let a loud moan that immediately grabbed Tanisha's attention.

That isn't Cordell's voice, and matter-of-fact, this dick ain't Cordell's either. Frozen in fright, Tanisha slowly looked behind her. Seeing a masked man behind her, she yelled for help. Attempting to get out of bed and fight the masked rapist/intruder off of her, Tanisha realized she was confined to the bed. One of her hands was handcuffed to the brass railing, and the masked intruder had her gripped firmly by the hair. Tanisha begin to yell for him to stop, crying and begging.

The masked intruder didn't stop. Instead, he went faster and faster, aroused, Tanisha's cries boosting his ego. When she began to get too loud, he punched her in the face three times until he had knocked her out, and then he pulled her back up by the hair and penetrated her at his maximum speed until he busted his nut. "Ahhhhhhhhhhhhhhhhhhhhhhhhhhh!" He moaned in a monstrous voice. That had to have been the most satisfying nut he had ever had. Quickly regaining himself and his energy, he pulled his pants up and made his way out of the apartment, hoping for a clean break.

Approaching her condominium, holding a bag in one hand, Bright hummed a song as she puffed on her cigarette. Seeing a masked man run out of her condominium alarmed Bright. "What the fuck?" She yelled dropping her bag to the ground. "Help, help, help!" Bright yelled immediately, running to her condo door to check on Tanisha. "I left that bitch handcuffed to my bed! Oh shit, oh my God, oh my God, oh my God, oh my God!" Bright panicked as she ran inside the condominium.

"Tanishaaaa!" Bright yelled once she got inside. When she didn't get a response, her eyes started watering and her heart raced with fear and beat loudly. Afraid to find Tanisha dead, Bright peeked her head inside of her bedroom. When she noticed Tanisha's pajama T-shirt raised above her behind and a sticky looking substance on her butt, Bright ran inside the room and fretted. "Oh my God, he raped her!" Bright continued to yell for help as she inspected Tanisha's body for blood, desperately trying to shake her awake. "Wake up, Tanisha, wake up...can you hear me?"

Moments later, Tanisha drunkenly lifted her head from the bed. She had a huge knot on her head and a black eye. Bright hugged her. "You've been raped, Choc," her voice trembled. "Did you see the guy's face?" Bright asked her.

Tanisha shook her head no and began to cry, "No, he had a mask on, and I couldn't get away because he handcuffed me to the bed." She showed Bright her hand.

Instantly Bright begin to feel horrible that she handcuffed Tanisha. "I'm so sorry, Choc." Bright kissed her on the forehead, holding her tight. "I handcuffed you to the bed so that you wouldn't leave. I can't believe this happened to you." Bright got up from the bed, retrieved the key, and hurriedly unlocked the handcuff.

Startled by Bright's comment, Tanisha massaged her wrist, looking at Bright, confused. "You handcuffed me to the bed while

I was asleep, Bright? Why would you do something like that to me?" The overflow of tears came out like giant rain drops. "If my hand was free, I could have gotten away, or at least been able to defend myself. Oh my God! That man raped me; he didn't use any protection and could have had anything, Bright!" Tanisha begin to crack up, thinking the worst. "No, no, nooooo, Bright, no! How could you; why did you?" Tanisha cried.

Before Bright could respond, her neighbor came inside and asked if everything was okay. Bright told her to wait in the living room and told her to call the police.

Bright directed her attention back to Tanisha to explain. She looked her in her eyes. "I'm so sorry, baby, I'm sorry. I had to make a store run, and I handcuffed you so that you wouldn't wake up and take anything to leave and get high. I didn't want you to run back to the streets." Bright wiped Tanisha's tears away. "It was all out of love. You know I would never do anything to intentionally hurt you. I love you, Choc," Bright said wholeheartedly.

Tanisha released herself from Bright's arms, angry. "Take something to get high? Have I ever stolen from you, Bright? No!" Tanisha punched the wall, causing her knuckles to bleed. "I would never steal from you, and you should know that." Tanisha fell on the floor and cried her poor heart out. "I'd never steal from you!"

"You're right; you've never taken anything from me, Choc. I'm sorry, baby; I'm sorry, but those drugs have changed you so much and I was afraid that you might leave while I was gone. I worry about you when you're out there!" Bright cried and then fell beside Tanisha. She hugged and rocked her in her arms, telling her how sorry she was. Holding each other the two cried together as they waited for the police to arrive.

"I got raped; he raped me, Bright, he raped me! It hurt, it hurt so bad! I just want all of this pain to go away!" Tanisha continued to sob.

The Next Day

When Bright stepped out of the hospital room to grab them lunch from the cafeteria, Tanisha stared at Cordell as he sat on the edge of her bed, watching the news. It had hurt him to learn that Tanisha had gotten raped. He didn't understand how someone had just let himself into Bright's condominium to rape Tanisha. When Bright told Cordell that Diamond had lost her key at their mother's house weeks earlier, it was enough information for him to start blaming and disliking her all over again. He had even exchanged words with Bright for handcuffing Tanisha to the bed in the first place, but later realized that Bright was merely attempting to keep Tanisha off the streets. "When I find out who did this shit to my girl, I swear, a nigga about to get the .45 in the ass, and when I get tired of hearing his bitch ass holler, I'ma blow his asshole out...on Crip!" Cordell told them the previous night.

Feeling Tanisha staring at him, Cordell asked her why she was staring at him.

"Cordell, I wanna go back to rehab. I'm serious this time. I need professional help," Tanisha said seriously.

Cordell smiled. "You serious, baby?" He sat next to her on the bed.

"Yeah, I'm serious this time, Cordell. I don't want our baby to come out addicted to drugs. I wanna be a good mother, and I want to get my life back in order. This life isn't for me."

"Pregnant? You never told me you were pregnant. How far are you?" Cordell asked nervously. He didn't want her to hold any more children that weren't by him in her womb.

Tanisha chuckled. "I'm not a week pregnant." She knew exactly what Cordell was thinking. "You're the daddy; I'm four months," she lifted her hospital gown to reveal her protruding belly.

Cordell stared at her stomach in silence, not really knowing how he felt, but he wanted to be sure the baby she was carrying was his this time. "Tanisha, be honest with me this time, all right? You don't have to lie to me, and I'm not going to put my hands on you. Have you been sleeping with niggas for dope, or do you have you a little smoker boyfriend?" He looked deep in her eyes.

"I swear on our relationship, Cordell, even though you've cheated, I've never cheated on you. This is your baby."

"Well, why I'm just now finding out?" Cordell replied.

"Because I wanted to get high, and wasn't sure I was going to keep it or not." She rubbed at her belly. "Life has been all bad since I started smoking dope, and I want my life back. I want you back, and for us to be the way we used to - happy and in love." She rubbed her fingertip down the side of his face.

Cordell nodded his head as a tear dripped from his eye and then slowly rolled down his face. "I want us back too, baby. For the first time ever, I'll be taking you to the rehab because you want to go. I'm proud of you, baby." He bent down and kissed her.

Tanisha held on to Cordell tight. "Thank you for never losing sight of me, and always loving me even when I didn't love myself," she cried.

****

The next day, Bright had the building superintendent change the locks on her doors, and even change the lock on her garage. The only person that had a key to the house was her. Diamond had lost her house key to the condominium at her mom's house. *So who could it have been that let themselves in my condo and raped Tanisha?* Bright continued to ponder.

Marion continued to come to Bright's mind, even though she had gotten the locks changed once before after he walked in on her and Shawn. "The rapist had a long, skinny penis," Bright remembered hearing Tanisha tell the detective in her hospital room. Marion didn't have a long skinny penis; his was thick. Shawn had a long, skinny penis, but he didn't have a key to her condominium, he was out of town, and would have never raped Tanisha.

After Bright's locks were changed, she called Cordell to check on Tanisha, called and spoke to her mother and then headed out to meet up with Dime. He had the dime, so now she had the time. Besides, she wasn't in the mood to be alone.

Weeks Later

Bright had just gotten back in the country with her boo, Shawn, after spending eight days in Italy in a romantic city called Venice, which was built on water in the middle of a lagoon. In order to commute, they had to take cruise ships and boats all over the city. Being with Shawn was like living in a fairytale that Bright never wanted to end; Shawn was her true Prince Charming. Everything about him was perfect, and Bright was madly in love with him.

Running inside the house, happy to see her mother, Bright was excited to give her all the new things that she had purchased for her while there, and she was dying to tell her about her unique, learning experience. She had sent three postcards home since she had been gone, and she couldn't wait to see her beautiful face. Noticing Deja's car parked in the driveway, Bright sucked her teeth. *The weakest link is here. Doesn't her ass ever go anywhere? Shit! Bitch still mad at me after I wrote her a damn twelve page letter, pouring my heart out and explaining me and Lil Jay's relationship entirely...DONE.*

After checking the mailbox, Bright flipped through the mail after she let herself inside the house. Opening a letter from the prosecutor's office, Bright knew it was pertaining to Treasure's case. Quickly pulling the letter out, she was anxious to see if they had given Treasure the maximum time. *Bitch tried to kill me twice now. Crawl in a hole and die, you dumb, stupid-ass, bitch!* The letter explained to Bright that Treasure was appealing her case, fighting to get a reduced sentence of seven years. Bright tossed the mail on the table, laughing, *Nope, bitch not if I can help it!* And then she skipped into her mother's bedroom. "Mommy, I'm homeeee!"

Inside her bedroom, Deja was lying across their mother's bed, watching T.V. "She went to the mall with Cousin Shanna," Deja rambled in a low and dry tone, not once removing her eyes from the television.

Bright walked around and slapped Deja hard on her behind, happy that she had spoken to her. She hadn't said that many words to her at one time in a year. "Aw, thanks, baby." Bright smiled, proceeding to walk out of the bedroom.

"Don't put your nasty-ass hands on me anymore, Bright!" Deja raised the volume in her voice.

Bright swung around and looked back at her sister. "Shut up, before I come over there and kiss you with these good, juicy, dick-sucking lips, Deja," she teased.

"Whore!" Deja nodded her head, and then directed her attention back to the T.V.

"I know you are, but what am I, I know you are but what am I?" Bright begin to mimic the tone of a child. She knew it was the fastest way to get under Deja's skin.

Deja got up from the bed and closed her mother's bedroom door. Bright pushed it back ajar, tired of fighting her sister.

"Deja, this is really getting old. Are you still upset with me over some dick? A dead nigga's dick at that?"

Deja nodded her head. "Bright, I've been over that and Lil Jay after you wrote me that long-ass letter explaining everything. Truthfully, though, I just dislike the person you have become."

"Really, Deja, seriously?" Bright put her hands on her hips. "Why, Deja? What have I done to you other than bust my ass trying to be there for you, protecting yo' ass, supporting you, and having yo' damn, back?" Her sister's words heart her heart.

Deja connected eyes with Bright. "Fine! You wanna know the truth...well here it comes!" Deja stood from the bed, threw the remote on it, and then faced off with her sister. "I dislike you because you run around here playing best friend and mommy to everyone else except your own kids. Do you ever call to check on them or to say hello, Bright?"

Bright threw her hands up in the air, and then headed to the stairs. "I'm done with this conversation, Deja. I keep telling yo' young, dumb ass that Larry took them away from me and there is nothing I can do about it!" Now leave me alone; I don't want to talk about it anymore." Bright began to climb the stairs.

"Stop lying, Bright. Stop it, please!" Deja yelled at the top of her lungs. She was tired of Bright running, hiding, and dodging the topic of her children. "Larry didn't take the twins from you. You've been lying all along, Bright. You gave them to Larry, as if they were pieces of paper, and never looked back." Tears rapidly rolled down Deja's face. "I communicate with Mrs. Lane and Larry, and I spend time with Lari and Lori every other weekend. I hold them, I kiss them, and I love them. They're beautiful, beautiful, children, Bright, and they look just like you." Her voice trembled.

"Deja, stop it! You don't know what you're talking about. Larry and his dumb, stupid ass Mama are both liars - "

Deja cut her off. "No, Bright, you're the liar, not them! Did you call them on their birthday to tell them happy birthday? They are two years old now, Bright."

Seeing Bright making her way back down the stairs, Deja blocked her at the last step.

"I went to their birthday party weeks ago, Bright, and I was sure you'd show up, call, or at least send them a gift...but you never did. They need you, Bright, like how Tanisha needs you, and how we needed Mommy when she was gone! Yes, I can admit that you've sacrificed a lot for us, and have been there. You've never let us down, and I'll be forever grateful to you for that, Bright," Deja said sincerely, holding her hand over her chest. "But why can't you just reach out to your own kids with the same love and affection and make sacrifices to get them back, huh? They're your kids, Bright. You birthed them." Deja's face was full of tears.

Without words, Bright brushed past her sister. "I ain't coming back over here no more! Bye, Deja!" Bright ran out the door as if she were being chased out.

"Until you can do right by the twins, we're no longer sisters! I'm taking Mama and Ray to see them too. I'm not gonna keep them a secret any longer, Bright!" Deja yelled as Bright climbed into her Infiniti and backed out the driveway.

How could Bright tell her sister that she didn't want her children back and didn't love them like a mother was supposed to love her kids? Bright resented them entirely, and if she had never seen them again in life, she would be just fine with that. Bright drove up the street cracking up into little pieces, because once again, there was a force standing between her and her family.

****

Later on that night, Bright was in her condominium alone, trying to drink her problems away. Bright was drunk out of her mind. On the phone with Diamond, Bright cursed her out for not being there for her. "You bitch!! How you in muthafucking Texas and I'm here going through all kind of unnecessary shit with my, stupid, dumb-ass sister, Deja - dumb, ass AGAIN. Do you know that bitch gets on my last nerve?" Bright slurred. "Well anyways, hurry up and get yo' ass back out here, bitch. I pay you enough to be here, gotdammit!" Bright burped. "Now hurry up and get fucking here! Good-bye, bitch!" Bright said before ending the call.

When Shawn called Bright and told her he was on his way over, Bright told him to hurry, because she wanted to have sex all night long. He told her he had a surprise for her and for her to be ready to go.

Baby, we just came back from Italy, I ain't going nowhere; I'll be here ready to fuck. Bright took a shower, scrubbing especially hard to remove the smell of alcohol, weed, and cigarettes off her. The shower had taken her buzz down. When she got out, she put on her favorite Victoria Secret body spray, oiled her body up, and threw on a sexy teddy he had brought for her and which she hadn't worn yet. When he knocked on the door, she opened it, showing her lingerie off. "Come get it, baby. I don't wanna go anywhere; I wanna make love all night long."

Shawn laughed. "Tia, meet my girl Bright. Isn't she dynamic?" Shawn introduced her to his good friend. She had just come into town from Detroit.

"Oh my God, Shawn, why didn't you tell me you were bringing someone?" Bright quickly grabbed her robe from the couch, completely embarrassed.

"I'm sorry, baby." He kissed her and came inside. *I was hoping to get it popping later on tonight, but it looks like you're already two steps ahead of us.* He smiled lustfully. "I came to take you out, but we can have a private party right here."

"Not cute, Shawn." Bright tied her robe tight.

"Don't cover up now; I like what I was seeing, didn't you, Tia?" Shawn looked at Tia.

Tia nodded her head. "Very nice, S-Man." She extended her hand to Bright. "I'm Tia, Shawn's good friend. I've heard so much about you." She smiled.

Bright sucked her teeth. "Funny, 'cause I haven't heard a thing about you." She looked at Shawn. "Can I see you in the bedroom for a minute?" She was quite upset.

"Have a seat, Tia, make yourself comfortable," Shawn said as he followed Bright into her bedroom.

Inside the room, Bright said, "What the fuck is going on, and who is that?"

"Relax. It's a good friend of mine who happened to be in town tonight, and I thought it would be nice if you guys met."

"That bitch was in there basically fucking me with her eyes, and you're entertaining it."

"Hold on." Shawn put his hands up. "I told you to be dressed and ready to leave. You're the one that came to the door all provocatively in ya birthday suit. We just both agreed how amazing you look."

"Shawn, I want her to leave," Bright said in a point-blank manner.

"And I want you to either come back inside the living room and entertain, or get yo' ass dressed so that we can go out for the night," he replied in the same point-blank manner. "But now that you bring it up, we have spoken about having a threesome, so what's up?" He pulled Bright to him by the waist.

"No, you've talked about it. I just listened."

"Okay, no big deal, I just thought you were in the business of satisfying your man." He kissed her on the neck. "I will have to do it one more time before I wife you up. Just a heads up."

"Nigga, you betta - "

Interrupting Bright, Shawn tapped Bright on her lips with his fingertip. "Now what I tell you about calling me a nigga?"

Bright bit her bottom lip, reminding herself that he despised being called a nigga. "Man, you better be glad I'm in love with yo' ass! If anything pops off, you bet' not ever ask me to ever do it again. Agreed?" She looked at him seriously. She didn't want Shawn in any sexual activity without her.

"You might enjoy yourself and decide to include it in our relationship," he teased her.

Bright proceeded to storm out of the room. She had no plans of hitting the town with any other woman with her man.

Shawn grabbed her by the arm. "If we're staying in, I like how you look under the robe." He untied it, and then gently pulled it off of her.

She stared at him, ready to cry. *What I don't do, another bitch will. Fuck it, I love him, he's good to me. I'm gonna finish getting fucked up, and let whatever happens, happen.* Bright nodded her head and then grabbed Shawn's hand and walked out of the room.

By the end of the night, intoxicated, the three ended up in Bright's bedroom, where they participated in a full-blown threesome. Waking up the next morning, Bright had a throbbing headache and extremely dry mouth. Getting out of bed, forcing her eyes on Shawn and Tia sleeping comfortably in her bed, Bright realized that their fairytale had finally come to an end.

Love & Insecurities

Over the weeks Bright had been on Shawn tough; things between them were still the same, but Bright didn't feel like he looked at her the same. Bright asked him if he was cheating on her, but he swore to her that she was the only one. He told her that he had something special planned for her in the coming weeks for their eighth-month anniversary and that she was going to be ecstatic. *Another trip out of the country, some money, a car, what? Nigga, I'm concerned about my place in your heart!* She wanted to yell and tell him. After seeing him make love to Tia the night they had the threesome, she worried because he was just as gentle and as passionate with Tia as he always was with her, and that killed her inside.

"Shawn, tell me the truth. Do you have feelings for Tia?"

"Bright, baby, please, not today. Let's enjoy our time together." He squeezed her tight.

"Why you can't just answer the question? Yes or no?" Bright sat up in bed and looked at Shawn.

"No, I don't, baby; I love and want to be with you. I just wanted to have that experience with you, and boy, how I wish I could turn back the hands of time. You have gotten so insecure, baby, and not only is it unattractive, it's annoying as hell!" Shawn got up to use the restroom thinking, *Damn, I wish I could hurry up and speed this process up. Bright is driving me nuts! If she only knew what I truly had in store…*

"Well, why were you looking all in that bitch's eyes and being all passionate and shit with her that night?"

"Maybe because we were in the heat of the moment, you ever think of it that way?" He came out of the bathroom.

"'Cause now every time we have sex and you look at me with all that heat and fire, it just doesn't have that same special effect anymore. It just feels so, blah," Bright rolled her eyes.

After another hour of the discussion, Bright told him that she had to go pick her sister up from ballet class and that she'd see him later.

Good riddance, Bright, and don't rush back! Shawn thought, pretending that he didn't want her to leave. *Maybe she'll experience some type of car problems that will prevent her from coming back tonight.* He laughed to himself. Shawn was tired of having the same old conversation.

When Bright got in her car, she sped off toward the highway to pick Rayonna up from ballet class. She hadn't picked her up since her and Deja's falling-out weeks ago. But Rayonna called her the following evening and asked her if she could pick her up because she missed her. "I'll come pick you up, Ray, but no talk about the twins, all right?" She told Rayonna. Rayonna told her that her lips were sealed. On the way, talking to Cordell and Tanisha on a three-way, Bright was happy to hear that Tanisha was doing well in her recovery and that she was feeling good about herself.

"Queen Bee, stop by the house and cook some grub. You know Deja ain't got it like you," Cordell teased.

"I'll cook for you if you come to the condominium. I ain't fucking with yo' evil sister, Deja, right now," Bright said sarcastically. Seeing sparks of fire and smoke coming from underneath her Infiniti, Bright became alarmed. "Oh shit! This muthafucka is smoking and has fire coming from underneath it! Let me call y'all back!" Bright panicked. Moments later, the hood of the Infiniti burst open, igniting a small fire. When the car begin to make a loud ticking sound, thoughts of the truck blowing up with Bright inside of it became her worst nightmare. Filled with terror and without further thought, Bright pumped her brakes, opened the door, and hurriedly climbed out, nearly being hit by multiple cars. Having made it safely to the shoulder, grateful to still be alive, Bright watched as her entire truck was engulfed in flames. *Oh my God, I could have just died!*

Summertime

Hanging out with Dime one night at his homeboy's grandmother's birthday luau, Bright stood in the backyard, pretending to be enjoying herself. She had gotten upset with Shawn because he didn't mention to her that his friend, Tia, was in town, but instead she had learned that for herself when she popped up at his house earlier that morning and found Tia cooking them breakfast in one of his T-shirts. Bright went nuts and Shawn tried to make it seem as if she was overreacting and that Tia being there was innocent.

"She's in your kitchen cooking breakfast in your fucking T-shirt and wearing your robe. We've spoken on the phone, talked a few times today, and not once did you mention that this bitch was here, and you want me to believe that this is innocent? Nigga, please! You two are clearly fucking!" Bright stormed out of his penthouse, heartbroken and angry.

So instead of sitting at home crying and arguing with Shawn on a Friday night, Bright decided to hang out with Dime at his homeboy's grandmother's birthday luau at her house in Compton. After Dime had introduced Bright to all his friends and their girlfriends, bragging about how beautiful and educated she was, Bright began to get some unfriendly stares. She didn't care; she just sipped on the Blue Hawaiian cocktails they were serving and smoking on her Newports, sitting fancy while they continued to whisper about her and hate. Throughout the evening, Bright continued to find herself watering up. Shawn had not called her or texted her one time since she had left his penthouse, and it made her feel awful. *I'm done with love after this, 'cause no matter what, every time I give my heart away, it just keeps getting handed back to me in a wet paper bag.*

"You all right, baby? Somebody fucking with you? You know I'll handle that shit." Dime walked up on her after talking with a few of his longtime friends.

"I know you will, baby." Bright smiled. "You always protect me and keep me safe. That's why I love you so much."

"You gotdamn right! Niggas will come up missing fucking with my bitch." Dime kissed Bright on her lips.

Interrupting their kiss was the lady who everybody called Granny, yelling out the back door for the guys to come inside and help her break a fight up. After all the guys ran inside to help, Dime gave Bright one last kiss and told her he'd be back. The loud yelling and screaming to break the fight up could be heard from outside.

Tired of waiting and listening to the drama, Bright decided to go inside and tell Dime to take her home. She had enough drama of her own. When she got inside, she was in awe at the fight that was taking place before her. All of Granny's granddaughters were viciously beating on a girl. Catching a quick glimpse of the girl's face when the fight had finally gotten broken up, Bright immediately recognized the girl's face, but couldn't recall where she knew her from. Her black eyes were so terrible that it made Bright cringe. Her eye was bulging out, black, and was completely sealed shut. She looked to be slightly dazed as she apologized to Granny and said her parting words. *I know this bitch; who is she?* Bright kept asking herself as the girl exited the house.

Moments later, the commotion began to start back up in the front yard, and everybody ran outside. The girls were back at it again, two against one, but this time the familiar-looking girl was working her fist into the eye of the granddaughter who had been dominating the fight inside.

"Dime, who is that girl; what's her name?" Bright asked him. The curiosity was killing her.

"Her name is Keisha Cones. She one of the most scandalous bitches in Compton. Bitch better be glad she ain't leaving out the yard on a stretcher," he replied.

Keisha Cones? Oh shit, that's Cousin Shanna's daughter! Bright remembered meeting Keisha once, briefly in '05 when her little brother Ramon had run away from home and ended up at Cousin Shanna's house. *Fuck that, that's family!* Bright thought as she quickly removed her heels, and then she kissed Dime on the cheek. "Sorry baby, but that's family. I'm not about to sit here and watch them jump on her like that," Bright told him, and she jumped into the fight, working her heel on the girl that was punching and pulling Keisha's hair from behind. "I got yo' back, Cousin!" Bright yelled out to Keisha.

When the guys begin to break the fight up, Dime grabbed Bright, confused. When Granny yelled and told Keisha to get out of her yard, Bright jumped out of Dime's hold and told him she was rolling with her cousin. He was steaming hot, and he told her that he never wanted to see her again. She was sure she'd be able to work her way back into his heart at a later time, but when it came to family, they always came first. There was no way she'd stand on the side and watch any member of her family get jumped on. She knew the experience all too well.

"On everything, good looking out, fam, for having my back!" Keisha said to Bright before they got in Keisha's car.

"Anytime, Cousin. That's what family is for," Bright told her as they climbed in her car to go to her house.

From then on, Bright, Keisha, and Keisha's older sister, Ryan, had begun to develop a close-knit relationship. Though Bright hung out and partied more with Ryan, since Keisha wasn't about the partying life, Bright admired Keisha on so many levels. She was a boss bitch of integrity and respect and accepted nothing less. Drug Queenpin, successful business owner...Keisha had major control in the city of Compton, and more money than people knew of.

Having been dealing with a drug lord and one of Keisha's mentors named Clint, Bright learned that Keisha was, in fact, a millionaire. Bright listened more than she talked around Clint and learned more about Keisha from Clint than she actually did from Keisha. She also found out from her big cousin, Ryan, that Keisha's involvement with two of the city's highest ranking gangsters, one a Blood and the other a Crip, led to one of Compton's deadliest Burgundy and Blue wars in history. Bright nearly passed out when she learned of Keisha and Lil Boo's involvement. Lil Boo was her old best friend Treasure's Burgundy fetish, someone that Bright later slid some pussy to, and it ultimately ended their die-hard friendship.

So in between her best friend, Diamond, being in and out of town, Bright would find herself hanging out with her cousins from Compton more.

Three Weeks and a new boss later

"Clint, daddy, I need some money, baby. I'm about to lose my house since I've lost my job going in and out of town with you. Take care of yo' bitch, baby. You wouldn't want me to end up on the streets now, would you?" Bright pouted, lying in the bed next to him. She was in Denver on an O.T. with her newest boss from Compton, Clint. Beside the trips and things he bought Bright, he was the hardest nigga to get money out of. Her bank account was getting low. Dime was no longer on her team. Big Poppa was now ignoring her calls. And other than the money she was able to blackmail Marion out of, Bright needed two new bosses to replace them.

"Looks like you don't have your priorities in line, Sex Kitten," Clint called her by the nickname he had given her. "This dick gon' be here for you, but you should have never allowed yourself to lose your job. It's always business before pleasure, baby, remember that," he told her. Clint was in his forties, very well-spoken, and a kept-together man. His gangster edge and salt and pepper goatee were the sexist things about him.

"Clint!" Bright stood out of the bed asshole naked, exposing the body that he liked to call perfect. "I'm serious, daddy, I lost my job and I know that you're married and everything, but I am also your girl. Take care of me, baby, don't leave me hanging." She looked at him seductively.

"I ain't gon' leave you hanging, Sex Kitten. I'll give you something. Now come over here and give daddy some good morning head before I go out and handle this business."

I know you better, nigga! Be nice, and I might make that missing Rolex of yours re-appear back in ya life. I sold your brand new iPhone to my cousin, Keisha, already, though, Bright thought as she sucked and slurped all over his medium-sized penis. On the last trip, Bright had stolen his watch and brand new iPhone when she realized that Clint might never break her off. She just couldn't imagine having given him all the pussy and head she had given him for free. When Bright finished satisfying Clint, he took a shower, got dressed, told Bright to order room service, and then left the room. After brushing her teeth and rinsing her mouth, Bright grabbed her substitute BlackBerry phone that she had been using after accidentally breaking her jail-broken iPhone. She called to check on her mother, and then caught up on her rest.

Later on, after taking a shower, Bright lay across the bed in the nude, just as Clint liked her to whenever they were out of town, and then returned Shawn's text messages. The two had continued to bump heads about his relationship with Tia, and in fear of getting her heart broken, Bright began to distance herself from him. In the middle of responding to Shawn's text about their eighth-month anniversary coming up, Bright caught a snatch of the conversation Clint was having on the phone when he entered the hotel room.

"Nigga, blow that bitch Keisha's head off. Creep, nigga, either catch that bitch in front of her salon or coming out of her house. But the shit needs to be done ASAP. You understand me?"

Clint didn't know that Bright and Keisha were related, and she preferred to keep it that way because she didn't want that to have any effect on her hustle, and she never revealed their relationship to Keisha. She would only try to talk her out of dealing with him. Keeping her game face on upon his entrance, Bright stood up, took his briefcase from his hand, set it down, and then passed him a cigar. "How about a glass of yak and a good massage, baby?"

"That sounds good, baby, but we going home a day early. My business here is done. Pack our shit." He pulled her by the hair as she passed him and then kissed her on the cheek.

"Don't start nothing," Bright purred. But inside she couldn't wait to get home so she could call Keisha and give her the heads up.

The Count Down

Two days, muthafucka, and somebody in the bitch's family better come up dead. If not, I'ma take yo' twisted ass out instead of yo' daughter. I think I like your baby momma. I'm down for being your little daughter's stepdad too. Terrence lay in his cell, staring at the picture of Shawn's baby momma that his people had sent him. He had a good chance of getting released from prison since a dead man name Jonathan Jordan's fingerprints were found on the gun that he had been stressing the entire time had been planted in his truck. Terrence didn't know an eighteen-year-old named Jonathan Jordan that was murdered last year on the Northside of Long Beach. However, his people were working on finding out who he was, and the people and gang that he was affiliated with.

His attorney told him this was a break in the case and that it was definitely something that they could use to their advantage. He was currently waiting to get the dead man's criminal background report released to him. "The worse his criminal record is, the better chance we'll have at getting you out of here," his attorney told him.

Terrence told Shawn that he wanted Bright left alive for him to kill when he got released, because as good as he remembered her dick-sucking skills were, he decided that he wanted her to suck his dick one more time before she died. There wasn't another person in the world that Terrence hated more than Bright Sheldon, and he got the biggest thrill out of playing the culprit in destroying her life. *Three more days till that eighth-month mark, homie.* Terrence continued to stare at the picture of Shawn's baby momma. He began wondering how tight her pussy was, and how good it would taste. *Y'all both deserve better.* He kissed the picture of the lady's pretty face, slid it back under his mattress, and then headed out to the yard. Niggas owed him money for drugs, and it was time for them to pay up.

Part 11

We're All We Got

Having been back home for two days, Bright continued to try and get in touch with Keisha. She had been calling and texting her since she got back from Denver two days ago, and she had not returned any of her calls. Stopping at Keisha's house, Bright banged on her door and called her name, but got no answer. She called her Cousin Shanna looking for Keisha and Ryan, and she told her she hadn't heard from either of them in days. In the midst of trying to find Ryan at some of the dope spots she was known to frequent, neither Keisha nor Ryan never came out and told Bright that Ryan was on dope, but after a piece of dope that her brother had accidentally dropped on the floor while distributing it disappeared when she got out of the truck, she figured it out for herself. She had even known that after she'd be missing in action for days, Ryan would call and have Bright pick her up from various locations that Bright could tell were dope spots.

Hopping back on the highway to Long Beach, Bright tried to call her cousin, Keisha, again. *Bitch, please answer the phone,* Bright thought while the phone rang.

"What's up, Bright? I'm right in the middle of breakfast. Talk to me," Keisha answered.

"Oh my God, you're alive!" Bright screamed through the phone, happy to hear Keisha's voice. "Finish your breakfast, cousin, and please, please, make sure you call me right after you done. I have something very important to tell you, cousin."

"As soon as I'm done, I'ma hit you," she told Bright, and then she disconnected the call.

Happy that she had spoken to her cousin, Bright headed to her mother's house to take her out to lunch. She hadn't spent much time with her since her and Deja's last altercation, and she missed her very much. "I miss you, Queen Bee. When you gon' come visit your mommy?" Her mother called and asked her the previous night.

When Bright got to her mother's house, she was glad to see that Deja wasn't home. So after getting her mother comfortably situated in her car, Cordell and Rayonna climbed in the back seat, and they all went out to eat at Applebee's. They laughed, talked, and enjoyed each other's time.

"Hey, why hasn't Shawn taken me to dinner yet, Queen Bee?" Rosette struggled to say.

"Because I'm still mad at him. He says he has something big planned for me tomorrow night for our eighth-month anniversary, so if he gets back on my good list, I'll be nice and allow him the honors," Bright teased. Besides being upset with him, she was still afraid that if her mother was around him too long that she'd bring up Bright's kids.

"Aw, don't be giving him a hard time, Queen Bee."

"I like Shawn for you, Bee," Cordell nodded approvingly. "But I'm starting to realize that you be into them L7, rich, conservative, niggas," he laughed, referring to the similar characteristics between Shawn and Larry.

"They say opposite attracts," Bright laughed. "We can't both be 'hood and be ending up in jail."

"As long as he protects you, loves you, and treats you right, I'm good," Cordell told her sincerely. He knew her hustle, but he was ready to see his sister settle down and be with one man.

Bright sucked her teeth. "He's a high-ranking black belt; he can definitely protect the girl," Bright giggled.

Rosette laughed. "I love my children. Y'all are something else," she joined in.

"Is he still going to come to my ballet concert with you Bright? And you're still coming too right, Cordell?" Rayonna put emphasis on the word still. It was her first performance, and she wanted all of her family there.

"Wouldn't miss it, little ballerina girl." Cordell winked at Rayonna. "Hopefully, Tanisha will be able to come too. She's been doing real good. I think she's really through with them drugs this time," he said proudly.

"She been in the program for four months, and she's due to have the baby in less than two months." Bright smiled. "I'm really proud of my Chocolate Drop."

"I been praying, son. She'll be all right. She misses her momma; she tells me that all the time."

"I been praying for her too, 'cause I need her to keep my hair braided up," Rayonna teased. Tanisha kept Rayonna's hair braided in all the latest styles.

Cordell looked at his mother. "I'm taking her straight to her momma after she gets out the program. She'll be clean, look good, have our new baby, and I'm sure her mother will forget how much she hates me and give her daughter another chance." He knew how much she missed her mother.

The conversation began to make her feel some kind of way, and she decided that it was time to go. "I have to meet up with Shawn, and Diamond will be back out here later, so I have to get home," Bright stood up and announced.

When Bright pulled up to her mother's house, Deja was getting out of her car. "Talk to your sister today, Bright. You hear me?" Rosette said as Cordell helped her out of the car.

"I'll do it for you, but I'm tired of having to always kiss her butt. She can speak to me too." Bright climbed out of the car, grabbing her bag.

"That's because you're the big sister, so do the big sister thing." Rayonna kissed Bright on the cheek and then said, "'Cause we're family and we all we got!" She struck a pose before running over to Deja.

Bright smiled at Rayonna. She was truly Bright's little sunshine.

Walking in the house, Bright realized that she hadn't gotten a return call from her cousin, Keisha, but that she had two voicemails from Clint telling her to call him ASAP. "Come meet up with me for the fifty grand, and some good sex. *Yeah, nigga, I see my threats to forward your wife the pictures of me sucking your dick or taking them to your house personally made yo' ass act right. Run me mines, nigga!* Bright laughed to herself.

"Hi, Deja," Bright said as she walked past her.

Deja so desperately wanted to yell, *Bitch, don't speak to me until you go see yo' kids!* But instead, she ignored her, since their mother was there.

In the house, Bright went inside her room to return Clint's call.

"You a cold little bitch! I can't believe you stole my Rolex," he chuckled into the phone.

"I can't believe you didn't give me no gotdamn money either!" She shot back. "Now like I texted you yesterday. I sold your iPhone, but I'm willing to give you your beloved Rolex back if you give me fifty grand."

"Damn, like that, baby? Wow! I thought we had something good going on," Clint said.

"I did too, but you could care less about me. Here I am fucking with a boss nigga, and I had to go to another nigga to keep from losing my house. After this, we're through!" Bright lied, sucking her teeth. She knew Clint was addicted to her and that he would start breaking her off to keep her on his team.

"How about I tell you I ain't giving you shit?" Clint shot back. He didn't appreciate the tone or manner in which Bright was speaking to him.

"Then I'm selling your watch and I'm dropping the pictures off to your wife at your house! You know I have your address," Bright snapped seriously.

"Look, let's stop arguing and make love. I miss you, Sex Kitten, and afterwards, I swear on my life, I'll give you the money, but you bet' not ever steal from me again. You understand?"

"Take care of yo' Sex Kitten, and I'll never have to steal from you again. Where we meeting up at?" She asked, ready to get her money.

After Clint gave Bright the address to meet him at, Bright walked down the stairs to leave.

Cordell looked at Bright from the couch. "Who was you cussing out on the phone, Queen Bee? Everything good?"

"I'm good now. I'm about to go get my money up from this dude named Clint, and then I'm going to holler at our Compton family about something very important."

"You need me to roll wit' you, sis, you straight?" Cordell yelled after Bright.

"I'm good, Cordell. I'll tell you about everything later. Bye!" She climbed in her Lexus and drove off.

On the ride to Compton, Bright spoke to Shawn.

"You ready for tomorrow, Princess Bright?" He asked her.

"As long as Tia isn't involved!" Bright snapped with attitude.

Shawn laughed. "Just get pretty. I'ma make sure you go out with a bang,"

"Go out with a bang? Hmm where am I going? Never mind. Let me call you back, baby, I have to run inside the post office," she lied, pulling up at the address Clint had told her to meet him at.

"Come over when you're finished. I miss holding you."

Bright smiled. "Awww, I miss you holding me too! I'll be there shortly. I love you." She disconnected the call and put her phone in her purse.

When Bright climbed out of the car she was abruptly struck over the head with a forceful object that instantly knocked her unconscious, and then she was dragged into a nearby house, where the horror of her life was soon to begin.

The Next Day

After making sure that Cordell was gone and that nobody was in the house except for Rosette, the masked intruder slipped in the house through the back door. Having seen Rayonna walk out of the house and start down the street, he knew that she wouldn't be too long or go that far, since Rosette was never left home alone. He had to move quickly. The plan was to smother Rosette in her sleep.

Having tiptoed inside of Rosette's bedroom, the masked intruder was upset to see her sitting in her rocking chair watching TV, laughing. *FUCK! This bitch is almost always sleep!* The masked intruder looked around the room, deciding to take the phone cord and strangle her, but when a truck pulled up in the driveway playing loud music, the masked intruder knew he had to change plans and make something else happen quickly. Having briskly walked into the room, the masked intruder forcefully pushed Rosette out of her chair, causing her to bump her head hard into the wall. He picked the TV up, snatching the plug out of the socket and then slammed it on the back of her head. *If that don't kill her, she's damn sure gon' be fucked up real bad. I'm sure Ice would be satisfied.* The masked intruder hurriedly ran through the house and swiftly out the back.

Blackmailed to Death

The day that Bright was dragged into the house, she was later slapped out of her unconscious state by Clint, demanding to know what she had told her cousin, Keisha, of their involvement or about the hit he had put out on her.

"Keisha? I don't know what you're talking about, Clint!" *Fuck, he figured out that we're related, but how?* Bright wondered in fright.

Having heard a conversation Keisha was having, Clint had coincidentally learned that the two were related. He had done and said too much in front of Bright, and he needed to find out everything Bright had revealed to Keisha regarding his hit to determine his next move. Not believing a word that Bright had said, he took her BlackBerry from her purse. After going through and reviewing Bright and Keisha's entire text and call history, Clint was convinced that Keisha was fully unaware of his and Bright's involvement. *Maybe the bitch was telling the truth,* Clint thought, preparing to walk out of the room. He had to make a few business calls.

"Get ya dicks wet on Bright, fellas, and don't forget to put your dicks in her mouth for a chance to experience the head of a lifetime," Clint said coldly, and then he exited the room laughing.

Bright had been raped anally, vaginally and orally repeatedly in less than two hours that day. When Clint returned to the room, Bright cried out to him. Bright couldn't take it anymore.

"Why you doing this to me, baby? I thought you cared for me."

"Bitch, please! I thought you knew your fucking position. But since you couldn't play it right, you've made me resort to me handling things my way. Now, where's my fucking Rolex at, and maybe I'll let yo' ass go." It was a twenty-year anniversary gift from his wife, and she had been asking him about it.

"Please don't let these men hurt me anymore, baby, please!" Bright cried for mercy, and then told him that his Rolex watch was in her glove compartment.

Clint sent his boy out to check her glove compartment. When he returned with his Rolex in his hand, he stood over her beaten and raped body smiling, putting her phone in his pocket. *Too bad I didn't know you were related to Keisha before things had gotten so far out of hand!* Then Clint looked in the direction of his homeboy, Beats. "Do whatever y'all wanna do with this slut, and then afterwards, get rid of her." As he walked out of the room, Bright cried and screamed his name.

"PLEASE, CLINT, PLEASEEEEEE, DON'T LEAVE ME HERE! I'LL NEVER, BLACKMAIL OR STEAL FROM YOU EVER AGAIN!" One of her rapists slapped her across the face and told her to shut up as he forcefully plunged his large penis in her butt.

"Ahhhh!" Bright cried with a face full of tears.

Clint walked out the door. *Sorry, Sex Kitten, it's much more complicated than that.* So besides her stealing from him and blackmailing him, Bright had been exposed to more information than he was comfortable with, especially since she was Keisha's cousin. Clint's driver opened the door for him to climb in the back of his truck. When he drove off the street, Clint grinned wickedly. *Keisha Cones, you're next.*

The next day, her hell was repeated all over again. Bright had cried and begged for them to stop and to let her go, but instead, while she was being raped from behind, another guy placed himself in front of her and forced his penis down her throat.

"This will help you shut that big mouth of yours," he told her, nearly causing her to vomit.

When they were finished with her, they left her lying on the cum-polluted mattress. Bright lay there in silence, degraded to the highest degree, feeling numb and empty inside. Bright was all cried out, and had no more tears inside. Staring at the wall, unable to blink, with a blank expression on her face, Bright believed that she was being raped for all of the false rapes she had cried in the past. *This is only the beginning of my torture and punishment before they kill me,* she kept saying to herself. She was prepared for the worst.

****

At the hospital, the family was in total distress. The doctors told them that in order to keep their mother alive, they would have to perform emergency surgery, and that in her condition, she only had a thirty percent chance at survival. Bright was nowhere to be found. They had been calling her since yesterday, to no avail. Cordell began to think the worst and was snapping left and right. He was the man of the family and he was on the verge of losing it. Deja sat in silence crying, holding her sister Rayonna's hand, afraid that they'd lose their mother and that something terrible had happened to Bright. Having strong faith in the Lord, Rayonna relied on Jesus Christ in her family's time of need, and she continued to pray her heart out.

Having been unsuccessful reaching Bright, Diamond called Deja, who told her to come to the hospital because their mother had fallen out of her rocking chair. Diamond arrived, working overtime to comfort the siblings, and even harder to locate Bright. *Bitch, where the fuck you at?* Diamond wondered. *You need to be here to see and feel this pain!*

"Deja and Cordell!" Rayonna stood up with a sudden burst of glowing energy. She grabbed both of her siblings' hands. "I just prayed, and y'all ain't gon' believe this, but God told me that he going to take Momma for a little while, but when he gives her back to us, she's going to be completely healthy again!" Happy tears trickled down Rayonna's face. "He's going to perform a miracle." Just moments earlier, her vision had been blinded and her ears had gone deaf from the world while God talked to her and showed her a vision. "I seen her in the vision. She's going to be able to walk and talk properly and everything!" She began to hug them.

"God told you that, huh?" Cordell shot, looking at Rayonna.

Rayonna nodded her head yes. "He did." Rayonna looked her brother in the eyes.

"Well I'm sorry to bust your bubble, but God forgot about our family a long time ago, Ray." Cordell got up and walked outside. Hurting, he was tired of the many tragedies that his family continued to encounter.

"I'm gonna walk around to give you and your sister space," Diamond told Deja, and then hurriedly removed herself from their presence.

Day Two

"Damn, bitch, I ain't never had nobody suck my dick so good before!" Beats told Bright.

"I like sucking yo' dick, too, 'cause you the only person that has been treating me right, and if I had met you before this, I'm sure I would have been sucking this big ole, fat dick every day and night." Bright was popping his dick in and out of her mouth and down her throat the best she could; her life depended on it.

"Every day and night?" Beats moaned in pure ecstasy.

"Wouldn't you like that?" Bright slurped loudly on his dick.

"Damn, I can't even imagine!" He loved the way she swallowed then spit his dick out then chewed on the head like it was bubble gum.

"Well, stop letting these niggas hurt me and let me go. We can start fresh, just you and me. What you say, baby?" She looked up at him as she sucked on his dick.

Beats came, and then slapped Bright in her already-swollen face. "Bitch, save all that fairytale shit and get this dick back up before I splatter your brains right now!" He pulled her up from the ground by her hair and then thumped her in the head with the butt of his forty-five caliber.

Tired of being beaten and raped, Bright had just about given up. *They have no plans of letting me go, and I'm not going out without a fight.* Opening her mouth as wide as she could, she bit down on his dick as hard as she could. Hands tied behind her back, Bright planned to bite Beats's dick off in the hopes that he'd pass out. She figured if her plan worked out, she'd have enough time to find a way to untie her hands and get out of there before the others got back.

Beats's screams went unheard, since they were isolated in a soundproof room. Bright bit and shook Beats dick as if she were a pit bull infected with rabies; she even began to growl like a dog. The gun fell from Beats's hand as the separation of his penis from his waist caused blood to shoot out and gush all over Bright's face.

Bright bit his penis completely off, then once he fell onto the floor, she spit it at him. "Dumb-ass nigga!" She wiped the blood from her mouth on her shoulders. Excited about her chance to get away, Bright stood up and kicked Beats in the ribs while he lay helplessly on the ground having a seizure. She ran around the room trying to untie herself. Unable to untie herself, she dashed up the stairs and was trying to use her neck and chin to unlock the door when Clint's driver pushed the door open and made eye contact with her. Looking as if she had seen a ghost, Bright gasped for her last breath…she knew it would be her last.

Clint's driver quickly observed the scene, pulled his gun out, and shot Bright in the head. Instantly, Bright tumbled down the stairs and landed flat on her back. The blood that rushed from her head caused her to lie in a pool of blood, eyes wide open and lifeless.

****

Come on, Princess Bright, you can't let me down right now! A precious life is depending on you at this very moment. Where are you; pick up the phone! Shawn paced the floor of his penthouse, dressed and prepared for the night's extravaganza. It was down to the wire. *Come on, baby, it's almost over, pick up, dammit!*

"She still hasn't answered, Tia." She came out of the room with her daughter in her arms. "I can't believe this shit!" Shawn snapped after his thirtieth failed attempt to reach Bright.

"Maybe she found out about me?" Tia said with a worried expression on her face.

"She couldn't have." He looked at Tia. "Look, go grab your things, and hurry, we have to get outta here," Shawn instructed. *This is not good.* He went to his safe, grabbed his money and their passports, and then they fled the penthouse.

"Going somewhere special?" A female voice asked after Shawn stepped out of his penthouse and approached the elevator. "BOOM!! BOOM!" Two stray bullets erupted from the gun, immediately knocking Shawn to the ground. One struck Shawn's head and the other ripped through his back.

"NOOOOOOOO! HELPPPPPPPPPPPP!" Tia yelled at the top of her lungs the second she saw Shawn's body hit the ground. Holding her daughter tightly in her arms with her head pressed up against her racing heart, Tia continued to yell and scream until help had finally arrived on the scene.

****

"We did the best that we could, guys. We revived your mother during surgery. Once we stabilized her, she had a seizure, and she has slipped into a coma. Your mother's heart rate is low, but it is still beating on its own. However, we did have to put her on life support to help her breathe. We're gonna do the best that we can to keep your mother around. We have more CAT Scans to perform to keep track of her brain activity, but I want you guys to be prepared for the worst. If we don't get any progress throughout the afternoon and night, which is very unlikely, your mother will go into a full vegetative stage by tomorrow afternoon. You guys are more than welcome to go see your mother now. Her room is directly across from the nurses' station." The doctor told them her room number. "I'm so sorry."

Inside their mother's hospital room, the children stood staring at their mother's body hooked up to a breathing machine and IV's.

Unable to see his mother in her current state, Cordell walked out of the room, saying, "See, Ray, I told you God forgot about our family!" Cordell punched the hospital wall, tears streaming from his eyes. "Let's go, y'all. I ain't coming back to this damn hospital no more, either; this place is bad news." He headed to the elevators to get to his truck.

"Ma isn't gonna die; God told me that she isn't." Rayonna looked at her sister. "Do you believe me, Deja?"

Trying her best to be strong for her siblings, as she had seen their big sister, Bright, do so many times before, Deja had gained a whole new level of respect for her sister, and she wished that she was there at the very moment to fill her shoes. Deja trembled, feeling as if she were about to pass out. In her heart, she knew her mother was in the process of transitioning to the afterlife, but how could she tell Rayonna the same? Trying to speak, Deja had completely lost her voice and could not get her words out. It was hard, and she just wanted to be alone.

After the girls kissed their mother's resting face, Rayonna turned to her sister, nodding her head. "Deja, she's not gonna die." Uncertainty began to pollute her mind, though.

Unable to speak, Deja wrapped her arms around Rayonna's shoulders and ushered her toward the elevator so that they could go home.

****

After making a quick call to Clint, his driver threw Bright's body in a giant garbage bag and then called Clint to find out what he wanted him to do with her body. He told him to get rid of both Bright's and Beats's bodies, but to put each in separate locations. "Fill that bitch up with acid to get rid of any DNA leading back to my camp." Clint told him.

Doing as he was told, his driver tossed Bright's body in the trunk of his car as if she were merely a piece of garbage. Then he climbed in his car and headed to Lueders Park to dispose of her body.

Once at the park, Clint's driver peeked at his surroundings. Noticing the coast was clear, he headed to the trunk of the car, grabbed the garbage bag with Bright's body, then threw it inside the dumpster. *Oh shit, I almost forgot the acid!* He thought to himself before getting back inside his car.

However, the sound of police sirens changed his plans. *I'll come back later; I ain't about to go down for a dead piece of pussy that I ain't even touch. Fuck that!* The driver thought as he got in his car and drove off.

Inside the dumpster, the garbage bag that Bright was inside of began to shift, and a faint voice began to cry out for help.

****

Death, just what the doctor ordered, muthafucka. I said I want a muthafucka to be dead, not almost dead! You better hope the bitch's momma doesn't make it. I keep telling you niggas, I ain't no joke. He had just gotten off his cell phone with one of his contacts after getting an update on Bright's mother. BOOM! "Sometimes never is better than being late," Terrence said out of the blue to his cellmate.

****

After biting and using her feet and legs to get out of the garbage bag, Bright leaned over the dumpster. Head leaking, feeling weak and unbalanced, Bright fought hard to get help. She wasn't ready to die, and she had a family to support. Falling out of the dumpster, Bright dragged her bloody body down the sidewalk until she reached the street, crying for help.

"Help, help me, somebody please help me," she continued to say. Her eyes got big as quarters when she saw a vehicle that looked like Clint's making its way up Rosecrans Avenue. "No, no!" She cried, terrified, then built up enough strength to stand. She wobbled in the middle of the street, waving her hands for help before finally collapsing in the middle of the busy street.

****

Tanisha had earned a weekend pass from the rehab, and she was looking forward to spending it with Cordell and his family. Momma Rose was on her deathbed and no one had seen or heard from Bright in days. The turmoil in the family was at an all-time high, and the despair in the house was thick. For once, Tanisha had begun to worry about Cordell returning to his old cocaine habits to ease his pain. The family was hurting about their mother and they were lost without Bright. She was the vessel that kept them solid, grounded, and together.

"Look, I'm about to drive around and see if I can find Bright. Stay here with my sisters, all right? I'll be back," Cordell told Tanisha early that morning.

Tanisha sat up in bed, rubbing her seven-month pregnant belly. "You sure you don't want me to go with you, baby? I really wanna be there for you."

"Naw, I have to pick up some money too," he told her.

Tanisha stood from the bed and wobbled to him. She grabbed his hands, rested her forehead on his, and looked him deep in his eyes. "You're my world. Your family is my family, and you guys are all I have." Tanisha squeezed his hands tight. "Let me be your rock, use me as your comfort, baby. I'm here for you. I love you...We're in this together."

Tears fell from Cordell's eyes. He held Tanisha's face, kissed her lips, and then walked out of the room. He couldn't bear losing his mother and sister, and he refused to continue sitting around, hoping and waiting for her to come home. He had to go out and find her.

Watching Cordell get in his truck from his bedroom window, Tanisha broke down and cried. Her heart ached terribly for him. She watched him struggle to remain strong, and knowing that he didn't know what to do and that she couldn't do anything to help him was killing her inside.

"Deja, Cordell, Tanisha!" Rayonna yelled through the house, nearly frightening Deja out of her sleep and causing Tanisha's heart to skip two beats.

"What's wrong, Ray?" Deja hopped up from the couch, almost going headfirst into the living room wall.

Tanisha quickly wobbled down the stairs.

Rayonna ran out of her mother's bedroom. "Momma woke up! She's up, and she's better now! Hurry, let's go to the hospital.

Cordell!" Rayonna called out for him again as she hurriedly put on her shoes. "Cordell, Momma woke up! I told you she wasn't going to die! Let's go!" Rayonna grabbed Deja's car keys and flip flops and handed them to her.

Deja looked at Rayonna sadly. "The doctor said that if Ma made any progress that they would call us immediately, Ray. They haven't called. I slept with the phone next to my ear." Telling Rayonna that broke her heart.

"I'm telling you, Momma is awake. I seen her in my dream, Deja. She woke up and she's waiting on us. Cordell!" Rayonna yelled up the stairs again.

"He isn't here. He went out to look for Bright," Tanisha told her. Her face was flooded with tears. She knew Rayonna was having a traumatic moment.

Deja grabbed Rayonna. "It was a dream, Ray. Let's have breakfast and give the doctors a little more time to call us."

"No! I don't want to eat breakfast, Deja, and I'm not going to wait on the doctors to call when I'm telling you that Momma is waiting on us!"

Looking at Rayonna, both Deja and Tanisha were at a loss for words.

"Forget it, I'll catch the bus to the hospital!" Rayonna ran out of the house.

"Ray!" Deja yelled after her as she slid her shoes on her feet and grabbed her car keys. "I'll be back, Tanisha." Deja quickly left to go after her sister.

After Deja left, Tanisha poured a glass of milk and then sat on the living room couch. With everything that had been going on, her mother begin to absorb her mind. *Maybe I should call her...* Tanisha grabbed her cell phone.

"What's up, boo boo?" Diamond walked inside the living room, unseen and unheard.

Startled, Tanisha asked her how she got in the house.

"The door was unlocked. Where everybody at...and how is Ma Rose?" A wicked smile appeared across her face.

"They went to the hospital to check on her, and Cordell went out to find Bright." She kept her eyes suspiciously on Diamond. She had given Tanisha an uneasy feeling.

"Yeah, what's up with that? That bitch just out of nowhere dropped off the face of the earth; where the fuck she at?" Diamond laughed. "Why you looking at me like that, boo boo? What, you don't like me anymore?" She sat next to her and rubbed her stomach.

Tanisha removed her hand off of her belly and then stood up from the couch, looking at Diamond strangely.

Diamond stood up. "Where you going?"

"To lock the door."

"Sit down, it's already locked. You wanna get high or something? What, why you acting like you can't talk?"

"You're acting real strange, Diamond," Tanisha said and began to call Cordell. She didn't feel safe around Diamond, for some strange reason.

Diamond stood up and snatched Tanisha's phone from her hand. "Girl, sit down! You ain't about to call nobody!" She pushed Tanisha roughly on the couch.

"Bitch, don't put ya fucking hands on me!" Tanisha slapped Diamond's hand off of her and proceeded to stand back up.

"Boo boo, sit yo' ass back down!" Diamond pushed her more aggressively than before.

Tanisha slapped Diamond and then ran toward the kitchen to grab a knife.

"Bitch! Why the fuck you slap me, bitch?" Diamond caught up to Tanisha, pulled her by the hair, and began pulling her toward Rosette's bedroom.

Tanisha immediately begin to defend herself, swinging, scratching, and trying to claw Diamond's eyes out, resulting in her busting Diamond's lip.

Diamond pulled a gun out and aimed it at Tanisha. "Fuck it, bitch, let's do it the hard way, then!"

Tanisha froze at once. "Why are you doing this, Diamond, and what do you want from me?" She looked Diamond in her unusually cold, dark eyes.

"Take your clothes off, NOW!" Diamond yelled, seeing the confused look on Tanisha's face.

Afraid for her life Tanisha did as she was told, tears falling from her eyes.

"Hold your fucking hands up!" Diamond admired her perky breasts. "You're always at the wrong place at the wrong time aren't you...boo boo?" Diamond reached out and begin fondling Tanisha's nipple between her fingertips.

"Why are you doing this to me, Diamond?" she cried, feeling extremely violated.

"Because you're always at the wrong place at the wrong time. But I have to admit that you have some good-ass pussy. That rape was intended for Bright, but like today, you were there."

Tanisha's mouth was wide open, confused. Her mind quickly began to travel back to the day she was raped in Bright's condominium.

"I seen yo' smooth, black ass all handcuffed to Bright's bed, and have been dying to know. Do you and Bright be fucking around?" Diamond stepped closer to Tanisha and kissed her lips. "How does she taste?" Diamond pulled her pants halfway down, revealing a penis. Terrence wanted Diamond to find someone to rape and beat Bright, but since Diamond was dying to feel Bright's insides and he wanted to torment her, Diamond decided to do the job.

Tanisha's eyes widened. *I have to admit that you have some good-ass pussy.* Diamond's words continued to replay in her head. *Diamond raped me...*

Diamond nodded. "Yeah, I raped, you, Tanisha, boo boo, but I don't want you to feel that I've only targeted you, because I've pretty much attacked this entire family, other than goodie-two-shoes, Rayonna. She's a tough cookie. In my old life, the bitches called me Shawn, but now the niggas call me Diamond. I'm in transition, boo boo. I like being a girl and being able to sleep with men, instead of being a masculine man, laid up in the bed with a bitch." Diamond had been getting hormone injections for full breasts, and had been taking female hormone pills. Shawn had always been known as a woman's man, but had always felt uncomfortable in his body and secretly desired to be a woman. His longtime girlfriend and baby momma was disgusted, having learned of his decision to transition from a man to a woman, and she had even threatened to take his daughter from him if he didn't get his act together.

Instead, Shawn left and sent her money every month. Later, she forgave him and allowed him to see his daughter, but only under the pretense of him being their daughter's godmother. She believed their daughter's knowledge of his transition would be too complex for her to understand. Shawn agreed. He had gotten nose and lip surgery for a more feminine appearance, and no one in his previous life ever recognized him. The only reason Terrence knew of his transition was because Shawn reached out to him to make money.

Tanisha looked down at Diamond's penis, forcing herself to swallow her throw-up. *This can't be happening right now, this can't be real. Diamond's a man!*

"I was the reason both of you bitches went to jail, and Cordell, too. He was easy. I'm also responsible for knocking Rosette's broke-down ass out of her rocking chair and busting her ass upside the head with her TV," Diamond smiled. "I would have rather killed Bright's ass, 'cause as much as I'd love to fuck her and make her suck my dick before my sex change operation, I was hired to fuck this bitch Bright's world up, but during the time I've known her, I've truly learned to hate that scandalous, manipulative, using-ass bitch. Unfortunately, somebody had to die in this family, or my little girl would have been killed, and I just couldn't have that." Diamond nodded. "Don't worry, though, Ice is gonna have Bright killed, or kill her himself, so you'll see her on the other side real soon. Now head to the dead bitch's room, boo boo, I'm going to take that pussy one more time." Diamond pulled the gun to Tanisha's head to motivate her foot movement.

Doing as she was told, Tanisha walked slowly, tears rapidly falling down her face.

Diamond laughed. "Oh, I forgot to mention, gurl, I even killed Bright's little boyfriend, Shawn. Can you believe that he was really going to propose to that wicked, ratchet bitch?" Diamond didn't understand how the men Bright dealt with couldn't see straight through her bullshit. "But having been successful in basically ripping this family apart, mainly the sisters, I have to admit that after I left that dope on the counter that I knew you'd steal," Diamond laughed, "I was disappointed that you didn't share or turn Cordell out. Why didn't you? Now I hate that muthafucka about as much, if not more, than I hate Bright. He really thinks he's something with his stupid ass, and that's the only reason that I'm going to kill you, Tanisha. To spite him. His ass gave me the most hell since I've been around."

Tanisha walked toward the room with her hands up in complete shock at the information she was learning. *You have to run, Tanisha, or this sick person is going to kill you!* A voice screamed in her head. She had a straight shot to the door.

"Now when we get in this room..." Diamond rubbed the gun down the crack of Tanisha's behind. "Don't get me wrong, I enjoy the loud, rough sex. The begging and screaming for me to stop arouses me to the max. Just lower it a bit this time, okay? I'd hate to have to knock you out again. Just try to relax, boo boo; you may actually enjoy it this time." Diamond slapped Tanisha on the ass.

RUN NOW!!! The voice in Tanisha's head shouted at her the closer she got to Mama Rose's bedroom. Without further thought, Tanisha took off toward the door as fast as her pregnant body would allow her to. Briskly unlocking the door, Tanisha slipped outside, yelling for help. Diamond was right on her trail, aiming the gun at Tanisha, trying to get a good shot at her. Sprinting across the street, Tanisha drew attention from the neighbors, begging for them to call 911. "She's a man; he's trying to rape and kill me!" Tanisha cried.

Running across the street, angry, Diamond began to shoot recklessly, when out of nowhere Diamond was hit full force by Cordell's truck, sending her flying into the air and landing headfirst into the pavement. Head busted wide open, the person they knew as Diamond had died instantly.

Relieved to see Cordell's face, Tanisha ran to him screaming and hollering his name. "Diamond is a man! She was the one that raped me, Cordell, and she pushed Momma Rose out of her rocking chair, too, and hit her in the head with the TV, baby. You were right, all along, she wasn't to be trusted," Tanisha fell into Cordell's arms, trembling and sobbing.

After taking his shirt off, Cordell covered Tanisha up as much as he could, glad that he had followed his gut instincts to come back home. "Everything is all right now, baby, I'm here," Cordell said, trying to absorb the chilling information that Tanisha had just told him, thinking, *This is wild! This type of shit only happens on TV. That he-she muthafucka better be glad that a person can only be killed once!* Cordell glanced at Diamond's dead body in the middle of the street before entering his yard.

****

"Where is my Momma?" Rayonna pointed toward her mother's hospital room in the intensive care department, devastated.

"I'm so sorry, sweetheart, but your mother expired this morning," the nurse told her.

"No, no she hasn't, .God said he was giving her back!" Rayonna's world began to spin around.

"Expired!" Deja yelled at the nurse. "Why hasn't anybody called to inform us of anything? The doctor said he'd allow us a moment with our mother if it resulted to this!" Deja was starting to lose her voice again.

The nurse looked toward the room. "The doctor called and spoke with the son. It was at his discretion. I'm very sorry." She began to tear up. This part of her job never got easier.

Deja cried, "We didn't even get a chance to say good-bye to her."

Deja hugged Rayonna and the two stood holding each other, crying viciously.

"He was supposed to give her back to us!" Rayonna cried.

"She's in Heaven now, Rayonna," Deja continued to tell her sister.

After speaking to the nurses, the doctor walked over to the sisters. "Your mother lived a very full life." He spoke in a comforting tone, trying to whisk them to the side and out of the walkway.

"My mother was only in her forties!" Deja cried. "She died way too young."

The doctor shot the nurses a puzzled look and asked them what their mother's name was. Clearly there was a big mistake.

"Rosette Clark," Rayonna told him. "She was in that room." She pointed to the room across from the nurses' station.

"The miracle case!" They all said in unison.

"Wait, what's going on?" Deja asked, puzzled.

Rayonna looked hopeful.

"We have a huge misunderstanding. Another patient passed away in that room this morning. Your mother had been transferred to another department. I just called and spoke to your brother, Cordell - that is your brother, correct?" The doctor asked. Once they confirmed that, the doctor walked them to their mother's new room in the recovery department, telling them a story of a miracle that Rayonna had previously told them she had envisioned.

Standing in front of their mother's hospital room, Deja's mouth fell wide open, seeing her mother in her current state. She was sitting up on the side of the bed on her own while holding the phone to her ear, smiling, laughing, and talking to Cordell. She was fully recovered, and her speech was no longer impaired.

Rayonna ran into her mother's arms. "I told you He said He was giving her back to us, Deja... not taking her home." Rayonna wrapped her arms around her mother.

****

Hours after emergency surgery, Bright was placed in the intensive care unit, where she had fallen asleep after being diagnosed with amnesia. She didn't remember her name, what had happened to her, where she lived, let alone any of her family contact information, so she had been reported as a Jane Doe. Medical staff were currently waiting on dental identification.

****

In a private section of the visiting area, Terrence had Jackie bent up against the wall, utilizing the ten minutes he had paid the guards to be alone with Jackie. Jackie was incredible, helping him to make the best of his time, whispering freaky whatnots in his ears and kissing him passionately in between biting him on his neck. "Slow down, baby! We gon' use our full ten minutes. Slow down!"

Terrence pulled her by the hair to keep her from nipping and blowing on his earlobe.

"Let me do my wifely duties, daddy," she told him.

Terrence had had his people send a four-carat diamond ring and card to her job asking her to marry him. Instead of calling him on his cell phone, she made a trip over to tell him yes. Terrence needed conjugal visits while he fought his case. He was tired of jacking off. "We have two minutes left. Make it last until the last second," he told her. He bit on her nipples and looked her intensely in the eyes. "You make me very happy, Jackie,"

"I love you, Ice,!" She rode him nice and slow, waiting for the final forty-five seconds so that she could allow his penis to hit her tender spot before making him cum. Looking at the clock on the wall, Jackie took off like a race horse in a horse race at the sound of the gunshot. Moaning in his ear, she said, "I love you too, baby, I love you so much, my dick, my dick, all mine!" She came all over him, making him cum two seconds before the tenth minute.

Terrence emptied himself inside of her. "Next time, I want every last second, you understand?" He pulled his penis out of her and pulled his underwear and pants up.

"Next time, baby, I promise," Jackie said as she followed Terrence back to the seating area.

When Terrence sat down, he said, "You ready to play your wifely duties and be a good stepmomma to my kids now? I got a few of them."

"Always and forever, baby." Jackie smiled, biting her lips. She was lustfully in love. Her man was in prison and still took very good care of her.

One Week Later

It wasn't up until her cousin, Keisha, came to the hospital to visit Bright that she miraculously gained her memory back. She had been in the intensive care unit at Kaiser Hospital, having successfully recovered from having a bullet removed from her head, and surgical stitching to her rectum. Though Bright's memory was clouded about the events that happened during her kidnapping, she pretended to have suffered from a severe case of amnesia whenever the detectives, doctors, and nurses asked her what happened to her and the names of the people that were involved. Bright was happy to be alive, she was afraid for dear life of Clint and his goons. She wanted them to believe that she was dead and gone, and she wanted nothing more than to forget those very crucifying days of her life. The experience was one of a torture chamber, and she didn't ever want to ever relive or revisit those harrowing moments in her mind ever again. Her cousin, Keisha's visit offered her the relief that she needed to move on.

"I knew there was something about your scandalous ass that I loved!" Keisha giggled. "I eventually found out what it was that you were trying to tell me too, boo, and from the bottom of my heart, I wanna thank you again for having my back. You're my angel," Keisha told her. After a few moments of silence, Keisha looked around the room to ensure their complete privacy and then bent down and whispered in Bright's ear. "You don't have to be afraid, 'cause I took care of that nigga Clint. I busted his muthafucking lips wide open, and knocked his teeth out his mouth with a hammer. Blood died a slow, painful, death, baby. I made sure he paid the ultimate price for fucking with me and my family." Keisha then kissed Bright on the forehead, stood back in an upright position, and smiled at her. "I'll be checking in on you, rellie," were her final words before exiting her hospital room.

Thank you, cousin; I love you! Bright cried, grateful inside; a tear mixed with many emotions rolled down her face. It felt wonderful to have a cousin that had gone to bat for her, especially one that Bright looked up to and admired so much.

Lying in her hospital bed, Bright was consumed in deep thought, and she realized that she was no longer living on her own fate. Had it not been for her mother's prayers, she would have been dead a long time ago. Approaching the age of twenty-one, Bright had been hospitalized three times from volatile attacks that all left her in near-death situations, all resulting from her lies, schemes, and her disloyalty toward others. Bright had seen the light for the third and final time, and decided that it was time for her to start living right. She feared that next time just might end up being too late.

The next day, having signed her release papers, both Cordell and Deja were anxious to fill Bright in on the chain of events that had taken place in her absence. It was mostly bad news, but they assured her that the good news would make up for all of the bad.

"Nothing has happen to my kids or anyone in the family?" Her children had been on her mind and in her heart heavily since her near-death experience, and she wanted nothing more than to see them and be in their lives; money had nothing to do with it. She also had plans on going to Treasure's court date to speak on her behalf. Treasure didn't deserve to be in jail. Her only crime was trusting Bright and being her friend. Bright wanted to change her life and do better, starting with her children and old friend, Treasure.

Deja's eyes watered up. "Things have happened, but your children and everyone else is fine." Hearing her sister ask about her children brought tears to her eyes and made her very emotional.

"Goodness, you're that NBA player, Larry Lane!" An approaching nurse yelled out, excitedly, immediately interrupting the sibling's conversation.

Larry spoke with a manner of deep, seriousness, and urgency "I'm sorry, no pictures and autographs right now, please. Excuse me, excuse me." He took wide, brisk footsteps to Bright's room.

Nervously, Bright began to hold her head down in shame. She wasn't ready to face Larry. *Who told him I was here? Why is he here?* Bright pondered.

Cordell stood by his sister's side. "Queen Bee, you ain't never gotta hold your head down in shame for nobody," he said seriously.

"I guess you're right, little brother." Bright pulled herself together, trying to mentally prepare herself for whatever Larry was about to toss in her direction.

Larry walked inside the room, and after immediately locking eyes with Bright, he looked to see if her hospital room TV was on. "Bright!" He rushed over to her and grabbed her hand. "I wanted to tell you before you seen it on the news. Our children have been kidnapped, and we're going to have to work together to get them back."

"No, no, no, no!" Bright began shaking her head repeatedly. She wanted her kids now more than ever, and now Larry was telling her that she might never be able to see their precious faces again, or have the opportunity to be the best mother that she could.

Seeing Bright at the brink of collapsing, Larry caught her and held her in his arms.

"No, Larry, they can't hurt my babies! They can't take them from me; I have to see them again! I have to! No, Larry, no, you have to get them back, nooo!" Bright cried desperately.

****

At the house, the family joyfully moved around the house, preparing for Bright's return. Feeling better than ever, Rosette had cooked her eldest daughter's favorite gumbo meal and invited her best friend, Gale, and cousin, Shanna, over, looking forward to having one of the greatest days ever.

Shawn nervously sat on the couch with Tia and her daughter, Alexis. Preparing to propose marriage to Bright, Shawn prayed that she wouldn't flip the second she walked through the door and saw Tia there. When Bright had first been introduced to Tia, she was on her last days, having discovered a deadly tumor on her brain. Instead of being depressed about it, Tia wanted to live her last days up to the fullest, experiencing and seeing different things, and ultimately getting her life right with God. Having reached out to her old childhood friend, Tia confided in Shawn about her health and her final wishes, and she had come to an agreement that since Alexis's father had been killed, Shawn would adopt her only child. When Shawn expressed his interest in marrying Bright and building a life with her, Tia wanted to meet and get to know her in the hopes that they would form an indelible bond.

But after having had a threesome, Bright made it well-known that she had no interest in building a relationship with or getting to know Tia. And because Tia had not mentioned her illness to anyone other than Shawn, she had begged him not to reveal it to Bright in fear of having her feel sorry for her and treating her differently. Though her illness was also a factor as to why Tia was always at Shawn's penthouse, more so, it was that the soon-to-be father and daughter could bond.

This was the reason for the big extravaganza that Shawn had spent months planning. The purpose was to bring all of their families together so that Shawn could propose to Bright, allow Tia the moment to announce her illness to her family and friends, and more importantly, introduce and ask Bright if she'd be willing to except Alexis in her life. It was planned accordingly and was supposed to be a joyous occasion where they would celebrate Tia's life and the life that Shawn, Bright, and Alexis would begin together. The following day, he was going to surprise Bright. He had their passports and he had a trip lined up for the two to celebrate in South Africa. When they were in Italy, Bright had told him that Africa was the next country that she wanted to visit. However, after Bright was kidnapped and he was shot by Diamond, the event was stopped from happening. But it didn't stop their union and chances at starting and living a happy life together.

"Here you go, son-in law." Rosette brought Shawn a cold drink over that he could take with his pain medication and then fluffed the pillow behind his back.

Shawn thanked her. He had just gotten out of the hospital and was still in a lot of pain. He was grateful that the bullet that hit him in the head had only grazed him, and the one to his back had punctured his lung, but did not kill him.

"God is good, and has been working some serious miracles for this family. Thank you, Heavenly Father. We are forever grateful and humbled to you," she began to pray as she walked back into the kitchen, praising Jesus' name.

"Hey, that's the famous basketball player Larry Lane on TV!" Shawn announced, nodding his head sympathetically as he said, "Poor guys' twin daughters have been kidnapped."

Rosette and Rayonna flew out of the kitchen to catch the news.

"Oh no! Those are my nieces! They've been kidnapped? Oh no!"

"Lord have mercy!" Rosette held her hand over her heart as she sat in her chair and watched the news.

"Wait, those are your grandkids?" Shawn asked Rosette, confused. He only knew that her son's girlfriend, Tanisha, was expecting soon.

She looked at Shawn with tears in her eyes after having watched Larry cry and plead for his children's safe return. "Oh Lord, you didn't know? Bright has twin daughters with Larry Lane."

Books by Mimi Renee!

Books by Mimi Renee!

Books by Mimi Renee!

Featured Author in the anthology

"I'd Rather Be Single"

Ink Game Publications

Presents

"Traces Of My Lipstick"

Website: www.inkgamepub.com

FB: http://www.facebook.com/mimirenee.thewriterchick

Twitter: https://www.twitter.com/Thawriterchick

Please post your reviews on line, and spread the word! Thanks for your support in advance!

Mimi Renee

Made in the USA
Charleston, SC
08 March 2016